HORRORS OF WAR

HORRORS OF WAR

TIM CURRAN

WEIRD HOUSE

ISBN: 978-1-957121-26-0

Text © 2002 - 2022 by Tim Curran

Cover Artwork and interior illustrations © 2022 by Brad Moore

Interior and cover design by Cyrusfiction Productions

Editor and Publisher, Joe Morey

Weird House Press
Central Point, OR 97502
www.weirdhousepress.com

CONTENTS

ILLUSTRATIONS

THE RAT KING

What the horrors of war are, no man can imagine.
—Florence Nightingale

Nervous? Sure, I get nervous as hell when people ask me about 'Nam and what it was like down in the tunnels. The things I saw in that awful suffocating darkness. My anxiety spikes, my hands shake. I get the cold sweats. They can't understand any of it. How acute your senses become until you can smell the enemy down there, feel them in the blackness, hear their breathing and the beat of their hearts.

Despite all of it, I never cracked up. I'm going to tell you about it—calmly, easily, rationally. When I'm done, you'll be convinced of my sanity.

Okay. When you went down into an unexplored tunnel system, your senses were just buzzing, every cell in your body at high alert, your nerves jangling like fucking wind chimes. You felt your way along inch by inch for trip wires and booby traps in passages the size of water pipes. Smeared with red clay and covered in mud, every second felt like your last. Your sense of touch got very sensitive after a while—I swear you could feel every grain of sand. Pebbles became boulders and roots were like tree limbs.

There was danger everywhere.

The gooks rigged trapdoor punji pits and grenade traps, tied deadly bamboo vipers and kraits from strings so they'd bite you in the face. They engineered ingenious little box traps that would dump scorpions and fire ants right down on your head if you tripped them. There were spring-loaded hatchways that would seal you in a cramped section of tunnel so tightly you couldn't even turn around. It was like being buried alive, your air slowly running out as you screamed and tried to claw your way free. Once, I got bit by a poisonous centipede that was a foot long, and another time, a green spider the size of my hand dropped onto the back of my neck and sank its fangs into me. I spent two weeks in the hospital fighting off the infection.

That was the life of a tunnel rat.

I was a small guy, thin and agile. My people were West Virginia coal miners, so crawling through narrow seams and tight passageways was second nature to me. That's how I became a tunnel rat. The motto of the rats was *Non gratum anus rodentum*, Latin for "Not worth a rat's ass." It puts things into perspective, doesn't it? Nobody was more expendable than we were. The running joke was that a rat's survival rate was about two minutes once they entered a tunnel.

My first gig with the rats was with the 5/3 of the 11th Armored Cav in 1967. It was a massive search and destroy op to root out the VC in the Iron Triangle and find their operational HQ. The brass called it Operation Cedar Falls. To us, it was just another tour in Hell. Above Xuan Loc, north of Saigon, we sniffed out one tunnel system after another. We destroyed dozens of them, locating caches of rice, SKS sniper rifles, crates upon crates of AK-47s and Chinese 9mm machine pistols, grenades and RPGs, hundreds of pounds of RDX explosives and factory-sealed cases of Russian radio-controlled detonators. We took all the goodies away from the guerrillas, and word had it that Charlie was pissed. We'd kicked his operations back six months.

A few months later, I was attached to the tunnel rat squad of the 168th Combat Engineers. As far as tunnels went, we came, we found 'em, we blew the shit out of them. That's how I ended up buddying up with another rat, Frank Sturcek. Despite what happened later, you have to understand that I didn't hate him. He'd never done me any wrong. Not really. Nobody hated him. He just creeped the squad out, disturbed them, made them want to sleep with the lights on.

He hated the Vietnamese. Not just the NVA or VC, the communist insurgents in general, but all Viets. He wanted to kill them all and entomb them in a common grave. He hated how they looked, how they smelled, the way they walked, the very sound of their language. He hated their dead fish eyes, sniping little smiles, and condescending manner. Mostly, he hated how they'd pretend to be your friend by daylight, but at night they were Charlie Cong. *Hey, you numba one, Joe. I washee your clothes and polish your boots and get you dope and sell you my sister. But tonight, Joe, oh you numba ten thousand and I kill you any way I can, you round-eye Yankee invader.* The rest of us accepted it as matter of course; Sturcek took it as a personal insult.

He woke each day from ensanguined dreams of slaughtering them, planning out his daily body count. When there was no tunnel action, I swear he physically and mentally withered. He looked like an old man after a few days without any contact. But once he went down into a system and bagged a few VC, he rejuvenated. He looked younger and rosy-cheeked, full of blood and piss and vinegar.

He was a predator and Charlie was his chosen prey.

Here's how he put it to me: "When they're in a tunnel, I can smell 'em, boy. My heart starts to pound, to hammer in my ears. I shake and tremble and get a fierce hunger in my belly. And that's no shit. My dick gets hard and my body throbs because I know I'm gonna kill me some gooks, shoot 'em in the face or slide my knife into their yellow throats. That's what it's all about."

He fed on their deaths. And that, too, is no shit.

He was a mole, a worm, a night crawler that was perfectly at home in the underworld. Believe me, they didn't call him The Rat King for no reason. The VC hated him so much they'd put a reward of 100,000 piasters on his head, which was about $10,000 American, a fucking fortune for poor Viet farmers that lived in hooches made of thatched straw and ate a handful of rice and a couple fish heads for dinner on a good day. But believe me, nobody ever collected it.

So, like I said, I didn't hate him. He just scared the shit out of me was all. But we cleared tunnels. Man, did we clear tunnels. We were hell on Earth for the VC/NVA all over Phouc Tuy Provence. We denied them their hidey holes, their supply caches, their ability to wage war against us. We killed them in numbers down in the passages where they thought they were safe. We flooded their networks, blew them up, made them unusable in myriad ways. Our real kick was using tear gas powder and det cord in combination with high explosives. We'd take ten-pound bags of CS tear gas powder wrapped in Primacord and blow them. The ignited cord gave an even dispersal of the CS agent throughout the tunnels. The beauty of that was it seeped into the walls and floors where the toxin remained active for decades. Once we did that, the tunnels were dead zones, completely unusable.

Sturcek and I went at it non-stop. Most of the tunnels we entered were nothing but wriggly crawl holes, ten- to twenty-feet long, maybe three- to four-feet in diameter. Awful, claustrophobic crawlspaces where VC sappers and snipers lived with their pathetic supplies. But now and again, you'd get into a real network, multi-tiered with five and six levels. It would take days to go through the entire thing.

The slopes were amazing, resourceful creatures when they put their minds to it. In some of the bigger systems that were designed to harbor and supply 5,000 men or more, you'd come across hospitals with operating rooms, primitive dental offices, gigantic supply caches, kitchens and eating areas, sleeping quarters and munitions factories where they'd pump out booby traps and anti-personnel mines (most of which were made from our unexploded ordinance).

One afternoon we dug into a sealed-off side chamber where thirty or forty Cong had been caught in a cave-in and suffocated. Another time, we found a makeshift tomb where hundreds of NVA soldiers had been interred. They knew how much we loved our body counts, so they'd drag their KIAs below to deny us. Something that drove command crazy.

Like I said, The Rat King had a real nasty death hard-on for the Viets and especially those hiding in the tunnels. He was very meticulous in every way. When he explored a system, he explored every nook and cranny and spider hole. That's how he was. He was the best I'd ever seen. I was good, hell yes, or I wouldn't have survived as long as I did, but old Sturcek was the apex predator of the subterranean world.

At first, I was amazed to work with him. I learned more in a week with him than I'd learned in months with other rats. But after a time…I don't know, he started getting under my skin. I began to fear him more than the VC in the tunnels. When he went after them, grinning with white teeth, bloodthirsty and starving for their deaths, I almost felt sorry for them. *Almost.* They were sheep and he was a wolf. I swear that he could see in the dark like a cat. And sometimes we'd be down there in that blackness, which was darker than anything you can imagine, and his eyes would shine yellow. I mean luminous, man, like there was a Halloween candle flickering in his skull.

After a time, I understood why the other rats didn't want any part of him, why they refused to go down into the tunnels with him. He was spooky as hell. To see him down there, to be with him, to feel the marrow-deep death vibes coming off him, it was almost too much. Sometimes he was a human worm sliding smooth and easy through the passages, something born to darkness. Then he would be a coiling, boneless snake slithering into air shafts and trapdoors. And sometimes a skulking midnight-black graveyard rat scuttling about noiselessly on all fours.

One time, I swear that I saw him emerge from a passage crawling not on the floor but over the roof like a spider. Another time, a rat the size of a tomcat jumped out at me, hissing. Sturcek seized it by the throat with his teeth. I heard it squeal as it died, the wet snapping of its vertebrae, hot blood spattering in my face. That sounds like wild exaggeration. I only wish it was.

When we went down into a new tunnel system, it was always dangerous. The first rat in was in a very precarious situation. Sometimes the floors were mined and sometimes, a trigger happy little zipperhead would pop up out of a spider hole and empty his AK into you. The first rat had to scan and search for trip-wires and devious little booby traps. Sometimes he'd find himself in a dummy tunnel—an empty counterfeit network rigged with short-fuse grenades and anti-personnel mines, hair-trigger booby traps and snake pits. They were built just to waste our time and kill as many Americans as possible. One wrong move and it was KFB—*Ka-Fucking Boom!*

The first rat had a perilous, touchy job. Only when he was certain things were safe, did he call in the others.

It was such bad news, that most squads took turns on who got the job of going first. Not in ours, though. The Rat King always went first. *Always.* He demanded that right. And once we were in and he caught the scent of the enemy, he liked to go after it alone. While we waited, he'd slip forward to do some killing. He liked slitting throats best, leaving a broken wide-eyed VC in his wake, a bloodless and shriveled thing that would look like he died of fright. Sometimes two or three—striking out at them in the dark like a mamba or a fer-de-lance.

I saw a lot of corpses down there. Hell, I made a lot of corpses down there. But all rats were virgins next to Sturcek. He was the real thing. The boogeyman, the devil in the dark. Wherever he went in the tunnels, he left a trail of dead VC and NVA. The longer I was with him, the more disturbed I became. Everything from his crazy eyes to his inhuman wrath to his superhuman feats down there began to get to me. Then, one fateful day in a system near the Song Rai River, the Rat King went off hunting on his own. After a time, he returned and said the tunnels were abandoned, but he'd found the remains of an American POW the gooks must have hidden down there. I insisted on seeing the body firsthand. I wish I wouldn't have. It was just some young guy, eighteen or nineteen, chalk-white, his throat torn out.

"That wasn't done by a knife," I said in the crowded confines of a little earthen room.

"No, something got to him."

"Down here?"

The Rat King grinned. His eyes were gleaming yellow in my flashlight beam, the teeth in his grinning mouth long and narrow like those of a sewer rat.

"There's things down here," he said in a low, growling sort of voice, "that no man has ever seen and lived to tell about."

I didn't doubt that. I'd heard wild tales like everyone else. I'd known a platoon tunnel rat with the 9th Infantry. He told me about a guy in their squad that lost his mind and got shipped to a nuthouse stateside. He went down into a tunnel outside Tay Ninh City and came scrambling out with glassy eyes, his face contorted into a silent scream. Twenty-three years old and his hair was streaked with white. He was shaking and sweating and shouting to the demo guy to blow the fucking tunnel. The demo guy armed a satchel charge and goodbye tunnel. Later on, the rat told them what he'd seen down there. He came across an ammo dump with three dead Cong laying there, all shriveled up like mummies…brown and flaking like maybe they'd been down there 200 years. When he prodded them with the barrel of his .38…they just broke apart. About then, the rat said, he smelled something sweet and hideous. Like honey, but so strong and so sweet it made you want to vomit. Something came creeping down the tunnel. He put his light on it, and that's when he went scrambling out of there, his mind ripped open like an infected sore. What did he see? Something big and black covered in hair like the bristles of a hog. He shot it…and it mewled like a stepped-on kitten.

"What the fuck was it?" I asked him.

But the rat didn't know. But his friend whose mind snapped couldn't be bribed, threatened, or coerced to go down into a tunnel again.

Stories, right? But when I looked at that POW in the tunnel, I began to wonder. And that leads to what I need to tell you about.

The infantry had found an unexplored system outside Duc Thanh, and as the tunnel rat squad, it was our job, of course, to check it out. I remember being very nervous and apprehensive about the entire thing. This was maybe a week after we'd found that POW. By that point, I was really afraid to go down into the dark with The Rat King. Everything was wrong about him. I kept thinking about that POW and wondering some real awful things. Like how the blood was still wet on his throat and the fact that maybe Sturcek knew more than he was saying about it. But he wouldn't kill an American. That's what I tried to tell myself again and again.

Anyway, we went down into the system. Just The Rat King and me. Let me proceed cautiously here. Since we didn't know what we were getting into, we went loaded for bear. Sturcek carried a .45. I toted a sawed-off M2A1 carbine in case we ran into the enemy in numbers.

He motioned me down after he'd secured the entrance. It was a typical tunnel in every way. The opening was shored up with a wood frame, but another than that there were no supports. The VC used a clay called laterite for their tunnels that had a heavy concentration of aluminum and red iron. It was easy to work with when it was damp, but when it dried, it was hard as concrete. Everything was slimy and dripping down there. Sturcek moved forward on his belly very carefully, using a mine probe—a long aluminum rod with a wooden handle that we used to poke around ahead of us for mines and booby traps that might kill us.

As the second rat, I moved about six feet behind him. We never bunched up in a tunnel because a single grenade could kill us all. My job was to check for loose earth or hollow spots that might indicate trap doors or hidden passages. Sometimes these could be dangerous—rigged with explosives or concealing a jack-in-the-box type hidey hole where a VC would spring out with pistol or an AK.

We crept forward about another hundred feet, and it was slow going. We came to a fork. Something I always hated—and The Rat King loved—because it meant we'd have to separate. This was a hot tunnel, and I knew it. The Cong were down there, and the heightened acuity of my senses told me that in no uncertain terms. I could smell them—a fishy, spicy odor combined with sweat and dankness. That's as close as I can get. I took the left fork and Sturcek took the right.

On I crawled, pausing as I probed and felt around for things that would kill me. I maneuvered my way down the tunnel the way the Viets did, by hugging the wall. Slime dripped on me, and clots of mud dropped into my hair, but it was the safest way there was. I was continually adjusting my eyes to the darkness. After a time, you began to notice variations in it. I kept going. There was standing water on the floor, and as I moved, my belly and legs became encrusted with muck. I heard rats scampering about. Things crawling and sliding around me in the darkness. It was as if the entire tunnel system was coming alive around me.

As I felt around ahead of me, I found that the floor dropped away, canting downward. It was a trap—the unwary would slide into a pungi pit below. A dead passage. I turned around and made my way back. I'd go to the fork and wait for Sturcek, then we could proceed together.

I was almost there when I heard something that made my skin crawl. It felt like my blood went to cool sludge and my guts solidified. I told you how unnaturally keen your hearing gets down there. Well, this was a loud, cacophonous sort of sound like having a trumpet blown next to your ear. It was a high, shrieking scream that echoed throughout the network, breaking apart into a pained, dog-like yelping that faded away until I wasn't even certain I'd heard it at all. I waited there, sweat beading my face, the breath rasping from my throat.

I heard no more sounds.

Was it The Rat King? Had he finally met his match in the darkness? Had something gotten him? The sort of thing no man has ever seen and lived to tell about?

I scrambled back down the tunnel, staying to the wall, moving as quietly as I could, but it sounded like thunder in the close confines. I knew that Sturcek wouldn't want me coming after him...but what if that scream had been him? I knew I had to go find out.

I crawled forward maybe fifteen minutes. I began to smell something, a gagging odor that I acquainted not so much with death, but maybe something that fed on death—a stink of wet feathers, dander, and decay. The way I imagined the wing of a vulture would smell. It kept getting stronger and stronger, my stomach creeping up the back of my throat.

Something was just ahead, and I knew it. I can't describe it exactly, only that the atmosphere of the tunnels had suddenly shifted from that of a relatively benign hole in the earth to that of a subterranean tomb. I felt insects crawling over my exposed skin, wriggling worms beneath my hands. Rats squeaked and bats flapped their leathery wings. It gave me the sort of feeling of suffocating hopelessness you get in the worst nightmares.

My stomach squirmed and spasmed with nausea from the rising stink that to me was maggots and carrion birds and flies, and the putrescent things they fed upon. And then...something worse: a persistent, meaty throbbing that I knew was the beating of a heart. At first, it was distant and low, but as I moved ever forward toward something I didn't even want to guess at, it grew louder and louder, then still louder. Its noise filled the tunnels until it was like a pounding drum in my skull. My bones seemed to vibrate with its awful rhythm. Faster and faster it went, thumping in my ears and my brain. It frayed my nerves to ribbons.

And as that graveyard stench filled my nostrils and the beating heart pulped my brain to sauce, I heard a voice, a wizened voice creaking like a coffin hinge: *"Don't come in here. Do you hear me? Don't come in here. Go back. You have to go back."*

But by then, it was too late. The flashlight was in my hand. We never used them much in the tunnels because they were like a beacon in the blackness for a sniper's bullet. I clicked it on. What I saw and what I was forced to do about it was what shattered my nerves.

There in a mud-dripping, fetid chamber, I saw The Rat King. No, it was not Sturcek, but *The Rat King*, what he became in the underworld—a gnarled, twisted, blood-dripping wraith with a gray, corrugated face and the bright yellow eyes of graveyard jackal. His teeth were long and blackened, red drool splashed down his pointed chin.

I saw the corpses of VC spread around him, all of them bled white. In two scaly hands like the claws of a buzzard, he held another VC, the throat ripped open. He—*it* had been feeding on him when I arrived. His grisly face leered and grinned at me like one of those devil faces you see carved into votive poles in the jungle that the peasant Viets make offerings to.

And all the while, his undead, noxious heart beat louder and louder until I couldn't take it anymore. I screamed. I shouted. I lost my mind. The next thing I was aware of was that I had emptied my carbine into him. The full clip. The Rat King shrieked and hissed, clawing out at me while freshets of blood poured from his mouth. Then he pitched over, stiff as a cadaver in a freezer.

But the heart in his bony chest continued to beat louder and louder. I drew my fighting knife and leaped on him, doing the only thing I knew that would kill his kind.

I had no choice.

Sometime later—minutes, hours—the chamber exploded with light as three other rats came looking for us. Their flashlights were on me, illuminating what I'd done and what I knew I must still do. *"Here! Here!"*

I screamed at their horrified faces, holding the still palpitating, throbbing organ I'd cut from The Rat King's chest, blood running through my trembling fingers. *"He can't die like us! As long as this still lives, he lives! Shoot it! Stab it! Burn it! Destroy it! Stop the beating of this hideous heart!"*

DER WULF

"And overall that tumbled plain lies the harvest
that the guns have gathered, the crops of flesh
that are man's toll to the beast he has made."
—Walter Owen, *The Cross of Carl*

Stalingrad was a witch's cauldron, bubbling and burning. Its flaming glow was visible thirty miles away at night. Rockets, bombs, and artillery shells rained down around the clock, creating mountains of rubble high as two-story buildings that were haunted by wild dog packs and strewn with thousands of frozen corpses. A blackened pall of smoke and suspended dust rose from the cremated remains of the city by day and lingered like a noisome fog at night. And still the snow fell, and the bodies piled up.

After four months of savage fighting between the German 6th and Soviet 62nd armies, Stalingrad was not a city but a great meatless cadaver rising up skeletal and raw and threadbare, its bones crushed and smoldering. Men fought with hordes of graveyard rats and slat-thin dogs amongst the ruins for scraps to feed on, sometimes feeding on one another and themselves. And though the great, seething charnel yard was an atrocity to some, to others—red-eyed things that crept slavering from the shadows—it was an opportunity.

13

Outside the shattered building, the wind howled and moaned across the gutted urban landscape, wailing like a wraith from a riven tomb. There was a thunder of anti-tank guns in the distance, the sound of screaming coming from down the street. And inside, debris and dust and a tense silence broken only by the guttural moans of the dying man. By the greasy light of a flickering oil lamp, Corporal Luptmann worked on him, though he knew it was hopeless. He took the final vial of morphine from his medical pack, filled a syringe, and injected it into the dying man's arm.

"Hold him now," he said to Sergeant Stein and Lieutenant Krantz. "Don't let him move."

There was no time to let the morphine work. The Russian stick grenade had blown his abdomen wide, and Luptmann worked with dirty fingers, sorting through purple bowel and pockets of yellow fat, pressing the loops of viscera back in place as the blood flowed and the dying man trembled. The gaping wound steamed, and Luptmann was glad for the warmth that unlocked his stiff fingers, making it easier to work. The light was so poor that he did this mainly by feel, locating the damaged artery and feeling the hot wetness gushing over his fingers. He clamped it and tied it off, but still the blood welled as he pressed a gauze compression bandage down on it.

"A waste of time," Stein said, fifteen minutes into it. "He's a dead man."

"Shut up," Krantz told him.

But Luptmann knew he was right.

Stein was a crude, evil pig, but he was certainly a realistic one. Colonel Hauser was indeed a dead man. He needed real surgery, not a fumbling attempt by a medic in the bombed-out shell of a Russian house. Stein walked over to join Kreig and Holz by the doorway. Luptmann and Krantz looked at each other, but said nothing.

Yes, this was how heroes died. Hauser who had fought in Crete and Belorussia and won the Knight's Cross for actions in Leningrad, was dying here in the dirty rubble of Stalingrad with his guts hanging out…and from a booby-trapped grenade fashioned by a fanatical Russian partisan in some dingy cellar. There would be no more medals or beer gardens or pretty girls for him. No snapping to attention when "Deutschland, Deutschland uber alles" was played, just this final cold entombment in a collapsing Russian hovel. The Fatherland's lasting gift for his sacrifice and duty.

He lasted maybe another twenty minutes and died. Luptmann still held onto the bandage, which was dyed red as his hands, watching the steam slowly cease to rise as the body cooled rapidly.

"All right," Krantz said. "You did what you could."

Now that Hauser was dead, Krantz was in command. He was tall and thin, blonde and bespectacled, his eyes gray as the winter-issue cap on his head. He looked from man to man, maybe for any that dared question his authority, and nodded.

"We…we should say something," Holz said, gripping a Mauser rifle tightly in his mittened hands.

Stein grinned with his bad teeth. "Okay, Hauser is dead. I'll miss him. *There.* Is that sufficient?"

Kreig laughed with a bitter, angry sound.

Luptmann stared down at the blood on his hands, staining his white snow shirt. "You're a shit, Stein. You've never been anything but a goddamned shit. Hauser saved all our lives a dozen times."

"Yes, Herr Doctor. How could I be so unfeeling?" Stein laughed.

Luptmann raised his red, steaming hands, maybe wanting to wrap them around Stein's throat.

Krantz shouldered his Schmeisser machine pistol. "There's no time for this. We have to get back. Take what you can off of him, then leave him."

They took Hauser's pack and rifle, his bayonet and bread bag, handed his scarred-up leather map case to Krantz.

The light was extinguished, and they went back out into the dead cold of Stalingrad. There was a booming of artillery fire in the distance, the moan of the wind, the sound of their boots breaking through the crust of snow. Stein led the way. He had been fighting and killing and maiming for two years now, but war had yet to erase his zeal. In the gray light, Luptmann watched him. He wondered when death would come for Stein and, if at that time, he would have to dip his hands into the man's belly or sever one of his limbs. He wondered, too, if he would put any special care into saving the life of a man whose soul was as desolate as the landscape around them.

They moved off, the breath frosting from their lips.

The city was a study in shadow. The hulks of gutted buildings towered around them, heaps of rubble spilling out over the streets. They stepped over the stiffened, naked corpses of Russian civilians and moved through the patchwork of night. Down an alley and past the shrapnel-pitted wall of a church. They dropped behind a snow-crusted row of hedges as a group of Russian children crept past, dragging the headless corpse of a dog behind them, which was no doubt headed for the stewpot. The children laughed and sang, mindless and desensitized by months of brutal conflict. Packs of them roamed the streets by night and, German or Russian, if they caught you sleeping, they'd slit your throat for a few crusts of bread or a ratty blanket.

Luptmann followed the others over the broken foundation of a house, his gas mask canister clanking as the wind bit into him. Sheets of snow blew through an open field. Crouching down, they crossed over to a block of ruins, and there they paused. Stein gave them a hand signal to stay put. Only Krantz crept forward. Stein and he whispered for a moment or two. Then Stein raced off by himself, moving from tree to tree, his greatcoat flapping in the wind. He sidled along a ruined house and then went inside.

Luptmann was aware of the wind that sucked the warmth from him, the breath in his lungs, and the beat of his heart. The house was where Boch and Ertel were waiting with the cook fire and the coffee they'd taken off an ambushed Soviet patrol that morning. What was bothering him, was that he could see the flickering flames of the fire and he shouldn't have been able to. Boch had arranged a tarp to block the light from prying eyes...but now it was very evident.

After a time Stein came back, and Krantz motioned them all to follow.

Inside the house, Luptmann saw that the tarp hung by a single naked peg from the rafters overhead. It was sheared open by three ragged cuts. A bayonet? Boch was lying near the wall, dead. He was slit from forehead to crotch, laid right open, split lengthwise like a stick of birch. His blood had frozen into red crystals around him. It was sprayed up the wall behind him, and frozen stalactites of it dripped from the ceiling. Despite the frigid weather, you could still smell his violent death—metallic, savage, and meaty.

"Boch, dear God, Boch," Holz said, turning away.

Luptmann didn't understand it. If the Russians had gotten him, why had they left the coffee and chocolate? His provisions and carbine? In Stalingrad, corpses were stripped immediately. But Boch had not been stripped. Just laid open, and Luptmann was thinking by something like a sword.

"Partisans," Kreig said. "It must have been partisans."

But nobody was believing that. Krantz had them search the house, that of it that still stood, but there was no sign of Ertel. Well, not exactly. A trail of frozen blood led to the kitchen and went out the back door, which hung by a single hinge and looked like it had been hit by a mortar round. Using Krantz's flashlight, they studied the door, the jagged scratches in it, the blood that led away into the snow beyond.

"Why would they drag his body off?" Holz wanted to know.

"They were hungry," Stein said.

It was an appalling thought, but not unheard of. There was very little food left in the city. People were eating dogs and cats and even each other now. Meat was meat.

"Partisans," Kreig said again.

That made Stein laugh. "Do you think so?"

He followed the blood trail with Krantz's flashlight. On the kitchen floor there was a single huge and monstrous print. Something had stepped in blood, and this was its spoor. It was not the track of a man. It was large and splayed out, and you could clearly see the marks of claws or spurs. There were a couple more tracks in the snow. The stride was immense.

"No partisan ever left a track like that," Stein said.

Krantz studied it closely. "Almost…almost like the track of a wolf."

"A very big wolf," Stein said.

Luptmann was interested in the pattern of the tracks. Not only was the stride immense, but whatever left it walked upright like a man. "A giant wolf that walks on two feet," he said, almost wishing he hadn't.

"Oh, you'd get on well with my grandmother and her stories of werewolves and ghosts," Kreig said, trying to sound amusing but failing miserably.

"The Wulf," Holz said. "It was here."

His words echoed off into the night, and nobody said anything for a time. Beyond the smashed door, the snow drifted, shadows jumping and prancing.

Horrors of War

You could almost hear death on that wind calling you out into the darkness, whispering your name.

"All right, goddammit," Krantz said. "We're going to see what this is about. C'mon, all of you. Stay together."

With a terrible sinking in his belly, Luptmann followed.

They moved off through the rubble and destruction, leapfrogging bomb craters that seemed to have no bottom. They passed a dog that was chewing on the face of a dead child, taking what the rats had left. Over piles of smashed buildings and around houses burned to frames. Luptmann saw a German machine gun crew frozen in the snow…though the gun was missing, an ice-encrusted corpse still held it.

Stein led the way through the wind, never losing sight of the trail. The snow had drifted it over in spots, but there was something almost primeval about the man: he could scent things like a dog. Maybe he lost the trail for a moment or two, had to cast about a bit, but he always found it again. Soon, they were in a neighborhood of deserted homes pocked and scarred by an artillery barrage. Many were roofless. There was a crumbling stone wall surrounding a high, narrow, and sagging house. Here, Stein stopped.

"This is it," he panted. "This is where the trail ends."

Luptmann peered over the wall. He did not like that house. It looked like a great dark coffin filled with night. It made a hollow open up in his belly. There was something forbidden about it that he could feel right down into his marrow like the lair of a child-eating witch.

"Look," Holz said.

Somebody had scratched crosses and hex signs into the stone wall, as if to warn people away from what lay beyond. The five of them stood there in their baggy white uniforms that were streaked gray with grime and spattered with old blood. Flakes of snow blew over the tops of their steel helmets and settled onto their bulky haversacks.

"Lead the way in then," Krantz said.

Stein was only too happy.

There was a rusting iron gate set in the wall, but it was very old and threaded with winter-dead ivy. It was wide open. The yard shivering in the shadow of that house was blown with heavy snow. Something had moved through it, though, you could see that. Something big. They stepped into the yard, the snow coming up past their knees. The house above them was shuttered and leaning, the walls weathered gray, holes punched in the roof, through which you could see the skeletal rungs of rafters. But it was in the snow itself that they saw something that stopped them: bodies scattered in the snow. Frozen gray hands thrust up from the drift with splayed fingers. Legs, arms, trunks. The face of a little girl looked up at them, eyeless and shining with frost. There had to be the piecemeal remains of a dozen here.

Stein grabbed an arm and pulled it up. There was no body beneath it. He tossed it aside.

"What sort of place is this?" Kreig said.

But nobody wanted to answer that. Luptmann was studying the limbs and faces in the snow, thinking things. That hollow inside him opened so wide he thought it would swallow him. This was beyond the carnage of war; this was something else entirely. All these body parts...not crudely tossed aside, but almost arranged in some unguessable pattern, if you could but see it. And he saw it. This was like an icebox, that's what it was. This was where the ogre stored its meat, keeping it fresh in the snow.

"Let's go in," Krantz said. "I've had enough of this nonsense."

Before he could stop himself, Luptmann said, "I don't think we should."

But he was ignored, at least by Krantz and the overeager Stein. Kreig and Holz heard him, though, and you could see the dread in their eyes aging them in ways the war never could. Luptmann felt an irrational, superstitious terror rise in him. Stein kicked aside the door, and they went in, one by one, Krantz shining his light about. The house had been empty, probably for decades. The floors were bowed, the walls rotted to the lathing beneath. Everywhere, settled dust and draping nets of cobweb, autumn leaves blown in the corners, a dusting of snow.

Stein moved down a corridor into what might have been a dining room once and still was, apparently. They saw it. They all saw it. The walls and bare floors were brown with old blood stains as were the ceilings. From exposed rafters overhead, dozens of limbs that looked salted and cured dangled from chains, swinging gently like hanged men. Ertel had been hanged with them, by the feet, slit open from crotch to throat, his blood gathered in a dented copper basin. The flesh of his face had been stripped away, his skull set with the punctures of teeth marks. His body cavity was hollow, emptied.

Holz made a strangled gagging sound.

Krantz said, "Dear Christ…"

And then something moved off to their left. Something growled, and they could hear claws on the floor scraping. Krantz put his light over there, and though they expected a rabid dog, they saw…a *boy*. He was naked and crouched on all fours, his hair long and stringy trailing down his back, his ears pointed and laid flat against his skull. His eyes were huge and liquid red, the lower jaw vulpine, the nose flattened out. He looked at them, lips curling away from sharp white teeth. With a low, bestial roar, he jumped.

Stein was ready, though. As the boy-thing leaped, he opened up on it, snapping a 7.92mm slug right through its throat that nearly tore its head off. It crashed into the hanging arms, set them swinging, and then hit the floor hard. It trembled for a moment or two, blood bubbling from its torn throat, its awful jaws snapping open and closed. Then it was still, blood pooling around it and steaming.

"What…what in the hell is that?" Holz wanted to know.

Stein kicked the body. "It's a sweet little boy that wanted to drink your blood."

Luptmann was offended by that mangled little corpse, yet his curiosity got the better of him. He kneeled next to it, taking in the peculiar anatomy that seemed as much wolf as boy. Those sharp teeth were made for tearing and rending, the hooked claws designed to hold onto prey and not let go. Everything was wrong. This child was not some unfortunate circus freak, he was beyond that. A mutation, a hybrid, feral and inhuman. Close as he was, Luptmann could smell the warm rankness of the child, and it disgusted him.

"Well?" Krantz said.

"If I had to put a name to it," Luptmann said, "I'd call it a—"

But the words evaporated on his tongue for there was a low, bestial growling. And it came from above. Krantz put his light up there. The swinging limbs cast darting shadows. Up in the rafters, three sets of eyes shined red and vicious.

"More of them," Kreig said.

Everyone slowly, slowly brought up their weapons. They had dealt with their share of rabid dogs in Stalingrad, and they knew that you made no sudden movements. You were careful, controlled; you did not startle. There were three more children clinging to the rafters…two girls and a boy. All of them were loathsome wolf-like things. The swinging arms made the shadows crawl over them, their eyes shining brightly in the momentary swaths of darkness. Their limbs were long, fingers narrow and clawed. They were all shaggy with a matted down of pale fur, their hair long and dirty, faces pitted with sores. Their mouths were open, needle-like teeth on display, gouts of drool hanging from their lips.

Luptmann had his rifle up, and it shook in his hands.

He knew that if he'd been alone, they would have fallen on him, torn out his entrails in moist tangles, and opened his throat, lapping up the blood that spurted out, bathing in it with great barbaric delight.

"Now," Krantz said in a quiet, but firm voice.

They all started shooting, blasting the swinging arms to fragments and peppering the beams overhead with rounds. Two of the children were blown from their roosts, faces sprayed from the skulls beneath. They hit the floor bonelessly, tumbling and shrieking. As the others got out of the way of those thrashing fingers, Krantz sprayed them down with his Schmeisser submachine gun, tearing them nearly in half. The third child, a girl, fell from above, but snagged herself on one of the hooks that had held an arm. It caught her in the throat and ripped right up to her belly, holding her. She spun upside down in a frantic circle, jaws snapping and claws lashing. Stein shot her in the head, gray jelly and bone fragments splattering against the wall. She was dead as the others, but continued to revolve on the chain in a slow dance macabre.

Holz fell onto his ass, hyperventilating. Kreig just kept backing up until he struck the wall.

And then a door at the end of the room swung open, and something crawled up a set of steps into Krantz's light.

Luptmann stood there, breathlessly, watching it.

21

Horrors of War

It was a woman…or almost a woman. A slender thing covered in lustrous white-blonde hair, a thick mane of it running down her back. Her fingers were long and thin and clawed, red with blood right up to the wrists. She was wounded, bleeding from a gash in her abdomen that painted her belly pink. As she pulled herself forward, she left a smear of dark blood.

"Kill her," Kreig said, nearly hysterical. "Do you hear me? Kill her!"

She reacted to his voice with a ragged, doglike snarl, her red bleeding mouth opening wide and filled with triangular fangs like shards of glass. Her face was oddly beautiful in some primal, animalistic way—the flesh pale and shiny, clinging tightly to a wolfish skull beneath. The eyes huge and translucent and running with tears, black holes flecked with veins of electric red.

Luptmann felt his insides run like wax. She looked at him, in him, perhaps *through* him, and he had a disjointed momentary image of her biting out his throat with those long teeth, her eyes rolled back in sensual delight. She kept staring. Her jaws opened and closed, a garbled voice coming out, and he thought she was trying to speak.

Krantz and Stein fired.

She rose up with a shrill roaring, her finely-muscled torso sleek and catlike. They could see the line of pendulous teats that ran from her breast to belly, the bullets that punched into them, opening her in a dozen hurting places. She shuddered and writhed on the floor, breathing out a hot yellow breath and slopping in her own blood, jaws sprung open with threads of tissue dangling from them, eyes wide, strands of dirty hair hanging in her face. Then she convulsed and vomited a stew of blood and bile to the floor. In it were tiny half-digested things that might have been the fingers of a very small child.

Luptmann just stood there with a buzzing sound in his head, unable to move. Finally Krantz took hold of him and yanked him out into the wind.

The siege of Stalingrad had been going on for four months by that point, and the German 6th Army was in complete collapse. Though warned by his generals of a bloodbath that would reach into the dread Russian winter, Hitler had ordered the 6th into Stalingrad. Taking the city would mean seizing a major industrial hub, and holding it would be a demoralizing and symbolic loss to the Soviets, and particularly to Joseph Stalin, in that the city bore his name. After a massive bombardment by German forces that caused a raging firestorm killing thousands of civilians and turning the city into a graveyard of rubble and burnt ruins, the 6th Army entered Stalingrad proper and then began the bitter, costly battle for every street and factory and house. Something the Germans called *Rattenkrieg,* the War of the Rats, a vicious war of attrition where success was measured not in feet, but inches and corpses.

After three months of carnage, the Wehrmacht had captured 80% of the city, but they did not hold it for long. A Soviet counterattack cut off the 6th Army and trapped them in the cauldron of Stalingrad with a starving, desperate civilian population. Vastly outnumbered, low on supplies, the Germans were encircled, and then winter came, showing its teeth. They died by the thousands of starvation, frostbite, and disease. And still the Red Army tightened the noose, pressing closer and closer, nipping away at the invaders, crushing them beneath the grinding, relentless tread of the Soviet war machine.

The Germans fought on, for there was little else they could do. They lost an average of 20,000 men a week, yet they kept at it, making the Russians pay for every inch of the ruined city as the Russians had made them pay. It was not a mere siege, but a violent and devastating clash of ideologies, a race war, brutal and monstrous at every turn. The Germans, low on supplies, dragged themselves from their broken bunkers each day, freezing and disillusioned, afflicted with dysentery and frostbite, typhus and lice, to fight for ruptured streets and wrecked factories, clambering over mountains of frozen corpses tangled in the barbed wire. They fought no longer for Hitler or the Reich, but for survival, for each other, for another day and another breath.

And the Red Army pushed in, crushing them. On the radio and blasting from huge loudspeakers throughout the city was the ticking of a clock and a voice morbidly reporting that every seven seconds a German soldier died in Stalingrad. It went on day and night, that infernal ticking accompanied by the funereal voice.

This was Stalingrad.

This was hell beyond hell.

And this was the netherworld that Krantz's platoon lived and died in.

Horrors of War

The smell of the roasting dog was mouth-watering.

After what they'd seen in the house, Luptmann thought he would never be hungry again, but the smell of sizzling meat caused his belly to betray him. It was a fine Alsatian, probably the pet of some German officer. Stein had shot it in the head, shaved its fur off with a trench knife, gutted and spitted it, whistling "The Stars that Shine in Germany" the whole while. Nobody knew really what Stein had been before the war, but they all knew what he was now: an animal. But even animals have their uses.

Finally, tired of the morbid silence and staring eyes and pinched faces, Krantz said, "That beast, one of those things from a fairy tale, yes? A she-wolf. She must have attacked Boch, killed him and been wounded, dragged Ertel off to feed her young."

Stein turned the dog on the spit, stabbed it with a fork, the juices sizzling into the fire. "What a tale we have to tell, and no one would ever believe us."

"But the bodies…they're in that house," Holz said.

"Let them be there," Krantz said. "We're getting out of this city. I've already decided that. To hell with this war."

They sat in the cellar of a bombed-out factory, grimy faces set and eyes unblinking. There was no talk, no complaining, and no joking. The usual camaraderie, despite the harrowing circumstances, was gone. Even Kreig wasn't bragging about the women he knew in Berlin, the girls he'd pimped along the Kurfurstendamm. Now and again, a heavy vehicle would rumble down the street above, maybe a tank or a motorized gun.

Smoking a Russian cigarette, Stein said to Luptmann, "Tell us a story, teacher. Tell us about Comrade Stalin. I like that one."

Though Luptmann wasn't in the mood, he did. A teacher. Yes, before the war he had been a schoolteacher. Sometimes he forgot. He cleared his throat, staring into the fire and reciting an absurd bit of Soviet propaganda. "For many, many years, the bear Stalin lived in a virgin forest. Then a Russian general came into the forest and tried to trap the bear. He put out a barrel of vodka and Stalin drank it, became very drunk, and came under the control of the Russian general. He made Stalin dance. Then one day, Stalin escaped and ever since he has been making generals dance."

"At the end of a rope," Stein laughed. "When the urge for a purge strikes him."

The dog was done, so declared Stein. He pulled it off the spit and sectioned it up. And for a time there were only the sounds of greedy fingers and chewing mouths, gamy meat sucked from bones and gnawing teeth. They ate the dog in its entirety, and when they were done, they sat around with greasy faces, picking their teeth with dirty fingernails.

Finally, Holz said, "We just can't leave the city…we have to link up with the company."

"Shit," said Stein. "What company?"

"They are gone, boy," Krantz told him. "Dead or captured, and one is the same as the other, is it not?"

And that was the story they kept hearing, from the moment they entered the city: the Red Army does not take prisoners, they shoot Germans on sight. Nobody knew if it was true or not, yet they believed it. And this is why, surrounded and beaten and starving, the small pockets of Wehrmacht invaders held out relentlessly, fighting to the bitter end, making the Soviets throw away a dozen lives for every one they took.

Luptmann was fond of Holz. All this war and atrocity, and still there was that boyish naiveté about him. It was refreshing really. But despite his shining eyes and idealism, Stein was right, there was no more rifle company. It had been smashed and decapitated and stomped into the frozen earth. Now there were only stragglers. Much like themselves.

It had happened at the Central Station railroad depot. The Russians, making them bleed for every inch, had dug in behind the platform, using smashed and overturned railroad cars as ramparts. The battle had gone on nearly two days. A surreal and deafening slice of war, littered with wreckage and the corpses of horses and men. The machine guns rattling and rockets whining and shells roaring, the ground shaking as artillery barrages were called in, and Stukas dove like birds of prey, dumping their ordinance. It went on that way for thirty hours as they tried to shake loose the Soviets from their holes.

Now and again, Colonel Hauser, bristling with ferocity over the inhuman tenacity of the Russians, would send in a shock troop, and there would be a clattering of small arms fire and the belching of a deeply-entrenched machine gun, then pandemonium as the Germans tried to drag off their dead. Shells and more shells were poured on the Russians until the depot and its train cars were nothing but a twisted labyrinth of metal and burning wood and pulverized sheets of concrete. The smoke was so thick you could not see ten feet in any direction. There was only the smell of gunpowder and burning bodies.

Surely, the Russians were beaten; surely, they were dead or had run off. Hauser ordered an assault, and it was just like the Russians to suffer in silence, sacrificing hundreds in order to draw the enemy in. And they had. Hauser's company had been reduced to half-strength after weeks of grueling, bloody house-by-house fighting, and what remained was drawn in, and then the mortar shells came down, backed up by anti-tank guns and machine guns. Soviet reinforcements showed at the worst possible time, firing truck-mounted Katyusha rockets on the Germans. They were called "Stalin's Organ" for the shrieking music they made as they came screaming in with devastating effect. When the smoke cleared, there was only Hauser and his small band retreating.

And they'd been retreating ever since.

That was a week ago, and now Hauser's men, minus Hauser, were no longer the elite Wehrmacht shock troops that had cut through the Soviet defenses like a hot blade; they were just the walking dead…ragged and emaciated and hollow-eyed, looking for a quiet grave to lie down in.

Krieg, who had been so long silent, said, "In my village, in Krinestadt, there was a tale told to us children by the old women. A tale of a child-eater. A woman who ate children in the forest. She was like our she-wolf…part woman and part animal. When she was captured, her stewpot was filled with child-meat. She was burned at the stake as a werewolf."

Stein laughed. "Yes, just like Stalingrad, burned at the stake. And we, my friends, are nothing but ashes." To illustrate this, he kicked some coals in the fire.

"It's The Wulf," Holz said, his voice barely a whisper. "That's what that thing was: The Wulf."

"Just a story," Stein said, refusing to discuss it.

But they all thought about it and could not stop thinking about it. *The Wulf.* A story that had been circulating for weeks, months. Some huge and hulking beast that walked upright, which showed only during the bloodiest of battles, was seen dragging off the corpses of the newly dead. If the tales were true, The Wulf scavenged not only the German dead, but the Russians as well. Many had claimed to have seen it…a shaggy, noxious thing with eyes that shone red in the darkness, a stench of warm carrion wafting off it. Even the Russian peasants had a name for it, something ancient and malevolent that had haunted battlefields for centuries: the *volkolak* or *volkulaku,* the eater of the dead and dying.

Luptmann said nothing. The city was dead now as were those that infested its corpse, and was it any surprise that the grim reaper was here in the form of a demonic wolf? Stalingrad was a madhouse, plain and simple. How long could you fight over rubble and ruins and fragments before you lost your mind? Days were spent fighting for a single house, a single hilltop, a single cratered section of street. In Stalingrad, men were livestock, cattle thrown against the grinding iron teeth of the meat-eating, corpse-chewing apparatus of death. And that apparatus ran around the clock, a sponge whose fuel was blood sucked up by the gallons and rivers and whose belly was stoked with cadavers instead of coal. Berlin had tossed division after division into the slaughterhouse of Stalingrad, and to what end? Men were formed up, herded, fed and watered, and then offered as sacrifice to that great, grim beast whose stomach was never full, who ate and tore and swallowed, always wanting more, never pushing away from the table.

Yes, in his disillusionment, Luptmann knew that he and all the others had been suckled on the sweet broth of propaganda, as all men in all wars were. They had been fattened and patted on the back and sent to slaughter, sent to fight for a smoldering carcass. And now? Nothing. Death and dismemberment, freezing and starving and hopelessness. No more Reich, no more Fatherland, no more Hitler and his false promises. Just this disemboweled city, burning and rotting, an immense graveyard haunted by monsters and men that were maybe worse.

The night was quiet, oddly still.

Horrors of War

Krieg kept watch, and they all slept in the chill darkness by the flickering fire pit. Luptmann dreamed of a little schoolhouse on a hill, the pastures dotted with sheep, the green Bavarian hills. He dreamed of home, of comfortable distances and breathless vistas. He saw clutching shadows and heard the low howl of a wolf. He came awake, and there was coldness and blackness. The fire had gone out. Somewhere, he could hear artillery booming, scattered machine guns firing. But here, in the husk of a gutted factory, there were the sounds of men breathing, of equipment shifting, and an awful smell of something that had been chewing on corpses and smothering babies in cribs.

"Kreig?" Luptmann whispered.

"Shut up," Krantz said. "There's...there's something in here with us."

And there was. Luptmann did not need to be told that. The silence was heavy and ominous. He could smell the thing that had dragged itself in here in the dead of night. A vile and malignant odor of rot and disease and worms. He could see nothing, but he could *feel* the thing, feel it nearby, hear its low and sibilant breathing, like air whistling through a pipe. Its breath was hot and rancid, nauseating. And then, as if it knew it was being heard, it growled low in its throat and began chewing with a sound of saws bisecting bones.

Stein said something, and everyone started shooting.

At shadows.

At noises.

Luptmann was the only one that did not fire. He studied the thing that slipped among them in muzzle flashes. It jumped around, leaping and bounding, but he saw it. A giant bristling with fur and obscene muscularity. Its eyes were crimson scarabs glistening with witch-light. Its jaws huge and blood-dripping, set with teeth like rapiers. It moved quickly, darting about, making a deranged and almost hysterical sort of laughter, like a hyena. Surely they had hit it, wounded it, drew blood. But if it was injured, you would not have known it. The men fired blindly, and that cannibal wolf demon was here, there, everywhere. It swung from the rafters by a single pawlike hand; it rolled through the wreckage like a ball; it danced through the air with unthinkable grace. Luptmann saw it crouching over Kreig's body, its snout buried in his belly. It tore out lengths of intestine and spat them in the air.

Then it had Kreig by the throat, shaking him like a cat shakes a dead rat.

They shot at it…or where they thought it was. It roared and slashed with its immense claws, laughed shrilly.

And then it was gone.

And so was Kreig.

"It scented us out," Luptmann heard himself say. "It smelled us at that house, and it followed the scent here."

"The Wulf," Holz breathed. "Dear God, The Wulf…"

What followed next was a nightmare even by the standards of Stalingrad.

Half out of their minds and much closer to being dead than alive, Krantz and his men burst the perimeters of the factory. They ran side by side, caring not one whit about snipers and Soviet patrols, partisans hiding in the ruins. They darted down streets and alleys, over heaped rubble, not entirely sure if they were chasing the beast or fleeing from it. The pavement was slick with ice the color of fresh bone. A cold, white moon brooded above. As they ran, they could hear the war calling out to them—booming and thudding and screaming. And they ran to it, desperate to be in its arms again, to smell cold steel and hot blood, smoke and cinders and the jigsaw puzzle wreckage of bodies. Because war was better than The Wulf, that horror from a demented fairy tale…infinitely better. They hated the Russians, and the Russians hated them, but surely men were men. Men would stand side by side, regardless of race or creed or political motivations, to fend off a walking, stalking nightmare.

Finally, they collapsed alongside a boulevard where the trees had been stripped of limbs by bomb blasts and stood out against the cruel sky like the masts of ships. They panted and grunted, sweat steaming and freezing on their faces. Everywhere, grotesque shadows lay in wait. The ground shuddered with the nearby death struggles of war.

Holz was the first to find his breath. "That thing…that thing…oh, dear God, that awful thing…"

And before anyone else could speak, Luptmann did. "That was a male, a male wolf…it was what killed Boch and stole Ertel away, not the female. The female was its mate. We killed its mate, its children. It has our scent and it'll keep coming for us, coming and coming..."

"You can't know that," Krantz said, clutching his Schmeisser.

"He's right," Stein said. "Our schoolteacher is right. We killed its...*brood* and it wants revenge; it wants blood. It lives for nothing else. Yes, if it was your family or mine, we would react the same. We must find it and kill it before it kills us all."

Holz stood up. "You're crazy! You can't know what it thinks or what it wants! You can't know any of that! You can't! You just can't know—"

Stein stood up and slapped him across the face. "Don't tell me what I know, you sniveling little girl! Don't you dare tell me what I know! I know death! I know war! I know blood and pain and horror! And *it* knows these things, too, by God!"

They all got up and started moving. The wind blew, and snow began to fall again, ice crystals stinging their faces. They came to a crossroads and, in place of the missing street sign, some deviant had nailed up the frozen corpse of a Russian on the signpost. Its arm was extended, index finger pointing, icicles hanging from it. Yes, that way, that way.

But what was that way?

There was no way to know. Luptmann thought maybe the river, the Volga. It was frozen solid now like concrete, he knew. In the fall, it had been so crowded with corpses you could have walked across them without getting your feet wet. When the river went to ice, the corpses were frozen in state. He had seen them...hundreds, thousands of them locked in black ice, like insects in amber. A mortuary sculpture of leering ice-faces and frosted arms jutting from the hard pack. But even that hideous comment on Stalingrad was infinitely preferable over the beast, The Wulf.

They ran again, and this time the war found them, named them as its own, recalcitrant schoolchildren that had run off. Now it had them; now it owned them. Bullets whizzed around them; mortar shells screeched over their heads. A barrage of rockets struck a leaning house and pulverized it.

"Move! Move! Move!" Krantz called out.

They were caught at the outer edge of a running battle, and Soviet elements had spotted them, seeing them not as stragglers but as a reconnaissance party scouting ahead of a relief column, perhaps. Bullets chewed up the pavement around them, drilled into trees and the shrapnel-gouged facades of buildings behind them. Buildings and trees burst into flames as incendiary rounds came down. They could hear tanks, big Russian T34s, rumbling in the distance. Incoming artillery rounds strobed with brilliant white flashes; the ground shook, buildings crumbled.

Krantz in the lead, they slipped through the hulks of buildings that were little more than frameworks of walls and chimneys waiting to fall. They passed what appeared to be a barricade of corpses, carefully arranged, then five or six Russian soldiers that were hanged from a tree. Deserters probably, executed by the NKVD. Ahead, ensconced on high ground, they sighted a tall red brick building more or less unscathed. As they approached it, a lone rifle opened up on them, and Luptmann felt a bullet glance off the side of his helmet, nearly knocking him senseless.

"Goddamn Bolsheviks!" Stein cried.

Without waiting, he ran at the building, rounds missing him by scant inches. He ran right up to a shattered window and tossed a stick grenade through it. There was a muffled explosion and screaming. Stein tossed another in there, and all was silent.

Krantz gave the order, and they entered the building, everything lit up now by burning wreckage. The first floor was nothing but debris and garbage, two dead Russians up against the wall. Both had died of battlefield wounds. The one to the left was missing most of his head, and the one to the right had his stomach blasted open by a grenade or shell. His body cavity was nearly empty, his viscera coiling out like snakes from a crevice. He was netted in it. Sections were frozen to his lap and boots and the wall behind him in a grisly network.

Stein prodded a more recent victim, a partisan, with his boot. He, too, was torn open, blood and sprayed tissue steaming around him. This was the one that had been shooting at them. Stein must have thrown the first grenade right in his lap.

"Kaput," he said, unzipping his trousers and urinating on the corpse.

Krantz led them up the narrow stairwell to the upper floor. There were two windows in the largest of the rooms which looked out over the courtyard. A defensible place. The Russians had been using it for a field hospital. The dead and wounded had been dragged away, but up against the far wall was a rat's nest of bloody dressings and bandages, overflowing bins of dirty sutures and surgical equipment, and…limbs. Several dozen amputated arms and legs frozen stiff like joints of beef. They had been neatly, almost meticulously, stacked, and there was something so positively absurd about this that Luptmann felt a chuckle claw its way up his throat.

Krantz found something better than limbs: a demolition pack. The sort of thing used for clearing bunkers. If the Russians came in any number, they could give them a fine kiss good night with it.

"They're coming," Stein said, peering out the window.

A band of Russians had followed them.

Luptmann took a look himself and, yes, there they were, moving through the trees, backlit by the raging fires, slipping out of a dry ravine, making for the courtyard. With usual Soviet overkill, the whole band came running through the snowy waste, firing automatic rifles and submachine guns at the building, liberally spraying down anything in their path without a true target in sight.

One of them slipped on the ice, and as he tried to rise, Stein pulled the trigger of his carbine and the man's head imploded like a water balloon. Krantz hosed them down with his Schmeisser, and Holzy popped off a few shots. Three Russians were cut down, and the others ran back for the ravine. But one, either suicidal or numb on propaganda, ran at the building again, firing his weapon. Stein tossed a grenade to him, and the soldier never saw it coming. It exploded in mid-air right before him, pitting him with shrapnel. Luptmann saw it happen and was again struck by the absurdity of the situation. Horrible, yes, but darkly humorous. For as the grenade exploded with a flash of light and a belching roar, it blew the man's arms right off, made it look as if he'd thrown them. No one was more surprised than he. He screamed and fell, made it maybe ten feet, a red and torn thing.

Stein laughed uncontrollably.

Then Holz started, and even old, dour Krantz began to giggle. Oh, the war had sucked them dry, had emptied them out, and this was what was left: bedraggled, weary automatons that found such carnage amusing. Luptmann laughed, too, despised himself for it, but laughed all the same.

"We either get out now or wait until they bring reinforcements," Stein said.

"We wait," Krantz said. "We need to rest a moment."

They heard snow crunching below. A lone soldier made an attempt to cross the courtyard, and then two or three followed. They did not fire this time; they snuck up to the building. Stein, still laughing, went over to the pile of limbs, grabbed two arms and, with expert throws, flattened two soldiers just that quick. They got to their feet, saw what had been thrown, and retreated. But by then, Krantz and Holz were in on the act, pelting their retreating forms with frozen limbs.

It was insane, it was gruesome, and being so, it was pure, unadulterated Stalingrad.

After that, they waited. Maybe twenty minutes or thirty, smoking and making jokes, firing insults at one another, despite the fact of what they'd seen and done and the fact that the Russians were surely still out there, probably waiting for a tank to smash the building with.

And then, a sound which shut them all up. Not the booming of big guns or the falling bombs which made the building shake from time to time, pounded dust from the rafters...no, not the war, but something else. Something far worse: a long, low howling that echoed across the frosty countryside.

The beast. The Wulf.

It heralded its arrival like a trumpet heralded that of an army. The Russians in the ravine started shooting, screaming, and there was no earthly doubt that it was among them. The screaming and dying went on for some time. And then there was only the sound of chewing and wet ripping, bones being snapped for salty marrow and heads opened like cans.

"It's coming for us," Luptmann said.

They looked at each other in the cool, frosted moonlight. Walking cadavers to a man, not the elite soldiers of the 6th that had swept through France and the low countries, just scavengers living off the corpse of Stalingrad. They had fought hard and for far too long, had been ultimately abandoned by Hitler to die in the wreckage. They lived on raw horsemeat and an occasional roasted dog. Yet, they *had* lived, and not for any grand ideal set forth in a posh Berlin drawing room, but for each other. Brothers bound by the bloody umbilical of war. And now, they knew, they would die together.

It was downstairs.

They could hear it panting, gnashing its teeth, smell the slaughterhouse stench of fresh blood and well-marbled meat about it. An animal and a man, neither and both, and something hideous beyond all such things.

Stein stood up. "Farewell, my brothers, tonight I slay the beast. I do it for myself and for you. But not for that pig, Hitler…fuck Hitler, I say."

It was a sobering moment. Stein, that lecherous human animal who slaughtered the enemy with such obscene delight, was going to meet the beast. To die for the others. And what could be said in the wake of it?

Nothing.

He ran down the stairs, and the beast howled with fury. Krantz grabbed his Schmeisser and ran down there, too. Holz could not; he was terrified. But Luptmann went. He got down there in time to see The Wulf take Stein in the reflected firelight. It was huge, hunched over like a storybook troll, but easily seven feet tall, sweaty and blood-stained and evil-smelling. Its eyes were lit like red lamps, reflecting silver moonlight. Stein put a few rounds in it, and it roared with anger. It slapped the rifle from his hands, taking his arms off at the elbows with its claws that were like razor-sharp scimitars. Then it howled and took Stein, sank its long, yellow teeth into his throat, nearly severing his head. It held his shattered body in the air, shaking it, letting his hot blood rain over it in some perverse baptismal, jaws open, tongue lapping, the deranged hyena-like laughter scratching from its throat.

Krantz screamed and charged it with a bayonet fixed on a Russian rifle, running it right through. It knocked him aside, slitting his belly open. The beast bellowed with an angry, cheated snarling.

Luptmann put three rounds into it, and it staggered back outside, screeching its rage.

He dragged Krantz back up the stairs, tried to doctor him, but Krantz wouldn't have it. "I'm done, old friend, simply done," he managed. "Now take my map case, and Holz…dear little Holz…the both of you leap out that window. But first, hand me that demo pack, eh?"

Luptmann understood.

The beast howled below and came charging up the steps. It was so huge, it had to bow its head to come through the door.

34

"That's right, you ugly heap of shit," Krantz said. "Come and get me, come and get me, Der Wulf…"

The beast needed no urging. Its brain, filled with hunger and death-lust, was simple and uncomplicated, a reptilian brain: eat and kill, tear and eviscerate. A horrid, hot stench blew off it that reminded Luptmann of what a tiger's den might smell like: meat and blood and yellowing bone, dirty straw and gnawed entrails, and the memory of primal savagery. The beast stalked forward, blood dripping from its stained and shaggy rancid-smelling pelt. Its snout was dyed red, gore dripping from the daggers of its teeth. It jumped on Krantz and stuck that snout in his face. It delighted in the kill, yes, but it fed on the suffering and terror it struck in its prey, it filled itself with this and gloated.

And as it looked into Krantz's defiant face, it saw none of this. If it had had a voice it might have said, *Where is your fear, little man? Where is your terror and loathing and madness at my accursed foulness?*

Holz jumped out the window into the snow, and Luptmann was right behind him.

They heard The Wulf, that abomination, howl with confusion. By the time they were half-way across the courtyard, the demo pack went and Krantz had his last laugh. The entire second floor went in a flaming eruption of brick and stone and mortar, and the building fell. They thought they heard the beast roar with agony as it was obliterated, atomized into a fine charnel mist.

They ran away from the war, toward the river. Two could feasibly slip through the Russian lines. But only two. With terror and pain and heartbreak, Holz cried and so did Luptmann, but they did not stop.

"I'll get you home, little friend," Luptmann said, meaning it like he'd never meant anything before. "I'll get you back home…I swear on the lives of Stein and Krantz and all the others."

And they ran on, hiding and sneaking and evading. For there was a world out there beyond the blasted cemetery of Stalingrad, and they planned on knowing it again, smelling its perfume and feeling its warmth, laying softly in its arms. Only then, would they shut their eyes and know peace.

THE CHATTERING OF TINY TEETH

"...there were worse things than rats and maggots
crawling in the unhallowed earth..."
—Henry Kuttner

1

It was a bad place, and fear was something you choked down with your daily rum ration. You lived with corpses and rats and severed limbs, the shattered anatomies of your fellow soldiers. There was always blood in your mouth and steel in your belly. And, of course, there were always plenty of stories. Tales about things that prowled No-Man's Land. Nightmare shapes that hunted battlefields from time immemorial. Things that dragged off cadavers, and not all of them walked on four feet. But they were just stories, and you tried not to listen.

2

When Corporal Stubbs saw old Brass Balls making his way through the hip-deep slime of muck and water that passed for the forward trench— or at least their minute corner of it—he knew there was going to be trouble.

"Here comes the frigging shit himself," he muttered to Piggy, who was licking the grease from a dented tin of sausages.

Piggy tossed the tin into the water, wiped his lips, and put a cigarette between them. "Lovely man, that one. Reminds me of me dear old dad," he said, blowing smoke through the slats of yellow-brown teeth. "If I but had the strength, I'd kiss him right on the arse."

Stubbs took the cigarette and pulled hard off it, spitting tobacco. "Glad you could join us, Sergeant-Major Bowes. Pull up a seat, why don't you? Would you like a cup of tea? Biscuits with jam? Do speak up, man."

Bowes was not amused. Rain dripped from the lip of his steel helmet. "Lolly-gagging and running your mouth won't win us this war, Stubbs. The quicker we pull together and set things right, the quicker you'll be home to your whore of a mother and your nightly bottle of gin."

"Did you hear that, Piggy? He called me mum a whore, of all things." Stubbs shrugged and flicked his ash, leaned against the parapet. "Guess he knows the old bitch, all right. God bless you, sir."

Piggy uttered a short laugh.

"Shut your pisshole, Stubbs. You, too, Piggy" Bowes said. He cleared his throat. The anger ran from his face then, like hot wax down the stem of a candle. A corrupt grin slit his features. "You lads look like you need a change of scenery. Right. I've just the thing for you." He cleared his throat again. "As you well know, things haven't been going well—"

"Haven't they, Sarge? Didn't notice meself," Piggy said.

Stubbs shook his head and sucked in a deep lungful of air that was rich with the stench of putrescence. "Can't believe you said that, sir. Why, take a look around. If this ain't Heaven, me boy, then just point the way."

Despite himself, old Brass Balls did look around.

And what he saw was Flanders. And more precisely, the famous sea of Flanders' mud. It was a colossal bowl of viscous sludge that stank and ran and fouled everything it touched. The rain kept coming down, and the trenches were filled with stagnant water that was flavored with blood, urine, and feces. Bodies floated in it. Parts of bodies. Countless rats that had tried in vain to reach the bodies and had drowned. And the rain fell, and the mud kept flowing, and the men kept dying. It was a gray world, gray and wet and stinking.

And that's what the sergeant-major saw.

Had he any humanity left after three years of the Great War, he would've wretched and then quietly lost his mind.

But he was right about one thing: things hadn't been going real well. Nearly a week before, some nit back at battalion got a real prince of an idea for an offensive. Troops were mustered and ammunition passed out. It began with a thirty-six hour artillery barrage of the German lines. Battalion figured that would soften the Hun up nicely. The smoke had barely cleared when some five thousand men of the British Expeditionary Force went up and over the wire and charged through No-Man's Land, hell-for-leather. Or maybe not so hell-for-leather, being that the terrain was riddled with chains of shell holes and great valleys from collapsing tunnel networks, all of which were separate bogs of mud. It looked like the dark side of the moon. The water was so deep in those polluted, filth-scummed pools that a man could drown in them carrying full fighting kit. They threw ladders and duckboards over them, and if nothing else, the mires became good places to die.

As it turned out, the Germans hadn't been softened at all.

The majority of the shelling had been concentrated on what was thought to be the German forward trench system, but was in actuality a series of dummy trenches dug by the Germans to delude their enemy. The ruse worked quite well.

Ultimately, when the infantry reached the high ground that bordered the German lines, hell conveniently broke lose. Hun flares filled the skies. Shells came screaming in. Bullets whipping. Machine guns clattering. All in all, the Brits lost over 2,300 men in a few hours of fighting.

Minor, of course, in comparison with what had happened at the Somme the year before. But costly all the same.

The Germans hammered the BEF all the way across No-Man's Land, forcing the survivors—most of them weighted-down with the wounded and dead—to retreat through a vicious artillery barrage. The boggy crater holes sucked down most of the bodies, and as for the rest, who could say? It wasn't even remotely realistic to send out stretcher-bearers into that hellzone. For the next eight, ten hours all that could be heard were the screams and moans of the dying and dismembered as they succumbed to ghastly, agonizing deaths. Which came not only in the form of their wounds, but from the armies of rats that prowled No-Man's Land.

Stubbs and Piggy were two of the survivors.

And now they sat in the muck, smoking and listening to the rain fall around them and rattle against the wire up yonder, thud against the sandbags, run in rivers down into the trenches.

"So, what sort of job have you for us, Sergeant-Major?" Piggy asked.

Sergeant-Major Bowes grinned like a cat with a mouse in its belly.

3

Vermin.

A constant of any war.

Anywhere there was garbage and human waste and bodies heaped like cordwood, there would be vermin. Flanders was no different. Vermin came in the form of wild dog packs that prowled No-Man's Land and dragged off bodies or parts of them. They came in the form of rats that devoured the dead and dying (they rarely went after healthy adults, but there were occasions). Rat bites were common as dysentery. And then there were the lice. Entire companies were crawling with them. The soldiers spent hours killing them, crushing them between thumb and forefinger. But the next day a new batch would replace them.

"Aye," Piggy said as they crawled on their bellies through the mud and debris, "I had the nits so bad one time, I tossed me shirt to the floor and watched it try to crawl away."

Stubbs knew it wasn't exaggeration; he'd seen it himself and more than once.

There were three others with them—Privates Benner, Sourton, and Pence—all green as summer grass, to a man. Stubbs could hear them back there, trembling like saplings in a high wind. One of them was whimpering. No matter. Soon enough he'd have his heart ripped out, and tears would be beyond him.

Piggy froze-up and lay stock-still, like a mannequin waiting to be dressed. He gave the others a hand signal to stay put. It was maybe thirty minutes until

40

sunset, but it didn't matter with the drizzling rain and heavy ground fog. Dark and dreary, was what it was.

Stubbs studied the terrain ahead, and it was merely more of the same. Blasted, blackened, gray with spreading pools of muck and standing water. The ground was so saturated, absorption was out of the question. There were shell craters, big and small. Most filled with water and many large enough to hide more than one man. Rats skittered through ditches and paused atop blighted stumps. This place had once been a forest, but was now denuded of both leaf and branch. The trees themselves rose like burned masts from the sodden ground, many split in two and scorched by fire.

"Onward and upward," Piggy said, and they began snaking their way forward again.

There were abandoned trenches full of heaped bodies. Collapsed tunnels and huge pits. Somewhere in the distance a dog howled. Piggy and the others could hear the Hun out there, joking in German, out on patrol or formed into burial parties, attempting to steal some food from the rats and dogs. There were bootless feet jutting up from the mud, some stripped right down to the bone. Dozens upon dozens of bodies cast about in every possible stage of decomposition. Stubbs saw a skull leering from the top of a leaning tree and three Hun skeletons in dingy gray rags peering over the lip of a bomb crater.

"What's this then?" Piggy whispered to them.

There was a shallow depression in the swampy ground and, in it, the form of a man face-down in the mud. He wore the long tunic of an officer and a Sam Browne belt that was riddled with tiny puncture marks made by rat's teeth. He was bloated up and noisome, but the really unpleasant thing was that his body was *moving*. In slow, boneless undulations it squirmed and shuddered. Piggy flipped him over, and he had been eaten down to the bone, his eye sockets thick with feasting maggots and his body cavity housing five or six hungry, busy rats. Piggy shook his head at the sight and shoved the officer away, a great flap of flesh falling over the horror in the hollowed belly.

One of the new soldiers started vomiting.

"Do as you will," Stubbs told him, "but be quiet about it."

"He's one of ours. Better grab his meat ticket," Piggy said.

Stubbs yanked the identity disc from around the corpse's throat and shoved it in his shirt pocket.

Just as the sun—what there was of it—faded behind the horizon, they found the set of abandoned trenches they were to set up the listening post in. Piggy directed the newbies in first. They slid into the water with silent cries. Dead Hun floated in the murk. It took some time to clear them out—they were so waterlogged and rotten they came apart like boiled chicken—and drag them off. But the stench remained. Stubbs had the newbies use their entrenching tools to help drain the slop, but after two, then three spongy putrescent corpses were unearthed, he gave up on the idea. Flanders was one huge and muddy burial ground. And the earth could only swallow so many bodies before spitting a few back up.

With the mist blowing down from the black hills to the east, it was hard to know where they were exactly. All Piggy could tell them for sure was that the Germans were just ahead and their own lines a few miles back.

It was a dark and shadowy spot brooded over by the skeletal remains of trees and singed rows of hedges that rode the squat and rolling hills. Like being trapped in a dead forest of craters and sharp dips. The mud was heavier. There were bodies everywhere. Parts of them scattered in every conceivable direction and very often caught in the trees overhead. That and the wreckage of splintered coffins, headstones turned to rubble. Stubbs figured it was an actual graveyard they were in, and an artillery barrage had blasted it flat and exhumed the dead in one form or another. The air stank of putrid decay. The mists smelled rank and evil. There was the husk of a church in the grainy distance, much of it reduced to crumbling masonry from the impact of shells.

Leave it to the Hun to dig trenches here.

"A churchyard," Stubbs said. "By all the saints."

He'd seen a lot in that war. He'd waded through corpses and death and disease on a daily basis, but, despite himself, something about this place made him uneasy. And it had nothing to do with the nearby Germans and even less to do with the obliterated dead. This place simply had a peculiar *feel* to it. The shadows seemed to creep, to prowl out of the corner of your eye…but when you looked, nothing.

Fucking Brass Balls, Stubbs thought. *A listening post out here. Damn.*

Piggy found a skull peering at him from the trench wall and dug it out. Stubbs took a look at it. It was pitted with teeth marks. Large ones. No rat or dog ever born had dentition like that. It sent a chill worming through him.

He gave Piggy a concerned look and then smiled at the dirt-spattered faces of the privates. "Well, if it ain't me old Uncle Dick. And thin as a rail he is," he joked, but his voice was low and cautious. "Don't worry, Unc, you and me will have ourselves a bite come first light. See if we don't."

The privates, all sadly numb now to war's atrocities and litter, giggled in the darkness.

But Piggy did not smile.

Neither did Stubbs. He studied the landscape with a wary eye. Knowing with complete certainty deep in the opaque depths of his soul that they were being watched, being studied. That something out there amongst the mud and bones and rubble was waiting for them. And it wasn't the Hun.

They were on higher ground here, and the water was only two, three feet deep. He could see that the maze of waterlogged trenches fed into a huge and gaping pit just off a way. Probably the remains of a shelled bunker and its assorted tunnels.

Christ, tunneling through a boneyard, of all things.

He wanted a cigarette, but there was no smoking out here. In the darkness, you could see the glow of a cigarette for a long way. Easy for a sniper to draw a bead on you. So, Stubbs waited in the heavy, rolling dusk and listened to the distant thunder of shelling, saw the yellow flashes of flares and the red glow of exploding rounds. Somebody was getting pounded good, and part of him almost wished he was there rather than out here. At least an artillery barrage was a known quantity. You knew what you were afraid of…but in this stygian, appalling netherworld you just couldn't put a finger on what scared you. What filled your belly with crawling worms and made your skin pebble with gooseflesh.

He waited.

He could hear the others breathing. Skittering noises out in the gutted remains of the churchyard which he knew were rats. Armies of bloated, gray-streaked rats big as cats. Their eyes shined like steel in the murk. You could hear them out there, chewing and rending and digging up half-buried things. The tear of flesh, the crunch of bone.

Horrors of War

At around three as he drifted aimlessly at the edge of sleep, knowing he had to stay awake, the drizzle stopped and the clouds parted like foam in the sky. A ragged crescent of moon washed down the pitted landscape in an eerie, ethereal glow. He could see the rats now, scattering at the intrusion of light. Blankets of mist clung to the earth, moving like wisps of smoke. He studied the shadow-riven forest of stripped trees. He was tired, his eyes would barely stay open, but he was certain he could see shapes moving out there.

And that's when he heard the sound.

Out in that rat-infested blackness, the sound of teeth chattering. It rose up and died away. Something in his chest dropped. His breath was locked down in his lungs.

"You hear—" he started to say, but Piggy's hand on his arm quieted him.

Through a burnt and ruined expanse of hedges he saw graves. Not old ones, but recent. Eight or ten graves in a row with mounds of earth piled atop them, into which crude crosses were sunk. They were Hun graves, he figured. And as he watched, the crosses began to tremble and jerk, finally falling over as if what lay beneath was trying to claw its way out.

But that wasn't it at all.

Stubbs caught an odor. It wasn't the stink of decomposition or violated graves: he was used to that. This was different, a black and filthy smell, flyblown, yes, but sharp and acrid. Piggy's hand gripped his arm tightly. Over at the graves they could see small, slinking forms. Hunched over and lithe, they pawed at the mounds of dirt.

His throat full of dust, something tight squeezing in his chest, Stubbs brought up his Enfield rifle, sighted in on whatever it was he was seeing. Human-like forms. But small and vicious like rabid animals, shapes snipped from black cloth. They frantically dug at the graves, five or six of them, snorting and grunting and chattering their teeth, and it was an awful sound. A sound to make your soul wither on the vine.

He had all he could do not to shoot.

"Don't, mate," Piggy said into his ear. "For the love of Mary and Jesus, don't draw attention to us."

And it seemed that one of them heard, for it stood up and peered in their direction. It looked like a child…or something pretending to be one. A child with a mane of long, matted hair. The moon glowered down on its face, and its skin was yellow as leprosy and corrugated, the eyes red and wet like fresh blood. Stubbs felt his insides melt. It looked right at them, mouth opening and closing rapidly, its horrible teeth chattering madly.

Stubbs didn't move for two, three minutes and neither did Piggy. The thing turned away and helped its kin exhume the Germans. In another five minutes, they had pulled two bodies from the rank earth. There was a thunder of small feet as they dragged them off into the shadows.

It was some time before Stubbs allowed himself to breathe. His knuckles were white as he gripped the Enfield. "Good Christ...Piggy...what... what..."

"Don't know...those stories you hear about—"

There was a splashing sound just down the trench line where it widened into the water-filled gully. Privates Benning, Sourton, and Pence, who were farther down and closer to it, came awake with a start. Piggy had let them sleep, knowing they needed it. But now they were alert and frightened.

"What was that?" one of them said in a dry voice.

"Jesus, that stink..."

And then it rose up all around them, the sound of chattering teeth. Like skulls clattering their pearlies in the gloom. Stubbs, half out of his mind, scanned the darkness with his rifle. In his head, there were insane images of battalions of war-dead skeletons rising up from the dank earth, chattering their teeth and rattling their bones. The noise was in front of them, behind them. It was impossible to pinpoint. Piggy sloshed through the muck to the privates, trying to calm them. Stubbs saw shapes mulling about the trench. He started shooting. Something dove over his head and landed amongst the others. There was screaming and shouting and awful, inhuman slithering sounds. More shapes slipped into the trench.

Stubbs cried out and skewered one with his bayonet, its toxic stink in his face. He ran it through, and still it fought and clawed just out of reach, attempting, it seemed, to force itself up the long blade at him. It was no child...it was a demonic thing from a grave.

More deranged faces rose from the gully of water, and the things darted forward with spidery limbs and fell on the soldiers.

Piggy was slashing at them with his trench knife, but there were simply too many clawing, biting, malicious forms, all slavering and tearing. He started wailing as the writhing shapes buried him alive. *"Oh sweet Mother of Jesus… Stubbs…Stubbs…get 'em off me…get 'em off…"*

And the last sight Stubbs had of his old friend and comrade was of him being dragged down into the gully, his screaming face submerging in the stagnant water.

And then suddenly Stubbs was alone.

He bolted out of the trench and off into the darkness, moving in what he thought was the direction of the British lines. But, Christ, it was hard to be sure. He fought through tangles of barbwire and swam through inundated bomb craters and crawled through fields of bones. But he kept going, certain he could hear them creeping and hopping behind him. His face twisted in a continuous silent scream, he listened for the sound of chattering teeth.

4

Sergeant-Major Bowes, who'd conceived of Stubbs' little adventure, didn't have it much better himself. Just as he'd had something unpleasant in mind for Stubbs and Piggy, battalion HQ had something unpleasant planned for him. Just before dawn as a light rain began to fall from the sky, he led a raiding party into No-Man's Land. Twenty men armed with Enfields and revolvers went over the parapet. Their faces were blackened beneath the rims of dented steel helmets. They carried hatchets and wire cutters and belts of grenades. The last four men carried ladders to breach shell craters and, most importantly, to lay over the German barbwire when they made their assault.

They'd been out maybe thirty minutes, making good time across the scarred and gutted landscape. At the Hun lines, they started cutting through tangles of barbed wire, making as little sound as possible.

Bowes was one of the first to go over the top and drop into the trenches, and they were empty. Abandoned except for multitudes of rotting corpses floating in the muck. He landed right on one, and it went to mush beneath his trench boots. And the smell…nothing new, but, Jesus, nauseating.

"We've been buggered," he told the others. "Goddamn if we haven't."

Gunfire rang out, and a few of his men screamed and sank into the muddy water. The sky exploded with bursts of flame. Parachute flares drifted down in showers of white and green stars. The ravaged landscape was turned to glaring daylight as the raiding party tried to climb back out of the trench system and reach No-Man's Land and its relative safety. In the distance, German artillery guns thundered, and trench mortars popped, and suddenly the air was electric with high-velocity shells hissing and screeching. They dropped amongst them with violent, earth-shattering eruptions of flame and debris.

Bowes called out for his soldiers to seek ground, seek ground, and he could see blackened taut faces and bulging white eyes in the flare lights, and then there was a resounding explosion, and three men not too far away were pulverized. Gore and bone shards slammed into the sergeant-major and dumped him into the muck.

There were blinding flashes and screaming. Rending explosions and rifle-shots. Men trying to escape through water-filled trenches and the stink of blood and meat, voided bowels and dying…everywhere, there was dying.

Bowes pulled himself from the mud and shoved men before him, up and over the sheared barbwire. He made it himself as more mortar rounds chewed into the trench system, detonating with plumes of fire and smoke. Muck and tainted water rained down. The concussion knocked Bowes face first into the moist, foul-tasting earth. A blasted tree took a round that tossed it up into the sky where it shattered into fragments.

Somebody started moaning that they were blind, blind, blind.

Somebody else wanted to know where his legs were.

The sergeant-major was drenched with blood, muddy water, and powdered down with dirt and ash. But he had to rally these men together before it was too late, he had to—

But then the earth erupted before him, and he was struck with clods of soil and water and wet things. More men were screaming, and maybe he was, too. Maybe he even blacked out for a moment, because he was on his ass and his arm was aching. A few shell splinters were lodged in his left bicep. Another flare illuminated the carnage of dismembered men. One of them stumbled back towards the German lines, holding intestines that sprouted from the smoking chasm of his belly. Another was waving his own severed arm madly in the air.

And then a blood-maddened, insane voice shrieked, *"Gas...gassss... gasssss..."*

And whoever was still in one piece and not raving mad were clawing for gas masks as the shells burst with dull, echoing thuds. Bowes pulled his on, praying the others did, too, as he thought of men he'd seen in hospitals, gas victims, vomiting out bloody chunks of lung. He could hear a warning bell ringing shrilly at the German lines.

By then, the gas was everywhere in yellow, miasmic clouds, clinging to the ground. Men were coughing and retching, and some were giggling and sobbing.

Well behind them now, from the Hun's advance lines, there were shouts and cries and gunfire. And what in Christ was that about? A counterattack? The Germans were surely under attack unless they'd shelled their own trenches.

None of it made sense, not really.

Another parachute flare sputtered in the sky, drifting earthward like a burning meteorite. Bowes saw that most of his men were dead. A few had gotten their masks on. Most were beyond hope. One soldier stumbled blindly forward, and he seemed to be carrying something. Why...it looked like he was carrying two or three *children*. But he wasn't carrying them; they were *clinging* to him like leeches, gnawing and tearing at him.

About that time, the sergeant-major heard the sound.

The chattering of teeth.

And then the real screaming began.

5

It was two days later, his arm in a sling, that Bowes found Stubbs. He located him away from the front in one of the myriad support trenches. He sat on a wooden bench, numbly filling damp, moldering sacks with sand. Other men with glazed, staring eyes did the same.

He stared at the sergeant-major, managed a morose and hateful grin. "Are you shell-shocked too, love? That's what we all are here." A morbid laughter came from his throat. "All crazy. Too crazy to be at the front. Did they tell you what happened to us out there?"

Bowes only nodded grimly. "I heard."

"Piggy's dead, Brass Balls. You bastard."

"I'm sorry," was all Bowes could say.

Command had told him everything. The captain was concerned about it all. He was certain that Stubbs was shell-shocked; had to be with a wild story like that. But as the captain told Bowes about it, you could see the dread in his eyes. Because it wasn't the first time he'd heard about such things. He looked even worse after Bowes related what he'd seen near the Hun lines.

"Right," said the Captain. "Bloody ugly business, that. Heard tales myself. Such things shouldn't be. This war is hard enough as is. I leave it to you to sort out, Sergeant Major. Right." Then he wandered out of the command bunker, looking very much like a man who needed to shit badly and couldn't find the latrine.

For a time, nothing more was said between the sergeant-major and Stubbs. They'd never liked each other. Stubbs, the volunteer. Bowes, the career soldier. But sometimes a kinship is formed by mutual experience, mutual suffering. Bowes lit cigarettes for the both of them, and they were good cigarettes, too, American ones.

Exhaling a cloud of smoke, Bowes told Corporal Stubbs what had happened to the raiding party. He told it easily and with complete belief. "…I survived by crawling back towards the abandoned Hun trenches. I threw my grenades at the little horrors and ran. I spent the night under a heap of wormy Hun corpses, but I survived. And now the captain has laid it all in my lap. He wants nothing to do with any of it." Bowes left out certain details, like the bit about the thing that leaped on him and how he slashed it to bloody ribbons with his trench knife. How he'd gripped it by its greasy, clotted hair and slit the head free and how that decapitated head had looked at him, *stared at him,* the teeth snapping hungrily.

"They said it was battle fatigue," Stubbs said in a wounded voice. "Treated me like I was half out of me mind. And maybe I was. Maybe I still am. But I could see it, sir; I could see it in their eyes."

"What did you see?"

"The *belief.* They believed me, and they were scared. Petrified at the idea of it."

The morning sun tried desperately to burn through the cloistral mists of fog and smoke which hung in the sky like congealed fat. There was a booming in the distance. The rattle of a machine gun; despite the horror each had witnessed, the horror that made the atrocities of war seem positively trivial, the battles still raged. The war had not stopped. It had not even slowed down.

Bowes dragged off his cigarette, scratched at a nit that nipped at his neck. "I've heard it before, you know. Those chattering teeth. In the past year or so…I've heard it on still nights out in No-Man's Land. Chattering and chattering."

Stubbs didn't admit if he had. He pursed his lips into a tight white line as he remembered his last sight of Piggy. "What the hell are they, Sergeant-Major?"

Bowes cleared his throat. "Ghouls. They are ghouls."

"Ghouls," Stubbs said, rolling the word off his tongue and not liking its taste much. "Ghouls."

Bowes nodded bleakly. "Yes, you see I was with Kitchener's regiment in the Northern Sudan back in '97 and '98. We fought the Mahdists tooth and nail at Omdurman and Khartoum. Egyptian forces were billeted to us. Good sort they were, but superstitious." Bowes licked his lips, spit bits of grit into the air. "Fine soldiers they were for the most part, but bogged-down as it were by centuries of tradition. There were places in the hills they simply wouldn't go. We had a devil of a time with them. Old burial places they wouldn't set foot in by night, said they were cursed, haunted. *Ghuls,* they said.

"Yes, that's where I first learned of the ghouls. How they would come out of their black holes amongst the old, crumbling tombs. A young Egyptian fellow told me all about it. Said the ghouls haunted the ancient crypts, lived in the decay and bones, fed on them. That there were places in Iraq, Persia, even the Sudan and Egypt, shunned tracks of desert into which no sane man would venture. These were the places the ghouls dwelled. He said that if ever I was out in the desert, in some lonely and desolate spot, and a child came out of the night, out of the sands and wind and called me by name, that I should shoot it on sight. Yes, and run like hell. Because they were like rats, human rats. Where there was one, there were dozens."

Stubbs said he believed it. Every last demented word of it. Because he

50

had seen. *He had seen.* "I wonder why they're here? This isn't Persia or one of them places."

"But the bodies, lad, so many bodies lying about. So much...*food* for them." He shrugged. "Maybe they've always sought out wars. Sought out the litter it produces."

Neither man said anything for a time. They sat and smoked and listened to the buzz of war and smelled the stink of it and saw the wreckage of it, thinking of worse things. Things that creeped by night. Things that fed on flesh and bones. Little things like children that were not children, but a dark and twisted secret of antiquity.

"The captain, as I said, has laid it at my feet," Bowes reiterated.

"And?"

"I have a few ideas of where they might be hiding, of where their lair might be. But I need a few able men. Men not afraid to shoot things that pretend to be children. Do you know any men like that?"

Stubbs grinned.

6

What the sergeant-major did was ask for volunteers.

For a special mission, he said. Those that he did get, he couldn't use at all, men maddened by war that volunteered for anything. And that left the raiding party at just Bowes and Stubbs, which wasn't quite enough.

The captain was aware of their operation, and it was he who steered them towards the far trenches where the trench mortar battery was located in an abandoned maze of ditches. It was a dreary and forsaken location. Stubbs and Bowes slugged through the mud and found it after some time.

They saw a heavily sandbagged dugout and a few forlorn men crouched out front, doing maintenance on the mortar tubes and plates. Two others manned a Lewis gun atop the parapet. They were a beaten, lean lot.

One soldier, a private, dressed in little more than rags, aimed an Enfield at them until he saw Bowes' stripes. Then he sprang to attention. "Sir! Sorry, sir!" he called out, his face covered with sores and dirt. His military bearing was almost laughable under the circumstances. "The lieutenant's inside, sir!"

Stubbs noticed there was a cross painted over the doorway but didn't

51

comment on it. Wearily, he and the sergeant-major descended the few creaking steps.

There was a small excavated room within, more sandbags lining the walls, a rough-timbered roof overhead. Seven or eight men lounged on the dirt floor or were splayed across ammunition boxes or heaps of mildewed blankets. It stunk of tobacco smoke, body odor, and rum in there. A few religious pictures were tacked up.

There was a small desk with a packing crate for a chair. A lieutenant with a bearded face and great gaping eyes like open wounds stared at them. He stood and returned the salutes of Bowes and Stubbs. "Gentlemen, glad you could come. Volunteers, eh? A special mission you say? Yes, the runner was here an hour ago and filled me in. Excellent, excellent." There was a rosary clutched in his left fist. A charred pipe hung from his colorless lips. He kept trying to light it, the idea that there was no tobacco in it was lost on him. "Men," he said, turning to those lounging about. "Have we any volunteers today? No? Yes? What's it going to be lads, eh?"

The lounging soldiers stared blindly at Stubbs and Bowes, wanting no part of them. They smoked in silence, passed a bottle of gin, ate tinned biscuits. Their faces were dead and emotionless, colorless masks pressed out by the ravages of war. It was hard to tell whether they were nineteen or forty.

Finally, one man with a shrapnel-scarred face said, "What sort of mission we talking here? Something bleeding dangerous, I hope."

"We're…" Bowes sighed, then drew in a quick breath, unsure how to broach the subject. "There's been a group of…*individuals* scavenging the dead. We're going to track them down, sort them out."

"The chatterers," someone said.

The lieutenant, pacing back and forth, said, "Chatterers? Eh? What's this then?" He turned away and started discoursing freely with his desk. "Hope they've got their own tobacco. Dreadful business…"

"Out there at night," another said. "You hear them."

Stubbs stepped forward. "The Jerries? *The Hun?* Is that what you're worried about, mate?" he said, with little conviction.

The man, slat-thin, scratched himself and stared into space. "There's worse things than the Hun…them that eat and chew. Them that chatter. Them that crawl and slink. Out theres—" he said, stabbing one white finger towards the doorway "—them that crawls and creeps and chatters. Them out there. Them that's hungry, yes. At night…we hear 'em clawing at the sandbags. That's why we hide in here. They whisper your name…"

The lieutenant was still trying to light his pipe. "Confounded business," he said, shaking his head. "Tobacco that won't light. Damp I should say."

Stubbs knew the man was hopelessly mad and paid him no attention. "That's right. We're going to clean 'em out. Rat-catchers and exterminators. That's us, love. In for a penny or a pound? Or would you rather hide in here? Sooner or later, they'll get in, won't they? Hungry as all hell, too."

One of the men hugged himself. Another began to whimper.

The man with the scarred face got up and crushed his cigarette beneath his heel. "I've had enough of this shit. Name's Keegan, Sergeant Keegan. Time to clean this mess up." He looked over at two men leaning against the wall. "Chalmers? Crumbly? What you say, then?"

They stepped forward.

"Better to stand and die," the one called Chalmers said, "than to sit and weep."

Stubbs patted them on the shoulders each in turn and led them up and out of the bunker. Bowes turned towards the lieutenant, saluted despite himself. He wanted to say something to the man. Anything. But the words wouldn't come.

He turned and left.

Behind him he heard the lieutenant rambling: "I say, this pipe's a bit of a scoundrel, isn't it? Well, no matter. Taste of the flame will soon sort it out." He tried to light it again. "Yes? Better…no, still not lighting, you rascal? Right. Give my best to the general. Tell him to stop by for a spot. Yes. Would it be imprudent of me to request more tobacco? Eh? What's that you say?"

By then Bowes couldn't hear him anymore. He was grateful for the stink of war. The stink of lunacy in the dugout was far worse.

7

Single-file, they passed through yet another blackened and burnt graveyard of trees.

They had Enfield rifles and Webley revolvers. Jackets of bombs. Lanterns swung at their belts. Trench knives were sharpened and bayonets fixed. Keegan carried the Lewis machine gun, his men loaded down with pan magazines for it.

"Aye, what we need is one those liquid-fire contraptions," he was saying to Stubbs as they walked across the gouged landscape. "Have you seen them, mate? By Christ, what a bloody show they put on! Saw the Jerries using one at Ypres. They strap these tanks of petrol on their backs what are connected to these hose-pipes. *Flammenwerfer*, they call 'em. Saw the Hun attack one of our pill boxes, those hoses spitting out twenty, thirty-foot tongues of flame. Saturated our positions. Cooked every last man to a bloody crisp. And, Christ, that stink in the air—like roasting meat on a spit. Great oily clouds of smoke."

"What did you do?" Stubbs said.

"We aimed for those tanks. Boom! Cloud of fire and no more Hun!"

The ground was hilly, torn, glistening like grease. A rain was falling, and mist seeped up from the ragged brown earth. There were sloping treed bluffs that had been turned into huge deadfalls from the shelling. And more bodies, of course, some wasted right down to skeletons. Others quite fresh and bloated. Stubbs saw a hand sticking up out of the mud like it was asking to be pulled out. They saw a Hun corpse upon which two mangy, filthy cats were feeding. They had stripped much of the meat from the face, tearing it off in raw filets and gulping it down.

Crumbly said, "Request permission to shoot the bastards."

"Denied," Bowes said.

They had a job to do, he told them one and all. Rats? Cats? There were worse things out here. Last thing they needed was to bring a patrol of Germans down on them. "We might find nothing today, lads," he went on. "And maybe part of me hopes we won't. But if we do…*if we do,* then we must be ready, eh?" He stopped them purposely, sensing they were getting close now. He passed out cigarettes. A pint of rum made the rounds. "You might see things today, lads. And they might be crafty, smart things. They might look like people, maybe. They'll certainly look like children…but, dear Christ, *they're not human,* get me? These things…they're evil…you're just prey to them. Remember that. They're no more human than pieces of walking meat. No matter how they look, how they act. You see 'em, you shoot 'em on sight. Is that understood?

Because if you don't, God help us. We'll never see home again."

And that was pretty clear, so on they went, trudging through the ravaged, blasted countryside.

Stubbs was thinking about the tunnels.

Both the allies and the Germans had dug miles and miles of tunnels through the Flanders mud. Many were abandoned. Many were not. Others had collapsed. The point being, the countryside was honeycombed with them. And what better system of conveyance for those little horrors than the endless passages? Those burrows could take them anywhere and everywhere. Out to the battlefields and graveyards and back to theirs lairs again. It was perfect. And he himself had seen them come up through the water to get Piggy. Apparently, they did just fine in the submerged, flooded blackness.

It was a thought.

About thirty minutes later, they struck on a disused, weed-choked road and followed it. The trees here were black and leafless, tangled with fingers of mist, but it was Autumn, and that was no surprise. It was from seasonal change and not war. The wind blew dead leaves underfoot and tossed them into cyclones in vacant, brooding fields. There were occasional shell holes, but no bodies. They saw few bones, and these were discolored, gnawed-looking.

But nobody dared comment on that.

Ten minutes later Keegan said, "Aye, look at this then."

They all did. A skeleton dressed in dirty rags was wedged between the trunk of a sprawling oak and a few enclosing limbs, fifteen feet off the ground. Its jaws were sprung open as if in a scream. Something had built a nest in the cage of ribs. From where they stood, they could see no injuries—no broken bones, no bullet holes or charring.

"What you suppose got him?" Chalmers asked.

But they all knew, somehow, it wasn't the war. "Maybe he starved," Stubbs offered. "Maybe he was hiding. Maybe he was so afraid of something, he never came down again."

They followed the road another twenty minutes and then there it was.

The abandoned village.

It was clustered over a series of yawning hills—little houses and crumbling brick shops, the grim finger of a church steeple lording above. A frost-heaved cobblestone thoroughfare snaked through it, but, like the road in, it had been reclaimed by weeds and wild grasses. It was a lot of things, that mist-choked place, but it wasn't quaint. A palpable pall of dread hung over the high-pitched roofs and leaning walls. Dark, empty windows looked down on the soldiers with a vacuous gaze, and whatever lurked in the dusty silence did not show itself.

"What happened, then?" Crumbly wanted to know. "Did they just up and leave, I ask? Was it the war? Is that what?"

Chalmers shook his head. "The war hasn't come within a mile of this damned place. It's not that."

And it wasn't. They all knew that.

The village had a bad feeling to it. A sinister, blighted feel. A strange and mephitic rottenness hung in the stillborn air that the stink of the battlefield could never hope to touch. This was cancerous, pestilent, unwholesome. Even the shadows seemed wrong. Too many or not enough. And quiet… so very quiet. Not a bird sang, nothing scurried in the woods that pressed in blackly from all sides. It was a huge and deathly stillness, a breathing hush of waiting and watching. The atmosphere of mortuaries and crypts.

But it wasn't empty.

Maybe there were no people, but there was *something*. Grim, hateful, and malevolent. Just a whisper of it, but it was there.

Bowes cleared his throat. "There was a Belgian fellow, a priest, used to visit the lines. Used to give last rites when our chaplain was injured by shellfire. A good bloke name of Vanderhoogen. You remember him, eh, Stubbs? Anyway, he said this village was abandoned thirty-odd years ago. People just wouldn't stay here." Bowes paused, studying the village as he would any other military objective. His left arm was still in a sling from the shrapnel he'd taken during the abortive and nightmarish raid a few nights before. He couldn't handle a rifle, but he had two Webley pistols on his belt, and now he sighted one in. "You know the bit—sounds and the like. Haunted, they said. Shapes moving about at night. Strange smells. No one was concerned until graves at the cemetery had been opened. They'd find bones in the morning scattered about, chewed-looking. Then a family vanished. Then another. Villagers fled. Said they saw hideous figures skulking about, small things like children but not children. Faces peering in windows at night. Red eyes watching from the shadows…"

Bowes went on, telling them he'd heard such stories other places and paid them no mind. Every empty town in every dark wood had some ghastly tale attached to it. But after what he'd seen in No-Man's Land, he started putting things together.

"And that's why we're here, lads. This place, I think, is where our problem originates. So, let's get to it then."

Crumbly said, "You sure bullets and bombs are the trick, sir? Maybe what's needed here is something more spiritual, eh?"

"They'll do," Bowes promised him. "We're hunting something flesh and blood. At least, I hope so."

8

The village.

The air was impossibly heavy as they made their way amongst the buildings, like some saturated envelope of menace. The rain fell, and the mud sluiced, and there was a chill here that had not been present earlier. Everything seemed to be decaying like flesh in a grave—collapsing roofs held together mainly by fingers of mold; walls punched with inexplicable holes through which oily darkness leered; shutters torn off, bricks going to powder, doorways warped and askew with unnatural angles. And everywhere, shadows pooling and flowing like rivers of absolute blackness.

"Can't say I like it," Keegan said, his face streaked with dirt and beaded with raindrops. "Can't say I like it one bit."

Building by house by shed, they checked out everything carefully. Even cobwebbed cellars and outbuildings. Places cut into the dank earth where the smell was of rank corruption, a high and oddly pestiferous stench of violated graveyards and plundered charnel houses. They didn't linger in such places long.

The truly unpleasant fact was that nothing had been touched or rifled through. Furniture, glassware, tools, lumber. It all sat untouched. Closets were hung with rotting clothing and piled with mildewed shoes. There were even a few hunting rifles, bottles of dusty liquor. The inhabitants had left in a great hurry, and none, not beggar nor thief nor recalcitrant boy, had *dared* come here to take anything. It was a shunned place. A haunted place. And this was more disturbing than just about anything.

The only thing any of the edifices had in common besides desolation were jagged claw marks furrowed into everything, shredding wallpaper and slitting open chairs. Doors were scathed by them, bed mattresses cleaved open, banisters gouged. But the most terrible thing were the prints in the dust—the footprints of tiny feet.

They found what might have been a tavern once. And in the dusty confines of the kitchen, a place that stunk of ancient blood and pain, they found a litter pile of bones in one foul-smelling corner. The bones were yellowed and punctured with teeth marks. And worse, the bones were human. And worse yet, they were the tiny bones of infants and toddlers.

"Bastards," Stubbs said, barely able to control himself. "Dirty murdering bastards."

Then they left the town and climbed up to the church that overlooked the village.

It was weathered a soiled gray, and the doors were missing. It brooded over both town and churchyard at the rear. The steeple was stripped and skeletal, the cross covered in something black and nameless. They went in and found it untenanted, save for the heaps of bones piled on the altar. And every last one methodically stripped of meat and sucked dry of marrow. It smelled dead and decayed in there like an exhumed coffin. The ambience was noxious and godless. Whatever worshipped at that altar of bones, did so in cloistered darkness. The soldiers mumbled prayers beneath their breath, begging for mercy and deliverance from that horrible place, from that festering and invidious atmosphere which seemed to crawl over their skins like grave worms.

Then they visited the churchyard.

Whatever had enveloped the town in dank, hellish sweetness, it was worse here. The atmosphere was a cauldron of sunless, eldritch horror.

Weapons at the ready, the soldiers followed a sunken road through the sucking, yellow mud. What they saw was a travesty. Headstones and funerary crosses had been tipped over. Stone angels had been smeared with excrement.

Vaults were flung open and emptied. Coffins had been dragged from their berths and shattered to kindling. And everywhere, bones scattered and pitted. Skulls laughed from the mud, were balanced atop sepulchers, and stacked in concentric circles. Rain poured down, and water ran from empty eye sockets. Even the squat bushes and denuded trees were decorated with femurs and ribcages and ulnas, crowned by jawless skulls. A necropolis decorated lavishly with the raw materials of the grave.

"This is their place," Bowes said in a hopeless voice.

And no one disagreed with that. They patrolled on, sweat-greased fingers on triggers as they moved amongst the open graves and ruined crypts. Suddenly Crumbly let out a piercing cry. The ground had given way beneath him, and he was up to his chest in a hole, pawing frantically to get out. The others pulled him free, content that nothing pulled him down from beneath.

Stubbs shielded himself from the falling rain and lit one of the lanterns. Down on his belly in the running mud, he lowered it into the hole. A tunnel led off in either direction. A stench of hot, gaseous dissolution rose up from it. "Aye," he said. "What I suspected. Honeycombed with passages. They probably dug right into the graves originally. And now? I'd say these hills are full of 'em, a network that starts here and connects with our own tunnels, those of the Hun, too."

The other soldiers were pale, thinking of what burrowed beneath them. Rain ran off the brims of their helmets, past dour unblinking eyes.

"Right," Bowes said to them. "Makes perfect sense. Now I couldn't order one of you in there. Wouldn't even think of it—"

"I'll go," Stubbs said. "Somebody has to."

No one disagreed or tried to talk him out of it. He took a Webley pistol from Bowes and two belts of grenades.

"Good luck," the sergeant-major said, shaking his hand as if in farewell.

Stubbs looked at the rainy faces of the others, knowing he'd never see them again. War was hell.

9

Lantern in tow, he lowered himself down into the wet earth as the rain pounded from above. The passage was small, and he had to creep forward on his belly, grenades on his back and revolver and lantern held before him. He pushed through the claustrophobic murk, a nauseous stench of subterranean rot washing over him.

He expected rats, but never saw a one.

There were places, maybe, even they didn't go. Forbidding places contaminated by a tenebrous, vaporous evil so complete, so utterly vile and contagious, they dared not tread. And the burrows beneath that accursed village were such a place.

Stubbs pushed himself along through the muck and slime like a reptile, noticing with some unease that there was no possible way he could turn around. Whatever underground nightmare he was inching towards, he was going there to stay. But it didn't bother him too much, because he kept thinking about Piggy. How he'd died.

The walls were narrow, sweating foul water and clumps of dirt. The blackness was thick and pungent, misting and hard to breathe. He had been squirming along maybe ten, fifteen minutes when he started to find fragments of bones and finally entire skeletons tucked away in the wet, earthen walls. Soon enough, the passage was studded with jutting leg bones and scapulas and skulls that protruded from the oozing mud. All of them were silt-gray and riddled by bite marks. But it wasn't just bones, but the soles of trench boots, ragged bits of uniform, discolored strips of belt, even a helmet or two, badly worried. Finally, the gnawed mummies of soldiers who as yet had not been completely stripped of flesh. Pipe stem arms and broomstick legs thwarted Stubbs's advance. He had to press them into the mud or snap them aside to continue.

Ossuary, was what he was thinking. Some great and dire litter, the remains of their feedings.

A skull hung from the dripping roof overhead. Stubbs dropped it a wink though he was thoroughly terrified. More than once he passed beneath the clawed, polished bottom of a casket that had yet to be plundered.

He heard strange echoes from time to time. The distant sounds of guttural voices or shrill cackling. And sometimes just the ominous and lunatic sound of breathing—like someone exhaling into an empty metal drum.

The farther he went, the more the stink changed from being merely rich and cloying with fleshy decay to something far, far worse. This new stench was overwhelming and all-encompassing, and it fell over him like a shroud. A film of it gathered over his skin and hung on him, polluted and noxious. It was the stink he'd noticed at the listening post that night with Piggy and the others—that immense black smell of utter putrefaction, not of dead things, but of living things so profane and debased they turned the very atmosphere to a tainted malignancy.

Yes, he was close now.

His flesh was creeping, crawling in shuddering waves, and he had to clamp his jaws shut and tighten down his throat so as not to start vomiting. That great putrid smell was *their* fouled milk, and it was spilled everywhere. It bled from the air like diseased blood.

He swallowed down hard, shivering, shaking, closer to madness than the war itself had ever been able to take him.

The tunnel was weaving drunkenly from side to side now. There were offshoots and burrows going in every possible direction. And more bones. Fresh corpses. Their death masks staring at him, warning him to get out. The passage began veering downward, and down Stubbs went, sliding through the slime and mud and then into a smothering channel that he had to fight his way through. Then it widened, and he fell suddenly into a gigantic cavern. It was dug from rock and soil, easily ten feet in height, three times that in width and length.

Pulling himself up, he held out the lantern. He was standing in two feet of accumulated muck that was equal parts excrement, bones, and filthy water. Hundreds of black beetles the size of cigar butts crawled and fed in the pooled waste. The walls and ceiling were honeycombed with tunnel mouths or cells like the chambers of a beehive. A dripping gray fungus hung down from them like Spanish moss.

He knew he wasn't alone.

He saw glittering eyes shining from those darkened recesses, saw stealthy forms sliding from their berths like eels. Heard the chattering of tiny teeth that were like roofing nails. And all around him, it seemed, chatterings and chitterings and squealings.

He was in their den.

Horrors of War

Yes, they looked like children—small, but hunched-over, moving with odd loping, hopping motions. Their naked skins were scabrous and sickly-yellow, their hideous little faces like living skulls, the skin drawn taut over the alien architecture of bone beneath. Wild, tangled mats of hair fell to their shoulders and beyond, hanging in greasy strands over their graveyard faces.

"Stubbs," they whispered in a single mechanical voice. *"Stuuubsss. Stubbs. Stubbs. Stubbs..."*

He shut them out, would not listen.

Some part of his brain that was still intellectually functional started wondering how many terrible stories these things had inspired—tales of bogies and dwarves and elves and forest devils. Because when he saw them, when he looked them directly in the face, he *recognized* them. They lived in the twilight of his psyche, images carried by all men as racial memory. These creatures, these ghouls, were ancient adversaries of mankind and had lived by night even as man had lived by day since the very dawn of the race.

When his voice came, it was dry, worn, but clear as crystal, "Yes, here I am, you disgusting little bastards. I've come for you, one and all."

And maybe he should've been afraid, but somehow, he wasn't.

He was a soldier, and he was a man, and these things were perverse; they didn't deserve to live. They began to advance en masse in his direction, calling his name, and Stubbs stepped forward and not because he wanted to get any closer to those chattering horrors, but because of what was *behind* them.

"Oh, dear Christ," he said.

In an elliptical depression carved from the far wall was another ghoul, but this one an adult. It sat on an altar, a throne of heaped human skins, bones, and dismembered limbs. A huge and flabby female with pulsing flesh, dough-white and horribly blotched with something that might have been a creeping fungus. A double row of teats ran down her torso, and from them, the squirming, maggoty bodies of her progeny suckled. She held them there, formless things with twitching limbs and mouths like lamprey that would someday walk and feast on the dead. A bitch and her brood.

She saw Stubbs and glared at him with red, lidless eyes, and there was such raw and unflinching hatred in them it turned his insides literally to sauce.

Everything seemed to run in him. His mind, too. Drawn down into some safe place where things like her could not possibly be.

She made a shrill squealing sound that pierced the air, echoed through the tunnels, and punched right through Stubbs like poison arrows. He could feel the fetid, hot blast of her breath. But distorted as it was, he heard the words: *"STUUUBBBSSS…"*

She was an obscenity, yes, but that oblong face smeared with gore was not the worst thing. Nor were those greasy, twitching growths that fell from her bulbous skull like living hair. Nor was the black tongue licking over spiked teeth. Or even that hideous voice that he could remember calling to him in a childhood nightmare.

For, as he watched, she was giving birth.

With clawed and leprous fingers, she was pulling a slimed and bloated larval form from her birth canal. A squeaking, writhing thing that made bile rise into his throat.

The lantern slid from his fingers, landed in the muck, but did not go out. It cast lurching, grotesque shadows as leaping things waded in at him. With the Webley, he dropped six of them in as many seconds. Then he started throwing the grenades, one after the other. The chamber became a hive of howling and screeching and dying. Inundated by her children, his flesh coming off in ragged strips, teeth sunk in far too many hurting places, he dove at the mother. With his left hand, he drove his trench knife deep into her swollen, undulant belly. And with his right, as she took hold of him and he lost his mind in the folds of her loathsome, necrotic stink, he shoved his last grenade into her mouth and pulled the pin.

There was a resounding explosion as her head blew apart into reeking jelly and he was filled with shrapnel. The children kept at him, shrieking his name, and then the world erupted into flame and light and raining earth.

10

Bowes and the others checked all the crypts.

They found more burrows and passages, many cut straight through solid stone. There were no limitations to the ghouls' depraved determination. He

63

and his men patrolled the cemetery, waited for some sign from Stubbs, and it was a long time in coming.

"Here! Sir, over here!" Chalmers called out, motioning towards the hole Stubbs had disappeared into.

Rain in his face, Bowes went over there and listened.

Yes, there and there and *there*.

Gunfire. Echoes of gunfire from some distant subterranean lair. And then the sound of grenades detonating one after the other. Bowes, grinned, though he was certain Stubbs would not return. Grinned because the corporal was giving them hell. He'd taken the fight to them, and now they were tasting the scorpion's sting, all right.

Keegan cried out and started pumping out rounds with the Lewis gun. Bullets sprayed wildly from the machine gun, tearing up dirt and pulverizing headstones. As Bowes watched in shock, little mottled hands dragged him down into the earth. And then Chalmers disappeared, and Crumbly's face followed it beneath the rank soil. And then they were coming from the earth, the ghouls, blind in the light of day. Coming for Bowes.

He heard his name whispered from the hole, echoing and echoing.

And then there was a sudden, enormous concussion from below like the roll of an earthquake, and the cemetery exploded into a rain of mud and bones and bodies and gravestones. And before blackness swallowed him, he thought, from some faraway place, of all those gases of decay built up in the tunnels below. And of the grenades igniting them.

And then the graveyard fell into a massive cavern beneath him.

11

It was dark when Bowes awoke.

Maybe he'd been awake for some time. Maybe drifting between dream and reality with surreal ease. His eyes flickered open, and he saw the stars overhead. The rains had finally lifted. The air smelled clean, fresh and pure. He was thankful to smell it one last time. His body was knitted with pain. His left leg was a mangled stalk twisted beneath him. His left arm was free of the sling but reduced to raw and bleeding meat. He was cut and gashed and bled profusely.

He knew he would not survive.

But he was a soldier, and a soldier's life often demanded sacrifice. Seven generations of Bowes had sacrificed willingly for Queen and country. And he would ask for no more and no less. He was a professional warrior, a career man, and as such, pride, duty, and dedication to cause were the only things that truly mattered in his life. As he lay there, he remembered India and South Africa, Burma and the Sudan. He'd given a good account of himself as a soldier, and he was content in death. A few lines from "The Young British Soldier" by Kipling visited him in his final hour:

> *"When you're wounded and left on Afghanistan's plains,*
> *An' the women come out to cut up what remains,*
> *Jest roll to your rifle an' blow out your brains,*
> *An' go to your Gawd like a soldier."*

Beautiful, Bowes thought. Simply beautiful. What more could a soldier ask for than a quick and painless death? Why—

The air went rank suddenly, smelled of foul things and foul deeds. He heard the chattering of teeth. He tried vainly to crawl through the slick mud up and out of the cavern, but it was hopeless. Quite hopeless.

Limned by moonlight, he saw a single ghoul. It came on with dragging, wet sounds, stinking of spoiled meat. An adult male, judging by the distended phallus that swung between its legs like a pendulum. It was raw-boned and skeletal, ladders and knobs of bone gaping under the slack and fungous flesh. He could hear its clotted, phlegmy breathing.

"Bowes," it said in a hissing voice.

With his right hand, Bowes dug the remaining Webley from his belt and fired three rounds into it. He could see the holes in its hide glistening. Could see the dire beams of moonlight shining through them.

Still it crept forward, cold and remorseless, dappled with mud and gore. Its lurid skull-face was grinning with a glaring appetite.

Bowes laughed. "You won't have me, you filthy bugger," he said.

With his right hand, he placed the muzzle of the Webley to his temple. As those knobby fingers reached for him, he pulled the trigger and, gladly, happily, went to his God like a soldier.

HELL FLIES

Into the jaws of Death,
Into the mouth of hell.
— Alfred Tennyson

Zero dark hundred and cold, godawful cold. That's when the dogs come out. Skinny racks of bones with hungry eyes and foaming mouths, they slink out of the darkness like jackals come to feed on the dead. Gnaw tongues from mouths, suck eyeballs from skulls. They chew the meat from necks and bellies, slavering the soft parts first. They're dirty and ugly, vicious scavengers that'll take your fingers off in one quick snap of their foaming jaws. Lots of Americans learn that lesson the hard way—*here, boy, there's a good dog*—that these are not the pooches they knew back in Cornfinger, Iowa or Brainsplat, Texas.

These are beasts, and they'll eat anything that doesn't run away.

Tonight is a real feast.

Out in the street, there's corpses everywhere—an easy baker's dozen of Johnny Jihads, grim-faced soldiers of the Mujahedeen, torn ass to Christmas by the chain gun on the Bradley. Those that didn't get punctured, perforated, and dismembered by incoming, drew heavy fire from the M2 .50-cals which cut them in half like black-clad paper dollies. Small arms fire and grenades finished the job. The former came in with such volume, the dead stood up and jigged the dance macabre, and the latter shook around what was left like puzzle pieces.

Now…here come the dogs, drooling for human jerky.

Half a dozen, breed unknown and unknowable. They seem to bleed from the night, slithery shapes, greased with shadows. They waste no time tearing into the buffet, slavering and slobbering, teeth grinding against bone and gristle. Lapping tongues licking up pools of blood.

"Fucking bullshit," Chap says. "Request permission to waste 'em, Sarge."

"Negative. We start capping rounds and every dune coon in the neighborhood'll know just where we are," Rye tells him. "The Americans came in, wasted some unfriendlies in this dead little village, and now they're gone. That's what we want our enemy to know. Ain't nobody out here. It's safe for them to come out for their dead, and when they do, we deliver their gamey asses to Allah."

"But…I mean, shit, listen to that," Shitbird says.

"Like music," Crazy Eight interjects. "Bite, bite, chew, chew…sweet-ass music."

"Zip it," Rye says.

But he's listening to that music, too, and it makes him smile. Why it's strictly dogs eating their own kind. Dog eat dog. Kind of funny when you think about it, and maybe, in a grand sort of way, it's karmic. "Fido's got to eat, too."

"Fucking sandbox," Shitbird says. "Fucking Iraq."

Down Home laughs. "Hell, man. Show respect. Our glorious coalition forces are fighting a war of liberation for the Iraqi people. Don't have shit to do with oil or soft money under the table in Washington. They said so on *Pravda*."

A few chuckles over that—*Pravda* being the nickname for Fox News, the state-sponsored propaganda channel.

The dogs go at it for about twenty minutes, all that chewing and ripping, then gradually it quiets.

"Sounds like they all done," Down Home says.

Rye laughs. "And not a single fuck is given that day."

Dogs eating the dead. It just ain't right, even if the dead are nothing but Hajis. The sound of it disturbs Chap because he remembers fighting in Fallujah in the afternoon heat. Dogs eating Haji corpses. Dust flying. The rubble. Everything burning from airstrikes, clouds of black smoke rolling around like sea-mist. Somebody crying out for CASEVAC.

Hell at ground zero.

The platoon was amped-up and wire-hot from the fighting, covered in grime and sweat, shaking inside and out, fingers trembling on triggers. House to house they went, methedrine eyes bulging from dirty faces. *Get 'em, boys! Waste them Ali Baba motherfuckers!* Then they kicked in the door of that house with the weird symbols painted on the walls, greasing everything that moved. The old lady started screaming at them.

They expected insurgents, but what they got was a young woman and two children. Too late. The three of them moved and they took about twenty rounds. Oh shit. This wasn't how it worked. Americans didn't waste women and kids. That's not how it was done. It wasn't in their red-blooded, all-American makeup, not part of their Hollywood pop culture programming. They were heroes, liberators, not killers. Surely not that.

Crazy Eight laughed and said, "Fucking bitches, where's Mohammed now? Wherein lies the false prophet as we lay down burnt offerings on the altar of the Lord?"

"True dat!" Ghetto sputtered. "Allah ain't come to salve yer wounds and stitch yer gut and save yer soul. He just ain't come, bitches."

"Fuck's wrong with you people?" Chap said, disgusted by it all. Nobody was sure if he was talking to the squad or the Iraqis.

"Check them fucking holes in 'em, yo!" Ghetto giggled, and it almost sounded like a whimper.

"All of you pipe down," the L-T said, trying to communicate with the old lady. He went to language school, and he knew his shit. Dead civilians. Oh boy, this was trouble.

She snarled at him in some guttural language that wasn't Arabic or even Persian, speaking riddles and casting spells.

Chap just stood there, shaking, disoriented, too little sleep and too much action. Too damn many amphetamines to keep him going. He stared at the bodies, and his stomach lurched, crawling the walls of his abdomen.

Jesus, dead kids.

Crazy Eight giggled because death turned him on and made him hard. And he got it, even if the others didn't: life was foreplay, and death was the climax.

The L-T gave up. What was the point? Sometimes these people acted like they didn't even understand their own language. He turned his back on the old lady for three seconds, but that was enough.

She pulled a knife and charged him. Crazy Eight pumped six rounds in her, nearly cutting her in half. "God has spoken," he said.

The old lady was curled up on the floor like a dead spider, her mouth hanging open. As Chap watched, a single grotesque fly crawled out.

"It wasn't shit," he whispers to himself, trying to forget that day as he supposes he'll be trying to forget it his entire life. "It wasn't even shit."

The dogs are gone now, and for one fatalistic, delusional moment, his stomach clenches like a fist because he thinks they were scared off, that something worse took their place.

But there's nothing out there, nothing on the scope.

The nights are the worst.

The sort of night you only get in the land of the sand where electric lights are an endangered species, and the darkness is not just shadowy but fucking black. Black like sewers at midnight. Black like the inside of body bags. Black as the souls of men who hunt other men.

As Shitbird grumbles about Betty Lou flashing her goodies to the boys back home and Down Home tells Sergeant Rye how he hasn't taken a seriously good dump in weeks, Chap leans up against the low stone wall, eying the dead through his NVGs. He's always watching. He secretly fears the darkness and does not trust what moves in it, so he watches and waits and keeps his M4 handy. The corpses are sprawled everywhere, in whole and in pieces. Thank God for the chill of the night, so he doesn't have to be breathing in their death-smell.

"Shit, Chap," Down Home says, ass in the sand, back up against the wall. "I got a carton of Marlboro reds that says ain't no movement out there until oh-three at the earliest."

Chap shrugs. "I'll take that."

Crazy Eight and Ghetto are ass-planted with them. Crazy Eight isn't talking, and that's a good thing. Ghetto rambles on about the hip-hop empire he's going to build from scratch when his feet touch American soil again. Everyone ignores him. It doesn't matter; he'll keep talking whether he's got an audience or not. Down Home just sighs.

Chap watches the dead in the streets because sometimes Haji headhunters lie in wait with Russian sniper rifles, expecting dumb Americans to sneak out and search the dead for maps or trophies. That's when they tag 'em. One minute you're clawing around in the dark looking for foreign weapons and trinkets, the next your brains are glistening on the cobbles.

Dusty, sore, and shivering in the night air, the ragtag remnants of 1st Squad wait because that's what Rye wants. Chap has already told him the futility of it all—with the smoking and swearing and general noise they're making, the Hajis were going to be keeping a very low-pro, but Rye doesn't care what he thinks. He's a sergeant, and if you ain't a sergeant, he likes to tell them, you ain't even a real soldier. So zip it, shut it, stow it.

"I'm serious, Sarge, I ain't shit in like forever," Down Home says.

Rye shakes his head. "Christ, you and your ass. I don't give a damn about your bowels, clown dick."

"What ya gotta do, dawg," Ghetto says, "is have one of them bean burritos at Dee-FAC. Step up to it. I shit green for three days after that, yo."

Down Home grinds his cigarette into the sand. "Sarge, would you tell him to quit with that shit?

"What shit?" Rye asks.

"That bullshit talk like he's a banger slinging rock on the corners. I grew up with that shit. I don't wanna hear it, I'm saying."

"Motherfucker's cold," Ghetto says.

"Both of you shut the fuck up," Rye tells them. "Quit stealing my oxygen."

That's how fucked up the war is. Ghetto is a cornhusker from Boogersnot, Nebraska. Somehow, out in the corn, he got the streets on him and went original gangsta. He wants to be a hip-hop mogul. And Down Home, an East L.A. homie, wants nothing to do with any of that. He wants a fat wife and a farm of his own. He even admits to liking country music. It was like they'd swapped personalities. Nobody could figure it. But sometimes in war, nothing makes any sense.

"Wait," Chap says under his breath, and everyone tenses spring-tight. They know he's onto something. The tone of his voice speaks volumes. "Something moved."

"Dog," Rye grumbles under his breath. "Gotta be a fucking dog."

"That's all," Shitbird says. The hope in his voice is practically heart-breaking; it could squeeze tears from a rock. He's got less than two months to pull, and he wants it to be an easy, smooth two months. He doesn't want to go home in a bag or with less than the necessary compliment of limbs or balls. Two months. He's already dreaming of being in the single digits.

Crazy Eight is peering over the wall now, too, scanning the darkness with his M249 SAW. It's got a full belt, and he badly wants to empty it. On slow nights when the others try to catch a few Zs or unwind, Crazy Eight will still be at war, talking about his weapon and what he can do with it, how it is an instrument of love and of death. How he must empty it each day, or he is not satisfied. He'll keep going on about it until some smartass—usually Down Home or Ghetto—says how it sounds like he's talking about his dick.

"Just gimme a silhouette, oh merciful God," Crazy Eight mutters. "Just one silhouette to pop in your name for greater glory."

"Shut up, you bug fuck," Sergeant Rye tells him. He's panning the streets with his NVGs, google-eyed invader from Mars.

"Not seeing shit," he says.

"No…wait," Crazy Eight mutters in a very low voice. "Something…saw something move…swore I did. You want me to shake some bushes? Show the infidels the hand of the Lord most mighty?"

"Hold fire until I say."

"You boys realize you're getting the jimmy-jammies over some dogs, right?" Down Home asks them. "They's just hungry. Didn't get their fill before, so now they's back. Gonna have a taste and be on their way. Simmer."

"He's right," Rye says. "All of you simmer down. You're louder than ten monkeys fucking a bucket."

But Chap is not convinced—he heard something out there. Something that makes no sense: a sort of whirring sound like immense insect wings.

Murph grunts. A cigarette hangs from his mouth as he holds his M4 up in fighting position. Like Crazy Eight, he's always ready to bust. He seems to enjoy it as if every frustration and disappointment in his life is out there in Haji form, and he will not be satisfied until he has killed them all. He's got an over-and-under, an M203 grenade launcher bracketed beneath his M4, and there's very little in life he enjoys as much as firing it. When the shit's flying and incoming is ripping up the real estate around the squad, he gets real excited as he sets grenades down on enemy positions with perfection. Same way a basketball fan loves to see his team sink one from half-court, *booyah!*

Once, Chap asked him how come he rarely said anything. Murph grinned and said, "When I speak, the enemy'll hear me. You can count on that. That's why I'm here: to talk to them."

Chap liked that. It was like some corny bullshit from a corny Chuck Norris movie. Screenwriter shit. The sort of braindead nonsense somebody comes up with that's never been in a combat zone.

"Anything?" Down Home asks.

But Chap isn't sure. Something out there doesn't feel right, and it makes his balls shrivel, the flesh at his belly creep with prickling waves the way it does right before contact with the enemy. He can't see anything through his scope, but that doesn't mean nothing's out there.

"Thinking about that crazy old bitch in Fallujah," Down Home says in a wounded voice.

Rye spits over the wall. "Well, don't."

"Ain't that easy, Sarge. See I'm not a cold, calculating natural born killer like you. I have respect for human life and all."

Ghetto barks out his trademark machine gun laugh. "You hear that, Sarge? That shit's for real, yo."

"Don't talk about it," Shitbird says as if the topic scares him. "Just don't."

Down Home shakes his head. "I wonder what she said to us...you heard the L-T; it weren't no Arabic she was speaking. Something else. Something bad."

Crazy Eight works a plug of tobacco in his jaw. "She was cursing us. Bringing death down upon us."

Chap's flesh gets to crawling. The very idea carries a terrible weight in his mind, and he's not really sure why. He remembers the sounds of her words— like something very old and very terrible.

Crazy Eight fondles the barrel of his SAW. "Hear the words that are spoken! Because of what we have done, we are cursed above all livestock and above the beasts of the field!" he rants, mangling Genesis 3:14. "On our bellies we'll crawl and eat dust all the days of our life!"

"This is the last warning you'll get, Jesus freak," Rye tells him. "Any more of that Sunday school, born-again, fairy-tale bullshit and you'll be cleaning shitters back at the base. You will never touch that gun again."

This is a real threat, a clear and present danger. Crazy Eight pulls back, hugging the SAW to his chest. Without it, they know, he does not exist.

"She say those awful words and, boom, bang, next night, L-T, he's just gone. Disappeared," Down Home says, knowing they're all thinking it. "Like some old witch spouting a curse."

Chap studies the street. Something's off here. Something has changed in the blink of an eye.

"Something happened," he says.

"Shut up," Rye tells him. "All of you just shut up. I'm hearing something."

They all are—a rumbling, groaning sort of noise that is building and building like an army of giants is heading in their direction. It's weird, inexplicable, and more than a little scary.

"The Muj," Crazy Eight whispers more to himself than the others. "A suicide army coming down on us. Bring it, motherfuckers. I'll light your asses up, praise Jesus."

"Quiet," Rye snaps.

Yes, at first it does kind of sound like an approaching army, one coming in heavy-duty vehicles or maybe—inconceivably—on horseback. But it's none of those things. This is the wrath of nature. It's angry, roaring, screaming out its lungs as the earth begins to shake and the wind blows up dust clouds that spin all around them. They feel it bite into their faces and turn the world into a revolving shadow-show.

"Sandstorm," Rye says. "Sounds like a good one."

"But there ain't supposed to be nothing!" Down Home says. "We all saw the weather! Supposed to be clear and calm! Supposed to be—"

"Heads down!" Rye shouts above the din.

The sand moves in, pushed by a pissed-off, insane maelstrom of churning wind that howls and screams, venting the pure wrath of hell. To Chap it sounds like millions of night insects cycling around them, swarming in black clouds. As if in evidence of that, the storm exhales a hot, noxious effluvium like a plague pit erupting with corpses.

Now the darkness is even darker—it's the blackness of deepest space where light does not exist. It's a shroud pulled over them. Raging dust-devils scrape exposed skin like sandpaper. Sand coats them, covers them, stings their eyes even with goggles on. It dusts their faces and fills their noses. Granules of it crunch between their molars. Though the night is cool, it brings a feverish crazy heat with it, sucking the moisture from them. Someone swears. Someone else screams.

And then, soon as it arrives, it dies out, and they shake themselves free of it like wet dogs. They brush it from their faces and use water from their canteens to irrigate their eyes.

"What the hell was that about?" Down Home asks, the tone of his voice begging for a rational explanation.

Veils of dust still roll around them, settling slowly to earth. It's a scary moment because if insurgents charge in now, they'd be in a real fix. Dusty. Confused. Disoriented. Not good. They pull the brain buckets from their heads, empty them out, finger-comb sand from their hair.

"Get those fucking lids back on," Rye snaps.

Helmets cover skulls again. Weapons are checked.

"You smell that?" Shitbird says. "Like something dead."

"Weird," Chap admits.

Around them, there is not just a two-foot drift of sand, but something like black cinders the size of jelly beans. They crunch under boots. Men shake them from their fatigues and packs.

"Fuck is this shit?"

Crazy Eight plucks one from the heap at his feet. He examines it in the beam of a Tekna penlight. "Some kind of bug. A fly...a fucking giant fly."

"What kind of shit is coming out of your mouth now?" Rye wants to know. A flashlight is a big no-no on a night operation. It's an open invitation to a sniper. Regardless, Rye takes it from his hands and scans the beam about. "Well, of all the goddamned things...."

Flies.

Big mothers, too. Thousands and thousands of them are spread around the squad, mixed with the sand, piled up like ant hills. Rye begins scooping them up with his hand, swearing under his breath. They have large gauzy wings, swollen purple-blue shiny bodies. Immense yellow owl-like eyes and nasty jagged proboscises that are threaded like drill bits.

"A sandstorm full of flies?" Down Home asks.

"It ain't right," Shitbird says, kicking piles of them about with his boots as if he's afraid they'll contaminate him. "It ain't fucking right."

Rye grunts. "Of all the crazy shit." He separates a single dead fly from the others. He presses a finger to the needle-like proboscis and jerks it away. "Goddamn...sharp as a tack."

Now the squad are finding the dead insects everywhere—crushed beneath them, in their hair, snagged in their equipment. Carefully, they pluck them free with shivers of disgust. Broken off proboscises are stuck in their tactical vests, belts, and pants.

"Dammit," Shitbird says. "Three stingers in my arm. I thought they were thorns. Shit."

Chap plucks one out of his neck, another from his cheek. "Fucking things."

"They ain't poisonous, are they?" Down Home asks, plucking half a dozen of them from his pants.

"We have been made unclean," Crazy Eight says. It almost sounds like he's sobbing. "Nimrod, Nimrod."

"Only Nimrod I see is you," Rye informs him.

Crazy Eight shakes his head slowly. "In the bible. It's in the bible. Nimrod, the Babylonian king. He sacrificed children. God sent a fly to him. It crawled up his nose and ate his brain."

"Tell him to shut up with that," Shitbird says.

Rye swears under his breath. "Goddammit, Crazy. If a fly went after your brain, it would fucking starve."

Shitbird giggles nervously.

But Crazy Eight is undeterred. "You don't get it. You are all blind to the curse upon us for killing that woman and her children! Look around you."

"Iraq. So what?" Chap says.

"Now! *Now!* But thousands of years ago this was Babylon, the ancient kingdom. We are guilty of the same sin as Nimrod, and God has sent flies to torment us."

"Shut the fuck up," Rye orders him.

Chap is speechless. *Unnatural,* he thinks. *It's unnatural.*

"Fucked up country, fucked up desert, fucked up sort of world," Rye says. "Goddamn freak show."

Shitbird keeps walking around in circles, brushing his hands over his armor and sleeves. "Christ, I can feel 'em all over me. Look at 'em all. We could've drowned in 'em!"

"Shut up, shit brain," Rye snaps. "Just dead bugs."

Ghetto sucks water from his canteen, spits out grit, then gags out something else: a fly. "Shit! In my canteen, yo!"

"Probably stuck to the spout," Chap tells him. "You washed it into your mouth."

Ghetto relaxes. It makes sense. "Wait…where in the motherfuck is Murph?"

Now everyone is looking around, tension rising, hearts pitter-pattering. Mouths are dry and eyes are wide. Rye takes a quick headcount. There are six men in his squad. Why is there now only five? NVGs are on. Everyone is scanning the streets, the dark hulks of bombed-out buildings as seen in pale, shimmering green. Shadows crawl and slither, but Murph is gone.

Chap is scared like the others. The fear is deep-set and real. Cold hands squeeze his heart, forcing blood to surge through his veins. Everyone's looking, searching. Fuck the perimeter. Fuck everything but finding Murph. He's a headcase, and everyone knows it, but he's one of them. A brother. He must be located.

He just couldn't disappear, Chap thinks. *Somebody got him.*

Insurgents. Gotta be. One of those peckerwoods is threading the shadows around them. Some of those Ali Babas are real good. They swim in the darkness like fish. They rise to grab a fly and sink away again, leave not so much as a ripple on the surface of the night.

Chap remembers the scream he heard when the storm set its teeth into them. Was that Murph? Did some sleek, black-garbed predator slide a knife into him and then drag his bleeding corpse away to instill fear in the others?

Crazy Eight is muttering under his breath about the mighty fist of the Lord smashing infidels. "Murph has been taken as sacrifice to the dark one," he says. "The king of vermin: Beelzebub. The lord of corpse matter."

Rye tells him to shut up. No talking. No swearing. No whispering. No fucking praying. This ain't Sunday school, he reminds them. It's a war zone. A combat deployment. To emphasize that, he raps Crazy Eight on the lid with the butt of his M4.

They sweep the sector. Fingers are on triggers and stomachs in throats. The enemy is here and not here. He is there and yet, somewhere else. Chap finds that his entire body is shaking. He's waiting for incoming, for the mortar shells to start screaming overhead like furies. He thinks of guys he's seen killed.

Of sucking chest wounds. Men drowning in their own blood or crawling in the dirt, missing limbs.

"Want me to call in back up, Sarge?" he asks. "Get that Bradley back here?"

Rye growls at him. "You stay off that horn, cheese dick. I'll tell you when I want reinforcements."

Rye keeps sniffing around for Murph, even though everyone knows that if they don't have him by now, the Hajis got him, slicing and dicing him, chopping his head off.

But that's not the case.

"Over here," Down Home says.

He's down on his knees in the sand. His mouth is hanging open. At the far end of the battle-scarred wall, there's a shape leaning up against it. Chap is one of the first there. His stomach leaping into his throat, he studies the shape—it's a man-sized sculpture of dust, dirt, and dead insects. Flies are stuck to it like it's a gigantic No-Pest Strip. Rye gets there. With shaking hands, he claws the flies free, revealing a shrunken sawdust-dry mummy beneath that slowly flakes apart in the wind.

Ghetto shakes his head back and forth. "That ain't Murph! Fucking thing's been there for centuries." He prods the carcass with his rifle. It's perforated with countless little holes like a termite-infested tree trunk. It can't be human.

Rye finds something at its throat and yanks it free: dog tags. "Poor fucking Murph," he says.

"Ain't possible...it just ain't possible."

As the others argue how it can't be, but it is, Chap walks off and sits down in the sand. He waits and then waits some more until it seems like he's been there a thousand years. The gleaming stainless-steel edge of reality has been dulled. Nothing feels right. It's like they're slogging through one of those dreams where your feet are so slow, they're encased in concrete. He keeps telling himself that this is really happening. It's here. It's now in the sandpit of Iraq.

Nervous, tense, sinister shadows clustering around them, he remembers that terrible night L-T Kattner disappeared. Lieutenant Katt. Oh, there were bad omens abounding. The platoon came in out of the field where they'd been duking it out house to house with insurgents, greasing extremists, getting greased, and chasing shadows and their own tails. When they reached the FOB, Foreword Operating Base, they were filthy, encrusted with blood and grime and dust, faces blackened by smoke, uniforms ragged, eyes like open sores. They did not speak. They smoked and grumbled nonsensically, eyeballing those who never went beyond the wire: big money civilian contractors and fobbits in their crisp, clean utilities.

Same old, same old. There were showers and cold Coke, air-conditioned connexes and a steady stream of bullshit. They served cheeseburgers and fries at Dee-FAC. Hot food. That was the ticket. That would make everyone feel better. Except that when they get there and queue up, guys start retching, vomiting out blood. The hamburger is full of worms. Nobody knows how or why.

The spontaneous vomiting is like a crazy catalyst.

That night, three guys on a recon patrol get smoked by friendly fire. Two others commit suicide at the FOB. A persistent and inexplicable smell of death blows hot and gassy from one end of the base to the other.

And throughout it all, the L-T complains that his connex room is filled with flies. That they follow him in clouds, biting and nipping. The squad thinks he's fucking with them, the way he does sometimes, but then they see the sores and hear the buzzing.

Sometime before dawn, the L-T disappears.

Stories make the rounds, of course. Hajis got him. He went shit-crazy AWOL and joined up with the Muj. He wasted himself on the FOB, and nobody found his remains yet. Chap doesn't buy any of it. He was one of the last to see him, and the L-T kept cocking his head toward the desert, as if he was hearing something out there no one else could.

Chap pushes it from his mind. Everyone is quiet for the longest time. No one looks at the crumbling remains of Murph. No one dares to.

Next to Chap, Shitbird says, "Goddamn flies. They're everywhere." Slap, slap, slap. "Keep biting me."

"Take it easy. They're all dead," Chap reminds him, feeling uneasy.

Stop it, he tells himself. *Quit trying to connect the dots.*

Shitbird holds a handful of dead flies. He casts them into the air like ashes. "Feel 'em. I feel 'em biting me...fucking *biting me*...." He giggles. "But I can't see them. Can't even see 'em...just feel 'em."

Crazy Eight is watching them. "The L-T was having trouble with flies, too. Welcome to the domain of darkness where the evil one rules, the Lord of Flies."

"Coming again," Down Home says.

The storm moves in, howling and moaning. They can see it with their NVGs: a gigantic rotating cloud of dust and debris. The ground beneath them seems to thrum with it. The sand at their feet blows around as if stirred up by a wire whisk.

Shitbird starts making funny choking sounds in his throat like he needs to scream, but has no air in his lungs. He gasps. He coughs. He sputters. He brings up his M4 and fires two three-round bursts into the shadows. There's nothing there. Rye grabs hold of him. Shitbird tries to fight free, manic and wild.

"Fuck are you doing?" Rye demands. "Get down!"

Shitbird knocks him aside. He's a little guy, but suddenly he's a powerhouse, full of venom and pure terror.

"There! There! There!" he cries out.

"Just the storm, man! Get your head down!" Down Home shrieks.

But Shitbird runs toward it, becoming a shadow. The flies have come. A black, buzzing tornado of them numbering in the millions, gathering, thickening, a living, dark mist that engulfs Shitbird in a whirlwind. The droning is cacophonous, ear-splitting like a thousand buzzsaws whirring at full throttle.

"THERE!" he roars. "I CAN SEE IT! IT'S COMING OUT THE STORM! OH JESUS CHRIST—"

His voice echoes all around them like a ghostly scream in a haunted house. The others try to restrain him, but he's hysterical, swinging his M4 around like a riot baton. By then, the others have pulled back in fear, in confusion. The flies cover them in a biting, needling, piercing cloudburst. They roll in the dirt, crying out, losing their minds in that tempest of vermin. But Rye is still on his feet and he charges forward, makes a mad grab for Shitbird...but Shitbird lets out a piercing scream and vaults six feet in the air. It's not possible. Not from a standstill. But up he goes, and up he stays, a grainy shadow in the flying sand. He dangles above them as if he's being held aloft. He swings back and forth like a corpse on a gallows, caught in a vortex of spinning dust and droning, hungry flies.

The others cry out, scrambling about, but not Rye. He remains unperturbed by this madness. Things are very black and white for a guy like him. He reaches for Shitbird in the storm, but Shitbird is dancing around in the air like Peter Pan, a shrill, nearly hypersonic scream cycling out of him.

Then there's a violent, wet crunching sound, and he literally explodes... like a water balloon full of meat and blood squeezed to the bursting point. What's in him gushes out with the force of a stream from a firehose, knocking Rye on his ass and splattering the rest of them with blood and bone chips.

Rye, mopping blood from his face, shouts, *"Pull back! Pull the fuck back!"* His voice shrieks above the sound of his whimpering/moaning/shrieking comrades.

And then Shitbird is gone like Murph, leaving an unsightly mess behind as evidence of his passing. The storm fades, and the night goes quiet except for the sound of the men. They are praying and sobbing and swearing, picking flies from themselves and broken off proboscis stingers from their faces and hands. Reality as such has been turned inside out, its noisome entrails hanging out for all to see.

The stillness is not only unsettling, it's downright disturbing. The world has stopped moving. It holds its breath and waits for what comes next. The moon high above in the hazy sky is a cardboard cutout. The shadows fused in place, night suspended. There is only this ice-locked, white-knuckled moment of pure terror. It goes on and on.

No one in the squad speaks.

They are afraid to even move.

There are countless evils in that war, but few that can climax this. So, they wait breathlessly, soundlessly, huddled together. In the distance, the sandstorm moans but never goes away, as if it's circling them. Dust blows about. Sand fleas nip, and hearts beat. Dead flies blow around them like crunchy autumn leaves. They are an easy target like this. One good spray from an AK will grease the lot of them.

There is no Charlie Mike here, no Continue Mission. That is the dynamic truth of the matter.

The ingrained, long-practiced fear and hatred of the Mujahedeen has been replaced by something much larger, much more oppressive and strangling. They all feel it. Not an hour ago they were warriors, believing (or made to believe) that their cause was not only just but righteous. With the disappearance of Murph and the stockyard slaughter of Shitbird, that has all changed. They are no longer badass life-takers and widow-makers; they are now little boys bunched together, shaking, wide-eyed, terrified of the dark and the nameless horrors that crawl in it.

All beady, frightened rabbits' eyes are on Sergeant Rye. He has the experience, the rank. Intolerant, long-suffering, pissy old Rye. He'll make the call. He'll tell them what to do next and how to feel about it. He grew up on a working hog farm in Arkansas. *We slaughtered porkers every spring,* he likes to tell the squad. *Dozens and dozens of 'em. Ham, bacon, pork chops, sausage. Shit, boys, we made cheese from the brains and soup from the blood, gave the snouts and ears to the dogs for chew toys. We used everything but the squeal.* He got involved in the harvest when he was eight-years old. Once a hog was in the gut harness, he held a tin bowl to catch the blood for soup after his granny slit its throat. He grew up in gore, and it continued during his hitch in the Army. He's one hard-charging, evil sonofabitch in a fight. Absolutely fearless.

Fixed by four sets of white eyes, he's drenched in Shitbird's blood, coated in sand and dust and fly fragments. He licks his dry lips and spits. "Seems we got ourselves one serious FUBAR sort of situation here. Question being, how do we get out of it intact?"

"You heard him," Chap says. "He said he saw something…that it was coming out in the storm."

"Bullshit," Rye says. "He was hallucinating."

"He saw something," Down Home says.

Rye sighs and lights a cigarette. "And what is this *something* you speak of, son? Has it got a name?"

Down Home lights up, too. "Things like it ain't got no name, Sergeant Rye. I only know it got Murph, and now it got Shitbird. We been cursed. That crazy witch in Fallujah done sold our souls to rock and roll. After wasting those kids, shit, we qualify for extinction."

"He speaks the truth," Crazy Eight says.

Ghetto starts shaking all over, like the song. He can't sit still. Something is boiling away in him, and he expands with the heat. Like a pressure cooker, he's got to vent that steam before he blows up. *"All right, goddammit! I don't want to hear no fucking bullshit! We're in a fucking fix and you're rolling over!"* he wails, the OG drained right out of him now. *"Somebody better fucking do something before it gets us all! I ain't gonna die like Shitbird! Rye…goddammit, you're just sitting there, doing nothing! If you don't have the balls to lead, then I will! The way home is that way! Let's move! Let's hump! Let's get this motherfucking train rolling!"*

Maybe it started as an insult for Down Home, but it quickly morphed into an accusation of Rye's ability (or lack there of) to lead, to do anything but piss yellow in his skivvies. So, Rye, fly-specked and cold with drying blood and powdered with sand, filthy like some bone-chewing troll crawling out of its burrow, leaps to his feet. He's fast. Wicked fast. He's twenty years Ghetto's senior, but that evaporates as he grabs him by the chest plate with one hand and slaps him silly with the other.

Ghetto cannot defend himself against the flurry of slapping hands that turn his wind-burned face red and stinging. Rye drives him down into the sand and jumps on top of him. "YOU DO NOT TELL ME HOW TO RUN MY COCKSUCKING, MOTHER-LOVING OUTFIT!" Slap-slap-slap. "I AM GOD OUT HERE! I AM THE SHEIK OF THE BURNING, FUCKING SANDS!" Slappety-slap-slap. "SO YOU SHUT YOUR PISSHOLE, CUNTING MOUTH, YOU BAGGEDY-ASSED, LIMP-WRISTED, AUTISTIC SHIT-SQUAT!" Slap-slap, slap-slap. "DO YOU UNDERSTAND ME? ARE WE ON THE SAME PAGE, YOU LITTLE ASS-LICKER?"

Ghetto is openly weeping by this point, sniveling like a spanked brat, blubbering boo-hoo. Covering his face and trembling. Hands yank Rye off him, and he shoves them away.

"Chap, get on that fucking net yesterday, and tell those shitheads I want fucking EVAC right goddamn now." Rye turns his evil eye on Ghetto, down in the sand, then to Down Home. "You get that sack of shit on its feet, and make it walk. Use its nuts for a pull-string, or wind it up with your thumb up its ass, but I want it fucking animated with a weapon in its hands."

Down Home pulls Ghetto up, but he can barely stand. "It's okay, bro. It's cool," Down Home tells him, but he might as well be talking to driftwood. The Ghetto they knew and loved and fought side by side with is gone now. He's been methodically exterminated. It's obvious from his body language that he's now a big doll that has to be led by the hand. He has to lean on Down Home for a few moments. Everyone is glad for the darkness because they don't want to see Ghetto's face. Not so much what's there—the red cheeks, the bloody nose, the slap-prints—but what isn't—the goofy grin, the mischievous eyes, all the odds and ends that comprised his soul. The death of Shitbird has stripped it all away, and Rye finished the job.

Rye's trying real hard to maintain his own dignity without shitting all over unit integrity more than he already has. He does not want them guessing the ultimate, ugly truth of the situation: he's scared to fucking death. That he duly pissed his pants when that unseen thing took Shitbird's life. He wants them to believe that he's still the same old evil-tempered, flag-waving, empty-skulled lifetaker with his brain down in his neck. The Pentagon pushes button A and he deploys, button B and he kills. He can't let them know that he's so goddamn scared that he's squeezing his ass cheeks together so he doesn't hot-squirt down his leg.

"You didn't have to do that," Down Home says. "He was just blowing off steam. You turned on one of your own."

Rye looks like he's going to give Down Home a good flash-blasting at the very least or an old-fashioned Arkansas beat-down, but he neither shouts nor raises a hand. "Save your pussy-assed, snot-nose, cry-baby shit for someone else, unless you want the same."

"You ain't touching me. You ain't touching anyone in this squad." Down Home's fighting knife fills his hand, the moonlight catches the edge of the blade. "Unless you want six inches of steel in your neck."

"You ain't got the stomach for it, little boy." Rye is grinning like death now. This is territory he knows well. "And don't brag yourself up about how tough you were in the ghetto, how many gangbangers you blew, or how tough you had it pimping your mother. This isn't street-corner spit-sucking. This is fighting man to man, not robbing old ladies and whining about the big bad white man."

"I'll fucking cut you!" Down Home hisses between clenched teeth.

"Then cut me," Rye sneers, gritting his teeth, breathing and blowing steam. His knife is in his hand now. He pulled it so fast, nobody even saw it happen. "Because if you don't, I'm going to slit you from girly balls to throat."

"Stop this," Chap says.

They're all concerned now. Down Home has a wicked temper when he's riled, but Rye is an expert with a knife. He's been stabbing and slitting the enemy since before Down Home was even born. He's a killer. And he knows he can quickly end Down Home's life in two quick slashes.

What could have come of this is unknown because Chap has made contact. "This is Charlie Delta Six! Requesting immediate extraction!"

The multiband radio in his hand squeals and crackles. There's static and shrill noise that goes right up everyone's spine like a black widow spider making for their throats. And then an explosion of screeching—the sound of Shitbird's death scream echoing out and out into the night.

After that, Chap refuses to touch the radio. It's down in the sand where he threw it. Nobody speaks. Nobody breathes. The sound of Shitbird's death cycles continually through their minds.

Finally, Crazy Eight lifts his SAW machine gun to the sky and cries out, "Oh, sweet Jesus, an abomination has crawled from the cellar of Hell! Show me your holy might that we might vanquish it!"

This doesn't even get a rise out of Rye. No, he stares out into the night, trying to get the gears of his mind turning again, because they're rusted and seized like old lag bolts. These are his boys. His shitheads. His ballbusters and life-takers and cherry-poppers. He needs to get them moving, redline them out of this kill zone before there's nothing left to mark their grim and grisly passing but boots and bones.

We're going to get out of this, he tells himself. *Back at the FOB, over hot coffee and hot food, we'll just shake our heads about this night.*

"That's just how it will work out," he mutters quietly.

"Listen," Down Home says. "It's coming back."

Rye feels a terrible glacial shiver envelop him. "Hell are you talking about?" he says, loud and boisterous, overflowing with sweet vinegar and sour piss, just as his boys expect. He's holding his M4 carbine up by the ghetto grip, eyes seeking unfriendlies. He goes over to the shrapnel-pitted stone wall, takes a quick turkey peek around it. "Ain't shit out there, home boy."

All eyes glue themselves to the rawboned silhouettes of Rye and Down Home. All except Ghetto, who stands there stiffly, dead from the neck up like a zombie in a cane field, his eyes peering out into the endless night at something no one else can see.

"You ain't listening, Sarge. The storm. It's coming back for more."

Now they're all listening, rabbit ears tuned in, and brains tuned down. Sure. There it is: the ghostly, mournful moaning of the storm, a sandbox demon encroaching the perimeter, sucking dust and grit into its lungs for a great screaming barrage that will blind them, peel exposed skin, jam equipment, and add ten merciless pounds to uniforms. What they really fear is not the sandstorm, but what hides in it.

"It's coming in, all right," Chap says. "And when it lifts, there'll be less of us."

"Shut your gob," Rye tells him. "We're getting out of here. Crazy? Take the point. Down Home, you let Ghetto pilot himself. I want everyone locked and loaded and ready to bust."

"And where is it we're going?" Down Home asks.

"Out into desert, shit-fer-brains. Birds'll be coming, and we'll need to pop smoke. I want open ground for evac."

But Down Home just laughs with a dry, crusty sound. "Got me this painful feeling, Sarge, that they won't find us where they're looking."

He doesn't elaborate, and Rye is glad for it. There are things he knows and those that he can't possibly know, but does. He feels them in his gut and hears their voices in his head. And all of it tells him one disturbing thing: they are lost. Out of space, out of time, out of reason. There is no exit and no evac from this sun-scorched, shadow-riven lick of desert hell. It's night, and the sun will never rise again. It's a perfectly crazy idea…but it gains traction in his mind, clarity in his soul. He hasn't heard a single truck rolling out there or a fighter-bomber burning like a wick through the sky, a dog barking or any big guns roaring in the distance. There's nothing out there but the whipping sand.

Not a damn thing.

He wants to fall to his knees and girly-cry, but he covers his terror with both hands and marches his boys deeper into the night. Suck it up and drive on. Forward momentum is what they all need; it will blow the dust from their brains and broom away the cobwebs in the attics of their minds. Sometimes, when the human animal thinks too much, analyzes its own predicament at length, it gets weak, it gets slow, it drowns in the byproducts of its own self-awareness.

For ten minutes, they push hard before the storm locates them.

They hear it getting closer, of course. Edging in on them like something primeval and voracious. It stalks them like a lion stalks a herd of wildebeest. When it shows finally, there's no defense. Just squat down, cover your face, wait it out. Pretend it's just a freak of nature, and not a demon from Hell wanting to harvest your soul.

It comes out of the night whirring and lashing, a black seeking cloud, a hurricane of sand and force. Anything loose is scraped up by it—dust, dirt, fragments of rock, sticks and thorns and pebbles. It blasts them, driving them face down to the earth, the wind sculpting dunes and waves that break and inundate them. It shrieks and wails like a hundred banshees screeching out their lungs at the same time.

And with it comes that utterly inexplicable smell of death, of roadkill steaming in the heat.

And the buzzing. That evil, sentient buzzing that fills their brains and crawls in their bellies. And the flies, of course. Oh, dear Christ in heaven, billions of biting, winging flies that cover faces and chew on arms and wriggle down necklines. The feel of them is pure madness. Men cry out and roll in the blowing grit.

Yet, somehow, in the eye of the storm, tucked down in that enveloping barrage, they hear Down Home screaming: "IT'S COMING! IT'S FUCKING COMING! *IT'S RIGHT THERE! I SEE—*"

But that's it.

The storm descends on them, blanketing them in sand as fine as sugar, dusting them down, burying them in it. Ten long, agonizing minutes later, the dust settles, and the survivors of 1st Squad shake the sand from themselves.

It doesn't take them long to find Down Home. They don't bother using NVGs. Flashlights are in hands. There's a hillside twenty feet away, and they locate him almost instantly. He looks like about two-hundred pounds of well-marbled sirloin steak that was fed into a woodchipper. They find his body armor, too. It looks as if it was dipped in liquid nitrogen and shattered into fragments with a hammer. They find one combat boot with a knob of bone sticking from it, his helmet, his rifle, and what might be his jawbone... everything else has been reduced to bloody mucilage, a glistening red human pudding.

And the amazing, utterly bewildering thing is that his remains are clean of sand and flies. They're everywhere else, but not on the hillside, as if something wanted the squad to see in graphic detail exactly what happened to him.

Crazy Eight drops to his knees before the eruption of gore. He fondles and gently kisses the barrel of his M249, belts of ammo wrapped around him like Christmas tree garland. "Even though I walk through the motherfucking valley of the shadow of death, I will fear no evil." Kiss, kiss, stroke, stroke. "I wear the armor of God and am invincible. I alone stand against the schemes of the Devil."

"Flies," Chap says. "Millions of them must have drilled right through him with those stingers."

"Shut your hole!" Rye snaps.

Chap keeps looking around, shining his light in every direction. "Ghetto... where in the hell is Ghetto?" he asks more than a little frantically. The tone of his voice suggests that he is close to cracking. "Where is he? *Goddammit, where's Ghetto?*"

Rye stumbles about, shining his light like the others. He no longer cares about drawing enemy fire. In fact, he hopes for it. Anything to prove that he's still part of this world, and not marooned in Purgatory. He begins to breathe very hard, shaking and sputtering until it all builds in him, and he shouts, "GODDAMMIT, GHETTO! YOU SHOW YOURSELF! YOU QUIT PLAYING FUCKING GAMES! THAT'S AN ORDER...YOU HEAR

ME? A FUCKING ORDER!'' And then he falls to his knees, making a half-choking sobbing sound that quickly becomes a hoarse giggling. And even that fades away as the night presses in.

Somehow, someway, they move. And they do it together. And the more ground they cover, the faster they go. *Hump, hump, hump.* They let their training do the walking and the talking: shit gets deep, escape and evade, live to piss about it another day. In full battle rattle, they move through dry ravines and mount rocky hillsides, cut across sweeping dunes and intersect scraggly thickets of dry brush. There are refugee camps out here, but they don't find them. They don't even find the Euphrates.

Yalla, yalla, yalla, Chap thinks. It's the GI bastardization of the Arabic word for hurry up, go, go, go. It echoes through his mind, and he allows himself to think nothing else. Maybe there is protection in ignorance, safety in avoidance.

He doesn't want to think about what's happening. There's something evil in that storm hunting them. Only you can't see it until it targets you.

Nobody knows anything now.

They trust in nothing.

They are no longer deluding themselves that they are proud warriors bringing freedom and light to the oppressed. All those GI Joe, John Wayne, cornball macho fantasies have faded now in the glaring death-light of reality, if they ever existed at all. Sour milk that the jingo flag-wavers back home suckle from the withered breast of the state.

Here is the situation: they don't know where they are, and they doubt that even crusty old Rye can get them out of it. They know to a man—or at least Chap does—that Rye is coming apart. He's erratic, unsure, conflicted. Undoubtedly unstable. He's leading them blindly through a nightmare countryside that's as repetitious as it is hostile—rocks and drifting sand, shadows and blowing moon dust, with the ever-present, heartbreaking moan of the sandstorm that circles them like a hungry predator.

They are lost.

And even the compass doesn't know where.

A sliver of moon glows above. Now and again, they see it blazing, and Crazy Eight starts rambling on about the Book of Revelation and Star Wormwood and the holy blood of the lamb. If he was ever there, he's gone now. Long gone.

Chap does not like the moon. He's seen it several times tonight, and it scares him. It's not moving across the sky as it should, east to west… it's moving *west* to east, as if time is going in reverse. But it can't be. It just can't be.

After what seems hours, Rye says, "There! Just ahead! I see something!" His voice is nearly hysterical with relief. "Do you see it? Do you?"

Chap sees it, and as they get closer, drawn to it, he begins to feel weak low down in his belly.

A village draped in night. The dead, immense silence of the place amplifies everything in surround sound: boots thud into the earth, equipment shifts and clanks, breath rasps from lungs.

Rye stops dead, sand blowing around his boots, his mouth gulping air like a dying catfish. His head begins to shake from side to side. *"It's not possible! It's not fucking possible!"*

But Chap sees that it is—they have hit the wall.

Crazy Eight falls to his knees, clutching his machine gun. "Ah, yes, of course! It must be so, as it was written so long ago! Ha, ha, ha! Yes, *'I will feed them wormwood and give them poisoned water to drink.'* And we supped well and filled ourselves with the bounty of Hell." He jumps to his feet, dancing around in a circle, seemingly pleased and terrified at the same time, stark raving and unpleasantly lucid. "Listen! You must all listen, for I am the voice of God, and now I speak! I tell you of the Great Dragon, the serpent, of Satan and the Devil! The deceiver! *Oh, Christ Jesus, the deceiver! He was thrown down to earth, and our sins have made a covenant with him!"*

Chap is not listening. His eyes blink. His heart beats. His blood pumps, and his nerve endings tingle. Other than that, he is not alive. He studies the village—the rubble, the ruin, the crowded buildings and houses gutted by artillery, everything smashed and broken, rendered to bones sculpted in sand. And before him, the bullet-scathed stone wall, and beyond it, the street strewn with dog-eaten Haji corpses. Only now, they have been skeletonized like Murph and buried in dead carrion flies.

"Insane," he mutters. "It's all insane."

His entire body itches from the bites of the flies. He peels off his armor, scratching his arms and belly and back. His nails tear open sores on his face, and the blood runs.

They have come full circle to their point of origin, and how do you explain such a thing?

And he is trapped in this netherworld with a religious fanatic with a martyr complex and Sergeant Rye, whose mind is as soft as a carved pumpkin two weeks past Halloween.

He begins to laugh at the hopelessness of it all, the despair, the soul-deep agony of the human animal. And particularly at the evil men do and the futility of trying to escape from your sins.

"Funny? Funny? Fucking funny?" Rye says, moving quickly and decisively, grabbing hold of Chap by the shirt and shaking him violently. *"Where is the humor in this? What is the joke? The guffaw? The fucking ha-ha?"*

But Chap cannot tell him because he cannot stop shrilling with laughter. Tears roll down his cheeks, and drool courses down his chin. His sweat dries in the chill of the night, and something essential dries up in his soul, like a puddle in the desert.

Rye tosses him aside and then falls to the ground, kicking and battering it with his fists, like a spoiled brat denied a sweet.

Chap walks in a drunken, loose-limbed circle. He giggles, sobs, moans, and titters. He pictures his mind as ice melting into slush.

And while they are both so distracted, Crazy Eight has left them. He answers a higher calling. Eyes glazed, heart hardened, and what's left of his mind focused and sharp like the tip of a surgical needle, he stumbles away from them and climbs atop the wall twenty feet away.

This is where they see him.

As the sandstorm begins to hum and buzz around them like a swarm of hornets, they brush grit from their faces and look upon him. He stands atop the wall, stiff as a post, the M249 SAW light machine gun balanced atop his shoulders horizontally, his outstretched arms parallel to it. Fittingly, his silhouette is that of a cross.

"GET DOWN FROM THERE, YOU FUCKWIT!" Rye screams at him. "GET DOWN RIGHT NOW! DO YOU HEAR ME, YOU MISERABLE PISS WORM?"

But Crazy Eight no longer hears anything in this world. He is deaf to it. He listens to the music of the spheres, voices from a distant realm. Chap expects Rye to charge him, yank him from the wall and beat him down. But he does not. The storm breathing fine sand in their faces, they watch Crazy Eight as the dust devil consumes him. Despite the noise of it, they hear his voice—tinny, crackling, and scratchy like an old record: *My words! My words! Hear the words of an angry God, oh serpent! Show yourself, that I might smite you with my almighty fist!* What he says beyond that is unknown, for the storm sucks him in. For a moment they can see a dim, indistinct facsimile of him…then he rocks the M249 in one ripping, sustained burst, shooting at something they cannot see and he cannot know.

"I SEE YOU!" he shouts. "YOU CANNOT HIDE FROM THE RIGHTEOUS!"

Chap shouts his name one last time, and then there is a cacophonous, ear-splitting droning that sounds like a plane coming through the sandstorm. Its noise rises and rises, piercing the night with hypersonic intensity until he has to cover his ears with his hands.

Crazy Eight screams, and there is a wet, splashing sound as he is divided into pieces, as if bisected by a chainsaw. Chap catches a blurry image of his remains being sucked up into the immensity of the spinning dust devil, which has stuffed itself with night and rotating debris, becoming a tornado of primeval wrath.

It hovers before them.

It fills the world.

A hot, fetid, vortexual maelstrom of not just sand and dust and scattered debris, but a graveyard cyclone of fragmented bones and crematory ash and corpse matter and billions of Hell flies, whirring like drill bits.

Chap and Rye clutch each other like lovers, clinging tight as they feel the awful suction of the thing begin to pull them toward it through the sand. It's a gigantic howling, shrilling, hissing entity, and Chap sees through his NVGs that it is not just whipping sand—there's something inside it.

"I can see it," Rye cries into the storm. *"It's...it's coming for me now..."*

He screams and wails, but it is drowned out by an even worse sound: a titanic buzzing that is so loud it's deafening.

Chap screams as Rye is yanked from him, held aloft like Shitbird, shaken violently, as if to take the fight out of him. Then he comes apart, pulverized, atomized by the swarming Hell flies into a red-gray mucilage of meat that sprays in every which direction. His head rolls through the dirt, a look of horror and agony frozen on its features.

Chap digs his way out of the sand. He shakes it from his goggles. He must see. It's more important than ever before that he see what comes for him. Because it *is* coming for him. He knows this as he knows his own heartbeat, his face, the feel of his skin.

"Show yourself," he says into the face of the angry storm, the M4 in his hands. Now he will see what has been killing them. "C'mon, goddammit!"

The sand cycles, and he sees a shadow in there, a skulking, horrible shape the size of a two-story building rising above him.

Fatalistic now, he rises to his feet. He is a soldier by training and perhaps even by birthright, a warrior. He will not die cowering from some crawling, Hell-born abomination. Even though his belly cringes in horror and his mind roils with terror, his brain feeling like it's rotating inside his skull, he steps slowly into the howling wind and flying sand, approaching the perimeter of the storm. Ten feet from it, he can see into its whirling guts, its shifting marrow. What he sees turns his blood to a cool, gurgling jelly.

The eye of the storm.

He sees the eye of the storm.

And he screams.

Not one eye, but *two*—two colossal, red, crystalline eyes whose prismatic lenses are steaming and ever-shifting. He sees wriggling, corpse-blue mouth parts, a vast cyclopean body—jagged like broken glass, razor-edged and black, made of pulsating segments—that would have dwarfed a tractor-trailer...and wings, four and possibly six sets of iridescent wings, membranous and threadbare like rotting curtains. They flap with dizzying speed, creating the demon wind, the blowing sandstorm, and that monstrous, gargantuan droning that shuts his mind off like a switch. The entire thing crawls with billions of Hell flies, they cycle out from it in twisters and agitated clouds and rippling typhoons, buzzing and buzzing, covering him ten inches deep until the world is shut out, and there is only the stark madness of his dreaming mind.

For many, many weeks after that, they keep Chap in the psychiatric wing of a military hospital. He does not know where. He does not even know who he is or what tragic series of events led him there. He only knows what they tell him—he was the only survivor of a night patrol in Iraq.

He tells them many things, but they do not listen. They claim he is violent, delusional, suffers from traumatic hallucinations and various neurocognitive disorders. He is strapped to his bed so he will not hurt himself, juiced up on Thorazine, Lorazepam, and Olanzapine, among others.

What he has to say, they do not hear. They all look at him with pitying eyes and blank expressions. They agree with what he says, but do not comprehend.

Sometimes he speaks quite coherently about the Lord of Flies and the sandstorm, the sins of his past, the threat of the future, but they do not hear him. They will not listen to his torment, his suffering, the knowledge that he is rotting like a corpse from the inside out, that he is pregnant with death.

At night, the Hell flies come out. They cover the walls, voracious and buzzing, tumescent with eggs. No one hears them but Chap. No one sees them but Chap. It is his curse because he looked into the malignant eyes of the Lord of Flies.

Usually around midnight, he becomes uncontrollable. That's when the Hell flies descend on him, covering him with crawling legs and biting mouth parts, dripping corpse slime and piercing him with proboscises. That's when he screams. Writhing with the sticky film they leave on him, he gasps for breath, becoming manic with what his doctors claim is acute delusional parasitosis.

But that's because they do not know his agony. The terrible gnawing from within as the implanted eggs of the Hell flies hatch and the maggots begin devouring him, squirming beneath his skin, feasting upon him and chewing at his nerve endings with morbid delight.

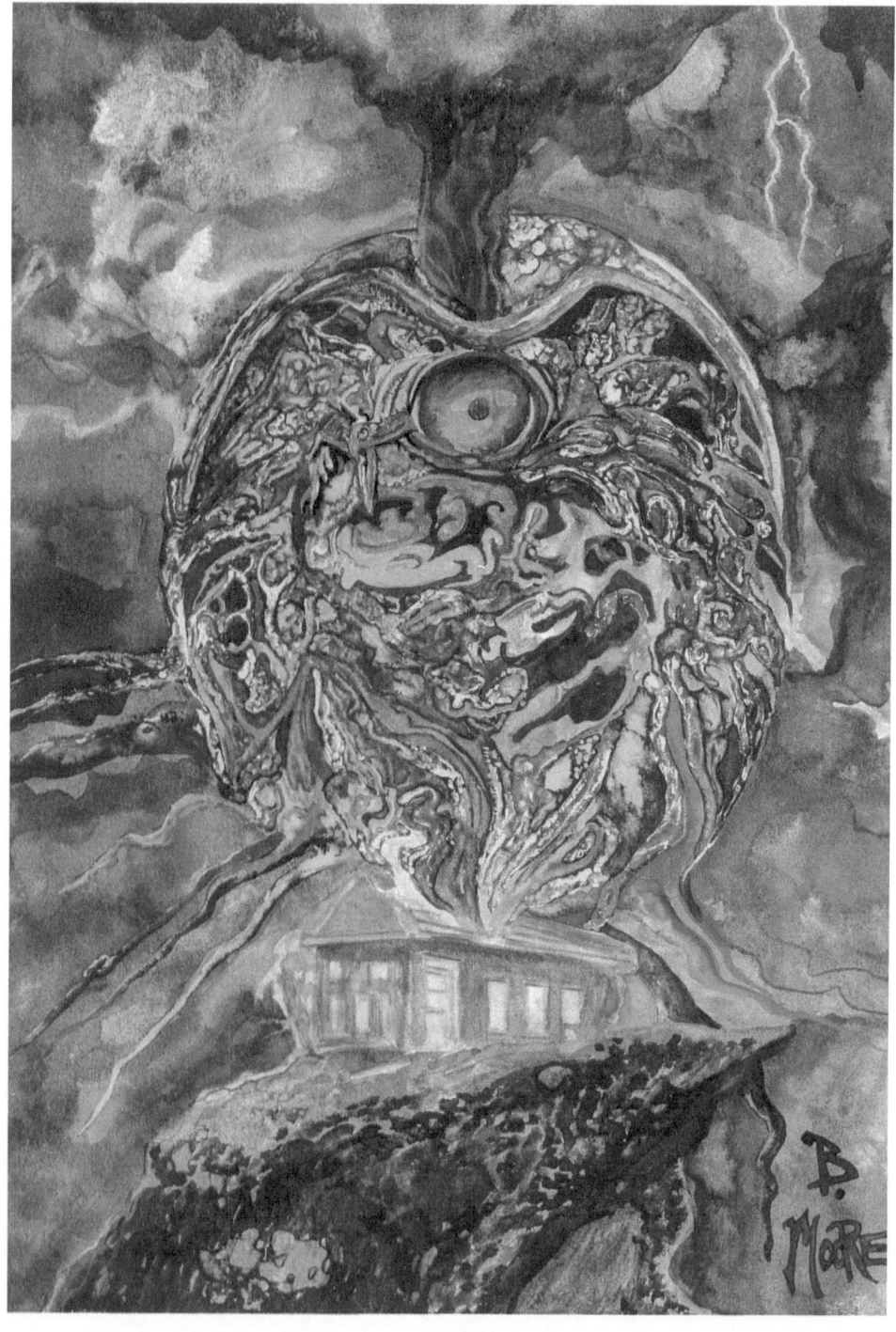

THE PROCYON PROJECT

Never think that war, no matter how necessary,
nor how justified, is not a crime.
—Ernest Hemingway

It was an easy gig, and Finn pulled it because he was a real, bona fide, small town hero. When he got back to Caneberry Creek from the Pacific, people couldn't do enough for him. They all wanted to hear how he'd given it to the Japs on Guadalcanal, as if he had taken them down single-handedly. Sometimes he almost believed it himself...at least until he woke sweating and shaking at four in the morning from nightmares of Japanese soldiers rushing by the dozens from low cave mouths, blood-smeared and fanatical.

Regardless, he did his best to sell himself as the hard-bitten, tough Marine and defender of freedom. It got him free lunches, dates with pretty girls, and even tickets to the latest flicks at the Rialto on Main. If they wanted to believe he was some hard-charging, bullet-eating, lean mean killing machine, so be it. He wasn't stupid enough to look a gift horse in the mouth. He played the part, and they ate it up. And all it had cost him was his nerves and his left leg.

He wasn't back even two weeks when he was offered the job at Blue Hills, which was a former pesticide plant that had been tricked out—as part of the war effort and something called the Procyon Project—as a weapons research facility for the Defense Department. What went on there was classified, strictly hush-hush, but it paid well, and all Finn had to do was check IDs when the workers and eggheads showed. It paid well and gave him plenty of time to read his magazines.

It was strictly creampuff stuff, and after Guadalcanal, he was more than ready for a life of leisure.

Just after Halloween in '43, he was pulling midnights because two of the guards had been drafted. He drove out to Blue Hills, clocked in, grabbed a cup of joe at the cafeteria, then made his way out to the guard shack. He was in luck. Manpower was in such short supply that they had called in a couple retirees to fill out the ranks. One of them was Chester DeYoung, another old jarhead from the old days. He'd seen his share of action with the Marine Corps during the Philippine Insurrection forty years before.

"Well, look what we got here," Chester said when he saw him. "Old blood-and-guts himself. What's a good looking grunt like you doing in a place like this?"

Finn giggled. Chester always gave it to him, and he liked that. He was about the only one in town who treated him like an ordinary human being. Everyone else acted like he was made out of glass. And he'd told Chester that more than once.

"Guilt," was Chester's answer. "They ration gas, collect metal, can't get panty hose or good beef, but you *really* sacrificed, and they know it. You gave a limb to keep the flag flying. But don't worry, son. You give it a year or two, they won't give a damn. You won't be able to pay them to listen to the stories of an old leatherneck. Take my word for it."

Finn found that both liberating *and* disturbing.

But that's what he liked about Chester. He had a way of putting things into perspective. Every time Finn told him about something that bothered him, Chester would sort it out for him and give him a new way of looking at things. Unlike his own father, who got up every day and stared at his son's medals on the mantelpiece like he was gazing upon the Ark of the Covenant itself. Finn was pretty certain old Dad liked the medals better than the guy who'd won them.

"How's it tonight?"

Chester shrugged, stretched. "Same, same, same. Check 'em in, and check 'em out. I'm so good at it I ought to bag groceries at the A & P. How you holding up, son?"

"Good, pretty good."

"Still getting the nightmares?"

Finn thought about lying, then he just nodded his head. "They've been bad lately. Real bad."

"They get that way. I know I had my fill, and now and again, I still get them. You can't go through combat and walk away from it pure as snow. Something in you forever changes. You just have to accept that and plod on."

Chester told him that the heavy fighting for the Sohoton Cliffs in 1901 still came back to him in his dreams. The ground was wet with blood. He'd never forget the men he mowed down during the assault.

"Sometimes it seems like a lifetime ago, and sometimes it seems like last week."

But, Christ, that was forty years ago, Finn got to thinking. *Am I still going to be dreaming about this shit in the 1980s?*

A sudden rumbling sound broke up the talk. It was coming from one of the main research complexes. The entire ground seemed to shake, then vibrate. Finn felt suddenly lightheaded, his guts clenching like a fist. He teetered uneasily on his artificial leg.

"Been hearing that off and on all night," Chester admitted. "Hell if I know what they're doing up there. Hopefully they won't blow us up."

Finn stepped out of the shack and leaned against it, sucking in lungfuls of cool, clean air. Crazy. That's what it was. The rumbling made him tense up, like when the shells were incoming on Guadalcanal. It felt as if his guts pulled up into his chest. That was bad enough. But the weird vibration made his head spin, his eyesight blur, and his skin feel like it wanted to crawl off his bones. There was something wrong about that.

"My neck gets sore when it does that," Chester said. "Goddamn old ticker skips a beat."

Finn worked his jaw. The fillings in his teeth made his molars ache like the metal was expanding.

"What the hell kinds of things are they doing up there?"

But Chester just shook his head. "Don't know, and maybe I don't want to know. Can't say that I care for it much."

Finn lit a cigarette to calm his nerves and steel himself. There was something very strange about this whole business. Suddenly, his scalp prickled, and it came again—that low rumbling that made the ground shake. It was followed by something like a high electronic squealing, then the vibrations. His head spun again. When he opened his eyes…it seemed like the world was moving, the trees writhing in the woods though there was no wind. And the stars overhead had changed. Instead of looking like tiny, white pinpricks, they looked much closer, like glowing, pulsating marbles.

Then all returned to normal.

"It gets you inside, don't it?" Chester told him. "I thought I was going to throw up the first time. I called up to Building A to see if something happened, but Doc Westly said they were just having some generator problems."

Generator problems, Finn thought. *That wasn't no goddamn generator. Felt like the fucking world was about to split its pants.*

He didn't really know what the Procyon Project was, but he was pretty certain it had nothing to do with generators.

Chester snapped his lunchbox closed. "Well, I best get going. The old woman waits up for me. Keeps the soup hot." He dropped a wink to Finn. "Worries about me heading into town and catting around with the girls."

"Sure," Finn told him, forcing a laugh.

Chester waved, and then he was outside the gate, moving pretty fast across the lot to his old Ford. He looked like he couldn't get away from Blue Hills fast enough.

Shivering, Finn didn't blame him one bit.

The first hour was easy. Finn sat around in the shack and listened to Kay Kyser live from the Aragon Ballroom in Chicago and paged through one of his mystery magazines, *Front Page Detective.* It was quiet, low-key, and boring. Just the way he liked it.

Around 1:30, he started making his rounds of the facility, keying in at the various watch clocks. Buildings A and B was where the research was going on, but there were a dozen other sheds and storage Quonsets that had to be checked. There were two guards on, as always: Finn and Jack Coye. Finn had the gate sector and Jack had the western sector, which included Buildings A and B. They had it all timed out. They'd start their rounds at 1:30, and by 2:15 they'd meet up over at the dispatch office, which was unmanned at night.

Ever since that weird stuff earlier—the rumblings and vibrations—Finn was feeling more than a little on edge. He was looking forward to running into Jack and having a smoke with him. Not only for the company but because Jack always seemed to know about things he wasn't supposed to know.

Jack usually made it to dispatch before Finn did. You could only go so fast with a wooden leg.

Although the various drives and parking lots of Blue Hills were strategically lit, it was still a damn dark night. The black forest seemed to be pressing up closer to the fence than usual. A crescent moon hung above the dark thickets and fields of tangled yellow grasses.

Finn felt like he was the last person on earth.

The damp seemed to be reaching up under his coat and crawling along his spine. He couldn't shake the chill that encompassed him. He was even getting the phantom stiffness in his missing leg again. Of all things.

He moved along the outer road, *gimping along,* as he liked to refer to it, checking the fence because they were real particular about their fence at Blue Hills. There was nothing to see, as usual, just lots of weeds and shadows and that awful encroaching darkness that Finn simply could not tolerate tonight. Maybe it reminded him too much of those black nights on Alligator Creek during the Battle of Tenaru when the Japs assaulted their positions all night long…or maybe it reminded him of the pooling shadows that seemed to ooze out of his closet door at night when he was a kid.

Whatever it was, it was really doing a job on him.

He patrolled along the outer road, scanning the fence with his flashlight, almost afraid of what the light might reveal in the long grasses. He felt tense inside, his heartbeat fluttery.

It should have lessened after he got back on the main road and made his way up to the boiler house, but it increased. Nothing felt right tonight. Everything was out of whack somehow, and he couldn't put a finger on what it was. When he got up near the dark hulk of the boiler house, he thought he heard a noise. A sort of *fssst! fssst!* sort of sound. The first time he paused briefly, but the second time it came, he stopped dead.

Hell is that?

He waited there, looking from the cars of the night crew parked in the grass to the boiler house itself.

Fssst! Fssst! Fssst!

It seemed more insistent now, and it was coming from over near the cars themselves. Finn approached them cautiously, ever aware of the .38 at his hip. His hand eased down towards the gun, fingers wrapping around the butt. As he withdrew it, a dew of sweat speckling his forehead, he panned the cars with his light. They were all dark and empty.

He saw something scamper behind a coupe.

It was large, too large to be a woodchuck or even a bobcat. In the back of his mind, he thought it had been a man scampering away on all fours. Swallowing, he looked around. What he would have given for some back up just about then. There were always the boys in the boiler house...but what was he supposed to tell them? That some night animal had him scared white?

Shit, Finn, we didn't think Marines were scared of anything.

Yeah, he could hear it now. Whatever this was, he would have to handle it on his own. He heard the *fssst! fssst!* sound again, and by then, he was shaking. His nerves weren't good since the Pacific. He had a habit of starting at the slightest sound. Even his sleep was thin, so thin it could barely be called sleep. A twig scraping against the roof or a dog barking three streets away brought him fully awake, eyes staring, muscles bunched and ready for action.

The .38 was shaking in his hand.

"Hey!" he called out, his voice scratchy and weak. "Hey! Who's over there?"

There was no response but that same *fssst! fssst!* which sounded a little too much like the call of a night grasshopper...except it would have taken about 10,000 of them to reach the kind of volume he was hearing.

Carefully, he edged around the cars, keeping the light in front of him. He had heard some very weird sounds in the Pacific at night, animals and insects that were truly disturbing, but this was beyond that. Now he heard something else. It almost sounded like a soft, meaty chewing.

"Hey!" he said with more volume now.

The chewing stopped. It was replaced by an almost throaty purring sound, then that *fssst! fssst!* noise, but louder now. Almost like a warning. It was coming from behind the Chevy in the back. Finn tried to swallow as he made his way over there, but there was no spit left in his mouth. The gun was shaking in one hand and the flashlight in the other, the beam bobbing frantically.

He moved around the Chevy, smelling a sweet, almost decayed sort of odor that stirred his guts. Then he moved around the back of the car and saw...he didn't know what he saw...only that it was enough to make him take two or three awkward steps back that put him firmly on his ass.

The light glanced off something.

Something that went *fssst! fssst!* and then rose up into the air on membranous wings that made a whirring sound like the prop of an airplane. It flew right over him and off into the darkness. He sat there, his breath barely coming, his heart pounding in his chest. Whatever it had been, it was nearly the size of a man but looked almost like an insect, a wasp maybe, except that it was set with sharp spiky hairs like needles and had three globular yellow eyes. *And* it had a mouth filled with backward curving fangs like those of a rattlesnake.

When he pulled himself to his feet, his light picked out the remains of what must have been a raccoon that was split right open, its entrails cast about like bloody clocksprings.

That thing...that bug...it had been eating it.

He stumbled back toward the boiler shack, bound and determined to tell the night crew what he had just seen, but then he stopped, knowing he couldn't. They would think he was nuts. Another crazy, shellshocked gyrine. They might not laugh to his face, but after he left they would be doing just that.

No, he wasn't going to say a thing.

Maybe he *had* hallucinated it. Maybe his nerves were more shot than he realized. Maybe the war had unscrewed something in his head.

But he didn't believe that for a minute.

He was late getting over to dispatch, and he knew it, but things weren't exactly easy after the big bug. Maybe outside he was no longer shaking, but inside he was still trembling, his guts coiled white. He had to key in at four different watch clocks before he got to dispatch, and his hand was shaking so badly at the first two that he could barely hang on to the key.

Finally, he just stopped, breathing in and out, forcing himself to calm down.

You survived a war, meathead, and now an overgrown hornet is giving you the heebie-jeebies?

He thought that sounded real, real good, but it didn't hold water. He had seen the teeth on that thing, and since when did insects have teeth? And the wings...now that he thought about it, there hadn't been a single pair but maybe two or three pairs. No, it was wrong in every conceivable way. Bugs did not get that big, and they did not have fucking teeth.

He keyed in at his last station and breathed a sigh of relief.

He couldn't wait to see Jack.

Jack would have some good gossip about all this weirdness, and he knew it.

Finn walked down the lonely, moonlit road, getting closer and closer to Building A and dispatch, which was housed in a Quonset just down the way from it. A cup of coffee and a cigarette, and he would start feeling human again. Things would make sense then.

The rumbling came again.

Oh shit, not again.

The rumbling noise grew louder and louder, sounding suddenly like huge waves crashing into a pier. The ground was moving, and again Finn found himself on his ass. The vibrations began right away. He could feel them in his bones, in his blood, in his tissues. It felt like the very stuff he was made of was going to fly apart at any moment. The nausea moved in rollers through his belly, his head spun like a top. When he blinked it away, he saw the world as he had never seen it before. It was grotesque and twisted, the trees like wriggling black fingers reaching up to luminous clouds in the sky, the buildings like leaning monoliths, the stars above incredibly bright and incredibly close, each of them pulsating and fleshy like beating hearts and opening like eyes in livid, blood-swollen sockets.

Finn screamed.

Then screamed again as he saw a flock of those horrible insects pass over the face of the moon, which was unpleasantly close and unpleasantly bloated like a slice of moist, rotting fruit.

Then it ended.

He got to his feet and hobbled the rest of the way to the dispatch Quonset. When he got there, he leaned against it, trying to catch his breath. He could not seem to find his center. He held on to the outer metal shell because he was literally afraid that it would happen again, and this time he really *would* fly apart.

After about five minutes, he was calm.

As calm as he was going to get anyway. He went through the door and found Jack Coye waiting for him. He was sitting by the radio, monitoring the air traffic out there. A cigarette dangled from his mouth. His usually robust face looked pale and pouchy. There were brown circles under his eyes.

"Crazy night," he said. "One hell of a crazy night."

Finn dropped himself into a swivel chair, pressing his hands flat against his legs so they would not shake. Jack poured him a cup of hot black coffee, and he sipped it slowly, dragging off a Chesterfield.

"You look like you seen a ghost," Jack said.

"Seen more than one," Finn told him.

"It's that...whatever they're doing over there. Some kind of generator, word has it. Some kind of energy source or something. Lots of weird stories making the rounds. I almost pissed my pants the last time they fired it up." He turned from the radio and looked at Finn. "Been getting to you, too?"

"Oh yeah," Finn said.

"Feel it in your guts?"

"Yeah."

"Your head?"

"Yeah."

"Makes you want to vomit out your stomach?"

"Yes. What's it about?"

Jack shook his head and lit another cigarette. He sat there smoking it. A long gray ash fell from the end onto his uniform coat. He didn't seem to notice. "Every time that machine up there kicks in, radio goes crazy. Everything cuts out. Nothing but static. But you should hear the traffic out there when it comes back on. Planes stalling out in the sky. Police losing their frequencies. Trouble over at the power plant. Maybe it's not related; I don't know."

Oh, it was related. Finn was certain of that. Whatever kind of machine they were developing or testing up there, it was like no machine the world had ever seen before. He had no idea what it could be, but he was starting to be very afraid of its potential. Every time they kicked it on, things went insane. The world changed; the sky changed. And each time it seemed to be a little worse.

And what about that creature eating the raccoon? he asked himself with a slight involuntary shiver. *What in the hell was that about?*

Again, he didn't know. All he knew for sure was that it looked like some kind of horrible insect, but like no insect of this world. Something out of one of his magazines—*Weird Tales* or *Amazing Stories*. He tried to tell himself it was unrelated to what they were fooling around with up there, but he wasn't buying it. And particularly after he saw that swarm of them when the machine kicked on just a few minutes before.

They were related, but in what way he did not know. It was simply beyond his comprehension.

"I don't know what they're doing, Jack, but they're putting out a lot of power. Power or energy like we never seen before."

Jack nodded, pulling off his cigarette. "The only scuttlebutt slipping out is something about a generator, a power source. That's the core of Procyon, I guess. Gotta be something big, though. I pulled day shift last week. We had brass from the Defense Department coming through and a general from Army Intelligence. I hear they had admirals from ONI and ONR here on Monday. This is big, Finn, real big. You know what else?"

Finn looked at him. "I'm afraid to ask."

"Way I hear it, it won't be just us handling security come next week. They're bringing in soldiers to man the fence."

Finn was liking all of this less and less. They already had MPs guarding the main buildings, but now the fence, too? "Well, I hope they don't blow us off the fucking planet."

Jack looked around conspiratorially, as if he was trying to see if anyone was listening. "Now, I don't claim to know what they got up there, but get this," he said in a whisper. "I got a cousin over in Puxley. He works at a meatpacking house. Apparently, they've been doing business here at Blue Hills."

"A meatpacking house?"

Jack nodded. "For the past month, they've been bringing over truckloads of meat and blood."

"*Blood?*"

"Yeah. According to my cousin, they've been delivering something like over a hundred pounds of raw meat and twenty gallons of animal blood two or three times a week," Jack admitted. "It would take a small army to go through that much beef on a weekly basis. And the blood...what the hell do they want with twenty gallons of animal blood?"

Finn felt sick inside. The scientists up there working on some kind of machine was one thing, but this was something else again. That much meat and blood suggested they were feeding animals. But there were no animals at Blue Hills. It wasn't a biology station or a medical research outfit; they were involved strictly in weapons research. Physics and electronics and the like. That's what the Procyon Project was about. At least, that's what people said.

Jack let that lay for a while. "You think that's strange? Well, get this. They've been getting deliveries of books and documents from some university out east. They come by special courier."

"What of it?"

Jack offered him a sardonic grin. "These aren't just any books or documents, friend. They're not technical manuals or blueprints or any of that baloney. These are special." He looked around ever more carefully now, ignoring the posters on the wall that said LOOSE LIPS SINK SHIPS and CARELESS TALK COSTS LIVES. "These are *magic* books."

Finn couldn't believe what he heard then. Not just magic as in pull the old rabbit out of the hat, but magic as in *black magic*. These were ancient, rare compendiums of arcane lore about vanished religions and forgotten gods, spell books that described how to summon things from beyond space and time.

"You mean like demons?" he said, his voice dry as chalk dust.

Jack shrugged. "Witch books, Finn. That's what they are. My source told me they got weird names like *Necronomicon* and *De Vermis Mysteriis*...that's

Latin by the way. These books are old, old, old. Very rare. They were banned by the church centuries ago. Only a few copies remain. Devil books."

"That's goddamn crazy. You sure your *source* isn't having a good laugh at your expense?"

Jack shook his head. His eyes were wide and unblinking, his face mottled with a grayish pallor. No, he looked worried, scared even. His was not the face of someone who had gotten off a good one.

"Those books are for calling up things…I can't even pronounce the names. Don't ask me to."

"But what's it all mean, Jack? What the hell is going on here?"

Jack shrugged. "I don't know. They got some kind of machine that sends out waves or something that make people sick. It creates some kind of energy that makes the stars go funny. They're bringing in blood and meat like they got a cage of tigers up there. And they're studying books on devil worship and witchcraft." He swallowed. "I'm afraid to connect the dots on this one."

"Me and you both, brother," Finn said.

They chatted for another thirty minutes, then separated to go make their rounds. It was easy and peaceful. Finn relaxed because there didn't seem to be any more activity coming from up on the hill, and that was a godsend. He keyed in at the watch clocks, taking his time, enjoying the night. He saw nothing weird. Everything that had already happened was slowly fading in his mind, and he was putting it in perspective—save for the big bug. He still couldn't make sense of any of it, particularly the things Jack told him about, but he knew well enough that some things were better off being left alone.

None of my business what they're doing up there.

Joe Heidigger had offered him a job driving a forklift over at the lumber yard last week, and Finn was thinking very seriously about taking him up on it. Maybe it was time for a change. Time to distance himself completely from the war and weapons. God knew he'd served; he'd done his part. Nobody could ask more from him.

The night was nice. Real nice. That was what he liked about the graveyard shift. The quiet, the tranquility. The crickets. The night birds. The lonesome cry of an owl. The solitude put you in touch with yourself. You could think and make sense of things.

He got back to the shack, poured a cup of coffee from his Thermos, and settled in. He had high hopes the rest of the night would be quiet. But when he heard the sound of running footsteps, he knew that wasn't going to happen.

Sighing, he stepped out of the shack and saw Dr. Westly right away. He was one of the Procyon Project scientists. His game was physics, Finn knew. In the flashlight beam, his eyes were wide, his mouth trembling. "Up there," he breathed. "It's happening up there…we can't stop it now. We *can't!*"

"Can't stop what?" Finn asked.

"The machine…it's self-augmenting! It no longer needs us!"

"You're not making any sense," Finn told him.

"We…we saw the potential for a new weapon. Dear God, but we did! It was a cutting edge fusion of theoretical physics, particle theory, and witchcraft theorem…yes, yes, *yes!* How could we know what we were playing at? The elemental forces of chaos we were tampering with?" By this time, he had grabbed hold of Finn and simply would not let go. His eyes were those of a lunatic, his face wet with rolling beads of sweat, his mouth contorted, his face twisted into a frightened mask of pure animal terror. "We let them through… yes, we did! But only the insects! I swear, it was only the insects! We had peered through the doorway of multi-dimensional reality into the very heart of a cosmic anti-world! We fed the insects with blood and meat, and they got larger and larger! They were not of this dimensional plane…don't you see? We couldn't contain them. They could utilize fourth dimensional space! *They flew right through the walls! Right through them!*"

Finn was getting frightened himself. "Doctor, you have to calm down."

"I can't calm down! I don't *dare* calm down! The machine is still active! It no longer needs us! It draws its energy right from the stars and the atoms themselves! Those *things* got into the machine! They took it over! They activated it! It runs because *they* will it!"

"The insects?"

"No, you fool! Those migrating minds from beyond! Those formless, shapeless entities that want to bring the horror through! The monstrosity from the throne of primal chaos! That living nightmare, primordial mass of nuclear cataclysm—"

Westly was out of his mind, completely out of his mind, and Finn wasn't too far behind him.

The rumbling starting again.

Shit.

The earth shook, and he heard a roaring sound from up on the hill as Westly continued to rant on and on. Then a shock wave of sorts knocked him off his teetering feet and nearly punched the wind out of him. It came with a great booming noise. It felt like Blue Hills had been picked up and dropped. He had the same sensation as you get from riding an elevator down many floors. The vibrations followed immediately.

From the vicinity of Building A and Building B, he heard screaming.

Finn got to his feet and hobbled up the road even though his belly was flopping and his head felt like it was filled with a storm of pillow down. He had a hell of a time staying on his feet, but somebody needed help, and he was going to help them.

The vibrations were coming from up on the hill, moving in oscillating waves that made him feel like his bones were hollow and he might drift off into the sky like a helium balloon at any moment.

"Don't!" Westly cried. *"Don't go up there!"*

"I have to!" Finn told him.

The world around him had become a threatening, evil thing. Nothing was right. The stars were drawing down again and the tree branches undulating like tentacles, reaching up towards the sky. Buildings A and B leaned this way and that, like narrow tombstones. They were wiggling like loose teeth. He tried to blink it away, but it remained, growing more distorted by the moment. The landscape became an abomination. He saw shadowy, dark structures like obelisks and spheres and cylinders rising in the distance. And then—

A whirring sound as swarms of those nameless insects filled the night sky and then a great flapping as of immense leathery wings, and he saw other things flying above him, just over his head...save that they were glossy and black, anthropomorphic but lacking anything that might be called faces.

Westly screamed at the sight of them, and Finn himself could only stand there, a numb and mute witness to the grim intersection of worlds.

The vibrations grew stronger and stronger.

The sky became a whirling, spinning vortex of thunder and flashing lightning. The rumbling became the roaring of freight trains, as if the mother of all tornados was bearing down on them. There was a deafening shearing, ripping sound, like static electricity crackling and popping. The air went hot as a funeral pyre, then cold as Arctic wastes.

It was like trying to breathe warm, wet oatmeal. Then a searing hot wind hit him, driving him to his knees next to the shrieking form of Westly. The wind was peppered with flakes of ash like a blizzard.

It came with incredible force.

The hill that Buildings A and B occupied had risen now like the cap of a monstrous mushroom, and as he watched, the roofs of both exploded into fragments with a blinding blue flash of light that carried the fragments straight up into the night.

Then the sky above them split open in a luminous aperture, like blazing sunlight seeping through a crack in a drawn shade. The hole widened, fanned out, consumed the sky and became a great and glowing gash of sucking, vacuuming wind that dragged both Westly and Finn along the ground, trying to draw them up into the cataclysmic heavens, which had become a huge and discordant vortex of spinning, twisting cyclonic matter.

Something was coming through that gash.

Something that had come to devour the world, to suck its blood and gnaw on its cold, yellow bones.

Westly went absolutely hysterical at the sight of it, screaming mindlessly, making strange signs with his hands. His speech was frenetic and garbled, but Finn heard this much: *"It's coming for us! It's coming for all of us! The primal nuclear chaos! Dear God, help us...Yog Sothoth, spare us! Nyarlathotep! Iä . . . ngai . . . ygg. . . . LÄ! LÄ! THE EYE OF AZATHOTH! I SEE IT! I SEE IT OPENING!"*

Finn just waited there, speechless, numb, helpless.

This was the end result of the Procyon Project, the ultimate triumph of weird machines and banned books and blood and meat—to call down this godless, hideous nightmare from the subcellar of reality, this writhing haunter of the dark, this seed of atavistic dread, this living atomic furnace. Yes, this was what they'd been trying to do all along. This was the power they were trying to harness and the force they wanted to weaponize.

They had been trying to bring this atomic, placental nightmare to term.

Finn thought for one insane moment that the full moon was being birthed from that gash. But it was no moon unless the moon had gone misty, indistinct and nebulous, a fluttering pale orb like a bleached and decomposing eyeball. And like a cyclopean eye, the thing began to iris open lengthwise, swimming closer and closer, filling the sky…and he saw something in there, something begin to unfold like the petals of a flower. Squirming, slithering things like fleshy ropes of afterbirth, unwinding and reaching out, growing and lengthening and dividing a thousand times until above the hill there was a forest of pulsing, whipping, transparent roots that seemed to reach for miles.

And beneath them…a phosphorescent chasm. A fungoid, hissing miasma that began to erupt and open like a mouth, slowly, ever slowly. A birth canal. There was something alive in there, a roiling river of cremating, pink hunger. Something alive with a glaring and ancient intelligence, a cold and alien hunger reaching out from some haunted charnel dimension. It had come to devour the world.

Finn heard a reverberating, wet mewling, like the agonized cries of some deformed, grotesque infant being born…

In mere minutes, the thing had divided and expanded like pestilential cells in a Petri dish, a great and squirming, tumescent web that was spreading over the heavens, the ravaged husks of Buildings A and B silhouetted against the flashing, blinding, awesome energy of its face.

It had not only filled the sky, but *become* the sky, and Finn was certain he was only seeing the barest fragment of its immensity.

Then there was a rending, rocketing explosion, and the sky sealed back up, and the thing which was engulfing the heavens let go with a huge and deafening eruption of force and matter and disappeared.

When Finn came to sometime later, the world around him was filled with smoke and fire. The destruction was everywhere. The buildings were gone. More so, the hills that held them were missing, too. A smoldering, blackened crater had opened up in their place. The land was flattened and gutted as far as he could see, thousands of trees blasted and felled. It looked like the dark side of the moon out there, gray and scarred and lifeless.

Westly was dead.

He lay there covered in a dusting of gray ash, his hands held before him like gnarled claws, his mouth hooked in a twisted grimace, his eyes bulging from their sockets.

Dazed, half out of his mind, Finn stumbled through flaming debris and a mist of greasy black smoke until he reached the place where the guard shack had been but was no more. It was here he fell to the ground, shaking and feverish. In the distance he heard police sirens and fire whistles.

Jack Coye was the first one to get to him. Like Finn himself, Jack was blown by ash, face smudged with soot. He gathered Finn in his arms. "Come on, boy, don't check out on me now. Talk to me, kid."

Finn smiled up at him. "Is it gone?" he said.

"Yeah…yeah it's gone."

Finn breathed in and out for a moment, then managed to sit up. "Whole place went up."

Jack nodded. "Sure, sure. Nothing left. But…did you see it? Did you really see *it?*"

Finn considered the question, then shook his head. He lit a cigarette, remembering that LOOSE LIPS SINK SHIPS and CARELESS TALK COSTS LIVES. "I didn't see a damn thing," he said.

Jack winked at him. "Good boy," he said.

MAGGOTS

Only the dead have seen the end of war.
—George Santayana

1

The few blazing sticks in the shallow pit did little to dispel the frigid winds that howled through the winter-dead forest. The trees were snow-heaped sculptures, the landscape blasted white with drift. Francois Jarny sat there, shivering, teeth chattering, hugging his greatcoat to him, for all the good it did. His knapsack was empty and had been for days, still he pawed through it with frostbitten fingers, hoping for a stray crumb of biscuit that he might have missed.

But there was nothing.

He had been hungry for weeks it seemed, at least since the Grand Armee had retreated from Smolensk, harassed by Cossacks and filthy peasants the entire way. Smolensk was a plague city, thousands smitten with typhus fever. So many dead that the locals were throwing corpses out into the streets.

That long? Jarny wondered. *Has it been that long since I ate some decent food?*

Studying his gnawed leather belt, he knew it was true. There had been a few crumbs of stale bread since, a thin soup of rotting turnip tops at a farmhouse, and, ah yes, the fine meal of roasted dog in Dorogobouche.

A starving, slat-thin hound, they had savored its juices and meat, gnawing bones and sucking out the marrow, making a soup from the poor thing's thin blood.

To taste of the meat. To eat of it.

Around him, huddled by small flickering fires, Jarny could hear men moaning and crying out, many dying from infected battlefield wounds, many more from fever and starvation. Each day there were fewer that moved on. Less soldiers. Less stragglers. Frozen corpses were iced to trees, standing upright.

Footsteps crunched through the snow. "Friend Jarny...what a terrible sight you are," said a voice.

It was Henri Boulille, his greatcoat hanging open, the blue tunic beneath streaked with dirt and dried blood. He grinned with yellow teeth. Jarny ignored him, knowing who and what he was.

Boulille squatted by the fire, warming his fingers as the snow fell in frigid sheets. "Why is it, friend Jarny, that you shiver with cold and hunger when there is food to be had? When there is meat that will fill you and keep you strong?"

Jarny stared at him with narrow eyes. "I do not care for your meat."

Boulille laughed. "Oh...tsk, tsk, Jarny...you wish to die in the Russian winter? You wish to never see the warm, green hills of France again? How terrible. How very terrible." He looked around. There were two other soldiers at the fire. One had fallen over, freezing to death. The other was delirious, speaking at length with his mother.

Boulille brought his foul, seamed face in closer. "What is it you think I eat, Francois? Do you think I chew upon corpses in the snow? That I gnaw upon their leathery flesh? Oh, but how mistaken you are! How terribly mistaken!"

But Jarny did not think he was mistaken. For he had heard the stories of Boulille and the others. He had seen them dragging frozen corpses from the drifts and heard the sound of knives and bayonets working at carcasses. There was a word for what Boulille and the others were, but Jarny would not let himself think it.

Boulille continued to speak, but Jarny would not listen. He could smell death upon his breath.

But to taste of the meat. To eat of it.

He was so hungry, so terribly hungry.

It had only been six weeks now since Napoleon's Grand Armee had marched into Moscow, fresh from their valiant victory at Borodino. 100,000 men. They marched into the city unopposed, only to find that the Russians had fled. The city was burning. Even miles out on the steppe, the sky had been blotted out by a black haze of smoke. The Russians had deliberately set their beloved city afire, then evacuated en masse. Those that remained were either insane or infected with typhus and dysentery, rat-bite fever. There was no food in the city. The water was contaminated. Two-thirds of Moscow was blazing, the air congested with smoke and ash.

But even there, in the hollowed, smoldering corpse of the city, Boulille had proven himself an apt survivor. The troops were starving, and Napoleon himself ordered immediate withdrawal. On the way out, Boulille had gathered the emaciated around him and led them into the ruins of a medical school. The only meat in the city was there in the dissection rooms. Boulille, no stranger to eating men by that point, had organized a feast. The men ate what they found pickled in specimen jars: organs, limbs, diseased masses of tissue. They fished meat from vats. They feasted, glutting themselves on white, bloated carrion.

Within days, most were dead from formaldehyde poisoning.

But not Boulille. He was fit. He was strong. A ghoul with chattering, yellow teeth sharpened on corpses, his eyes black, lusterless shoe buttons betraying a void of seething madness in his brain.

And now, here he was, full and fat and rosy-cheeked, making obscene offers of meat to Jarny. Who, at half his age, was a stick-thin, trembling thing with mad eyes and hollow cheeks, the skin bitten off his lips, his leather belt well-chewed, ribs thrusting out beneath his lice-infested tunic, which hung on him like a winding sheet.

He was so terribly hungry.

But one taste…one taste and you will never be a man again. You will be a thing of graves and gallows.

But to taste of the meat. To eat of it.

How it came to be, Jarny could not say. But his next awareness was of stumbling through the snow on broomstick limbs, Boulille supporting him, holding him up like a father with a favored child. They moved among the dead and dying. Men crying out. Men boiling with typhus fever, steam rising from them in a mist of pestilence. Corpses jutting from the snow, dead-white faces sparkling with frost. The meat stripped from throats and gouged from bellies.

"Come, friend Jarny," Boulille said, grinning at the death around him here in this fine kitchen of hell with abundant foodstuffs laid out upon the cutting boards of ice. "Walk with me. Soon you will know strength…and wisdom."

Jarny had some delusional half-memory of being deposited in the snow before a blazing fire. His eyesight was blurred from starvation. He could barely move his limbs or think a coherent thought. There were men around him. Soldiers he knew. Brave men. Cowards. Officers. Enlisted rabble. Yes, circled around him, all grinning like desert-picked skulls, faces streaked with grime, eyes huge and black and empty, grease glistening on chins, gore hanging from mouths.

"Eat, friend Jarny, good friend Francois Jarny," they said. "Fill yourself."

Jarny, dangling somewhere between dream and waking nightmare and harsh reality, remembered Dorogobouche. The Grand Armee, tattered from malnutrition, disease, and exposure, fought a rear-guard action out of the city as the Russians reclaimed it. The streets were clogged with the mangled carcasses of horses and human corpses frozen in stiff white heaps, both of which had been flayed before death by ravaging gangs of cannibals that haunted the bones of the city. Everywhere, smoke and flames from shelled buildings, burning powder wagons. Naked peasants huddled around fires, yellow-faced and pockmarked from typhus fever and rat-bite, dancing madly until they dropped and were ground underfoot by their fellows. And through it all, the hunters of men skulked in cellars and ruins, waiting to rush out and claim the wounded. To roast them on crude spits. And it was no fable, for Jarny had seen it. Seen their firepits. Seen their smooth, white faces and glistening, hungry eyes peering from pockets of shadow.

Boulille had fed quite well in Dorogobouche.

But even then, starving, Jarny refused to think of it.

But to taste of the meat. To eat of it.

The fresh corpse of a soldier was laid in the snow before him, charred and crisping from the flames. And it was the bayonet in his hands that split the pig open until the redolent, hungry smell of fine, juicy meat enveloped him in a hot, salty cloud of appetite.

After that…they all feasted.

Knives and bayonets hacking. Slabs of steaming, dripping meat shoved into greedy mouths. Faces glistening with grease and yellow fat grinning up at the moon. Lunatics luminous with profane delight. Bellies filled. Fingers licked. Entrails divided. Bones gnawed of scraps and sucked of marrow. Then nothing left in the snow but that blackened, rent carcass, broken and scattered in all directions.

Jarny had never felt so strong or so deathless.

2

Months later, Paris.

Warm, sultry.

Jarny, more dead than alive, searching for food. For the dead.

There were few cemeteries in Paris by that point, most having been banned because of the foul odors and seeping rot that began to contaminate the air and streets and cellars of nearby neighborhoods. By the late 18th century, the miasmic stench of putrefaction could be smelled across the city, where it hung in a pestilential haze and was thought to be the cause of one epidemic after another. The cemeteries were closed. The largest of which, the Cimetière des Innocents had been shut down in 1786.

The Cimetière des Innocents had once been the main burial ground for Paris. Located next to Les Halles, the central Parisian market, on the corner of rue Saint-Denis and rue Berger, the dead had been heaped there since the Gallo-Roman days. In 1786, when it was closed down with all the other smaller graveyards, the dead were taken to the newly opened catacombs at Denfert-Rochereau, far south of the city. Jarny knew this well, for his father had been one of the laborers. Night after eerie night, a grim procession transferred the draped remains from the Paris cemeteries to the catacombs.

All that remained now were St. Parnasse, le Cimetière du nord Montmartre, and the Cimetière de l'est, known as the Père Lachaise cemetery. And this is where Jarny went. To his favorite hunting grounds at the junction of rue des Rondeaux and avenue du Père-Lachaise. Standing at the cemetery gates, heart palpitating with strange desire, driven by depraved forces, he listened for watchmen. His teeth were chattering. But it was not from the chill evening air, but hunger.

Quiet, you must be quiet, he told himself.

Yes, this was secret. How clever he had been this night, as every night. All of Paris in an incensed uproar because some skulking ghoul was violating the tombs of their dead, yet he, Francois Jarny, had slipped out of the sleeping barracks with a shovel in his hand, right past the guards with their drawn bayonets and breech-loaders. Now he stood before the cemetery gates, panting and delusional, a cold and sour-smelling sweat beading his face. He stood there with his hands wrapped around the uprights of the fence, trying to fight what was inside him, what slithered and shifted in his belly, making an insatiable hunger roll through him in queasy waves.

Some worn shred of humanity in him would not allow it. Not again. This time he would not give in to it. This time he would be master of his own flesh. He would not weaken; he would not lose control.

"I'll kill myself if I have to," he said under his breath. "I'll do whatever it takes...do you hear me? You won't make me do this, you won't...make me do it..."

And that's when the pain came. It brought him to his knees, squeezing tears from his eyes and making his mind spin until he could do nothing but moan and thrash on the concrete. The pain was like razors sliding through his belly, needles bursting his stomach, nails and tacks filling his entrails until he begged for it to stop. Dear God, anything, anything just make it stop, *just please make it stop—*

And then it did.

Jarny lay there, dripping wet with perspiration, the agony slowly subsiding until he could breathe again and his heart stopped hammering. He was being taught a lesson and knew it. He had to learn not to ignore the hunger, not to fight against it.

He coughed out a black, oily mass of phlegm and then felt better.

Using the uprights, he pulled himself to his feet and pressed his moist, feverish face to the fence. The wrought-iron was cool. Like death.

Picking up his shovel, he scaled the wall and dropped down on the other side, panting. Not from exertion. Not really. It was something else—Père-Lachaise: a winding maze of crypts seemingly piled one atop another, like some morbid excrescence of graveyard stone. The hunger bloomed inside him like funeral orchids. It wanted, it needed, it desired. Jarny moved along through the battalions of leaning headstones and moon-washed sepulchers. The cemetery was a study in silence, a marble forest that held its breath. Tree limbs creaked overhead; rats scratched in the darkness.

As always, he deluded himself. It was the only thing that kept him comparatively sane.

He tried to convince himself that if he wandered in circles long enough, maybe he would get confused and not be able to find the grave. It was a pleasant ruse, but it did not work: for the hunger knew where the grave was. It could smell the black soil and oak box, what rested within. It had the scent, and like a bloodhound straining at its leash, it led him there. A small, conservative tombstone the color of a blanched skull. Jarny looked up through the intertwined tree branches at the sullen eye of the moon, but there was no solace there.

Something hitched in his belly.

Spikes were driven through his stomach wall.

"Yes, yes," he said. "Quit being so greedy."

He touched the stone and silently read the name there: ELIZABETH DUPREE. She had drowned in the Seine. Fifteen years old, she had been in the ground nearly a week. The hunger increased in his belly. Yes, she would be seasoned properly.

Forgive me, he thought. *Forgive me.*

He took the shovel and cut away the sod. That was easy enough; it hadn't the time yet to properly take root. He rolled it away and began to dig. At first, he dug into the soil almost languidly, as if he planned on never finding what was buried below. But the pains kept rising and falling, and he began to dig through the wormy, black earth in earnest, taking it down foot by foot and squaring off his excavation as he went. Three feet, four, five.

The hunger rolling though him made him practically giddy now.

He kept digging, his pile of dirt getting larger as the moon slipped across the sky. And then…the shovel struck wood. Breathing hard, drenched with sweat and black with earth, he began pawing the soil away from the polished box. When it was clean and gleaming with dirty moonlight, he raised the shovel over his head and let out a wounded, agonized cry, breaking the catches one by one.

Jarny hoped, God how he hoped, someone would hear him, that the noise he purposely made and his cry of loathing would bring someone. The gate swinging wide, men with rifles rushing through the grass. Finding him, seeing him for what he was.

Yes, yes, yes, seeing the thing I am and killing me, shooting until their guns are empty and—

The pain again. Not a full-fledged attack, not an out and out violation, but more like a groping of filthy, unwanted hands, an obscene kiss in the dark. Shaking, tears running down his cheeks, he gripped the lid of the box and threw it open.

The stench.

Oh, the high foul stink of it.

It came rolling out of the casket in a mephitic cloud, green and wet and sickening. Jarny fell back against the side of the grave while his stomach lurched and roiled. Thick and noisome and utterly offensive, it was also… *delicious.*

He lay there, shaking his head, in complete denial of the perversions to follow. Bile climbed his throat, spitting hot and acidic onto his tongue. He couldn't do this. Dear Lord, he couldn't do this *again.*

But the hunger was a living thing inside him, huge and silver-toothed and unwieldy. It was so irresistible that it blotted out who and what he was, made him into a host, a vessel with hooked fingers and teeth and insatiable desires.

The corpse of Elizabeth DuPree was not a pretty thing after nearly a week in the damp, rank earth. Her white lace burial gown was mottled and water-stained from seepage, a dark mildew had grown up her neck and over her cheeks like a beard. Her folded hands were likewise meshed with morbid fungi. Her face was sunken, lips shriveled away from the teeth so that it looked as if she were grinning.

Please don't make me do this, don't make me touch...that...

But then, as always, Jarny's will was no longer his own.

Things like defiance and self-control no longer existed. They had been crushed beneath the stark and vile immensity of the hunger and the need of what lived inside him. He was just a vehicle, a machine with no conscious volition of its own.

And that's what made him jump into the casket, on top of the corpse, feeling it and smelling it, disgusted beyond earthly bounds. He pressed his face to that of the dead girl until her putrescence filled him and the hunger went mad inside him. His tongue came out and licked her blackened lips, tasting the powders and chemicals the undertaker had used on her, and something beneath all that, something repellent and nauseous.

He dragged the body up into the moonlight, dumping it on the damp grass.

And what was inside him said, *Fill us...we're starving...*

There was no more waiting.

Jarny sank his teeth into the gelid flesh of her throat, yanking out moist flaps of fetid meat, chewing and tasting, driven insane by the textures and revolting flavor on his tongue. He tore her gown away, gnawing at the greening meat of her thighs and belly, tearing at her cold breasts and nibbling at her mottled buttocks. He licked and sucked and tore. He used his teeth and his hands, shredding and devouring and spitting out gobs of black juice that ran from his mouth. The taste was disgusting, the feel of rotting meat sliding down his throat made him feverish and disoriented. And when he was full, satisfied with his charnel meal of pulp and bone and graying meat, he screamed and mutilated what was left, tearing the corpse asunder and rolling in the scraps until its feel was his feel and its stink was his own vile perfume.

And then it was done.

Jarny slowly came back to himself, ribbons of decomposing tissue

123

hanging from his mouth, his uniform splashed with drainage and oozing black ichor. The sickly-sweet stench of putrefied meat clung to him in a ghastly bouquet. His first impulse was to scream and his second was to vomit. To throw out his guts and everything that was in them: that warm and slushy mass resting in his belly. But he didn't dare. For *they* would not allow it. They would never have that, never have him denying him their feast of grave-meat.

Show us, they said. *Show us.*

So Jarny stood up, unbuttoning his filthy tunic, revealing the yawning hollow in his side that was eaten away and infested by a squirming mass of white maggots. No ordinary graveworms, these were impossibly fat and pale and sluglike, a coiling and slinking mass even then lengthening and thickening and bursting with eggs from the feast he had given them.

It was enough.

They were happy.

Excellent, they said.

Whimpering, Jarny retreated from the plundered grave as the worms inside him grew fat and lazy and torpid. As they went to sleep, he ran from the cemetery, a hot wind of dementia blowing through his head.

3

By the time they marched into Vilna, Napoleon's Grand Armee had been reduced from 100,000 to barely 5,000. Weakened to a deplorable state by fevers and plagues and starvation, the bitter cold did the rest, and this in a matter of weeks. Jarny, now having supped upon the meat of men, was not like the others. Strong, vital, full-blooded, he fought the Russians and peasants at Boulille's side. While the others fell dead at his feet from exposure or cowered in the trees, Jarny fought like an animal, taking sheer savage joy from the men he killed. When he emptied his rifle, he drew his saber and charged into the Russian ranks, slashing and hacking, delighting in the screams of the enemy and laughing with merciless sardonic humor at their pleas for mercy.

His saber felled a forest of men, leaving a writhing carpet of carcasses underfoot. Limbs were scattered, heads rolling free, bowels spilled steaming to the snow. There was purity and glacial joy in the killing that he had never experienced before. There was nothing finer than the saber laying open one's enemies and staining the snow red. And there was no sweeter joy than having their blood sprayed over you in reeking gouts, splashing over your face so that you could taste the life you had taken, knowing it, feeling it, filling yourself with its hot wine.

Jarny saw his enemies as cattle to be slaughtered, to be brought under heel and blade, swine to be carved and smoked over a hot fire. And while the others died in numbers, laid low by fever and famine, his belly was full. And who could know of the secret joy he felt bursting into the miserable huts of peasant farmers with others of like appetites? The screaming, the cutting, the rich heady aroma of spilled blood? The slabs of juicy meat roasted on spits, entrails cooked on sticks over hot flames? He lived for the kill, the feeding, and his prey was abundant.

Then, just outside Vilna, a Russian reprisal. Musket balls whizzing through the air and shells bursting, men screaming as they were cut down in the snow. The air was wet with a fine mist of blood. Everywhere, bodies and parts of them scattered about in a gruesome hodgepodge. Jarny was hit by shrapnel as he jumped over the shattered anatomies of his fellow soldiers in a vain attempt at escape. The shrapnel nearly tore his right leg off, shearing open his belly and filling his gut with burning fragments of metal. Unwilling to die, he crawled through the snow, dragging his viscera behind him in freezing loops. He left a trail of blood and slime.

After that, his mind fell into a fog.

He and dozens of others were dragged into Vilna, seeking food, shelter, and medical aid. But there was none to be had. Vilna had been ransacked by peasant riots and fighting. The typhus plague had swept the city, and corpses were heaped in untidy, loose-limbed stacks right out in the streets. The population was starving, diseased, and filthy. They crowded into stinking little huts infested with cockroaches.

Jarny was dumped with the rest of the sick and wounded in the field hospital at St. Bazile. It was an awful place, even by the standards of the day—crowded, steaming, and stinking. Jumping with lice, men were packed in wards shoulder-to-shoulder, sometimes right on top of one another on floors that were a seething pool of human waste infected with disease germs. Typhus raged, as did influenza and dysentery. The wounded and ill literally drowned in their own vomit, blood, bile, and excrement. The corridors were stacked with thousands of corpses. So many that a crude maze-like path had to be opened through them. Rats fed on the dead and dying. Broken windows and ruptured walls were stuffed with torsos and limbs in a grisly rampart to keep the polluted air from infecting the living.

Jarny was thrown in a tight, close room with hundreds of others that were delirious from hunger and fevers. The floor was covered with rotting straw fouled with urine, bile, and feces. There were bodies everywhere, many rotted right to mush. He was tossed atop the wormy, spongy mass of a bloated corpse. A corpse infested by...*maggots*. And no ordinary maggots were they, he soon learned, but a race of graveworms with a perverse communal intelligence, a single overriding need to infest and feed. Jarny landed on the body of their previous host, in fact, who was too rank and polluted by that time to be of any further use to them.

So they entered Jarny.

They came in through his eyes and nostrils and mouth, up his ass and through the numerous holes in his hide where sharpened staffs of bone jutted forth. They filled him, infesting and breeding.

You won't die, they told him. *We won't let you.*

And that's how it began. He did not die: they would not allow it. They repaired him, rebuilt him, and soon he was well again...as well as a man can be that is little more than a host for hundreds and hundreds of worms.

Out in the streets of Vilna, as the plague overflowed every house, every barn, every makeshift morgue and spilled out into the streets, it was a horror as well. Constantly harassed by Cossacks and insane peasants, Napoleon pulled back as the Russians poured in to fight, leaving the sick and dying behind to their gruesome fate. By the end of December there were 25,000 people in Vilna, nearly all of them stricken with typhus fever. By June, only 7,000 would still be alive.

Jarny was one of them.

But by that point, colonized as he was, he could no longer call himself human. What the worms had given him was secret, and what he would have to do for them was a horror.

And it was always the same: *Feed us.*

4

It was in the streets and all over the Paris papers the next morning: the awful, slinking ghoul had struck yet again. This time it had violated the grave of a young girl. The body had been carefully unearthed then savagely mutilated, torn to fragments in a deranged frenzy. Parts of her were scattered over the walks and dangling in the trees.

He learned of it as did all, and hearing it, remembered that once he had been a man named Francois Jarny. A human being.

5

When he woke in the barracks several days later after another hideous night of mania, sweating and shaking, the worms had been busy. They had spun a cocoon of new, pink flesh over the gaping hollow in his side. It was their gift to him, so he did not have to look on their wriggling, industrious masses.

Yes, a gift and it filled him with a loathing that was absolute.

He vomited bile into the basin, then, wiping his mouth, he fell against the tub, shaking and whimpering. He could still smell the grave-ooze on his hands, his breath.

After the tears had finally dried up and that stark insanity stopped scratching inside his skull, Jarny stood up and allowed himself to look at the patch of pink skin just below his ribs. It was very shiny, almost waxy-looking. And warm. Very warm, almost hot. He pressed the flat of his hand against it, and it gave like a water balloon, something sloshing beneath it. He couldn't help himself—like a child intrigued by a scab, he pressed his fingers against the patch of skin. The new flesh was squishy, flaccid. When he applied pressure to it, his fingertips sank into it like it was not human skin but the flesh of a soft, rotting peach.

He pulled his hand away, fingers stained with a dirty, brown liquid like tobacco juice. The smell was horrid, like the drainage of gassy corpses.

Horrors of War

There was revulsion, of course, a deep-set, physical revulsion that had become an almost common thing with him, a natural rhythm, like happiness and sorrow. He subsisted on a daily diet of it. Knowing that he was host to them. That they owned him. That they would make him violate more graves, feed upon the rot within, stuff himself with it like a glutton at a buffet. He was infested by grave worms, and there really was no way out.

They were small, and he was large.

They were weak, and he was strong.

But he was one, and they were a multitude, forever starving. Forever demanding.

They felt what he felt. Tasted what he tasted. Knew what he knew. And, oh yes, they could see what he saw. They could look through his eyes and make him experience things as they experienced them. And to Jarny, there was no greater horror in this world beyond the feasting itself. To look out through his eyes, *as* them, feeling their lust and depravity and knowing their cold, cutting hunger. To become a corpse-worm appraising a shank of greening meat and not feel repugnance or simple disgust, but a joy and pleasure that was almost sexual. A noxious hunger, an overwhelming, chemical desire to crawl over the offered putrid mass, to bore into it, to chew and suck upon the grave bounty, and, yes, meet others of your kind in those moist, tainted depths, to mate, to spawn, to lay your eggs in hot, pearly masses within.

That was horror…to do such things and *love* it.

He couldn't even kill himself, because they would not allow it. They would repair whatever damage he incurred and make him walk again, a mindless cadaver, a shell that existed only to find and feed upon the carrion they desired. Not that he hadn't tried again and again. But they always patched him up and would until he was so polluted by their larva and waste, that he would be of no further use to them…except as food.

He could feel them wriggling about in his side, repairing the damage he had done. They did not punish him. The feel of them slinking and slithering inside him was punishment enough.

Already, they were hungry, and he would have to feed them. Such was the penalty of resurrection and morbid symbiosis.

Jarny thought it was months now, but maybe it was years. It was hard to remember. Yes, he had a fine, new sheath of pink skin at his side... but what of the rest of him? He was bony and pale, tiny, red lumps of infection broken out all over his body. They were soft to the touch, filled with discolored pus. He was rotting from the inside out, and the maggots kept him alive, kept him going even as they drowned him in their own diseased filth and poisoned wastes. For he was their home. A home that needed constant maintenance. But they were ambitious, diligent; they would not let him fall to disrepair.

Not just yet.

The *La Gazette* reported that the ghoul had been active again. This time at the cemetery of St. Parnasse. Watchmen of the *Gendarmerie Royale* had fired at the creature, but it escaped over a wall. They claimed it had the face of a wolf or perhaps a hyena.

Jarny laughed at that.

Laughed and remembered Henri Boulille...and hated.

He stood before the mirror, looking at the cadaverous thing he now was: hollow-socketed, sallow, gums pulling back from yellow teeth sharpened on corpses and gray bones. The worms moved within him, digging and tunneling and forever burrowing. He could see their plump shapes just beneath his skin. Down his arms and over his chest, like peas pressed beneath the flesh of his face and in constant, busy motion, writhing through his honeycombed tissue.

Yes, he looked at himself in the mirror.

But what looked back was a monster.

6

The horrible destruction of the Grand Armee in Russia was final testament to the vulnerability of Napoleon's forces. As the tattered, ragged remains retreated through Poland, the Russians continued to harass them, circling ahead of the scattered army of the living dead and practicing a scorched earth policy. They burned villages and farms, slaughtered animals, and heaped wells and ponds with the carcasses of men and cattle. Food was scarce. Water contaminated. Peasants began to join the remnants of the

Grand Armee, forming a wandering parade line of refugees that stumbled along, at a distance, behind the broken, zig-zagging march of soldiers seeking France. And as they moved, they spread typhus and influenza in their wake.

In many of the fractured, smoldering villages they came to, the peasants burned their dead in great pyres, already infected by forward units of the Grand Armee. They huddled around fires, burning dung to keep pestilential vapors at bay. It did them little good.

Jarny often walked alone.

The other men knew what he was by then, an associated of Boulille, the corpse-eater. They shunned his company. Often he could hear them speaking: *Regarder là, il est Jarny, l'ami de Boulille. Il mange les cadavres des hommes, remplit son ventre de charogne.* Yes, they were right. He was a friend of Boulille's, and he *did* eat the corpses of men and stuff himself with carrion. How right they were.

Other than his appetites, he was no more or less appealing than the others. Covered in lice and sores, his greatcoat a soiled, threadbare thing, his tunic crusty with urine and excrement, bloodstains and the grease and fat of his nocturnal feedings, he was a hunched-over goblin with hollow cheeks. Face dirty, teeth chattering, and cataleptic eyes staring, forever staring, the mind behind them was diseased by what it had seen, what it had done, and what it would yet do.

Jarny was mad and infested. Jarny was a ghoul.

As he wandered alone, far from the others one day, he came upon a filthy, little hamlet. A woman in rags was stirring a pot over a fire. Her eyes were like wet glass set in a yellow, pocked face, her narrow, decaying teeth jutting from sallow gums. She was insane, and Jarny knew it. She motioned him over, and he drank from her foul well. Afterwards, she offered him a tin cup of soup. It was quite good, though the meat was seasoned unpleasantly sweet. And too familiar to the taste.

She giggled as he ate, scratching through the snow like an animal to the dirt and roots beneath. Finally, in perfect French, she said, *"Ah! Je vous avais attendu, ami Jarny! Un autre dit vous viendriez! Ici… mon mari et enfants sont morts de la peste, ainsi j'ai fait un potage hearty fin à partir de leur chair et os!"*

It wasn't roots she was scratching for, but to show him the well-boiled bones of her family. Those of her husband and children, from whom she had made a special, hearty soup anticipating his arrival. Yes, Boulille had been there, instructing the mad woman to expect another of similar appetites.

The column, as it were, marched on, and bitter winter gave way to slopping, wet spring. With the warmth and wetness, the typhus fever raged and dropped dozens of men each day. The dysentery worsened, as did the influenza. Diseased men leaned against others just to make it another mile, a few more feet. The pestilence was blowing through Eastern Europe on a hot wind of plague. The lice were unbearable, breeding in the warmth and damp. Jarny's flesh and clothes were teeming with them. As he tried to sleep at night by his pitiful fire, they nipped and bit and made him tremble and sweat on the moist ground. The ragged clothing of the soldiers actually *moved,* they were so infested.

One night, a soldier named Betrand jumped up in a mad frenzy, stripping his clothes off and throwing them into the fire. They burned with a popping sound, the noise of hundreds of lice being incinerated. Hopping about in the mud, naked, he was delirious, slapping and scratching at his emaciated, lice-bitten body, calling out, *"Grêle vers la France ! Grêle à Napoleon!"*

Another man raised his musket and shot him dead, so the others might sleep. His body did not lay long before soldiers and peasants slipped out of the shadows and dragged it away to be quartered by bayonets and roasted. This was what they had become. No longer were they the Grand Armee. Now they were beggars and criminals and scavengers, skulking things less than men. Filthy with their own waste, human rats that spread disease, parasites that fed upon one another.

Tormented by thirst and hunger, the stragglers marched ever forward through the rains that turned the fields and roads to rutted mud holes. Pools of standing water were putrid with the corpses of men and animals. Only the mad sipped from them.

It was to these ponds of carrion that Jarny was driven by what burrowed inside him.

Horrors of War

At night, while the others were scattered away from him, he would seek out especially deep pools of rank water that were seething and steaming with dozens of waterlogged corpses and carcasses, greening and flyblown as they broke the oily surface in putrescent tangles and staffs of jutting, white bone. He would dive amongst them, peeling mucid flesh from fungi-slicked skeletons, gnawing on jellied hides and innards boiling soft with rot. These were the ponds he swam in, bathed in, and filled himself with.

And this, ultimately, was the hideous creature called Francois Jarny that returned to France.

7

After days of stuffing himself with whatever was convenient—gas-swollen rodents and flyblown dogs found in alleys—the maggots led Jarny on a wild chase down into the sewers where they smelled something delicious, something ghoulishly tantalizing.

Beneath the metal grating, it was a place of stagnant waters and sucking, black mud, sewage and rats and rotting things.

Amongst all that misting decay and nauseous stench, they had scented something they wanted.

They pushed Jarny on and on. He slopped through the smelling muck of those winding, echoing tunnels, scattering vermin, his arms specked with insect bites and curious rashes. Long after midnight, in a clogged, leaf-covered backwash where leeches clung fatly to his legs, they found what they wanted.

The corpse of a little boy.

Jarny had seen his face in the papers. Everyone had. He disappeared, and no one could find a trace of him. But they could not smell like the maggots could. Once he decomposed sufficiently, they could scent him easily. Jarny dragged the boy's gas-bloated body out of the foul water and laid it on the concrete embankment. By moonlight, the child was an atrocity. He was so badly distended that the buttons of his little shirt had popped free. Delicious.

He looks delectable, the maggots said.

132

Jarny frightened off the rats that had been nibbling at him and did what he must do.

In the wan light of the leprous moon peering through a sewer grating, he licked the boy's bluing face, touching him and squeezing his puffy bulk, like a butcher appraising a fine cut of beef, deciding how best to cut it. The maggots went wild within him, biting and pulsing and digging into the loam of his intestines. And Jarny was pushed, as always, into higher realms of depravity.

Revolted and insane, he tore open the boy's belly with his teeth, swooning as a nauseating, sickly-sweet cloud of corpse-gas blew into his face. Then he was biting and tearing, screaming into the night as he sank his teeth into pulpous flesh. He buried his face in the putrescent mush of the boy's abdomen, yanking out soft entrails with his teeth, sucking down rivers of carrion-slime, tearing and ripping until his jaws were sore and his face oozed with corpse-jelly.

Panting and gagging in the rank, sluicing water, he shook with fevers. Gore dipped from his mouth. His body convulsed. The maggots, of course, were oblivious to his discomfort. *Show us…let us see,* they told him.

He stood and let them look through his eyes. Their delight was carnal and voracious. The boy was little more than a mangled, gray-green heap of mildewed meat, marrow-sucked bones, and shattered, gnawed wreckage.

Now finish, Jarny, they said. *The sweet-meats, don't forget the sweet-meats.*

With a loose brick, he broke open the boy's skull, gnawing and licking at the jellied gray matter within, spitting out beetles and worms that dared defile this rarest of cutlets. At first, he was gently passionate with the sweet-meats, but soon the ravenous ghouls within pushed him to new heights of frenzied gluttony. He yanked the buttery-soft meat out in rancid handfuls, shoving it greedily in his mouth, chomping and feeling it crush to a sweet, juicing paste beneath his teeth. He smeared it over his face and danced madly in the dappled moonlight. In the end, breathless and horrified, he licked the skull clean as a soup bowl.

And then, satisfied, the maggots went to sleep.

Jarny scrambled up out of the sewers and vented his horror in a whooping, hysterical scream.

8

He lay awake that night.

Barely breathing.

A vile-smelling juice ran from his pores like sweat. He stank of corpses and graves. Inside, he was infested. As the worms slept off their hideous repast, Jarny lay shivering and polluted with their wastes and drainage.

It couldn't go on much longer.

9

The next day he was summoned before Captain LeClerq. He was a stern, gray-haired man that had absolutely no tolerance for anyone. But he had a soft spot for Jarny. They had both survived Napoleon's invasion of Russia and had crossed the Neiman together, the Russians laying waste to what remained of the Grand Armee as they crossed the freezing river, hundreds cut down, hundreds more drowning, but the majority rafting across on corpses. They had both received the *Légion d'Honneur* for their valiant actions.

"Sergeant Jarny," LeClerq said, not looking up from his daily reports. "You have, no doubt, heard of this ghoul haunting our cemeteries and of the vile thing he or it has been doing."

"Yes, sir." Jarny waited, at full attention, the maggots looping in his stomach.

"All Paris is angered. There are cries from the highest offices."

Yes, Jarny was certain of that. He could just imagine the vociferous outcries of condemnation coming from the plush salons of the aristocratic and the social-climbing upper bourgeoisie. Were they truly offended? Truly outraged? Probably not. Decadent to the core, these people lived lives of leisure while the masses starved in the streets. They frequented the salons and cafes of the Champs-Elysées, talking at length of poetry, art, and politics. Many subjects they were equally ignorant of. But when something like this happened…they feigned outrage…but secretly delighted in it. Anything to escape the self-imposed, dull sameness of their regal prisons.

The vegetable sellers, ragpickers, rat-catchers, and common tradesmen of the Les Halles and the rue de Venise were probably the ones truly incensed. They and the prostitutes who sold themselves nightly for fifty *centimes* or a head of cabbage to eat. Yes, incensed probably, but not surprised. Not in this city.

"I suppose they are angered," Jarny said.

LeClerq removed his spectacles. "Come now, Jarny. Please speak openly."

Jarny sighed. "That is...sir...I wonder if these people are truly angered or secretly relish the gruesome details."

"Ah! You speak of the culturally elite? The privileged? The aesthetics? It is well you have no political ambitions, Jarny. But I prefer, as do you, to think that I serve the all and not the few. It is important to remember this."

"Yes, sir."

"But this business at hand...it is a most..." He paused, studying Jarny through his wire-rimmed spectacles. "Are you well, Jarny?"

"Yes, sir. I but slept poorly last night."

LeClerq merely nodded...though for one, trembling instant, Jarny was certain that the man suspected him, that he was about to stand up and cry out for Jarny to confess his evil sins, to admit to what he was. But he did not.

"Monsieur Betreaux was here, Jarny," LeClerq said with a certain gravity behind his words. "Betreaux is the Police *Commissaire* for this quarter, as you probably know. What he told me was most disturbing. You will not read of it in the newspapers or scandal sheets. His men at St. Parnasse Cemetery...they claim they fired at the ghoul...and he was a soldier."

Jarny felt woozy, his head spun, and his eyesight seemed to blur. "But... but," he stammered, "such a thing...it is impossible...."

"Yes, Jarny. So thought I. Until I was given this." LeClerq dropped a small brass disc on the desk. "Do you recognize it?"

Jarny tried to lick his lips, but it would have taken rivers. He swallowed, tried to stay on his feet as his world careened madly around him and the maggots gnawed hungrily at the lining of his stomach. Of course he recognized the disc: it was a button. A button from a military infantry tunic. Why, his tunics had the very same buttons....

"I told Betreaux I would personally make an inspection of every tunic in the barracks." But LeClerq waved that away. "But I will not. I find the idea distasteful. Besides, it would create a certain amount of suspicion, yes? So you and my other sergeants shall do it. Check your platoon, Jarny. Check their tunics."

Look at me, you fool! Can't you see guilt, the horror, the madness in these eyes?

"Yes, sir. I shall."

Jarny saluted and turned to the door, amazed that he was able to stay on his feet, amazed that he did not fall to his knees and cry out his obscene crimes. If only he had but the strength.

"And Jarny?"

LeClerq studied him with typical flat indifference. "Watch your men closely."

"Yes sir."

"This fiend must be found and destroyed."

His eyes welling with tears, Jarny said, "I couldn't agree more, Captain...."

10

A popular pastime in those grim days was to visit the Paris morgue. Passers-by and the morbidly curious would enter that forbidding stone building, immediately making for the display room. Here, behind a large viewing glass, arranged on slabs, were the unclaimed corpses laid out like meat in a butcher's window. Engulfed in a sweet stench of decay and less definable odors, the curious could study, at their leisure, the bloated, white bodies fished out of the Seine, the crushed remains of workmen, suicides with throats burned by the rope, and street women found hacked in dim alleys, their eyes glazed in horror.

All were laid out naked in grisly splendor, there being no secrets in death. Tacked to the wall behind were personal articles: trousers, coats, petticoats, hats, scarves. It was thought that if a particular heap of moldering meat was no longer recognizable, perhaps an article of clothing or a favored watch might be.

It was not, of course, a pleasant place.

But pleasant or not, people stopped by in droves. For unlike many

136

other Parisian exhibitions, this one was free to the public. At any given time of the day one might glimpse workmen with their satchels of tools standing about, gnawing on fresh loaves of bread from nearby vendors. They stood shoulder-to-shoulder with high-born, melancholic ladies in their silken gowns and lacey parasols, self-styled intellectuals and street poets chiming graveyard verse, upscale businessmen with top hats and walking sticks, dozens of giggling girls fresh from the mills and shops who moved around in rosy-cheeked swarms.

They all came: lower classes, bourgeoisie, intellectuals, aristocrats. They looked upon dead faces that were swollen blue from the river and eaten to the bone by fish; faces waterlogged to the point that they were coming apart, faces that were sliced, jabbed with holes, eaten by rats and dogs, burnt and mutilated by forces unknown; faces that were like so much molten wax, heated by the sun and infested with larvae, until their soft, pulping flesh literally slid from the skulls beneath. And, now and again, the face of some young woman who'd thrown herself into the Seine only to find exquisiteness in death: lustrous sweeping hair, flawless marble skin, high, skullish cheekbones, lips pulled into a soft, gray pout, life encapsulated and death personified in the ravishing beauty of the charnel. The undertakers often made death masks of these poor girls. One of these became known as *L'inconnue de la Seine,* and was copied and sold in great numbers, decorating sitting rooms and parlors across the country.

By day the morgue was a thriving place, by night just as still and quiet as the flyspecked faces in the display case.

And it was here, in the dead of night, that a man named Francois Jarny came, driven by what starved within. It was not his first visit to the maison des morts, as it was known. He knew there were troublesome attendants in the cellar where the most select cuts were to be found. But the maggots were smart. They made Jarny hide in a broom-closet until first one attendant slipped off for his lunch and another napped in an empty office.

The buffet was open.

The maggots, of course, had Jarny bring an iron prybar with him. After a bit of straining and grunting, he popped the door to the cellar and went down the sweating steps. The postmortem room was of no interest to them…though there were certain lingering odors that were positively succulent.

In the cold room, Jarny opened the drawers set into the wall. The fare was adequate. The crunchy flesh of a burn victim. The rheumy eyeball of a suicide. The soft fingers of a drowning victim. The sweet belly fat of a strangled infant. Snacks, mainly. Appetizers. Enough to drive the maggots into contortions of rapture, but hardly enough to sate them. They kept at Jarny, filling his bowels with shards of glass.

Feed us, they said. *We need real meat. Find it.*

In one of the last drawers, he found what they wanted. A murder victim exhumed from the cloying soil of a cellar floor. A woman. She was wrapped tightly in a stained, gray sheet like a Christmas present. Jarny hefted it from its chamber and shook it. What was inside sloshed about lusciously, as if the present were filled with a thick mint jelly. He opened it slowly, teasing and almost seductive. The maggots appreciated a fine presentation. Much of the woman splashed out in a repellent surge of juice, watery meat, and sludgy tissue. The stench was pure, joyous putrefaction: gamy and yellow and marvelously brined in its own heady juices. Perfectly repulsive and perfectly appetizing.

Taste her, they said, *sip her.*

Jarny, a wet, distorted scream breaking in his throat, dipped his fingers into the gelatinous mass of her remains, as if she were fondue. He sucked them clean, nibbling at the green, mossy bulge of her throat, yanking her blackened tongue from her mouth and licking it like it was still alive… then chewing upon it. As the hunger rose up inside him and his mind was thrown into a blank, gray haze, he began ravenously tearing and snapping at the goodies.

And, the maggots said: *Behind you!*

The sleeping attendant had stole back in, stealthy thing that he was. He stood there with a look of absolute, revolted horror on his face. "You!" he shouted. "You! What…what in God's name are you doing?"

Jarny grinned at him, corpse-slime running from his mouth, a flap of stringy tissue hanging from his jaws. *"Je mange la chair des cadavers!"* Jarny told him.

His fingers curled into malicious claws; he jumped up with a demented, gibbering shriek. But the attendant was a stout, powerful man. He snatched up the forgotten prybar and put it to use. As Jarny raged and howled, the prybar rose and fell, swung by a man whose soul was sickened by what he saw. It shattered Jarny's left arm, cleaved open his head, smashed-in his ribs. He hit the floor, and the attendant, worked up into a maniacal hatred, continued to swing his weapon.

Finally, panting and dizzy, he looked down at the ghoul. Jarny was still alive, eyes wide and glassy and aware, but he was broken, bleeding, his neck snapped, and his body splayed limply. Blood was running freely from all orifices.

As the bar came up for the death-blow, Jarny smiled with red-stained teeth, saying, "Thank God, Thank God...."

Francois Jarny no longer moved.

11

But he was not dead.

He only waited while the worms attempted to put him back together again. But his wounds were massive, grievous; it would take many days, and they could not bear the idea of starving all that time.

At midnight the next evening, a new attendant came on shift. He saw to all the trifling tasks his job entailed. When he was finished, and quite alone, he peaked in the drawers at the cold cuts, looking for anything that might be of use. When he reached Jarny's berth and looked upon that white, grinning face, he gasped.

Jarny saw him through filmed yellowing eyes: the long cadaveric face fanning out with deep-set lines, the narrow discolored teeth, the dead gray eyes. He knew this man, God yes, how he knew this man. Just the sight of him made Jarny smell the powder and battlefield stench, feel the cold and nits biting him.

"Oh, ho, ho," said Boulille, "friend Jarny, good friend Francois Jarny. So you are the ghoul of the cemeteries, eh? Tsk, tsk, my old friend. What a state you are in."

Jarny did not speak, but inside his head he spoke to the maggots: *Look at him! He's fat and healthy and cunning! I'm ruined, but he is perfect...for a host.*

Yes, they said with great, breathless fervor. *Yesssss....*

Happily, Jarny waited. He did not wait long. Alone, ever obscene and deranged, Boulille thought he would sample a scrap of meat from his old compatriot of the Napoleonic Wars. As he sank in the knife, Jarny sprang up with the last drop of vitality available, seizing Boulille by throat. Oh, but how Boulille fought! He jumped away, dragging Jarny right from his berth. He fought, he tore, but Jarny would not release him. They fell to the floor in a heap, Jarny on top. And then, black toxins running from Jarny's flesh and dripping from his nostrils and ears, a heaving muscular convulsion swept through him, and he voided what was inside. He vomited a foamy, peristaltic river of slime and worms, hundreds and thousands of worms that kept pouring out in moist tangles with each convulsion. They were fat and white and glistening. They covered Boulille's screaming face and thrashing body.

But not for long.

They entered him. Through his mouth and nose and ears, through tiny cuts and abrasions. They wriggled up his ass and worked their way down the head of his penis. Wherever there was an opening, they swarmed. And many of them just tunneled straight in, melting into his flesh until he was no longer Henri Boulille, craven cannibal, but merely a host for something ancient, evil, and undying.

Jarny hit the floor, quite dead.

Boulille collapsed beside him.

12

By the next evening, following a cursory examination, Boulille was placed in an unused drawer. The maggots gave him the semblance of death, for it suited their purposes. And now, he could begin his new life amongst the sepulchers and mortuaries and graveyard damps.

Boulille did not lose consciousness.

He lay there, praying for the darkness, for release. But it was far too late for that. Infested by the grave worms, globby masses of eggs laid in the hot, charnel earth of his flesh, he was forever theirs now. When they hatched, the new generation got right down to work, setting things right.

The next night, Boulille sat up and walked. He left the morgue in search of a fresh grave…but not too fresh, of course, for the maggots liked their meat well-grayed and well-softened.

And this, then, was the final vengeance of Francois Jarny.

1867: THE SKULL EATER CAMPAIGN

"As long as I live, I will fight you for
the last hunting grounds of my people."
—Red Cloud, 1866

1

Major Lyons assembled the raiding party after what was found half-buried in the drifting snow at Crazy Woman Creek.

He assembled the party on direct orders of Colonel Carrington of the 18th Infantry and commander of Fort Phil Kearney in the northern Wyoming Territory. Carrington told him to put together a force of hunters and killers that could bring the perpetrators of that particular atrocity to ground. Carrington was thinking it was the work of Red Cloud's Oglala Sioux warriors riding the vengeance trail.

But Lyons knew better.

For he had seen the bodies at Crazy Woman Creek, the remains of a reconnaissance patrol of the 7th Cavalry. He had commanded the relief column that had gone out in search of them when they were three days overdue. In a clearing, the horse soldiers were found jutting from that ocean of bitter white, blanketed by a fresh down of January snow. They were riddled with arrows, crusted with blood, their eyes wide and mouths frozen open in silent screams. Whatever had taken them, it had been damn quick.

But it hadn't been the Sioux.

At least, not any ordinary group in Lyon's way of thinking. The Sioux would kill quicker than poison, slit throats as a parting gesture, strip away weapons and provisions and scalps.

But they did not devour the bodies.

2

The ragged peaks of the Bighorns were monuments and cairns rising up in the black, blowing night. They sucked frigid winds and heavy snows deep into their ancient lungs and exhaled them, inundating the raiding party in a whipping, biting blizzard.

But the raiders struggled on. Forty men plastered in snow and stiff from the wind. The storm hit them hard, trying to shake them off the high ridges and narrow cuts, like ants from summer leaves.

"Crazy Snake" Boone McComb, Chief of Scouts, rode ahead of the regular Army columns, flanked by his scouts. He wore fringed buckskins, a heavy beaver coat, and a bearskin cap pulled down low over his protruding brow. His hair and beard were long and white, his eyes just as dark as smoldering buckshot. "Yes sir," he was saying, "haven't seen a storm like this brew since the Bitterroots, Montana Territory, back in '52. Clear, calm day as I recall. Then up comes Mister Blizzard, howling and screaming and calling m' mother everything but a Christian woman. Weren't long and there came a war party of Blackfoot. Bloods they was, whooping and hollering and thinking they was going to be roasting some fool white ass over a fire."

"What happened?" Corporal Wood said from behind him.

"Eh? Ye with me then?" McComb said to him. "I see that ye are. Well, I won't get into specifics fer the here and now, but let's just say m' battle axe got stained red that day and m' musket was so hot I branded half-dozen of them Injuns with it when I split their skulls with the stock! God bless them heathen savages, God bless 'em! But they found out as many has that Boone McComb has got a tough bark to him, he don't split easy!"

Captain Cheevers looked to Major Lyons, shook his head. But Lyons did not acknowledge him. Maybe at times he grew tired of Boone McComb, too, but there was one inescapable fact: as a scout and guide he was incomparable.

Cheevers had been something of a boy wonder during the War Between the States, leading bloody cavalry charges straight into the heart of Johnny Reb bands and scattering them to the four winds…those that weren't slashed, hacked, or shot outright that was. At the close of hostilities between the North and South, he had been under General Carleton with Kit Carson, riding hell-for-leather against the Navajo, Kiowa, and Comanche of the Southern Plains.

He was a real soldier, he told Lyons again and again, not some used-up, moth-eaten, hide-smelling old beaver trapper like McComb.

As far as Cheevers was concerned, Boone McComb was filled with more ripe shit than a Kansas City privy.

So, true to form, McComb went on nonstop, and the storm took his voice, pulled it up into the high polar altitudes, froze it solid, shattered it, and let the fragments drift down over the troopers as they trudged forward. Bits of his voice bounced up and down the column, echoing up into the pine-covered slopes and down into the lowlands between. Things about wintering in a high cave in the Tobacco Roots with only a she-grizz for company, being at Zachary Taylor's side when he kicked Santa Anna squarely in the ass during the Mexican War, and how he'd sold his six Ute wives for black powder and jerky one lean year.

As usual, McComb's tales ran high and randy.

But no one seemed to be listening, not even Wood. The world was silent and white, vision down to a few rods at best. The troopers were wrapped in heavy trade blankets and overcoats, leaning into the howling wind. Their eyes squinted from beneath the brims of Jeff Davis hats. Around them, snow blew thick and impenetrable as pillow down. It powdered the men, dusted the horses, hung in sheets in the air. And the only sounds were sabers rattling and equipment shifting and the plodding of snow-clotted hooves. Yes, and maybe the mountains themselves, sighing and breathing with a cool white hiss.

McComb's scouts were cutting for sign far ahead in the blizzard. They were good, those boys. Born manhunters. And the very fact that they were hot on the trail of an Indian war party in that raging storm was testament to this.

Major Lyons had complete faith in McComb and his Indian scouts.

That they would find what they were hunting, there was no doubt. Lyons only wondered what in God's holy name that might be. Six hours before, he had marched his command out of Fort Kearney into the Bighorns right into the belly of a blizzard to find and destroy the perpetrators of the atrocity at Crazy Woman Creek. Five hours before that, Lieutenant Teague had preceded him with a reconnaissance party to lay the groundwork for that grand retribution.

And now, the wind in his face and the mountains wearing the blizzard like a blanket, Lyons only hoped that when he next saw Teague and his troopers they were not corpses.

It had been Colonel Carrington's idea to send Teague's party well ahead of the main force, and Lyons did not like it then, and he liked it even less now. For there was death in the snow-choked air, and with each mile, its grim psychic odor grew stronger and stronger.

3

Every man in the column, veteran and greenhorn, knew what they were facing. How the Lakota Sioux and their Cheyenne and Arapaho allies operated. They had fought long and hard for their rights against intruders. And though the tribes often fought amongst themselves and enemies like the Crow and Blackfoot, they could present a very cohesive front when it came to killing the white men who threatened their ancestral hunting grounds. They would ride out in small raiding parties, harass and confuse the whites, torment them with guerrilla warfare and—when the soldiers grew tired—lead them into traps, attacking with devastating main force units.

Nobody knew that better than Boone McComb.

"Yep," he called out. "God's country! That's what this is! The hot blood and horny gut of the world itself! Breathe in that air, ye pilgrims and mother-rapers! Like feeding at yer mama's tit! Makes ye glad to be alive! Makes yer business harder than a fighting cock! Oh, to be sure! To be sure, ye sonsofbitches! Ha! And the fighting tribes know it same as I do! They'll fight fer it, hell yes! Snow'll run red and bodies, both red and white, will be heaped like jackwood afore this is over! Goddamn Powder River'll be the biggest bone pile in history! Glory to that!"

"Can't somebody shut him up?" Cheevers said to Major Lyons, but Lyons simply ignored him.

The snow blew, and the wind whipped, and McComb shouted out bits of half-remembered psalms he'd learned at his mammy's knee long before he'd come to the Rocky Mountains and become a heathen savage like his tribal brethren. When he was feeling lonesome or nervous, he had a habit of talking loud and long, letting his voice echo through the high peaks and desolate pine forests. It was a habit that had stuck through these long and lean years.

And right then, squinting into the storm, he *was* nervous. For he knew how vulnerable the column was, how green was the blood of its inexperienced men, and how quickly death could come galloping out of the white wastes. Because death was out there, and he could feel it down in the marrow of his bones. He could smell it and hear it in the hush solitude, a scream on the far side of silence.

As they entered a deep-cut wooded hollow, a drifted white meadow opening before them, he was no longer rattling on. Something had gripped him and shut his voice off. He raised an arm to halt the column.

Listened.

Horses spluttered and men mumbled behind him. A perfect down of snow fell. A stick snapped in a thicket off to the left. He could hear...yes, horses coming. And not with a gentle canter, but with speed and urgency.

"Get ready," he called out to Lyons.

The column tensed.

The scouts came riding in, blue-coated skirmishers trying to keep up with them. There were three of them—Five Wolves, Him-That-Rides-Tall-Horse, and his brother, Snake-Hawk. They wore blanket coats and feathered campaign hats, dangling pigtails braided with beaver fur, their faces brown and lined as blasted desert rock. Five Wolves was Crow from the Musselshell, the other two Osage out of western Missouri. Neither tribe had any love of the Plains Sioux. And the Crow, like the Blackfoot, had never accepted Red Cloud as their leader.

They rode right to McComb.

Five Wolves spoke first in sign, saying that many Indians were coming. Then he spoke: "Plenty come soon, but they wear no paint and make no war. They come fast, they come out of fear."

Which McComb did not like to hear at all, because very little could spook the Nations up here. Crow, Blackfoot, Flathead, Sioux…they were fierce warriors and lived for the hot blood of combat.

Lyons said, "No sign of Lieutenant Teague's party?"

"No more sign of 'em than a squaw's heart, Major," McComb said. "White men up here, I'm thinking, are just as rare as that. Bet ye there ain't a beaver man nor hump hunter within fifty miles of this place."

"No white men now," Five Wolves said, more than a little cryptically.

He was bothered by the approaching Indians. Very bothered. But only McComb saw that, and seeing it, was more disturbed than ever. He turned to tell Lyons that something goddamned strange was afoot, but one of the skirmishers, a green and scared little boy named Oates, called out: "Indian war party! About a hundred of 'em riding down on us!"

"Wait!" McComb called out. "Just wait one danged minute, ye idiots—"

But nobody was waiting.

They had heard *Indian war party,* and that was all they needed to hear. Men sprung from saddles. Horses were picketed. Sergeants rallied their troopers, setting up defensive perimeters and kill zones amongst the trees. Men rushed through the snow, and you could almost smell the fear coming off them, thick and yellow. The scouts weren't waiting with whites coming to arms; they went for cover and drew their Hawkens rifles, and McComb rode on his black gelding, shouting and swearing and trying to make them all see reason. But at the height of the Indian Wars, there was no reason and no rhyme. All red men were savages, and no tribe was innocent.

"Take cover!" Lyons called out to him.

McComb did, knowing that what was about to happen was a mistake. After he picketed his horse, he rolled into the snow next to Lyons, trying to make the man see reason. "Five Wolves says it ain't no war party, Major! They ain't blacking their faces against us! Just some reddies on the run! We don't need to shoot fer chrissake, not yet! Let's see what this is about…."

148

But Lyons didn't want to hear such talk. "It's about the lives of forty men under my command, McComb. And I don't take such a responsibility lightly."

"But Major…if ye'd listen.…"

Cheevers was sighting in his carbine. "Why don't you shut up for once, McComb?" he said, his breath frosting in the still air. "If you don't have the belly for it, just keep your fool head down. This is a shooting war."

"A *shooting* war, ye say? Well, I don't care fer that, ye misguided, shit-eating crowbait!" McComb said. "I'm about to piss in m' boots outta plain fear!"

But it was pointless, and he knew it. Cheevers was a West Point squirt who'd cut his teeth chomping down the Rebs, medals and ribbons and gee-gawgs galore, and knew about as much about the fighting tribes of the High Plains as McComb himself knew about menstruation. And Lyons, as experienced as he was, could only see red scalphunters about to overtake his command. The troops were scared, and they would have shot daylight through their own mothers at that point.

Shit.

And then the Indians showed.

Not a hundred of them, but more along the lines of twenty. They came rushing down the hillside at full gallop, but like Five Wolves had pointed out, it wasn't fighting in their blood but *fear*. Fear of something behind them that they were riding hard to escape from. Right away, McComb saw it was no war party. These looked more like hunters than warriors. They wore no paint, no war-bonnets or war-shirts. They shrieked no battle cries or war songs, held no feathered lances or war clubs high. Hell, their ponies weren't even painted for the taking of lives.

And, dear Lord, they had women and children riding with them.

"Wait!" McComb called. "Fer the love of Christ and the saints hold yer fire! Hold yer fire! *Fer fuck's sake, don't be shooting!*"

The first shots rang out.

An old man with blowing white hair took a round in the throat that spattered gore on the riders behind him. His pony took a volley and went down squealing, trapping him beneath it. A woman was blown from her mount. A young rider's head evaporated in a crimson mist. Bodies were dropping, ponies collapsing into the red snow. Rifles were loosing rounds, and men were shouting, clouds of gun smoke fuming in the air with a sharp stink of burnt powder. And the Indians were screaming and dying, greasing the snow scarlet as they died in numbers.

They never had a chance.

McComb did not fire.

He turned away from the slaughter, appalled as always by what men of his own skin were capable of. The unnecessary carnage. The wanton cruelty. The tribes could be cruel, too, but never without reason, never out of fear shriveling their guts, never because their bellies were filled with yellow marrow or for the needless, sadistic thrill of it. There was no honor in that. It was how whites fought, with worms in their bellies.

All he could hear was the shooting and the dying, and all he could feel was the pain it caused him.

Gunfire. Rounds flying like wasps. Powder fumes. Sergeants calling out. Men firing until carbines clicked on empty chambers. Whooping cries of satisfaction from green troopers who had not fallen to buck fever, but rose to the killing, like sharks to blood and bait. And out there in the snow…good Christ…the dead and dying and the suffering.

And then it was over.

Lyon called ceasefire, and the soldiers stood around with smoking rifles and pistols blazing hot in their hands. A few of them fell into the snow when they saw what they had brought forth, vomiting their guts out.

"A fine piece of shooting that was, boys," McComb called out into the void. "Ye just cut down a harmless hunting party on the retreat! Medals to ye all!"

One of the troopers was sobbing. Others giggling. Most shocked into sullen silence. As the veils of smoke lifted, they could see that the ponies were all down, punched with bullets, dead or close to it. Their riders were trapped beneath them or sprawled loose-limbed on the killing grounds, faces blown clean, chests drilled by rifle balls, blood and spilled viscera steaming in the snow.

McComb saw a child, a girl of maybe ten, lying in the bloody snow. She'd taken a round right through the left eye. She lay there in her elkskin dress and buffalo robe, limbs twisted and blood cooling, hair blowing in the wind. A tendril of smoke came from her burning eye socket.

Cheevers stepped forward to say something and McComb knocked him out of the way. "God bless ye, one and all," he said. "Goddamn porkers."

The snow fell, and the wind moaned; the dying cried out, and the living wailed out their horror.

4

Boone McComb.

Frontier tradition had it that he was born with a pistol in his left hand and a hatchet in his right, that he knew how to skin a beaver before he could walk and that his mamma had forgone the tit and jug-fed him straight Tennessee corn whiskey. It was probably bullshit, but he himself encouraged the telling of wild tales and reveled in the fact that he had become something of a living legend. For although it was a well-known fact that he was a crack-shot with a Hawkens rifle and hell-on-earth with a Green River knife, many considered him to be at his finest when he began spewing a good story. He spun yarns like a spider spun webs, and it was anybody's guess what was real and what was out and out nonsense.

One thing was for sure, though, and that was the fact that there was none better than Boone McComb at scouting and pathfinding and stalking.

If you were going up into the high country, traversing through the sacred lands of the fighting tribes and you wanted to live to tell the tale and not have your scalp decorating the lodgepole of some randy young buck…then the man you wanted was Boone McComb.

Indian fighter, fur trader, beaver trapper, buffalo hunter, explorer and guide, he was more Indian than most Indians. He could track lint through a hailstorm, find game where none existed, smell water ten miles away, and speak no less than seven Plains Indian languages. And if all that wasn't enough, he was an honorary chief of both the Flathead and Shoshone Nations.

He had been there, and he had done it.

When the American Fur Company had its last real rendezvous in 1837 in Wyoming's Green River country, McComb had been on hand with Jim Bridger, Kit Carson, and hundreds of other trappers. During his tenure as a guide, he had led countless wagon trains down the Oregon and Santa Fe Trails and had hacked passages through the Sierra Nevada and Colorado

151

Rockies with his bare hands. He had taken part in Jean Nicollet's expedition to the Plains between the upper Mississippi and Missouri Rivers with John Freemont, and nobody, with the possible exception of Bill Cody, had been better with a buffalo rifle.

The tribes themselves either loved him or hated him, but there wasn't a single warrior in the Nations that did not respect him.

The Sioux called him *Sosho-Witke,* "Crazy Snake."

He'd picked up that particular tag when Lakota hunters had come upon him one afternoon some thirty-five years before after a group of marauding Blackfoot had killed the other two beaver skinners in his party. They found McComb sitting by a fire, his buckskins red with Blackfoot blood, roasting rattlesnake on a spit, and shouting out a long monologue on how he was the equal of the Blackfoot Confederacy and had first met them in peace, but would meet them next in war. The Lakota hunters threw Indian sign at him and ran off, not liking this insane eater of snakes.

But the name had stuck.

And maybe Captain Cheevers despised him, thought that "Crazy Snake" Boone McComb was not a real soldier. But then again, maybe Cheevers had never set his eyes upon a real soldier before, a God-honest bullet-eating, blood-pissing manhunter.

But Major Lyons knew lightning corked in a bottle when he saw it.

And that's why he trusted nobody but McComb to lead them up into the Bighorns and what waited there.

5

Sick with it all, McComb stood there with his scouts, who were not surprised by any of it. They knew the way of whites, and they knew them all too well. Five Wolves, who was McComb's blood brother, looked impassively on the carnage as only an Indian could. *"Siha Sappa,"* he said in pidgin Lakota.

McComb nodded. "Aye, Blackfoot they is."

The Blackfoot were considered by many to be the most fierce and bloodthirsty tribe on the upper Missouri. They had no equal in battle. They fanatically resisted white incursions into their lands with a hatred that sometimes even paled that of the Sioux. Fiercely independent and often barbaric, they were enemies of the Crow and the Sioux, just about all the tribes of the Rockies and Plains. McComb had no love for them and had barely escaped their attentions with his scalp intact more than once. But to see them gunned down like this...well, it was an atrocity, that's what.

"I feel that this will not go unpunished," he said to Five Wolves.

Five Wolves nodded, his face implacably grim beneath the brim of his campaign hat. "There is no honor today. We have made council with death."

"You speak with a straight tongue, m' brother. I fear a place has been made ready fer our bones."

"You have said it."

McComb was not a man who lived his life in fear of the supernatural, like many whites and many more Indians, yet the massacre before him—which could have easily been avoided by clear heads and calm hands—made him wither inside. Made him believe that the blood spilled on this day would be demanded anew as expiation in the final hours of each man there. He had seen too much in his many years not to believe that there was a big medicine that no man could know or name. As an honorary chief of the Flathead Nation and blood brother of Chief Many Horses of the Bitterroot Valley, McComb had once climbed a hill and fasted, calling upon the powers of earth, sky, wind, and water in the traditional summoning of the personal spirit guide. And after six days, his own had appeared in the form of a great and shaggy albino ghost buffalo.

And it would come for him, he knew, at the hour of his death, and its spikes would be red with his own blood for all that he had shed.

What say ye to this, White Spike? he thought at his spirit guide. *I say I tried to stop it, but what say ye? Am I just as guilty? Are m' hands just as red, old friend?*

Under Lyon's orders, the horse soldiers had formed a wide and trembling ring around the remains of the hunting band. Men were ready to start jerking triggers if the Indians made one wrong move, but McComb knew that wasn't going to happen. All the men were dead, several of the squaws and children. The old women gathered up the surviving children and hugged them beneath their buffalo robes. The young women were inconsolable as they wailed their eerie dirges to the sky, weeping over the dead braves, their husbands and sons that had been cut down by the white devils. Using flint knives, they were crudely chopping locks of lustrous, black hair from their scalps and tossing them into the wind. They cut their hands and faces, screaming and crying out in the Piegan Blackfoot tongue, cursing the unfairness of the Great Mystery and cursing the killers that had brought this pain into their lives.

The troopers watched this, and more than a few of them were pale at the sight of it. Their hands were shaking on their rifles as the Blackfoot women went mad with remorse and grief, slashing and gouging themselves, smearing their faces red and shrieking in high, screeching voices.

"Good God," Private Chandliss said. "What are they doing?"

"They're mourning their dead, son," McComb told him. "It's their way. Their souls are in agony, and they will force agony upon themselves and cry out so that the Great Spirit will hear them and guide their dead into the hereafter."

A young woman in a blanket coat whose face was a mask of wrath and pain, painted red and glistening, looked upon a trooper named Karnes and screamed at him in her native tongue. The trooper, not much more than a boy, took a step backward. "Hell is she saying?" he asked, feeling the hatred punch into him like knives. "Hell is she saying?"

Five Wolves looked at him. "She is calling for your death. She says we are life not worthy of life, praying we die in the dirt like dogs. Those are her words."

McComb knew that to these boys, who were used to white women weeping softly at caskets, this was all savage and horrifying. But it was the way of the tribes. The Crow, Flathead, in fact all the tribes of the Upper Plains mourned in this way. Grief to them was brutal, organic, and uncompromising. The women often retreated to desolate areas where they sang their mourning chants throughout the day and night, cutting themselves and screaming. It often went on for weeks and weeks.

He felt a great pity for what he was seeing, but he knew that had this been a true battle and the whites had been killed in numbers, the Blackfoot women would have dragged the white wounded into the trees and done unspeakable things to them. It was their way. Their fallen, still-living enemies were subjected to cruel, sadistic tortures that were unthinkable. The women would spit in their faces, empty their bladders and bowels upon them. Gnaw their fingers off. Emasculate them with their teeth. Cut out their tongues and gouge out their eyes with sharpened sticks, skin them like animals, peel the meat from their faces. And if the bellies of their fallen enemies had been laid open, they would yank out the entrails and chew on them, roast them over fires and slow-smoke the carcass they belonged to.

Those rare few that escaped the clutches of Blackfoot women told stories that turned the stomachs of even the hardest-bitten mountain man.

McComb knew that very well, for he'd once escaped from the Blackfoot himself...and still wore the scars.

The woman who had screamed at young Private Karnes was now grinning at him with blood-stained teeth and muttering something at him in a guttural, growling voice that sounded more animal than human. He looked like he was ready to vomit or pass clean out. Perhaps both. Her eyes fixed on his, holding his gaze hypnotically, she brought up her flint knife, screamed with volume, and severed her left pinkie finger at the second joint and threw the bloody digit at him.

Karnes wavered, then went down cold in the snow.

"Savages," Cheevers said. "Nothing but mindless savages...."

The woman who'd sliced her finger was sucking on the stub, two perfectly bright red rivers of blood running from the corners of her lips and to her chin. She was smiling.

"Look away, ye damn fool," McComb told Cheevers. "This is a private affair. Not fer white eyes. Look away or they'll do worse."

As they carried on with their rites of mourning, the other women were crossing themselves.

"Christians for God's sake?" Cheevers said. "Do my eyes deceive me?"

"Many of the tribes have been Christianized," Lyons told him.

And this came as a shock to him. These were red savages...what could they know of a white man's god? What could they know of the mercy and goodness of the Lord Jesus Christ? These pagan beasts in their black buffalo robes and wolfskins, necklaces of bear claws and animal bones?

McComb could read his thoughts just fine, for some books were well-thumbed by simplicity. "Aye, heathen Christians, sir, that's what these are. They get their bleeding fingers on ye, ye fine tit-fed stripling, and they'd skin yer foul hide with a bone knife and recite the Gospel of St. Luke whilst they did so."

"That's sacrilege, sir," Cheevers said.

"Nope. Only sacrilege here, m' cocksure friend, is a young fool what won't admit to his own grievous shortcomings."

Cheevers was glaring at him now, his hand on the hilt of his campaign sword. "I'll remind you to watch your tongue, McComb."

"And I'll remind ye to kiss m' dirty backside, ye pork-eater."

Lyons interceded at that point. "That'll be enough. From both of you." When Cheevers had stomped off, cooling his ire and letting the wind blow the steam from his cheeks, Lyons got in close to McComb. "I know you don't like him, Boone. Precious few of us do…but please don't be baiting him. We have enough problems. Fool or not, he's an officer, and you can't belittle him in front of his own men."

McComb laughed full and hearty. "Belittle him, Major? Why he's a positive Christian saint. I worship the very ground he walks on. Goddamn tenderfoot."

A few of the troops overheard and chuckled under their breath.

"Boone…"

"Easy, Major. Don't sprain yer hump," McComb said. "I don't like him, but I ain't gonna wade into his liver with m' knife and such."

Maybe it would have gone beyond that, but the Blackfoot women started screaming out with hell fury. The two Osage scouts, Him-That-Rides-Tall-Horse and Snake-Hawk, had dragged several corpses off into the brush, and they were whooping and hollering. Several of the old vets amongst the horse soldiers knew what it was about and were chuckling over it. They understood the way of the red man all too well and had, on occasion, done what the Osage were now doing.

"Dear God," Cheevers said.

"Stop this!" Lyons called out. "Damn it, stop that!"

The Osage each had a Blackfoot male corpse face-down in the snow and were kneeling on their backs. They yanked the heads up by the hair and, using their skinning knives, slit a line around the skulls until the scalps were loosened. Then taking hold of the dripping flaps, began to yank and pull until the scalps came free with hair locks intact.

They held their bloody prizes up for all to see, shaking them in the wind, uttering shrill war cries.

"McComb! Stop them!" Lyons said as the Osage went after more corpses. "This is unacceptable!"

But McComb laughed, having practiced the art on many occasions himself. "It's out of m' hands, Major. Blood and killing ye wanted, and blood and killing ye got. And these boys are half-starved fer hair. It's their way." He looked over at the Blackfoot dead. "All gone to Jesus now…all of 'em…."

The Blackfoot women screamed and raged, and the Osage shouted their joy into the white underbelly of the world as they sawed more scalps free.

6

The Indian Wars.

They began, technically, in 1862. It was in that dark year that the Santee Sioux of Minnesota—embittered by starvation, crop failures, broken treaties, and desperation forced upon them by the U.S. government—ran loose from their barren reservation and set in motion a series of bloody encounters that left some 500 whites dead. Men were mutilated, women raped and disemboweled, children nailed alive to houses and trees. The settlements of Western Minnesota and Eastern Dakota flew into a state of panic. Under their chief, Little Crow, the Santee were finally crushed by a white militia at Wood Lake. The surviving Sioux fled to the reservation and 2,000 of them were rounded-up. Thirty-eight were hanged, the rest imprisoned. Little Crow himself was captured and later killed.

His skull, tanned scalp, and wrist-bones were put on public display at a museum.

The Indian Wars were in full swing.

By 1864, the Sioux had been joined by the Arapaho and the Cheyenne, making raids into Nebraska. Under Colonel John Chivington, a Methodist minister, Cheyenne villages—most of them peaceful—were razed, their livestock slaughtered, their inhabitants killed or sent to reservations. Soon, the Colorado Cheyenne and Arapaho were on the warpath. Whites were killed wherever they could be found. A ranch outside Denver run by a family named Hungate was raided by the Indians. The family was murdered, their bodies viciously mutilated. The corpses were taken to Denver and put on display, fanning the flames of Indian-hatred.

By this point, the whites were wild with rage.

They wanted payback, and they got it at Sand Creek, Colorado. Under the sadistic command of Colonel Chivington again, some 700 volunteers from the 3rd Colorado attacked Black Kettle's Cheyenne and Arapaho encampment. Over a hundred men, women, and children were massacred. Children were used for target practice, beaten to death as they begged for life on their hands and knees. Women were trampled to death, men dragged to ribbons behind horses. Wild with blood-thirst, the soldiers viciously mutilated the corpses, scalping and skinning the young and old. The genitals of men, women, and children were taken as souvenirs, male scrotums to be used as tobacco pouches. Fingers were sliced off and collected in rawhide bags. Indians of all ages were disemboweled, some while they were still alive, their hearts and livers wrenched free. The private parts of women were slit off and stretched over saddlebows and knitted together into chains which were worn around the brims of hats while the soldiers rode in rank. Saddles were draped with the still glistening scalps of children, and it became a contest to see who could get the most. And several particularly creative ghouls, having threaded female breasts and genitals onto sharpened sticks, rode through the carnage shouting in glory as they raised their bloody human trophies high for all to see.

But Chivington's orders were very clear and followed to the letter: *"Kill and scalp all,"* he said, *"big and little; nits make lice."* The proud militiamen, their hands red with innocent blood, rode into Denver, their saddles strung with scalps, decapitated heads, and body parts sliced from women and children.

Kit Carson, who was no lover of Indians—and his campaigns against the Navajo, Kiowa, Comanche, and Cheyenne attest to this—said of the massacre: "No one but a coward or a dog would have had a part in it."

The shock waves from the Sand Creek atrocity rolled throughout the Plains. Some 1,600 Northern Arapaho, Cheyenne, and Sioux warriors rode roughshod through Colorado, burning ranches, attacking forts, capturing wagon trains, and slaughtering many more than had been killed at Sand Creek.

While the whites planned out their punishments which would ultimately bring the tribes to their knees, the large Sioux tribes of Montana, Wyoming, and the Dakotas—thus far, unmolested—watched the white incursions. They had already decided to defend their sacred hunting grounds by any means necessary. And their leader, Red Cloud, was a born fighter.

When Forts C.F. Smith, Kearney, and Reno were built along the Bozeman trail into Montana Territory, Red Cloud's War began.

Banding together the various Sioux tribes—Oglala, Brule, Miniconjou, and Hunkpapa—along with their Cheyenne and Arapaho allies, Red Cloud amassed his forces and began randomly attacking the forts on the Bozeman. War parties slipped along the walls, imitating the cries of wolves, picking off sentries one by one with well-placed arrows. When they could not get at the soldiers themselves, they attacked wagon trains and wood-cutters and cattle herders, stealing horses and mules, and setting block houses afire. Many dressed in captured Army uniforms, raiding and burning and killing, disappearing completely when large cavalry units closed in.

They were ghosts, and everyone at the forts was scared.

Red Cloud, with a force numbering 2,000, was intent on closing the Bozeman Trail and Forts Kearney, C.F. Smith, and Reno at all costs to protect his people and the herds of buffalo that were their lifeblood.

A young infantry captain named Fetterman, who had recently joined the Kearney staff, boasted that the untrained Indians were no match for the might of seasoned U.S. forces. "Give me a single company of regulars, and I can whip a thousand Indians," he proclaimed boldly. "With eighty men, I could ride through the Sioux Nation."

Fetterman got his chance in December of 1866 when word was sent to Colonel Carrington at Fort Phil Kearney that a woodcutting detail was being attacked by Indians. Fetterman was given command of a relief expedition of exactly *eighty* men. An ex-Civil War officer and a real fire-eater by all accounts, Fetterman rose to the occasion bravely, never knowing he was riding into a carefully-engineered trap laid by Red Cloud and his crafty, blue-eyed war chief, Crazy Horse.

When Fetterman's troops reached the woodcutters, there were no Indians about, and Fetterman was angry that he had been denied the chance to slay the savages. Then, led by Crazy Horse, the warriors appeared like ghosts. Whooping and hollering, they caused mass confusion and panic as they darted around on horseback, shooting and letting arrows fly, waving red blankets around that frightened the soldiers' horses. This was a decoy party, and Fetterman rose to the bait.

He gave chase and in doing so crossed Lodge Trail Ridge, which put him out of visual contact with the fort. At which point, Crazy Horse's warriors ran no more. They wheeled around and made to fight. And this was when Fetterman saw the jaws of the trap close in on his command as a thousand Sioux, Arapaho, and Cheyenne braves rushed in from all sides, appearing literally out of nowhere. They swept in with arrows and small arms fire, war clubs and lances, and within a matter of minutes, Fetterman's relief expedition was wiped out to the last man.

Reinforcements arrived, but the Indians were gone, and the snow was heaped with the corpses of soldiers. They had been mutilated most viciously. Noses were sliced free, hands cut off, entrails yanked from body cavities. Skulls were shattered, brains placed on rocks along with eyes that had been gouged free. Private parts were severed and shoved into mouths, and every available inch of the bodies themselves were pierced with arrowheads and spear-shafts. All had been scalped, and several had their heads removed and put in buffalo-skin bags—a traditional sign of disgrace and dishonor that the Sioux reserved for cowards and dogs.

After the Fetterman Massacre, Red Cloud's fame with the fighting tribes was assured. Many more joined him, and his big medicine was legendary. Traffic on the Bozeman Trail was effectively halted, and the myth of white military superiority was laid to rest.

The snow ran red, and the Seven Council Fires of the Sioux burned bright as the bloodiest years of the Indian Wars on the Upper Plains came to pass.

And it was under this yoke of simmering violence that Major Lyon's raiding party rode.

7

After the massacre of the Blackfoot, nobody said much.

Not even McComb.

The greenhorns amongst the troopers were not so green anymore; what had been lily-white and pristine had been dirtied now with a stain that would never wash clean. So be it. Maybe it was for the best. For the sooner they learned all about death in Powder River country, McComb knew, how it felt in your heart and tasted in your mouth and how its stink clung to you, the sooner they would realize what they were up against. And now that the troopers had been dipped in red, they had a pretty good inkling of that. Not that McComb really believed it would save their greenwood asses, because the death that was waiting for them up here in the mountains was literally beyond comprehension.

It was something inexplicable and well beyond his own meager experience of these hills and draws and the shadows that haunted them. And that reached back more than forty years and damn closer to fifty.

Sometimes when he squeezed his eyes shut, he heard not only the wind in the trees and the whisper of snow, but the rumble of the hooves of the ghost buffalo that would come for him in his final hour.

And mayhap I'm just too goddamned old fer this stripe, he thought more than once. *Mayhap I should find m'self a rocking chair and a porch and ruminate m' days away with the rest of the old fools.*

He was riding well out front of the column now with his scouts, just beside himself by what had happened to the Blackfoot. He was, of course, no friend of that particular tribe, but he knew who and what they were, what their customs and traditions were and what these things demanded of them.

Major Lyons, apparently, did not.

Overcome, perhaps, by guilt he had tried to help the Blackfoot women. Offering them horses and food and help with their dead and wounded, but such a thing was like offering Satan a crucifix. The women wanted no help from the white devils who had committed such a crime. The more Lyons tried, the louder they screamed and wailed. Nothing but the gruesome, slow deaths of the soldiers themselves would be acceptable to them. Finally frustrated by it all, Lyons had ordered his men to ride, leaving the women in the hollow.

"They'll die out there," he said to McComb, "and there's nothing I can do about it."

McComb wanted to tell him that there *had* been, but it was too late now. He didn't, of course, see no reason to rub salt into the wound. Sometimes the only way children and fools learned that a stove was hot was by branding their hands upon it. Maybe Lyons would take something away from this, but probably not.

"They won't die, Major, not unless they want to," McComb told him, knowing just how crafty and wily were the Blackfoot. They would live, and while they lived, they would devote every ounce of energy they had to asking the Great Spirit to punish the white transgressors who had brought death into their clan.

And maybe, just maybe, the Great Spirit would grant this.

If not, the Blackfoot weren't above taking matters into their own hands.

McComb's worst brush with the tribe had been in 1848 when he'd been scouting Two Medicine River in Montana Territory for beaver at high summer. A huge, male silvertip grizz had come upon him quite quickly, before he even had time to pull his Hawkens. The bear savaged him with its lethal claws, laying open his back and ribs, upper arms and shoulders. It seized his head in its mouth and tossed him. Fate intervened here before the beast made a meal of him. He tumbled down an embankment, rolling through a hillside of briars, and into the river, where the current washed him a mile downstream. Bleeding and battered, with only a knife and a medicine bag on his belt, McComb stitched up his ragged lacerations best he could with catgut and buckskin thread and began a tortuous six-day crawl through the brush. Drinking from puddles and eating roots and berries, his wounds crawling with maggots, he finally made Cut Bank Creek.

And it was here that a Blackfoot party had found him.

There was no mercy to be had. For reasons unknown, they took him to their encampment and beat him senseless. Then he was turned over to the women, who tied him to a post and dug in his wounds with sticks and whipped him with willow branches until he passed out. That night, they untied him and left him lying in the dirt, perhaps thinking him too weak to escape. But wrong they were. Before the festivities began anew in the morning, McComb crawled out of camp, made the creek again and followed it for days until he came upon a group of friendly Crow sneaking through Blackfoot country.

He still bore the scars of the evil grizz *and* the tender attentions of the Blackfoot. He had no true mercy for either, but he believed there was necessary killing and that which was unnecessary.

Five Wolves at his side upon his paint, McComb steered them deeper into the white desolation, his Osage scouts cutting for sign just ahead. Never had he known these mountains even at dead winter to be so bereft of life. Such silence was not only unnatural, but spooky. Nothing stirred. Nothing even breathed. And his scouts were only too aware of it. An inexperienced white would not have noticed it, but McComb did, and it lay on him like a killing frost.

They were expecting something, just as he was.

And like him, they did not know what shape it would take, only that it would be something born of horror.

As they rode, picking their way carefully up wooded hills and down into snow-choked hollows, he could feel the dread growing in him, thick as canebrake. There was fear, he knew, you could understand, such as that of marauding Indians or hungry, wild animals, and then there was the kind you could not understand. That which began as a pale seedlet in your soul, nourished by anxiety and the unknown, finally bursting free of the stony, moist soil and filling your mind with a garden of black, reaching growths that strangled off things like reason and sanity.

And this is what McComb was facing.

Knowing that every mile brought them closer to the black, beating heart of the very thing that had sent the Blackfoot running into the sights of the horse soldiers.

In the eerie silence, the wind moaned through the empty thickets and mounded bluffs, dead trees breaking the drift like headstones and spires. Shadows that were alive with a crawling vitality spilled down from the organ pipes of the high elevations. Something eldritch and pestilent existed up here, and McComb and his scouts could feel it growing thick as cobweb, closing in around them like a dark fist anxious to squeeze the breath from their throats.

McComb and Five Wolves came down a slope into a valley floor. Everything was cloaked in a thick mantle of snow. Rocks, trees, all sculpted white. Flakes of snow drifted in the air, a lonesome, bitter wind picking up drift and creating spinning whirlwinds. The Osage were just ahead now. The hooves of McComb's gelding broke through the crust of snow carefully, its breath rolling out in white clouds.

As they mounted a pine-clad hill, the snow was disturbed by the passage of horses. Many of them. The scouts checked it out and told him they were the horses of Indians, that they were unshod. The hoof prints of soldier's horses were always shod.

"War party come this way," Five Wolves said.

"Aye. And I'm getting the feeling that they rode right through Teague and his boys," McComb said. "Be a lucky scratch if we find even their scalped corpses."

The wind had drifted over most of the tracks. They would appear and disappear at irregular intervals. His heart clenching in his chest, McComb steered his scouts ahead, up higher into the forbidding hills. The rises were heavily forested, the trees slouching under blankets of snow. Sinister shadows spread out over the drift like blood from slit arteries, flowing and pooling.

The Osage rode up over a grade and then, seconds later, they rode back to its crest and motioned him forward.

"Now we see," Five Wolves told McComb in sign.

Yes sir, he thought, *we surely do.*

Moving carefully, he brought his gelding up the rise, brushed snow from his face with one fur mitten. He gripped the reins with it, leaving his right hand un-mittened and free to get at the rifles in their scabbards, the Colt pistols under his robe, the tomahawk and knife on his belt. The world was a soundless void around him, cold and blown by snow, almost alien with its complete lack of life. No birds cried out, no wildlife stirred in the brush, nothing but the soft moan of the wind, the rustling of the pines and the creaking of branches.

Cresting the hill, coming through a gust of churning snow and blinking it away, he saw what his scouts saw, and a raw, fearful ugliness was born in his stomach.

"Shit," he said under his breath, tightening rein and stopping his horse.

The trail of the war party was visible where it vanished into a thicket whose branches were woven tightly to either side and overhead like a tunnel of brambles. And set out before it…rough-cut maple limbs that were driven into the snow and down into the earth beneath, and on each was speared a human head. McComb knew whose heads they were.

Teague. Colter. Bolek. Perry. Hyderman. The heads of the white soldiers of Teague's reconnaissance party.

Their bodies were nowhere in sight, and neither were the bodies of their Pawnee scouts.

McComb climbed off his horse, and Five Wolves followed him.

The heads were impaled up high, so they stared right into his eyes. Their faces were gray and seamed, sparkling with frost and spattered with drops of blood that had gone black. Mouths had been stitched shut with black gut, and eyes were staring, bulging sightlessly and filmed over. Icicles of blood hung from the stumps.

All of them had been scalped.

Up on their horses, the Osage were singing low, mournful songs.

"These here to scare us off," Five Wolves said.

"And it's working," McComb told him. "A warning."

"You have said it."

Because that's what it was, a warning. The war party had gotten the jump on Teague's men and decapitated them, speared the heads to frighten off the main force that they knew was coming. McComb had seen such things before. He studied the trees around them, the white-clad mountain peaks. A shrieking wind rose up, scattering drift and shrilling through the pines. Bony branches rattled and scraped. What he had been feeling for so long now had gone positively black in his belly, boiling away like a poison.

"We have to get rid of these afore the bluecoats see them," he said. "Only Lyons needs to know."

With Five Wolves' help, he yanked the stakes out of the ground and tossed them down into a hollow deep with snow. When they returned, the Osage were cocking their heads and listening to something on the wind. McComb heard it only for a moment…an unearthly chanting of many voices that faded quickly away.

Swallowing, he thought of the ghost buffalo.

8

Two years before, after Five Wolves had returned from a buffalo hunt to discover that his wife and three sons had been butchered by the Sioux in his absence, he felt his blood go to black ice and his soul wither like wildflowers beneath autumn's first frost. He walked as a man, yet he was not a man, only a ravaged husk. There was no fire in his heart and no music in his soul, only a cloven and gutted emptiness inside him that not even time, the great healer, could hope to fill with warmth and understanding.

The great hoop, the circle of life, had been forever ruptured, and he was severed from it much as an infant is severed from its mother at birth by the cutting of the cord.

He attended the funeral and though embittered with grief and remorse, he showed no pain, shed no tears, just moved silently, as was the way of his fathers, the *Absarokee,* the Crow Indians. As was traditional, he chose the location of his family's funeral scaffolds in a shaded stand of cottonwoods on Hanging Woman Creek. And as was also custom, the women of the tribe sewed up the bodies of the fallen in buffalo shrouds with their medicine bundles and carried them up to rest on the catafalques, draping beaded pelts and pendants over them.

And that night, and for many nights, Five Wolves mourned at the scaffolds.

They were formed of four lodge poles driven into the earth and anchored in places by cairns of stones. Atop, were cradles of boughs that supported the death-bundles. Bleached buffalo skulls were set on poles before them as totems.

He sang songs to them by day and night as they began their journey to the other world and the embrace of the Great Spirit. One rainy night as he shivered in his buffalo robe, a pack of wolves approached, scenting the meat of the dead. Five Wolves frightened them off, but one remained that stared at him from the fringe of the creek with huge, glistening eyes. Eyes that looked very much like the eyes of Five Wolves' long dead father, Fox That Speaks. Five Wolves walked towards this lone wolf, and it did not scamper or run but moved almost casually up to a hilltop where it howled but once and then disappeared. Five Wolves was frightened, for the wolf was his spirit guide, but as frightened as he was, he knew that the Great Spirit was speaking to him in a voice of mystery.

The next day, heeding the supernatural, which to him and all Crows was but another branch of the natural, he built a sweat lodge of willow reeds and sequestered himself within. Only his medicine pipe and medicine bundle went with him. For three days and three nights, he fasted naked, sweating and dreaming, and finally well past midnight on the third day, his eyes snapped open and there came clarity.

He heard the howling of his spirit guide.

An eerie wind that was chilled like the grave itself blew into the lodge, whistling through the reeds and making him shake and stirring the coals in his fire pit. Steam rose from them, a steam that boiled and coalesced into fantastic forms and phantasmal shapes that paraded around, within and without him, opening his eyes, filling him with the wine of the Great Mystery and making him drunk upon it so that he could finally see through the ether of the now into the ether of the what-will-be.

A vision.

He saw a place of gray shadows and black, shattered ice and a cold frost-smoke that blew over hundreds and thousands of death scaffolds that had grown up from the dead soil in a profuse and leaning forest. The ground was pitted, scarred, bleeding a foul mist that formed itself into the shapes of leering, crawling devils and night-haunts. The world was a graveyard, and this was the inheritance of the Crow, a world leeched of life, like a carcass leeched of blood. No man nor beast prowled the craggy landscape, nothing left its print in the dank crust of soil. There was only the death-fog and the pale, cadaverous light of the skull-faced death-moon above. Mold grew up the scaffolds in graying wreaths. Shadows crept, and shades of the long-dead bled up from the ground in noisome tangles, drifting over the bones of the Crow.

A graveyard had overtaken the world of light and life.

And then weaving amongst the clustered, crowded deadwood of the catafalques and scaffolded tombs of rotting cerements and thrusting, yellow bones, there came a death army on horseback. Ghosts. The evil dead. They were skeleton warriors dressed out in threadbare hides and moldering pelts, carrying shields and bows and battle lances. They wore the scalp headpieces of wolves and buffalo, and the only thing alive about them were their red-litten eyes, which were pathways into the netherworld white men called hell. There were dozens and dozens of the death-riders, and they seemed to be rising on horseback from a barrow trench in the earth, which was like a great wound that smoked and seethed with a pale, blue phosphorescence.

Five Wolves shook and sweated, wanting to scream as he smelled the stench of grave-spices and sweet putrescence that blew from them in a wind of cremated ashes. He saw the thin, charnel moonlight shine through numerous holes in their bodies, heard the chattering of their teeth and the rattling of their bones, the ghoulish scratching and gnawing of the vermin that lived within them. But worse, he heard them calling out in windy, moaning voices that echoed from subterranean depths of utter night.

He heard them call his name.

This had all happened in September, what the Sioux called the Moon of the Black Calves. The time of year when the buffalo calves lost their immature woolly coats and traded them for the dark brown pelts of adults.

For many days, Five Wolves was haunted by his vision. He spoke of it to tribal elders and shaman, and they all told him that, in time, the truth of it would be revealed to him. For many months afterwards, he woke in his lodge sweating and trembling from dreams in which dead things that looked like his wife and sons reached out for him from split-hide shrouds that writhed with grave worms. He was, essentially, a haunted man.

Then a year later, from his vantage point on a high, rocky bluff, he watched the long knives building their fort on Piney Creek. The fort that would soon be known as Fort Phil Kearney and right there on sacred Sioux lands... lands that had long belonged to the Crow before the Sioux forced them out. Five Wolves watched the bluecoats all day and well into the next, as he suspected many Indians did from their discreet hides. The soldiers were quite industrious as they mowed grass down and erected blockhouses, surrounding their encampment with a high wall of logs. Sioux warriors harassed them every step of the way, killing and scalping, but the whites never stopped until the fort was complete a month later.

It was as he watched the long knives that Five Wolves finally understood his vision or, at least, part of it. The Sioux had killed his family during the Moon of the Black Calves, September. And it was during this moon cycle that he was also given his vision. And one year later, again during the same cycle, he watched the soldiers build their fort, with which they would make war upon the Sioux Nation. Like many Crow, Five Wolves was more or less friendly with the whites. And like all Crow, he hated the Sioux that had murdered and plundered his tribe and stole their ancestral lands. Though he did not understand the whites, he knew they hated the Sioux as he did, and he decided then and there that he would help them with their extermination of his tribe's most fearsome enemy. For things had come full circle, and the hoop was no longer severed, but made one.

He did not completely understand his vision of the world become a graveyard—though he thought it was what the Sioux would do to the Crow Nation, turn *their* world to a graveyard—but he knew that the murder of his family at the hands of the Sioux was allowed by the Great Spirit so that he would have his vision at Hanging Woman Creek and join the bluecoats in destroying his mortal blood-enemies.

This was how the circle of life was reestablished and how Five Wolves became part of the order of the living and not the march of the dead. He had purpose and vision and the blessing of the Great Spirit. His duty now was a holy one. He would spill Sioux blood for the blood of his family and, more importantly, for the blood of his slain and misused people.

It was prophecy.

9

As they rode higher into the mountains, cutting for sign through drifted valleys and along ridgelines blown clean of snow, McComb began to wonder if he was fixing to die. For all he could seem to think of was what had passed, what had been and would never be again. He saw faces and places that he would never see again. Maybe he was too old, and maybe his spirit guide, that ornery White Spike of the ghost-world, was sniffing his trail and closing in for the kill.

Back in the old days, all a man needed was what he carried in with him, what he stowed on his horses and mules. His trap sacks and parfleche, a good buffalo robe and a fine set of buckskins, powder horn and bullet pouch, pistols and rifle, a fine set of knives and throwing hatchets. A good wind and a fertile river valley. A bit of luck and a fine Indian woman to warm his robe at night and help him with his hides. A man could live then. Free and easy, nothing but open sky and green earth and a heap of beaver plews to pay his way come rendezvous time.

But then the soldiers had come. And with the soldiers, the goddamned settlers from back east. More and more of them, fouling the air and crowding the land and stripping away the life of the mountain men and tribes alike. McComb didn't even like to think what ten years would bring to this country or twenty.

Jesus.

It was all dying. The beaver trade had collapsed, the buffalo were being hunted to extinction by hide hunters, and the old glory days of laying your traps and working your lines were all but finished.

There was deep remorse in McComb over this. And guilt. For he knew that it was men like him that had the paved the trail for the others to follow and, in doing so, had signed the death warrant of their own lifestyle and that of the tribes themselves, whether friend or foe.

And knowing this to be true, he thought: *M' fate is clear, is it not, old White Spike? I will pay fer m' transgressions. I have planted m' crops and I will reap said harvest.*

He was riding with Lyons again, out front of the column, his scouts far ahead. Lyons had not seemed surprised when McComb told him of the fate of Lieutenant Teague's party. He had said very little of it, accepting things the way a man had to in this country. For suffering and death were simply a part of life.

McComb was not rattling on, chewing leather as was his way.

Like the snow-blown world around him, he was silent and waiting. Making ready for what was out there, what was closing in on them even now. His senses were hypersensitive, acutely alert. He was hearing the horses and rustle of equipment, the rattle of sabers and the swish of overcoats, but he was also hearing how the wind spoke, what it was saying to him. How it swept earthward from high elevations and whispered down trailheads and through lonesome hollows. His eyesight was keen, preternaturally sharp, dissecting shadow and bole and drift for the tell-tale signs of an ambush, his nose ever-casting for the scent of things that feasted on human flesh, the eaters of men.

For they were here…somewhere, and soon now, his instinct told him, they would show their hand.

Only good thing, way he was figuring it, was that the wind was blowing northwest straight on to southeast, which put himself and the troopers downwind from what was out there, and that would make it nigh on impossible for those bugaboos to scent them proper.

Listen.

Yes, riders.

Horses on the march, making a good clip. It was clear as a bell to him, and maybe you had to live in those mountains for years on end to hear it, but it was there, all right. He could hear it, and he could feel the hooves coming, the distant, minute vibrations they made that traveled through the hooves of his own mount, up its legs, and into his own body.

"Hear that?" he said, turning to Major Lyons directly behind him. "The scouts is coming in."

Lyons held up his arm, halting the column.

Captain Cheevers said, "I don't hear a damn thing."

If the situation had not been so dire, McComb would have laughed. For Captain Cheevers was a comical sort. Certainly, he was a good soldier and a brave one, but he was also a fool. The sort of fool only the Army could breed in numbers. Cock-sure, arrogant, all flash and show, but deaf, dumb, and most certainly blind.

He was something, all right. Dressed in tanned knee boots and fringed gauntlets, buffalo coat thrown wide to show off his fancy pearl-handled Colts, broad-brimmed, black Stetson set on his head at a jaunty angle, and a red silk neckerchief at his throat...he was like something from a wild west show back east. His mustache and beard were chiseled sharp enough to slit a throat, and his face was that of a Roman bust. All pomp, circumstance, and conceit, just strutting like a stud rooster, tail feathers bright and pretty and fanned high.

McComb figured it was gonna be a hell of a job keeping this boy's topknot from decorating a Sioux scalp-pole.

"Well, I'll be damned," he said. "Now ye might have been the terror of the Tennessee graybellies and been hellfire-and-brimstone against the Comanche down on the Staked Plains...but up here in God's country, son, the proper marrow and hot blood of the world, I figure ye couldn't find yer own butthole with one well-oiled finger."

"I've had enough of your—"

"I'm sure ye have, ye randy young moonling, but afore ye dismiss me as being full-to-slopping with grade-A pigpee, do me the favor of *listening*. Shut with yer jelly-jaw and yer cock-talking and just use yer ears. Them being those hog-flaps to either side of yer head, son."

"There's nothing out there, you old fool," Cheevers said. "I don't hear a thing."

"Then you ain't listening, son," McComb informed him. "And if you don't listen out here, you die."

Cheevers was many things, but mainly he was a warrior. And he was certainly no tenderfoot to be spoken to like that. And particularly by some old beaver trapper like McComb. True…he could *now* hear the sound of horses coming in, but that was all.

He sucked in a short breath, said, "I'll admit my ignorance of the Sioux—"

"Good fer ye, son! Good fer ye!" McComb said, right over the top of him. "I like an officer what admits he's ignorant, and ignorant ye surely are. Just as dumb as sun-dried goat dung, yes sir. I've been out here on m' hook setting traplines and scraping hides since '23. I know m' business, and ain't afraid to admit as much. But you stick with old Boone, boy, and I'll learn ye yer trade, sure as the Sioux Nation shits in the woods, I will!"

Cheevers grimaced. "I know my trade, sir."

"Do ye? Do ye really, pudding foot?" McComb shrugged under his furs. "Well, I suspect that if ye did, ye would not only have heard m' scouts coming in, ye would have smelled what I've been smelling fer quite a piece now."

"Which is?"

"Restless pony herds and wood smoke from council fires, yes sir."

Cheevers clearly did not smell a thing. "Listen, you old—"

"Enough," Major Lyons snapped, "enough."

McComb laughed. "That boy don't know a fat cow from a skinny bull."

Cheevers bristled.

Lyon's beard was as gray as silver dust, his eyes hard and narrowed like deep-cut creek beds from too many years of fighting. He did not like Cheevers, and all knew it. The only reason Cheevers was along was because Carrington had ordered it. Cheevers had an uncle who was a state senator from Indiana, so Carrington had to carefully consider his political future.

McComb studied the sky that was just as white as fresh bone. The heavy-timbered hills. All and everything. He seemed to see something there he did not like. The troopers to a man were bundled against the storm, but McComb, knowing that country too well, kept a hand free to make a play for the brace of Colt pistols at his waist.

The scouts were coming in now and not practicing their usual stealth. Their calico stallions were snorting and crunching through the snow, vaulting fallen timbers and pounding up through little, snowy hollows. As always, they rode right up to McComb.

"What do you see, m' brothers?"

Snake-Hawk pursed his leathery lips. "Injun village up ahead," he said in a low voice. "Plenty ponies and teepee, but...."

"But what?" Cheevers asked.

But the Osage would not look upon him. In fact, they would look at no one but McComb, whom they saw as one of their own. Unlike whites, they were not easy to read, years and years of bitter wind and weather having rendered their faces as emotionless as polished stone.

But McComb could see something there, and he did not like it.

"What did ye see?" he asked Five Wolves.

Five Wolves' face was wet with melting snow. Flakes lighted off his nose, beaded to water. "I see no life down there. War party...it ride through and leave silence behind."

There was something else bothering him and the other two, but McComb knew it would do no good to press the matter. Things would be spoken of when the time was right, but not before. It was the Indian way.

"See here," Cheevers said. "Quit talking in that gibberish and tell us exactly what you saw down there, dammit."

But Five Wolves would not, and neither would the Osage. To them, Cheevers was a non-entity. He would have to ride with them, fight with them, gain their trust through bloodshed and buffalo shit before they'd accept him. To them, he epitomized all that they despised in whites...all show and no substance.

"Don't waste yer breath, pudding foot. Yer not their kind of boy," McComb explained to him. "No sir, they will not come to yer council, white man. They don't care much fer yer medicine, and ye speak with a tongue that's more crooked than a crawling kingsnake."

Cheevers was ready to draw his saber, but Lyons stilled his hand with a look. Because sometimes, despite how much of a dandy you were, it was better to shut your mouth and open your ears.

"I guess we better take a look," McComb said, something crawling in his belly like inchworms. "If that's to yer liking, Major."

"Column, ho!" Lyons called out.

McComb and his scouts led the way. The snow became thicker and wetter, the smell of smoke more pungent. As they rode, McComb could smell death, new death, but something much older, something hideous and awful.

He did not like it at all.

Because he knew death came quickly in Powder River country.

10

As they rode down into the Indian camp, the snow fell in heavy, moist clumps. Thick stands of pine drooped under shivering blankets. Deadfalls, outcroppings, and bushy knolls were chalky sculptures. The column trudged forward, horses spluttering and men coughing into their hands. Skirmishers and flankers clutched Springfield rifles, watching, seeing, anticipating. They crossed a stream bubbling up through plates of ice, and the village was right before them.

McComb saw teepees set out in a little windy meadow, like the sharp bows of ships sinking into a shifting, white sea. He saw racks erected to dry hides and smoke meat, buffalo furs draped over willow frameworks. There were tripods set over dying fires, pyramids of wood. This was no temporary encampment.

And what struck him right away was the silence.

No barking dogs or giggling children, no elders or squaws gathered, braves with rifles watching with wary eyes.

Nothing.

Just wood smoke in the air, the sound of the wind circling and moaning, logs popping in the fire pits, lodge covers flapping.

But McComb was hearing something else: a dark, whispering silence that was so loud it was screaming. That was the sound of the village—a perpetual, droning hum. A neutral sound of emptiness that was eerie and unearthly.

Kneeing his mount into a walk, he followed his scouts through the camp, the soldiers spreading out behind. They saw the bodies soon enough. Like at Crazy Woman Creek, the corpses were stiff as deadwood in the snow, slit and hacked and eviscerated. Pools of blood had frozen into red crystals. Everything was covered in a down of white, like flour spread over the floor of a slaughterhouse.

"Dear Christ," was all McComb could say as he dismounted.

"What the hell happened here?" Cheevers wanted to know.

"Something came through here, son," McComb told him in a hiss of whisper. "And whatever it were, it was making meat."

He could hear some of the men getting sick now.

He was looking at dozens of bodies and parts thereof. They had been stabbed and skinned, faces peeled from the skulls beneath, arms and legs torn free, bellies opened, and throats ripped out. Loops of internals were cast in the snow, frozen now, like dead snakes. Children and babies had been shattered against rocks, warriors riddled with bullet holes and sheathed with arrows. Women were impaled on stakes thrust into their privates. And every face, every single clawed and blood-spattered face was locked in a screaming death mask, eyes wide and jaws sprung.

And they had all been scalped.

Many partially devoured.

And worse, the crowns of their skulls were split open, and what had been inside had been sucked neatly out.

"This was a Crow camp," Major Lyons said, his voice dry and very old now. "What in Christ...who did this?"

But McComb and his scouts were not saying.

McComb examined bodies, saw a hand thrust from the snow with a knife locked in its grip. He tried to pull the body up, but there was no body. Just an arm in a buckskin sleeve, a knob of bone jutting from where it had been torn from the shoulder socket.

Cheevers was walking amongst the carnage in tight, little circles. "Skulls...

all the skulls have been opened, emptied," he kept saying. "The brains... where are they?"

"Somethin' et 'em," one of the soldiers said.

McComb examined a bloody head. The flesh had been stripped back from the forehead like the skin of an orange. Just below where the skull was cracked open like an egg, there were indentations set into the bone: deep, ragged punctures.

"Teeth marks," he found himself saying.

Major Lyons swallowed.

Whatever had roared through here had come with not only spears and knives and arrows, but with teeth and claws and grim appetite. A merciless storm that pulled bodies apart, gutted them, plucked limbs free, and devoured what remained. The Crow had been killed not just for sport... *but for food.*

McComb and Lyons went into a teepee that was painted with symbols and animals. The smell that greeted them was that of roasting human meat. An old Indian—possibly a medicine man from the pipes and drums and collections of dried herbs—had been scalped and chewed on, his body dumped into the fire pit. McComb and Lyons pulled his smoking, blistered remains from the flames, blackened rungs of rib jutting forth, like barrel staves. He broke apart in their hands.

Systematically then, they went from teepee to teepee.

Many were collapsed, stomped down and yanked from the lodge poles themselves, but others were filled with treasures: blankets and buffalo robes, food and rifles, moccasins and fine skin shirts, medicine bundles and ceremonial shields...things that were valuable in that hard country. Things no warrior in his right mind would leave behind after a raid.

It didn't make a spit of sense.

"I've never seen anything like this," Lyons admitted. "Leaving all this behind...what sort of red devils are we dealing with here?"

But McComb silenced him with a finger pressed to his lips.

He cocked his head, listening, listening.

Lyons heard it now, too. An echo of something carried on the winds from the high country: a ritual chanting that was shrill and hollow. Then the storm swallowed it. But what they heard was enough to set gooseflesh creeping at their spines, to fill their veins with a cold sludge.

The scouts, up on their mounts, heard it, too.

They studied the snowy hills and peaks, mouthing silent words. To a man they looked scared, absolutely terrified.

"What is it, m' brother?" McComb said to Five Wolves.

But he would only shake his head. "I will not speak of it."

"Hell kind of animals would do something like this?" Lyons wanted to know. "Slaughter like this and…and eat the brains, the bodies?"

"I don't know," McComb told him. "Not yet. But we better cast a wary eye, because whoever they is, they's watching us and have been fer some time."

Lyons gripped his Henry rifle so tight his knuckles were white. He looked up into the mountains, into the trees, the shadowy runs. "Let's bring these bastards to ground," he said.

Sergeant Hope came over, saluted. "Sir, we found a pony herd in a draw yonder."

"Leave 'em," Lyons said.

Hope looked shocked, but did as he was told. Generally, if horses could not be brought to safety, they were killed to deny the enemy their use.

Lyons turned to McComb. "The scouts…they're acting strange."

"*Scared* is the word fer it, sir. Hell, yes," McComb said. "Those three are real bullet-eaters, but something has 'em spooked sure as shit in a shinebox. And I don't like it one bit.…"

The sergeants cried out for men to come to horse, and the column rode out of that cemetery, pretending they couldn't hear things on the howling wind. Things like whispers and laughter and the sound of their own names being called.

"The vultures will feed well this night," McComb said.

11

It was Five Wolves, scenting the forest around them, that first caught the odor of the stalker up on the ridgeline. The Osage caught it next, then McComb himself. They pinpointed his position quite easily from long years spent stalking game in the forest.

And such a smell…upwind from their adversary, it was a rank odor of moldering hides and bones gone gray in shallow graves. McComb in his many years had known red scalphunters to scent themselves with everything from elk shit to the musk from the sex glands of big grizz…but nothing like this. He could not imagine how such a revolting, aged odor could bring them any closer to their prey unless said prey happened to be full of maggots.

McComb and Five Wolves went into the trees while the Osage stayed in the cover of a dense stand of pine with the horses.

Now the hunt was on.

A pistol in one hand and a Flathead tomahawk in the other, McComb crept forward through the snow, staying in the deep-knit shadows of the aspens as he edged closer and then closer still. He was a wolf hunting his prey, smelling it and feeling it out there, reaching out with his mind until he could touch it. And whatever in the name of God it was, it felt like nothing his senses had ever come up against before…not hot-blooded and virile like a warrior, but cold and squirming like worms twisting in graveyard earth.

But he couldn't distract himself with wild flights of fancy.

Be the wolf, he told himself. *Its pelt covers you, its hunger is in yer belly, its teeth are yer teeth, and its remorseless eyes are yer own.*

It was a trick a Shoshone man-killer name of Silver Knife had shown him years ago. You wanted to be a great hunter? Then you *became* a great hunter, you became a ferocious and blood-hungry wolf, well-muscled, silent and stealthy, not a stumbling, fumbling city-smelling whiteman out on a Sunday picnic. Silver Knife did it with a sacred wolfskin covering his body. He crept right up on animals and men, slit throats and took meat, counted coup and gathered scalps. And nobody had been better. So good was he that superstitious men, both white and red, had called him a Skin-Walker, a shifter of shapes.

McComb paused.

Five Wolves was moving up the hillside directly opposite of him. Their plan was to squeeze this scalphunter between them, take him alive, then put the knife to him, and make him answer a few select questions.

But the scent had disappeared.

The wind died suddenly, barely breathing now with a hiss up in the high branches. The snow fell calm and even, flakes the size of quarters drifting down like something from a penny postcard. Tensing, McComb became the wolf again and moved between two aspens whose boughs were heavy with snow. They brushed his back. He made no sound, every muscle standing taut and ready. He was cresting the ridgeline now, the heavy pine forest beneath him and white-washed river bottomlands to the other side. He was looking for a snowtrail. For that sneaky bastard had been snaking along the hill up here, and he must have left sign.

There.

Footprints cutting through a drift. The scalphunter had moved through here, all right, but whence did he go then? There was a perfect, unbroken crust of snow lying amongst the trees. Unless the shadows were coveting it, this sonofabitch either flew off or took to the trees.

McComb was uneasy now.

This was not the familiar terrain of stalking a man. This was something else. A man whose trail appeared, then disappeared. Beneath his bearskin cap, McComb's scalp was itching with sweat. He forced himself to breathe slow and even, to shake off the panic that scratched in his belly.

Then the stink came at him—black and dirty, like meat thick with flies.

He caught sight of a stalking shape slipping through the trees. He moved after it, his tomahawk and pistol just as greasy as lard in his fists. Staying to the trees, being the wolf, he let his nose guide him in and then—

Crack!

A big bore rifle. Five Wolves' Hawkens. Had to be. McComb heard something fall in the snow ahead, thrash about like a stepped-upon snake, then go quiet. He launched himself out of the cover of the trees with the war-cry of the Crow's, which had brought the gooseflesh to many a Sioux or Blackfoot buck: *"Hooo-kiii-hiiii!"*

His cry shattered the silence, and it was like the mountains woke up, shook themselves, and everything seemed to come alive at once. The wind whipped and howled. Snow whickered through tree branches. Five Wolves let out a battle cry, and whatever he had tossed lead into let out a keening, unearthly wail, like that of an earthbound wraith breaking free of a tomb. And at that precise moment, a shadow that was crooked and quasi-human in shape leaped out at McComb, appearing suddenly from a gust of snow.

He went down on one knee, bringing up his tomahawk, and caught a fevered glimpse of something hulking and snow-covered, dressed in ragged skins and flapping hides, its face gray and seamed like pine bark, long, white hair writhing like snakes. Its yellowed teeth had been filed to sharp points.

Good God, not a man.

An apparition.

It swung its war club at him, and he swung his tomahawk at the same time, the shafts of both weapons colliding with a jarring impact that rendered his arm senseless right up to the shoulder socket. But the big Navy Colt .44 in his hand barked and put a round right through his attacker's chest, tossing him or *it* sideways and into the snow. McComb had killed plenty with his Colt Navys, and when you took a round from a .44 at close range in the chest, you did not get up again.

But as the wind pushed away the cloud of dark gray smoke, there was no body.

There was no blood.

McComb whirled around in the snow with his Colt, trying to find the thing which jumped him…but there was nothing. And in the snow all around him, there was not so much as a drag-mark or footprint. The only prints were his own.

He didn't wait to find out what that meant, for he was smart enough to know when he'd had a brush with something beyond his ken. As he vaulted off through the snow, ducking beneath branches, it felt like his chest was filled with the flapping wings of blackbirds. It was sheer adrenaline and terror, and he recognized it as such.

He found Five Wolves right away.

He had apparently been luckier, for his shot had taken down his attacker and kept him there. But Five Wolves did not look satisfied at the kill. Though his face remained unreadable, his eyes were filled with doubt, uncertainty, and something pretty close to horror.

"Got him, did ye?" McComb said, breathing hard with the exertion of the past ten minutes. "Aye, cored him sweet and proper."

"Him not dead," Five Wolves said.

McComb looked down at the body in the snow.

What in the Christ was this?

The head was like some exaggerated, wolfish skull, plaits of dirty, black hair streaked with white hanging down in knotted strands. The face itself was shriveled and waxy-looking, the color of rotten tallow, set with a deep-hewn spiderwebbing of wrinkles that cut right into the skin like razor cuts. Everywhere, dry and split open as if from immense age, like that face had belonged to nothing that had lived recently, but maybe had been stripped from a head that had dangled in the desert wind from a scalp pole for decades.

But that was hardly the worse part.

"Like...like three faces," McComb said, trying to wrap his brain around it.

There was a jagged, bloodless gash cutting through the scalp and down the forehead to the bridge of the nose where it split into two separate lacerations like branching lightning, a stitch-work of black gut holding it all together. It wasn't simply an elaborate wound, but sections of three separate faces *sewn* into a common whole. Like something from a sideshow horror house... absolutely grotesque.

"Hell is that?" McComb wanted to know. "Not a man...maybe three of 'em, and they weren't human exactly to begin with."

Five Wolves said nothing.

Like the thing that had jumped out at McComb himself, this scalphunter was wearing a patchwork of dirty hides, some of which were tanned and hairless and some of which were thick with animal fur...and some of which were its own skin, threaded together with the rest, threadbare and ragged. Other than that, it wore rawhide leggings speckled with mold, and stiff moccasin boots. A rancid, flyblown stink came off it as if it had been rooting around in graves that were none too fresh. A scarf of shaggy scalps was thrown around the neck along with a necklace of bear teeth. One stiffening fist still held the tomahawk that had been meant for Five Wolves, the blade dark brown and clotted with hair and tissue from recent use. It was raised to strike.

But man or beast or unholy composite...it surely had to be dead.

The Hawkens fired a .50 caliber ball that could drop a bull buffalo in its tracks. Five Wolves had caught this thing right in the head, and the result of that was that the entire left side of the skull was gone beneath that hanging hair. McComb could see the brain in there, pale gray and convoluted. A great, meaty, fist-sized chunk of it was missing. A few tendrils of smoke were still issuing from the wound itself with a burning stink.

No, this *fellow* was dead.

You couldn't survive a blast like that.

But McComb, having seen very well what had attacked him, was none too quick to throw dirt on this one.

And then the jaws parted with a clicking sound.

The puckered lips were pulled back from teeth that were pitted and black. The mouth grinned like a dead carp spoiling on a riverbank. The eyes opened then, and McComb saw they were yellow and mucid, set with tiny, black, pinprick pupils.

Five Wolves began to wail some ancestral dirge.

And McComb, who'd waded through his share of corpses, found that his mouth was so dry he could not speak. He was dizzy with a mad, rioting terror in his head that sounded very much like the wind that moaned through the trees at that precise moment. His limbs felt rubbery and weak, and for the first time in many long years, he felt a scream of absolute hysteria crawl up his throat, needing to vent itself. And in his head a voice, his own: *Ye ain't seeing this, ye crazy deluded old fool! Fer dead is dead, and the dead don't move, and this thing is dead as greening meat, and ye know it, so snap out of this here hallucination already!* But it was no hallucination, and he knew that as those eyes stared into his own, and he could see something not necessarily alive in them, but something *aware,* something smoldering with an evil that was grim and foul beyond reason.

As Five Wolves dropped to his knees in the snow, shrieking out some madness to the Great Spirit, there was the distant sound of approaching riders, and the wind screamed like an animal that was being put to death. At that moment, it seemed like there was only McComb and that horrible scalphunter. The jaws snapped together and began to chatter madly, snapping and snapping. Beetles were crawling in the hair, a knot of slow-crawling worms rising up from the exposed brain.

And somewhere, somewhere up in the haunted, wind-blown dead lands of the mountains, there came a chattering of teeth, as if from a hundred living skulls. Like what was up there was answering this abomination down here.

McComb did scream then.

He screamed out all the pain and dementia in his brain, cocking and firing until he was lost in a mist of powder smoke and that thing in the snow was no longer moving, its head blasted to wormy fragments.

Five Wolves and he stumbled madly down the hillside, and as they did so, as the shadows and drooping tree limbs enclosed the thing in the snow, McComb looked back once and only once. Then he followed Five Wolves down to the horses, nearly mad with fear.

12

Night.

They huddled around the fires, frightened to a man, but not daring to say so. On Lyon's orders, they made encampment in a sheltered break. Each troop was dismounted and dismissed. Picket lines were formed in the trees, white canvas tents put up in orderly rows. Sentries were posted, and picket guards watched the horses. Wood was gathered and fires built. Five Wolves and the two Osage scouts had gone out hunting and returned with two fat elks, which were promptly slaughtered and dressed-out.

Then the sun went down and night locked in.

The darkness beyond the fires was shifting and impenetrable. Anything could have been out there. And every man in Lyon's command was very aware of the fact. The moon peered out from a ragged curtain of clouds from time to time, but not enough for anyone's liking.

"Horses are acting funny," Sergeant Hope told Lyons. "Can seem to settle 'em down."

Lyons sighed. He could hear the horses whinnying and spluttering, straining at their leads and pounding the snow crust with their hooves. Whatever was bothering them, it was starting to get to the picket guards as well.

"Mayhap they caught scent of something," McComb said, smoking his pipe by the fire, the orange glow of the flames licking across the crags of his face.

Horrors of War

Nobody commented on that, and nobody seemed to want to. It was all bad enough up here with the cold and the snow and the creaking silence of the drooping white forest around them. The shadows beyond the fires seemed to actually creep like living things.

Everyone was tense and expectant and maybe McComb more so than the other whites. He refused to relax so much as an inch. He kept his weapons handy and ready, for that was how you survived in that country. You slept with one eye open and a pistol in your hand. He had two Colt Navy .44s at his waist, a knife, and two hatchets slung inside his beaver coat. His Henry rifle had been removed from its buckskin harness and leaned up against some camp trappings not three feet away. He was very aware of his weapons, not just physically but psychically, the way a man is aware of the fingers on his hands.

Stroking his long white beard, he dug a burning ember from the fire and re-lit his pipe, pressing tobacco down into the shale bowl. He watched the men around the fire through heavy-lidded eyes, feeling their nervous tension and knowing that such a thing could be disastrous out here. When a man lost his nerve, he soon lost his life.

"Well, there I were, gentlemen, high on the Popo Agie—which if ye reckon to m' tongue, is north of the Sweetwater and south of the Horn," he said, blowing out a cloud of smoke from his nostrils. "Yes sir, there I stood, knee-deep in hides with a skinning knife in m' hand and m' balls swinging in m' breeches. Just a-washed down in blood and hump fat as I were a-graining m' skins, a dozen dead spikes heaped about m' feet, all gone under sweet and pretty from m' old Hawkens. Now if ye ever hunted the buff, then ye know it's no sweet shine. Ye can't nary hunt spike without bathing in their blood and guts and meat-smell. Yes sir. So, I was scraping m' skins, and all sudden I hears a rumbling and a grumbling like an empty belly, and what were there? Just a bull grizz, had to have a ton on 'em. Musta scented old Boone, what with the blood-stink and all. That old grizz stood up on his hinders clear to seven mayhap eight feet and growls something fierce. M' gun weren't nowheres near. Just m' knife and them dead spikes. At that moment, gentlemen, I prayed to the Lord above and wished I'd had dog-earred the Good Book a scant more often. Nothing to do but die. So, I say, well Old

Ephraim, yer fixing to spit me, are ye? And that big grizz, he grinds his teeth and licks his chops. I say, these here spikes are yourn if ye let me scamper off with m' hides and m' life. That bear, sociable old fang he were, he do the damnedest thing. Lifts his hinder like a hound and squirts piss on m' buckskins. Off I run. Now I didn't smell so good back then, what with the pee-stains and shit-splatches in m' breeches, but after that? Hee-hoo! Every she-grizz on the Horn wanted to rut me hard and proper. And that's a true story."

That one got a wily grin from Major Lyons, giggles from Privates Wood and Chandliss, and a sour look from Captain Cheevers. Five Wolves smiled and so did the Osage.

"Think that's funny, do ye?" McComb allowed himself a chuckle. "Well, weren't so funny, not at all. Mayhap, someday, I'll tell ye about that old painter what woke me with a stream of yellow cat pee in m' face."

More laughter. McComb was simply trying to distract them, and they knew it. Thing was, it worked for a time, and everyone relaxed a bit, allowed themselves to sigh and maybe think about tomorrow or what kind of grub might be on the griddle back at the fort.

"I do certainly miss the old ways," he told them in all honesty. "This a-hunting of mankillers is delicate work, all right. Years back, I had me a good run of it. Lots of plews, a few good wives, a fine rifle. What more could a man ask? Sit about the fire chewing boudie, smoking honeydew, and sucking on the old baldface John Barleycorn."

"What's boudie?" Private Chandliss asked.

"Crow-guts, m' boy. Buff intestine. Ye clean it out, turn the fat side innard and stuff it with meat, roast it. Like a sausage. Real fine etin'. Ye'll never meet a white woman who can fix it proper. No sir."

Captain Cheevers had been listening the whole while, drawing off a thin cigar, and that sour look had never left his face. The fire reflected off his dark eyes, his waxed, cavalry-style mustache with the upturned ends. "That's your problem, McComb: you live in the past. Just like the tribes, you're part of the old and not part of the new."

"Careful with that, my fine young shavetail," McComb said to him, staring into the fire. "Remember where yer boots are stepping and yer head might be laying. It were these fine members of the old and not the new what supplied yer grubsteak this evening. Ye should be thankful."

"The old ways are dying."

"Yer souring m' milk again, son." McComb packed his pipe and re-lit it, blew out a cloud of smoke that danced over the fire. "Mayhap, sonny boy, ye can tell me what's so grand about these new ways. I'll smoke a piece and listen to ye and yer brass-balled wisdom."

Cheevers was unshaken by the old beaver trapper's smart-mouth or the grins his words brought to all around the fire, even the scouts. "The world is changing, McComb. Men like you are relics. You are the dust of the old world that will be stomped by the progress of the tomorrow to come."

"That's fancy-talk, yes sir. M' business is getting hard just listening to ye," the Chief of Scouts said. "I bet when ye shit yer drawers there ain't no smell, and when ye piss in the wind, ye don't taste the spray."

"All right, gentlemen," Lyons said. "We got enough problems here."

Cheevers didn't seem to hear his commanding officer, though. He had one hand on the butt of a pistol at his waist. A hatred was boiling in his eyes, and everyone there could see it.

McComb laughed. "Go ahead, ye simple squeeze of shit. Pull that iron. Be the last thing ye do this side of the grave." He pulled off his pipe, his craggy face looking as old and wise as the mountains themselves at that moment. He sighed. "Tell ye what. Tell ye all what. I seed all of the new I wanted some months ago. Ye all are familiar with that lick of hell called the Fetterman Massacre. Well, I were there. No, not with that cocksure ass-digger Fetterman. He turned his command into worm-meat, by and by. No, I scouted fer Captain Ten Eyck and his relief expedition. I saw them bodies out there. Goddamn, nothing but scalped meat. All them brave boys gutted and gouged, limbs and heads, brains and livers scattered about. Fetterman was a fool. He killed them boys. No sir, I seed all I need of the new, Cheevers. If that's yer new, it ain't worth shit on a stick."

Cheevers promptly got up and left the fire.

Nobody seemed to mind.

It was time for food, and everyone was ready. They feasted on roasted elk steaks and marrowbones, hardtack and bacon, tins of Blue Hen tomatoes and army biscuits. Lots of black coffee. For a time, there was silence, only the wind up in the trees and forks scraping steel plates.

McComb ate as much as three men, and when he was done, he burped with satisfaction. "I wear the wolf in m' belly, boys. Long have I been possessed of a fierce hungerment."

Lyons rolled himself a cigarette when the meal was done and plates cleared, the fire fed fresh logs. "What's the matter with your scouts, Boone?"

They had not eaten a thing. They had stalked and killed the elk, brought them back for all to consume, yet had not touched so much as a short rib. The three of them started into the fire with great concentration.

"They ain't got no wolves in their bellies this night," McComb said, but did not elaborate and did not need to.

Major Lyons retired to his tent, and McComb sat about chatting with Five Wolves in sign and the Absarokee tongue. It was a grim discussion, and it went on for some time as Private Wood and Chandliss listened and watched, but did not dare interrupt.

When they had both lapsed into silence, Wood said, "What...what were you and the Indian talking about? If you don't mind me asking, sir."

McComb smiled. "About m' days as a hump-hunter, son. A hide-hunter and how it were fer me. Yes sir, heavy in horn and hide was I, but not exactly wise. Then upon a hilltop, under the teachings of Chief Many Horses, I fasted and called fer m' spirit guide, ye see. After some days out came this ornery ghost buffalo. It became m' totem, and never again did I hunt that fine animal nor its brethren."

This was true to a certain degree. But their personal spirit guides were not all that was discussed. They also touched upon other things. And what they were he would not repeat to any white man. At least not yet.

He filled his pipe, locking his eyes with those of Five Wolves, then those of the Osage scouts. What passed between them no man knew, but it was akin to dread, to fear, because something inexplicable in the atmosphere of that sheltered draw was suddenly heightened. McComb himself could not put a name to it. He only knew that it moved up his spine like cold fingers and made his scalp prickle, the way it did sometimes when death was so close he could smell its mortuary breath. He watched the smoke from the fire rise up into the trees above, making the boughs shift and creak. Stray flakes of snow danced in the firelight.

"Be a long night, I reckon," he said, exhaling smoke.

"You have said it," Five Wolves told him.

In the pale, shifting moonlight, McComb studied the big pines ringing in their little hollow. They were frosted white by the snow and the pallid moonlight itself. The wind was blowing, but not fiercely. It had a clean, evergreen smell to it. Amongst the trees themselves he could see gloomy, shifting shadows. They could have been just about anything or nothing at all. The trees were very tall, very old, very full. They looked savage, primeval. He had spent his lifetime in these mountains, but never before had he visited a place that felt so empty…yet an emptiness that was unspeakably alive.

What the hell is happening here?

He and Five Wolves shared another ominous look, then he cast his eyes over to Private Wood. "Son? Would ye be so kind as to fetch Sergeant Hope fer me."

As the kid scrambled away, McComb winked at Private Chandliss so as to reassure him that all was fine. But it was not. He had tried to shrug off his interpretation of the atmosphere, but he simply couldn't. The forest felt haunted now, filled with spirits. They were crawling in the shadows, viscidly alive and hungry.

Hope crunched over the snowpack. "What is it?" he asked.

"I have a feeling we are not alone out here," he said.

And he needed to say no more, because out there in the riven darkness there was the sound of breaking branches and forms rustling through the fir boughs. The subtle noise of feet breaking the crust of snow. But it was a covert sound, a calculating sound of stalking. Men started murmuring throughout the camp, and it was like some deathly pall had fallen over them all.

McComb took up his Henry rifle, and the scouts took up their muzzleloaders. All across camp was the sound of men taking up arms and making ready for what might come next. There were nervous whispers, the rattling of sabers and the sound of bolts being worked on rifles. The moon had risen higher in the sky, but its light did not dispel the creeping shadows, it only intensified them. Loose siege lines were formed, but in the shifting light of the fires and the ebon darkness they were weak at best. The sergeants tried to rally the men into a cohesive unit with whispering voices, but the fear of the forest had settled too deeply into them.

Private Wood was standing with McComb and his scouts, but Chandliss had been placed farther down the line to fill the gap. The noises of movement out there were louder now, and they seemed to be coming from every direction, like the camp was ringed by hostiles. The air was no longer cool and clean, but warm with a moist smell of black soil, wet fur, and rancid hides.

Out in the darkness there was a low growling. Like a wolf.

"Oh Jesus," Private Wood said.

"Easy, boy," McComb told him, his eyes panning the darkness. "Don't get spooked. Not yet...."

There was more growling. Then grunting sounds, like feral pigs.

Major Lyons had formed his command into a circle, and the sergeants were slowly marching the men towards what waited out there. Maybe it would have been safer to wait, but already men were panicking, and command was breaking down.

Somewhere, there rose a hollow, bestial howling. An unearthly baying that was from no animal, but almost human in tone.

The shadows were moving from the trees.

"Back!" someone shouted. *"Pull back!"*

More howling, more growling and stealthy movement.

Somebody started shooting, and pandemonium ensued. Sergeants shouted to bring discipline, but nearly every man there was operating on sheer instinct fueled by superstitious terror. Rounds were flying. Men screaming and cursing. Long-armed shadows darted amongst them. There and then gone. Troopers were down in the snow firing, shooting as they stumbled backwards towards the fires. Men tripped over one another, discharged their weapons into the sky.

McComb sighted in on advancing shapes, fired and fired again. He saw them drop, then rise again, snarling things that moved in and out of the darkness. Snake-Hawk and Him-That-Rides-Tall-Horse fired, primed and loaded, fired again. But it was hard to get a bead in the blackness, to know what you were shooting at or if it was even a living thing and not a stump or deadfall.

Five Wolves rushed to the fire and returned with a flaming log and tossed it out at the shadowy perimeter. Twisted shapes darted and jumped, bullets and rifle balls thudding into them. They howled and shrieked, roared like wounded animals. McComb saw a shape that was manlike...though hunched-over and shaggy. It looked like a warrior wearing skins and some kind of flapping wolf headdress. He caught a glimpse of a face that looked like a screaming, waxen skull, its eyes like raw meat.

He fired.

The figure dropped, then vaulted back off into the darkness.

Then it was over, the sergeants shouting for men to stop shooting. The air was heavy with drifting smoke and burnt powder. Major Lyons and a few others grabbed burning logs and advanced towards the trees. The snow was beaten down from the passage of many feet, but there were no bodies. Not even any blood. Just a few tufts of fur and a dirty smell of embalmed things that quickly dissipated.

"We hit them, I know we hit them," Lyons said.

"Some do not die so well," said Snake-Hawk.

Roll call was sounded, men shouting out their names. No one was injured, no one had really been attacked. The hostiles had merely moved in and out of the lines, daring the soldiers to give chase. Ghosts.

Sergeant Hope came running over, saluting Lyons. "Major...Private Chandliss is gone. We searched camp. He's just not here."

"Send out a reconnaissance party," the major ordered. "Find him."

But McComb, standing there with his scouts, knew that it was a waste of time. Chandliss was gone. Those that had breached their lines had taken him, and he would never be found. Not by night. He wondered how many more would be missing by sunup.

And high in the mountains, a wolf began to howl.

13

Morning came with a frost mist in the trees and hollows, ice crystals shining in the snow. The smell of evergreen was strong, only overpowered by the smell of grain and horses, leather harnesses and wood smoke, frying bacon and boiling coffee. Men were bustling about, making ready for the ride after breakfast. It could have been any midwinter bivouac, any morning after any maneuver in the high country. But it wasn't, and everyone there felt it.

Two more men, night-guards, had turned up missing by sunrise.

But they did not go missing long. Five Wolves and the two Osage began cutting for sign immediately, and within the hour, as Lyons' troopers stumbled hopelessly about through the trees, they found them.

"You wanna tell me what in the hell does something like this, Boone?" Lyons wanted to know, sickened by it all.

McComb looked up into the trees. The missing soldiers—Scopeman and Holliwell—were about thirty feet off the ground, impaled upon the sharpened limbs of a mammoth pine like insects on pins. Their corpses were side by side, the limbs thrust through their backs and out their chests. It was anyone's guess what could have carried them up there and then had the strength to skewer them like that. Or if those boys had even been dead when it had happened.

"Can't say," McComb told him. "But I'm guessing that before this ride is through, we're gonna know."

Lyons narrowed his eyes, clenched his teeth. "There will be a reckoning for this," he said. "May God have mercy on whoever fucking did this, because I will show none."

He looked once at his Chief of Scouts, at the Indians, swore under his breath, and stomped away. He did not issue an order for anyone to climb up there and pull the men free, but then again, the idea was ludicrous: the nearest limbs were fifteen feet up, and the bole of the pine was slick with ice and snow. Maybe one of the scouts could have done it. Maybe.

Breakfast passed in silence.

Lyons watched his men eat but had no stomach for food himself. He stood there, staring up into the mountains as food was eaten and coffee drank, and then the sergeants rallied the men and broke the camp down. The troopers went to the picket line and saddled their horses, packed equipment.

"Fall in!" Lyons called out, watching the parade line form. "Count off!"

The count went down the line, and when it reached the end, the bugler sounded boots and saddles, and troopers scrambled about under the watchful eye of their commanding officer. As scared as they were, as concerned as they were about what might come next, they knew Lyons was in a foul mood, and they maintained a rigid discipline.

"Prepare to mount!" Lyons called out into the chill air. He raised his saber high, brandishing it. "Mount! Right by twos! H-o-o-o-o!"

The scouts led the troops out of the bivouac, Boone McComb out front in his furs, a buffalo rifle cradled in his arms. The troopers swung right by twos, forming a column with Captain Cheevers leading the way.

Lyons, on horseback, watched them ride out in formation. He did not know what to expect next. Had they been facing a conventional enemy, he would have had nothing but faith in his command. He knew they would fight. Though many of his men were green, still many more were veterans of the War Between the States. But this enemy...it was like none he could comprehend. He was no fool. He saw what was in the eyes of Boone McComb and his scouts: fear. And it took a lot to frighten them.

And what could inspire that was what worried him.

14

The troopers rode in silence.

Stark, apprehensive silence.

Fear had taken root in them now and would not let go. It thickened their blood and quickened their hearts, submerged their minds into a dirty half-light that was bright enough to die by but far too dark to see the hollow-eyed shadows until they swarmed out and teeth were sunk in throats.

McComb felt it, too, but his was of a more virulent variety. Blessed ignorance was beyond him now. He had seen what they were up against and knew very well the sort of hell they were riding into and what it would exact from them.

And there was little he could do but pray in his heart and grip his pistols all that much tighter.

He was riding out front of the column again, because these men needed him more than ever now, and he would not abandon them to what waited out there.

It had been seven hours now since they broke camp. They had halted only once, an hour ago, when a shallow stream was found bubbling through plates of ice. The men filled their canteens and ate some cold rations, hardtack, jerky, and dried apples. A morral of oats was given to each horse. There was little speaking and absolutely no camaraderie.

The snow was whipping around them fine and bitter like sand and chipped ice, stinging faces and hands. The horse soldiers kept the brims of their hats down low to prevent snow blindness and kept pushing forward, higher and higher, along the edges of ravines and gorges, below wooded slopes and jutting cones of volcanic rock. A column of ants pressing ever forward, the blizzard shrieking and lashing around them, creating wild shapes and leaping shadows. The wind was piling up snow into four-foot drifts, inundating horse and man until they were white-mounted effigies. It blew and sang, wailed mourning dirges and promised every man that, *yes,* there was death out here. Gruesome, macabre death, rattling like bones in the stark belly of that storm.

The scouts warned McComb of going any farther. Telling him in no uncertain terms that what had claimed the Crow village would claim them as well. For it was out there even now, circling like wolves around a fire, smelling human meat and lusting for it.

But McComb did not pass this on to Major Lyons.

Not yet.

Five Wolves had found a game trail the war party had used. It cut down through a narrow valley and up into a rough, mountainous stretch of hillocks and scrub brush. The storm lessened for a few moments, and visibility began to return. All around them were slopes fringed with jackpine and cedar thickets squatting under burdens of snow. Barren knots and mesas of gray rock thrust from the whiteness, casting deep shadows over the landscape.

What struck McComb was the silence.

All he could hear were the men and horses, the wind sighing up in the trees. No hawks crying out in the sky, no coyotes howling. No elk breaking for cover. Just that uncanny, enveloping silence. He pulled a chunk of venison jerky from his parfleche and chewed it slowly, feeling eyes watching from hollows and shadows.

They rode on.

A meadow opened before them, its sterile whiteness broken only by clumps of juniper and fingers of yellow devil grass breaking the frosty crust. A river cut through it like a jagged scar.

McComb let the jerky fall from his fingers.

He smelled something, heard something, *knew* something.

The chanting.

Those high, unearthly voices chanting. It was coming from everywhere, spooking the horses and making the men nervous.

He tried to swallow again and again as he felt his hide began to curl. "Here's damp powder and no way to dry it."

Lyons looked at him.

The storm returned with a vengeance, a churning blizzard engulfing the column. And it couldn't have arrived at a worse time.

The scouts and flank guards came charging back across the river. Men were shouting. A rifle cracked and then another. One of the guards galloped out of the storm, fell from his saddle and the battle, as such, began.

It started with the sergeants calling out and swearing, telling the men to dismount, to create siege lines. Troopers hid behind logs and brush heaps, bringing their rifles to bear. Others wildly dove for the nearest cover available. Rifle balls were buzzing around like hornets, dropping troopers and thudding into the flanks of horses. Visibility was negligible. They could see a swarm of shadows rushing at their position, but little else. Major Lyons, still mounted, returned fire as men around him fell and gushed red in the snow. Most of the soldiers were in kneeling or prone positions now, greeting the advancing war party with a deadly barrage of rifle slugs and musket balls.

A few men panicked outright, running this way and that. But most of the troopers held their ground. Armed with the new Trapdoor Springfield .50-70 breechloaders, they kept shooting and shooting.

McComb carried two rifles with him.

One was a sixteen-shot Henry repeater, and the other was a Sharps buffalo rifle, .50 caliber. He joined his two surviving scouts—Snake-Hawk and Five Wolves—who had set themselves up behind a rock outcropping with their muzzleloaders. Him-That-Rides-Tall-Horse was lying out in the snow now, being trampled with the others beneath the hooves of the approaching war ponies.

McComb began levering and firing as that shrieking horde rode in on them, swooping down with a fanatical mania that was disturbing even for the Sioux. McComb hit three of them, another more than once, but still they came on, riddled with holes and howling for the blood of white intruders. They rode in and out of the blizzard, ghosts again, nightmare shapes that appeared and disappeared.

Major Lyons had two big service revolvers in his hands.

He was frantically blasting away at shadows...shadows that howled like beasts. He dropped one, then another, but as he advanced for the kill, they were gone. A tomahawk came spinning end over end through the snowy air, barely missing him and thudding into Sergeant Hope's head, splitting the crown of his skull wide open. He fell over straight as a plank, the snow around him pooling with scarlet ribbons.

The entire episode took on a weird, surreal tone as ghost Indians broke through their lines, shooting and throwing knives and hatchets, tossing spears and letting arrows fly. They dove from their mounts onto screaming troopers, hacking and clawing and biting. Others were caught in crossfire that knocked them from leather...but they did not stay down. Roaring and whooping, they rose to fight again.

They were not men.

What the soldiers saw they could scarcely believe.

Black shapes on horseback, on foot...hulking things in hides and flapping skins, buffalo robes and tattered wolf skins. They wore necklaces of animal bones and blackened human ears, scarves of scalps and the headdresses of wolves and bears, some of which had long pelts attached to them and others which were just fanged skulls. Their faces were hidden beneath tanned death masks made from their victims, cut away so their own gaping jaws were free to bite and tear.

What the troopers saw of those faces, were more beast than men.

It was madness, sheer madness.

Guns firing and blades whirling and arrows punching flesh. Men were shouting and screaming, begging God for deliverance. But there was no deliverance, for hell had rode down on them now, and its belly was empty. A young sergeant bayoneted a warrior a dozen times, and he rose again and again, taking the sergeant down with claws and teeth. Taking a knife, he slit open the sergeant's head just below the hairline from ear to ear, skeletal paws jerking the bloody scalp from the skull beneath.

Lieutenant Cheevers, saber in hand, cleaved the arm off another warrior, then thrust the blade straight through him. The warrior grinned, teeth chattering, and Cheevers let out a cry and stumbled backwards. The warrior reached behind his back, grasped the bloodless blade and pulled it through and out, haft and all. Cheevers, half out of his mind, pulled a Remington .44 pistol and put a ball through the warrior's left eye socket. The warrior seized up as gray debris and bone blew out the back of his head, then he folded up into the snow, lifeless. His revealed face was a composite mask of human skin and reptile hide sewn together. His mouth was stitched shut, strands of gut thread trailing down to his waist.

Other warriors had been blasted nearly to fragments, but still they moved and raged and stalked. A single gray arm crawled through the snow, propelled by a mottled hand that was sparsely furred. A decapitated head with the vulpine jaws of a wolf fastened its teeth on a soldier's leg, biting and glaring up at the horrified man with insane red pits for eyes. Another soldier literally smashed a warrior to writhing scraps with the butt of his Enfield rifle-musket...but still those disembodied skeletal hands gripped his throat, throttling his life away.

McComb watched the carnage around him, ghost warriors swallowing bullets and blades but refusing death. Their skins were ragged canvas, the flesh of their faces hanging in loops. Grunting and growling and snapping at one another, they fed on downed troopers that were not even dead. Brain-eaters, flesh-eaters. Cannibal-demons.

A mounted warrior carrying a feathered spear came pounding over the rocks, and McComb brought up the Sharps and blew the bastard right off his mount. And he should have been dead.

But he wasn't.

The .50 caliber ball had blown a fist-sized entry wound into his chest and an exit wound easily twice that size out his back. As he pulled himself up from the snow, McComb got a good look at what he had shot. Like the others, he was dressed in a hodgepodge of draping animal and human pelts, withered scalps hanging from his throat in black-haired wreaths. His hair was long and white, knotted with sticks and leaves and dead insects. And he wore a human corpse-mask of fissured, gray skin which ended at his mouth, gnarled, yellow fangs on display.

But what horrified McComb the most, was that through the ragged eyeholes of the mask he could see that the warrior's own eyes were sewn shut.

He was blind.

Yet, blind or not, he knew where McComb was, and he came at him, jaws sprung open, a beard of moss dangling from his chin to his chest. *"Yi-yi-yi!"* he shrieked.

"Jesus Christ..." McComb managed.

Drawing a skinning knife, the warrior moved in with a loping motion for the kill. McComb pulled matching pistols and drilled him again and again. But it did no good: he might as well have been trying to kill the wind itself. The warrior leaped, smoke billowing from a dozen holes. McComb dodged to the side, but lost his balance and went face-first into the snow. He rolled over quick, but the thing was on him, those long, yellow teeth jutting from blackened gums, his breath like tombs. His human death mask was blackened and split open in a dozen places...and the face behind it was like something from a freak show: a malformed and flyblown patchwork of human flesh, dark and pale and seamed gray, all sutured together.

As the warrior brought the knife up for a killing blow, McComb jabbed the iron barrel of a .44 Colt into his mouth and jerked the trigger. The top of the warrior's head blew into confetti, and he fell straight back, just as dead as anything McComb had ever seen.

Shapes moved in and out of the storm, chattering their teeth and feeding on the fallen. McComb could hear sounds of feasting: wet, meaty chewing noises and teeth scraped over bone.

Crawling through the snow, his head thrumming with white noise, he listened to men screaming. Many of them were not dead...they were being eaten alive.

15

Fifteen were killed.

Another five were badly wounded.

Five others had disappeared completely.

The storm had blown itself out, and the meadow was stained red with blood and blackened by powder. Plumes of smoke hung in the air, gently dispersing in the breeze. The bodies of half-eaten men and dead horses were heaped in the snow. And the smell—of new death and old—was raw and sickening.

Lieutenant Cheevers and many of the others were rocking themselves in the snow, mumbling, crazed, and staring. The stiffening remains of the warriors were cast into a pit dug from the snow. Logs and kindling were heaped over them, set ablaze. But some were not dead as such. Flaming arms and torsos steaming with greasy, black tendrils of smoke kept trying to work themselves free. Soldiers—some giggling, some shaking, some vacant-eyed and insane—kicked the offending parts back in, fed the fire. The limbless torso and head of one warrior kept muttering in some guttural tongue that not even McComb was familiar with. It was not an Indian dialect, not in his experience. It lay there in the snow, chattering its overlapping gray teeth and speaking. Its death mask was gone, and what was beneath was worse. Strands of greasy, black hair fell over the elaborate scarification and stitchwork of its face. A gash running from the corner of its lips right up to its left ear had been sewn-up tightly with black sinew, pulling its entire face to the side in a grim rictus.

It stared up at McComb with one mucid, yellow eye that was filled with a blind, unreasoning hatred.

"Burn it," he told the soldiers gathered there. "For God's sake, burn it."

Into the fire it went, muttering on and on as the flames engulfed it.

McComb found Major Lyons, pistols in hand, yelling out orders, refusing to let these horrors disrupt his command. His eyes were glassy, red-rimmed pits.

"I talked with m' scouts," McComb said to him. "Ye need to hear what they said."

Lyons had a bad tic in the corner of his lips. "Yes?"

"Skull-Eaters," McComb told him. "They call them the Skull-Eaters, fierce living dead warriors that only show in the coldest winters…"

He told him then the story of a Sioux medicine man named Silent Crow.

198

At least two centuries before, he had challenged a tribal shaman, saying that he and only he should be their spiritual leader. His power was greater, he boasted. To prove this, Silent Crow, using ancient and forbidden knowledge, had called up fifty warriors. Warriors he had stitched together out of odds and ends of any available carrion, whether man or beast. The warriors killed many, but the Sioux managed to destroy them. And Silent Crow was sealed up alive in a cave, along with two others: Bearskin, his war chief, and Tongue-of-Serpents, his wife.

"But, they say he didn't lay still," McComb told the major. "That old Silent Crow, dead as old bones, came back from his crypt and brought an army with him. And that's who we're fighting."

"It's…it's goddamn insane," Lyons said, looking like he wanted to weep. Then his eyes stared into the pit of burning things, some of which still moved. "Why…why now? Why here?"

So McComb told him what Five Wolves had said. That Silent Crow had been called forth with some very bad medicine, probably by the Sioux themselves, and the reason for that was to avenge themselves against white savages who were murdering their people, killing their buffalo, and raping their lands.

Major Lyons thought about it for a time.

He sent Sergeant Nix and four troopers back with the wounded. Which whittled the raiding party down to eleven men, counting the scouts. The dead were crowded together and covered with blankets.

"According to tribal tradition, Five Wolves tells me, Silent Crow's lair is a two-hour ride up into the high country, that it's a taboo place. But he and Snake-Hawk are willing to take us there and die with us."

"They are very brave," Lyons said, meaning it.

"Question is: Are we up to it?"

Studying the treeline, Lyons said, "We'll have to be. We have to run that ghoul to ground."

"Not just him, Major," McComb said. "But his war chief and that wife of his. Five Wolves says that she is some sort of straw-witch or conjuror. She is the source of his power, so sayeth the old tales."

The scouts were sitting in the snow, wailing shrill songs and cutting their hands and faces with their knives, smearing the blood over themselves.

"What are they doing?" Lyons asked.

McComb did not smile. "They're singing their death songs."

Lyons called for boots and saddles, and the sergeants told the men to come to horse. The order of march was already established: McComb and his two scouts out ahead, followed by two skirmishers, then the main body… or what was left of it.

This was how they rode into the land of the dead.

16

A ride of two hours that became four in the teeth of the storm, and the raiding party found the graveyard.

A Crow cemetery.

Normally, such a place was forbidden to whites and non-tribal members. If you defiled it by entering, the Indians would hunt you, put you down in the worst possible way. Snake-Hawk was Osage. He would not cross it. He feared ghost warriors as much as the living Crow. But he knew that what they were facing was no common enemy. McComb spoke to him at length, and he finally looked to Five Wolves.

"These are your people here," he said. "I will do as you say. Only as you say."

Cheevers and the others didn't care for any of this, leaving it all up to a red savage hamstrung by countless generations of superstition. But it had to be this way. McComb was more Indian than white by that point. And without him and the scouts, they'd never find the lair. Not before nightfall. It was all in the hands of Five Wolves.

"Listen to me, m' brother," McComb said to him. "Long have you ridden by m' side. We have made good medicine together and have been as brothers. The only way to put that devil Silent Crow down is to cross these sacred grounds. But without yer blessing, we will not. How say you?"

Five Wolves thought about it a long time. "You ask me to defile the burial grounds of my fathers to avenge white deaths, my brother. Whites who have stolen my hunting grounds and made the little ones fall with the coughing sickness. You ask me to spit on the memories of those who have fallen…how can you, as my brother, ask this?"

McComb looked him straight in the eye. "Listen to me. Ye know m' heart is open, and I speak with a straight tongue. I have fought by yer side and would die by it. Those are m' words. They have always been m' words. But this is not about the whites. Silent Crow will kill all…men, women, children, the whites, the tribes. *All*. Ye saw what his warriors did to the Crow village. Those were yer people. I ask ye now to avenge their souls; I ask ye to feel their blood-hate and let it become part of ye. Yer fathers and the Great Spirit would want it so, I think."

It looked like Five Wolves was going to forbid it, but perhaps driven by necessity and the purity of his vision of the world become a graveyard, he finally said, "We will ride through. No one must touch anything. If they do, if they defile my fathers, I will have their blood. Those are my words."

So, the column of eleven, led by Crazy Snake Boone McComb and his scouts, made their way through in utter silence. Snowflakes danced in the air like motes of dust, and the wind moaned amongst the graves. Five Wolves sang a high, wailing dirge, begging the ghosts of his ancestors for forgiveness.

The blizzard had pushed drifts through there, but it was still very clear the sort of place it was. The cemetery was hilly, set with snow-capped mounds of earth and dead oaks. A winding, narrow trail led through the menagerie of death. The bodies of Crow chieftains and their families were laid out on willow scaffolds decorated with war shields and antelope hides, feathers and the skulls of sacred animals—beaver, wolf, bear. The bodies themselves were all little better than skeletons wrapped in elaborately beaded pelts of beaver and buffalo, sewn-up in soft hide shrouds that had rotted through the seasons to rags. Skulls leered at the soldiers; skeletal arms bearing bracelets and weasel pendants dangled from drooping, threadbare cerements.

The dead were everywhere.

But no one had been interred there in many years.

There were dozens upon dozens of crumbling scaffolds and four times that number of deerhide berths strung from tree limbs like dark cocoons with rawhide or hemp rope. These were the graves of warriors, common tribal members. Some trees had as many as six or seven of these suspended graves and were adorned with wolf skins and feathered staffs, medicine bundles in fringed buffalo calfskin bags, and ceremonial masks representing the animal totems of the men's societies. Burial moccasins erupted from shrouds, and mummified, bird-picked faces still bore the earthen reds and yellows of funeral paint.

Warrior's berths were strung with bows and arrows, favored muskets or lances, hand-painted buckskin shirts. Sometimes sacred medicine pipes and embalmed raptors.

The scaffolds were crowded between the trees, and the trees were thick with growths of shrouds and mummies and leering skulls. The dead ones seemed to leer and reach, dangle and hang from every bough and platform.

The riders had to duck down in their saddles to avoid being brushed by cadaver fingers and trailing limbs.

And where there weren't hide berths sprouting the dead, the trees were garnished with animal bones and eagle feathers, draped with snake skins and flapping buffalo pelts, strung with sacred porcupine quill tapestries and the spreading antlers of elk and deer.

McComb rode through, his hands free of buffalo mittens, clutching rein and rifle. He saw all those wasted faces, the disintegrating belongings, the altars of long-decayed food left out in wooden bowls for the Indian's spirit guides. He saw a woman with a fleshless face and long, tangled, black hair holding a tiny, withered infant.

Knowing they had died together in childbirth, he was saddened.

Finally, they reached the outskirts of the burial ground.

And when the last white had ridden free, Five Wolves went down on his knees in the snow, wailing and mourning. And then, in the Crow Tongue, he called out: "I ask forgiveness, my people. For you are my blood, my flesh, my soul. When I, too, fall, this will be my home. May my ancestors forgive my sacrilege. But my mission is just. Know this. For soon I will lay alongside you in the bosom of the Great Spirit. These are my words. Hear them."

Then he climbed back on his mount, and they rode away from that disturbing, ghoulish place, and the storm hammered down on them, and, to a man, they knew what was coming next would be profane beyond words.

17

The snowstorm was raging again.

The troopers, clutching rifles, were bent over in their saddles against the screeching wind. Soon enough, the scouts located a trail beat into the snow. It started abruptly and cut through a stand of pines. And on the other side, a sheer face of rock rising two-hundred feet above them. It was craggy and leaning, perforated with cavelike mouths and frosted in white.

The raiders stopped there, looking up, listening and hearing that weird, high chanting, echoing from deep within the passages.

"This must be it," Lyons said.

The scouts muttered to one another fearfully.

McComb dismounted, studying the cave mouths like they were the lairs of ogres and trolls. They were round and perfect, obviously artificial, the lowest set an easy twenty feet off the ground and the highest well over a hundred feet above. He fingered his beard and touched the scars and ruts of his old face, knowing they would get no older. At the foot of the cliff face, jutting from the snow, there were heaped bones…what looked to be hundreds of them. A mountain of grinning skulls, shattered ribcages, ulnas and femurs and vertebrae and reaching metacarpals, frosted white. This was the litter pile of what waited inside. The remains of their conquests, the various battlegrounds and graveyards they had plundered.

It ended here.

Three jawless skulls had been set out on stakes hammered into the earth. All of them were brown from age and carved with complex ritualistic designs that looked like witch-sign. The two to either side were human enough, long, black hair still hanging from the scalps. But the one in the center had belonged to a monster. It was larger than the others, lewd and misshapen. The bones were all wrong, ridged and thrusting. The orbits huge and up-turning, jaws thrust out in a vulpine snarl and set with hooked teeth, like those of a viper.

"What the hell did that belong to?" Lyons wanted to know.

Cheevers stood there, looking angry. "It's a sideshow gaff," he said. "Something made out of other bones. That's all it is."

"Couldn't be nothing more," McComb said. "Just a gag."

But nobody was laughing.

Five Wolves stood by McComb's side, studying the boiling, white sky and the snow-draped mountains. "It is a good day to die," he said.

Horrors of War

Major Lyons put three men on picket duty with the horses, and the others prepared to enter the mouths. Five Wolves and Snake-Hawk picked through the mounded bones, climbed the sheer face with coils of rope, tying them off above at separate passages, and slid down their lengths.

Lyons went up one with three soldiers, and McComb went up with his two scouts and Lieutenant Cheevers. The hope was that they would meet up again inside.

McComb led the way, pushing through the opening on his hands and knees, the others coming in behind him. The passage narrowed incrementally, and he had to crawl on his belly like a snake, clawing through snow and ice. In places, the passage was drifted from floor to roof. It went on that way for some time. The roof brushed his back and the walls his shoulders. Then, gradually, it widened, and he was able to crouch, then stand. He lit his oil lantern, and Snake-Hawk lit his.

That's when they saw the Skull-Eaters, lined-up and waiting.

The passage followed a gentle incline into the ebon belly of the mountain and to each side of that narrow tunnel, mummies. Leaning against the walls… the Skull-Eaters. But all silent and dead as wax effigies.

All of them were dressed in filthy fur robes, the rotting hides of men and animals, beaded war shirts with bone hair-pipe breastplates, all of which were mildewed and frozen and hanging in moldering strips. It was hard to say which were garments and which were their own skins. Necklaces of ears and bones, scalps and leathery entrails were strung around their necks and thrown over their shoulders like sashes. They clutched rifles and spears, hatchets and tomahawks, war clubs and skinning knives in hands that were human, almost human, and others that were hairy and clawed, like those of beasts.

"These ain't no sideshow gaffs, I reckon," McComb said. "No sir."

Lieutenant Cheevers was trembling and sweating. He teased aside a strand of hair from his brow with the barrel of a pistol. "This many, dear Christ, this many…how could it be?"

But nobody knew.

Their faces were mostly hidden by tanned human death masks, but those that weren't were much like the other Skull-Eaters McComb had seen: sutured assemblages of animal and human tissue, sometimes the segments of several disparate faces sewn together along with strips of snakeskin and wolfskin and bearskin. Many had their eyes stitched shut, and still others had their lips sewn up, threads of jute hanging in strings. And down the line, he saw many with the feral jaws of wolves...or something like wolves.

"Death," Snake-Hawk said morosely. "Death is all around us. It calls our names and prepares a place for us."

McComb said, "Dead, just dead."

But he didn't believe it, and neither did anyone else. He looked and looked and could not turn away. Yes, they looked like sideshow gaffs, all right, things thrown together out of human and animal parts, passed off as monsters in a house of horrors back east. But there was no getting past the bloody scalps they were clutching or had strung from their hide ponchos like medals.

How long they would be dormant was anyone's guess.

McComb pushed on through that silent, sepulchral jury until the tunnel ended and they found themselves in a huge grotto hewn from solid rock. The ceiling was thirty feet above them, the walls a hundred feet apart. Water was dripping. And there was a black putrefied stink twisting in the air. The walls were not walls as such, but carefully built ramparts, erected not with bricks but jawless skulls. Thousands of them stacked and interlocked, like puzzle pieces. Some were gray with age, going to powder. Others were still splattered with brown whorls of dried blood.

McComb held up his lantern, shocked.

Shadows found those death heads, made them shift and move, blink and grin and slide from their perches.

The floor of the grotto was merely another litter pile of human remains.

Yellow skulls riddled with teeth marks, rib slats and ulnas, pelvic wings and scapulas. They were set with black mold and rivers of frost. Among them were weapons and boots and arrows and clothing. The three missing soldiers had been dumped there, gutted and gnawed, their skulls opened like cans. There were Crow Indians, too...dozens of them, broken and bloody and cannibalized.

"Let's go," McComb said, leading them through that mortuary and into another passage.

The bobbing oil lamps made distorted shadows creep around them, sliding like snakes and grotesque phantoms. The air was thin, dry, and cold. Specks of dust and ice danced in the lantern's glow, and everything stank of blood and meat, rainy crypts and spices.

Then the tunnel abruptly ended, and they were in a small chamber.

In the center was a hole leading below, and out of it wafted a stink that was hot, black, and wormy.

"Now we get a taste," McComb said. "Now we get into the guts of it."

18

Battle was joined.

It started with an eerie, disembodied chanting that grew to a feverish pitch, and then the undead were awake in the cavern with Major Lyons and his three troopers. There was no time for fear or shock, really; this was survival, and the four of them turned and faced what shambled out to feed on them. But what were they? Ghosts? Revenants? There were a dozen of them, and they all wore heavy hide shrouds over their heads that had been intricately stitched from dozens of discolored skins and scalps trailing locks of black hair. The shrouds hung down to their knees, moccasin boots and buckskin leggings beneath. They brandished battle lances, tomahawks, knives, and war clubs. Several had bows and quivers of feathered arrows.

They came forward, grunting like boars...then stopped.

Lyons held a hand up, warning his men—Pearson, Coyles, and Standard— to remain still, to remain quiet. The Skull-Eaters did not seem to know where they were. He watched them fan out, jabbing and slashing the shadows with their weapons. Every now and again, stopping and waiting as if they were listening.

And he knew that was exactly what they were doing.

Eyeholes had been cut in the shrouds, but in the light of the burning lanterns he could see that they had no eyes, that their lids had been sewn shut. Yes, blind. Like many of the others that attacked them in the storm, completely blind.

It was chill in the cavern, but Lyons could feel sweat trickling down his face, steaming. His men were trembling, and he supposed he was, too. He could smell the fear coming off them.

The Skull-Eaters kept circling around, squealing with delight as they searched for their victims.

They'll never find us, he thought, *if we can…only…be…quiet.*

But that was asking a lot. For he could hear his men breathing, straining against their muscles to remain motionless. Two of the Skull-Eaters were gradually moving in their direction. Closer, closer. They were chattering their teeth.

Then Coyles made a gasping sound.

The Skull-Eaters moved in on it immediately.

Lyons and his troopers opened up with carbines and Colt pistols, drilling holes into the advancing flesh-eaters, and it barely slowed them down. They shrieked their war cries and rattled their yellow bones and charged forward. Pearson was skewered by a lance and driven to the ground. Arrows were loosed from bows, and Coyles and Standard were pierced again and again, and they, too, went down. Blood foaming from their mouths, they looked back at Lyons with rage and panic and defeat in their eyes as the scalphunters fell on them with knives and tomahawks, slashing and chopping while their dying screams echoed through the cavern.

His pistols empty and smoking in his hands, Lyons tossed them aside.

There was an arrow in his shoulder, and another had laid his cheek open, but he was beyond pain. He was fighting with instinctual hatred now. He tossed his oil lantern at the Skull-Eaters, and a mushrooming cloud of fire consumed three or four of them. Burning and crackling, they did not go down, but rose from the flames blackened and crisped and even more obscene than before. They charged him with tomahawks raised, trophy scalps and threadbare shrouds smoldering, plumes of nauseating smoke rising from them.

Lyons let out a rebel yell and rushed right into their midst, swinging his saber and casting them aside like deadwood. A war club glanced off his skull, and a tomahawk opened his ribs, but he fought on, slashing and dodging until his attackers lay in writhing pieces at his feet.

The other scalphunters who had fallen on Pearson, Coyles, and Standard were busy eviscerating and mutilating the corpses of the troopers. They had slit free scalps and opened bellies and peeled faces from skulls. They wore glistening scarves of bowels, and gore spattered their shrouds and painted their clawed hands a brilliant, glistening red.

But there was no time to hack them down.

Because in the blazing light of the oil lanterns, another had come.

Looking upon this one, Lyons shriveled momentarily with fear. For this one was special. He did not think it was Silent Crow, but perhaps his war chief, Bearskin. And he was right. Bearskin had barely been human in life, and he was far less than that in death. Like some hideous troll, he was stitched together out of human and animal hides, draped with rotting pelts and trailing skins, a ragged and fearsome thing that was corrupt with decay and riven with vermin. His face was a patchwork of human skin, animal hide, and reptile tissue sutured into a whole that was garishly stretched over the jutting bone and rotten hollows of his skull.

One eye was but a socket writhing with worms, the other filled with a huge, pustulant yellow eye lacking a pupil. And it was this eye that leered at Lyons. The mouth opened, and graying teeth filed sharp as awls gnashed together. A voice that was guttural, clogged with grave earth, spoke first in the language of the Sioux, then in English: *"I will feed upon you, white man,"* it said. *"I will gorge myself on your blood and meat and decorate my lodge with your skin and entrails. I will rape your daughters and your wives; I will wear their scalps and string the bowels of your children around my throat."*

Lyons stood his ground, terrified, yes, but more repulsed than anything. Some things should crawl like worms and not walk like men, and this was one of them. Bearskin stepped forward. Tiny, sharpened bones had been inserted ritualistically into his skull and now jutted forth like the spines of a boar. On his head, he wore a headdress made of a dozen human deathmasks stitched together with gut. Locks of hair dangled from the scalps and hung in his face.

The stink coming off him was a horror itself.

"Come and get me, you sonofabitch," Lyons said, raising his saber.

Bearskin let out a chilling cry and raised a feathered war club, his other hand curled like a claw, the nails long and splintered and yellow.

He leapt.

Lyon dashed into meet him. He dodged the trajectory of the war club once and then twice, slashing Bearskin open at the chest and gut. Then the war club struck him in the face, and the orbit around his left eye shattered, blood and tissue slopping out, along with his eye from a tangle of optic nerve. Blinded, in agony, he struck with his saber and slit Bearskin's face open to the bone from jaw to brow. The wound pulsed with a hiss of gas, exposing a nest of green, segmented worms that threaded through the skull beneath. Then Bearskin had him, crushing him against rancid, crawling hides, trying to squeeze the life out of him, pressing him tighter and tighter.

Lyon's mind exploded with black dots, and with one last effort, he brought his saber up and, as luck would have it, right between Bearskin's legs where it sliced through rancid meat right up into the gut-sack.

Bearskin cried out and released him.

Black ichor splashed from the wound, spilling onto the floor of the cavern and sizzling. Bearskin was injured, and Lyons went at him, swinging his saber, aiming with one good eye, hacking and cutting at that horror until limbs were severed and that face was bisected and then bisected again. With a scream of violation, Bearskin went to his knees, and it was then that Lyons cleaved his head free with a final burst of strength and kill mania.

Bearskin's decapitated head continued to shriek and chatter its teeth, a vile yellow fluid running from the mouth. The headless body stumbled about drunkenly, raining worms and carrion beetles. And Lyons, his head filled with a sibilant white noise, crawled from the chamber into another tunnel, his mind gone to a shivering sauce.

19

Picket duty outside the caves.

Pinley, Johnson, and Kreese, privates all.

They were more frightened than they had ever been in their lives. There was terror associated with being sent to Indian country by the Army to begin with, but what they had seen and what they now knew distorted everything that they had ever held dear. They were shivering things that started at the whisper of the wind, the crack of a stick.

And then the singing began.

"Do you hear it?" Johnson said.

But the other two did not dare admit to it. It came floating out of the darkness at them, a high and wavering voice that was purely female and purely evil. Like the voice of an insane woman in a lonely cemetery, singing a mourning dirge over the graves of her children...eerie, strident, and filled with grief.

It was everywhere, echoing and echoing, bouncing around them and making them feel the cold like never before. They could hear footsteps crunching through the snow as that voice got louder and louder and more melancholy. But there was nothing, nothing...only the wind and the snow and the shadows.

And then—

"Shit," Pinley said, bringing his carbine up.

A woman came walking out of the shadows as if she'd been born from them. She held her arms out to them, and she was absolutely beautiful. She wore a thigh-length dress of fine, white antelope skin. Her legs were long and brown and well-muscled. Her cheekbones were high, her lips full, her eyes dark as bottomless wells, sparkling with the last rays of the sun. Long, black hair that was impossibly lustrous hung down to her waist. A scent of lilacs and honeydew came off her.

Johnson and Kreese went right to her.

There was no man who could not have been seduced by her beauty and enchanted by the siren call of her voice.

"No!" Pinley warned them. "Keep away from her! Keep away!"

But they no longer heard him, and as they got close to her outstretched arms, Pinley saw the feral appetite in her eyes. How those hands with their long, lovely fingers were scaly and thorny, the claws of a beast. Then she reached out to them, and they screamed as her claws opened their guts. Both men collapsed, blood seeping into the snow and steam rising from their opened bellies. The woman that was not a woman at all but something grinning with fangs, cadaverous and crawling with snakes, held their entrails like the strings of marionettes as she dragged them through the snow, closing in on Pinley.

He fired three times.

And in each muzzle flash he saw her change into a crotaline, slithering thing that lusted for his blood.

Screaming away his mind, he dropped in the snow, and when her shadow fell over him, it was cold as ice in a grave. Her smell was that of roses rotting in a sealed tomb.

Then her hands were on him.

20

On his belly, McComb lowered his lantern down.

Lord in heaven…what sort of place was this?

He saw more bones and rocks, but knew there was something revelatory awaiting him in that pit. Posting Five Wolves and Snake-Hawk above, he and Cheevers dropped down there. They fell maybe ten feet, and there was another cavern just off to the right.

Cheevers carried the lantern, and in a small, cell-like alcove, there was a sarcophagus. Bones and skulls, putrefied furs and skins were heaped around it. Strange pictographs and writings were etched into the walls. The sarcophagus was cut from the corrugated stump of some gigantic, primordial tree and propped against the wall like a mummy case. It was elaborately carved with serpents and devil-faces, glaring eyes and writhing bodies, mystical formulae.

McComb went to it.

He knew, God yes, *knew* it belonged to Silent Crow, the architect of this atrocity. He put his hands on it, and his fingers crackled with blue arcs of static electricity. It did not feel like wood, but like hide, like skin. It was moist and supple and warm, pulsing beneath his fingers like living tissue.

"Help me," he said.

Cheevers set the oil lantern down and came to him. Together they hooked their fingers beneath the lip of the lid, pulling and grunting. Sweat ran down their faces, and their breath was expelled in frosty clouds.

And then—

That wicked, disembodied chanting reverberated through the passages and honeycombed tunnels, raging louder, rolling through the subterranean netherworld like awful thunder. It had potential and grim momentum.

Cheevers and McComb stared at each other with wide, unblinking eyes.

They could hear echoing sounds now. Footsteps, dragging sounds, screams and shrieks and gunfire. There was no more time, no more time at all. They had been lucky thus far, but that was drawing to a close now. The Skull-Eaters were waking up, and the soldiers were dying. A sickening wave of heat rolled through McComb's belly as he saw his own grisly death play out before his eyes.

The ghost buffalo was close now.

Together then, straining and pulling…the lid came off in their fingers, clattered ominously to the floor.

Silent Crow.

Just like the others…not even a man.

His tree-trunk casket was filled with a wet, green heat. Tendrils of steam wafted into the air with a hot, fermented odor of malarial swamps and rotting leaves. Roots and tubers and shoots grew from the casket, in and out of him.

"Dear God," Cheevers said, lantern held high, painting the horror in that blossoming earthen box with sputtering tongues of murky, orange light.

Silent Crow was decked out in blackened hides and skins held together with sinew and catgut, garishly decorated with the tiny bones of birds and reptiles, dyed livid reds and yellows. His breastplate was set with claws and quills and feathers. There was a choker of jawless infant skulls at his throat, each of them burnished brown and ancient, etched with black mystical symbols. Gray, long-fingered hands were pressed over his bosom, clawed and curled. His hair was long and matted, intricately set with beads and braids and rodent bones.

And that was all bad enough, but that face swimming in shadow.…

It was made of convoluted flesh, gray and pink and raw red. It was ritually scarified, half-moon shapes sliced to the bone beneath and tattooed with glaring, horizontal white bands and black crescents beneath the hollow, sunken eyes. The skin at his forehead, chin, and cheeks was pebbly, beads having been injected into the dermis in bizarre, intricate patterns. Slats of wood or iron had been inserted beneath the flesh of his brows and lower jaw, giving him a grotesque, demonic look. A tusk of yellowed bone penetrated his nose and fed into his cheeks at either side like a ring.

Here was the face of the undead, the ghoul-king, the hell-spawn infernal—a morbid crazy-quilt of high, jutting bones, gouged hollows, and plated reticulations painted in reds and oranges, greens and blues. A face that looked, if anything, like a flesh and blood representation of a tribal fetish mask.

McComb brought up his Colt .44, pressed the barrel to that lewd face.

And Silent Crow woke up.

His eyes became blazing, yellow orbs of hell-fire with pinprick pupils. With a demented laugh, he jumped out of the casket, knocking McComb aside and taking hold of Cheevers. Standing now, he was even more hideous. Towering and gaunt, seemingly stitched together and surgically sewn, the sleeves of his hide shirt were tacked with human scalps from wrist to shoulder, flaps of black hair dangling like fringe.

Cheever was powerless in his grip.

The flesh around Silent Crow's mouth had been slit carefully away in an irregular oval, blackened gums revealed and a mutiny of overlapping teeth filed sharp as pikes.

McComb let out a mad cry and fired at the medicine man three times. The balls blew holes in him, clouds of dust and filth fuming out.

Then Cheevers dropped the lantern.

The chamber was plunged into a darkness that was tight and suffocating.

McComb shouted, cried out, expelling terror from his mouth.

Cheevers made a gasping, strangling sound, and then McComb heard his bones snapping wetly, his blood splashing to the earth, the nauseating noise of his skull coming apart. Then teeth on bone…and a sucking sound.

McComb began shooting wildly, the muzzle flashes burning in his retinas. He bumped into walls, fell over rocks, crawled madly about, trying to find a way out. He plain panicked and was not ashamed of it.

Then light.

Five Wolves was there.

Snake-Hawk at his side.

Silent Crow bounded out to meet them. Snake-Hawk, feeling the hot blood of his race, plunged at him with his hunting knife, and Silent Crow nearly took his head off with a slash of his claws. Then Five Wolves let out a cry and fired his Hawkens with one easy, smooth motion. The .50 caliber ball drilled Silent Crow right in the chest, lifting him up and tossing him ten feet. He let out the shrilling cry of a hundred screeching voices and rose back up, unstoppable, relentless. He dove at them, his mouth filled with wolflike fangs.

Horrors of War

It was then that McComb remembered the pistols in his hands and used them.

He put two .44 caliber slugs into Silent Crow, and that was enough to drive him to his knees, and he skidded on the earth. He looked up at them with his corpse mask of a face, clawed, yellow fingers reaching out for them. A blood that was black and foaming exploded from his mouth as he screamed at them with a vile, shocking hatred that was poison to its roots.

McComb emptied his pistols into him.

Five Wolves brought his tomahawk down with everything he had. And with such force it lifted him off his feet. The tomahawk cleaved open the crown of Silent Crow's skull, black blood and worms and a gray slime of brains bubbling down his face. And then he came right up, knocked McComb aside and lashed out at Five Wolves with one fist. Five Wolves brought his arm up to protect himself, and that fist snapped his wrist clean as a dry twig. He went down, and Silent Crow became a seething swarm of coffin-flies and retreated into a nearby tunnel.

"Are you all right?" McComb asked.

"My arm...but I can fight."

There was no time to mourn Snake-Hawk.

They went into the passage. It was small and cramped. McComb vaulted through it, knowing he was down to knife and tomahawk himself now. Once again crawling and slinking and worming his way through dirt and rocks and then finally snow, digging through it like a rabbit until...until his fingers broke through a crust of ice, and the world was above him, cold air in his face.

Somehow, he was above the cliff now, a sheer drop to either side. He could see the picket guards below. They had been eviscerated, their horses disemboweled.

McComb cried out into the night, into the blizzard and setting sun.

He was not alone.

Silent Crow was coming up behind him, a million tortured and possessed voices chanting his return. He came forward in a churning storm of trailing hair and flapping hides, mummified animal parts and scalps, jagged teeth chattering, blood smeared over the mask of his face. The tomahawk was still sunk in his head.

McComb pulled his knife, slashed and cut.

And Silent Crow sank a tomahawk into his shoulder, dropping him into the snow. As he came on for the death blow, chattering and cackling and speaking in a dozen discarnate voices, McComb brought the blade of his knife up with all his strength, taking Silent Crow's hand off at the wrist. He let out a deranged wail, and then there was the echoing report of a rifle, and a slug punched through his head, shattering his skull like a jelly jar.

Silent Crow broke apart.

He became moths and flapping birds and chittering insects. Fog and smoke and mist and death-smell.

Cradling a smoking Hawkens rifle in his arms, Five Wolves was there.

"It is not over, my brother," he said. "He still lives. And we shall seek him to his grave."

21

The catacombs.

High above them was another cave mouth set into a ridge of ice-locked stone. Both wounded and bleeding, but clutching knives and tomahawks in death-grips, McComb and Five Wolves moved through the snow towards the mouth. The way was marked by a drifted path set with jawless human skulls on stakes to either side. They followed them up and up, brothers in life and brothers now in war to the death.

"This is cold doings," McComb said under his breath.

The storm had ended, and the breeze was light, but cold and whispering. The stars had come out overhead as had the moon, their light reflected in the crust of the snow.

As McComb neared the cave mouth, he saw it was lit up inside by a guttering, yellow illumination. He ducked inside with Five Wolves at his heel, both bleeding and sore, but tense and ready for battle. What they saw was a winding catacomb that seemed to twist on and on into the mountain. Its floor was littered with human bones and frozen slime and scraps of flesh gone black. The walls were tacked with the leathery skins of men, women, and children. All of them had been slit free in a single pelt and tacked up, like the hides of bears. Many were so impossibly old that they had split open and were

215

flaking away like rotting shrouds. This was the slaughterhouse of man-eaters, a human charnel barrow.

Torches were lit and set out at irregular intervals. The light was dull and flickering, the air greasy with smoke and the stench of roasted human meat.

And as they pushed deeper into the labyrinth, the reason for that became quite apparent. Huge pits had been hewn into the uneven rock floor. They smoldered with an offensive stench, filled with the blackened bones of men. McComb looked down into one, seeing a ribcage basket, a shattered skull, a pelvic girdle, assorted tiny bones that may have belonged to children. Smoke rose up from them, like steam from a witch's cauldron.

Five Wolves began to sing a mournful dirge beneath his voice.

McComb went tense as a spring.

The trophies of the kill were everywhere. Mummified human heads hung in clusters of eight and ten, cables of gut inserted through their ears and pulled clean through, the heads knotted together like beads on a necklace. All of them shriveled, gray, and eyeless. These clusters—and there were many—swung back and forth on hemp ropes tied off above. Limbs that were brown and smoked dangled amongst them. Skeletons gone yellow with age were wired together and likewise suspended.

"Graveyard," McComb said. "A stinking, goddamn graveyard, I'm thinking."

"Your words are true," Five Wolves said. "The world become a graveyard."

There were stone slabs set out and all of them dark with old bloodstains and some that were not so old. Bits of dried tissue and meat were stuck to them, whorls of blood sprayed up over the skins on the walls.

They moved on, ducking beneath arms and legs and heads, squeezing between skeletons, kicking their way through heaped bones and skulls, many of which broke apart under their boots, like delicate crockery. The catacomb turned to the right, began to widen, and the stench of burning meat and cremated bone was simply unbearable. It made their eyes water, their throats constrict. The smoke was heavy and pungent, like river mist. The torches burned, casting a thin, yellow light that reflected off the smoke and limned the ghoulish trophies hanging from the roof.

And then before them were five or six baskets of threaded sinew. Each larger than a man and each filled with bones…human bones and animal bones—femurs and ulnas, scapulas and the slats of ribs. The skulls of adults and children stacked like bricks, but also those of wolves and beavers and bear. All of it wound up in the linked vertebrae of snakes, human arm and leg bones protruding in every which direction, like spikes.

McComb was not a man given easy to fear, but he felt like he had blundered into the lair of some cannibalistic ogre from an evil fairy tale. It was chill in the cave, but sweat had popped on his face, ran down his spine.

They slipped beneath the baskets and saw the cadavers of four women hanging over one of the firepits by nooses of hemp. They were puckered and brown and dried like jerky, slowly smoked and seasoned over the flames. They were Indian women, long tresses of black hair hanging over their faces, which were shriveled like raisins. McComb had to wander if those poor ladies were even dead when it began.

The stench was revolting.

The catacomb canted upwards and terminated into a large cavern. A great tongue of stone led out into it like a bridge and to either side, a sharp drop to a shadowy hollow that was heaped with human corpses, many fresh and bleeding, dumped atop others that were little more than skeletons in rags of skin.

"Listen," Five Wolves said.

McComb did and heard it, too. A low, coarse grunting as that of pigs rooting in the mud. And many, many of them. All grunting and snorting and squealing from below. He could hear the sounds of flesh being torn in wet flaps, of teeth gnawing on bones, of hooked fingers digging through the carcasses. He dared look down into one of the crevices and saw…he could not be sure at first…just slithering, crawling things that moved like carrion worms amongst the heaped husks. These were not the living dead, but something possibly worse. Something that was alive and fleshy.

Children.

His brain told him it could not be so, but those things down there were small and childlike in form, human maggots feeding off the dead. He saw their faces in the guttering light…greasy, smeared with gore, impossibly white with the huge black eyes of nocturnal burrowers. They were chewing on entrails and nibbling on bones, gnawing faces from skulls, scratching with scaly fingers and growling and hissing at one another, like wild dogs.

Lunacy.

McComb thought he was mad. He had suspected it for some time now, but this proved it…Five Wolves and the Osage had said that Silent Crow had a wife, Tongue-of-Serpents, a suitably vile name for the vile creature which must have given birth to those crawling ghouls below. He did not know this to be true, but in his heart, he did not doubt it.

"Look upon it no more," Five Wolves told him.

The things down there had no interest in them. They were content to feed upon the dead. Five Wolves led them farther out onto that tongue of rock that was raised above the pits below, and they found Silent Crow.

At the sight of him, sprawled on some kind of makeshift bed of bones and straw and refuse, they made ready for battle; their spirits burned brightly and made ready for the kill. But it was unnecessary.

"He's gone under," McComb said. "Nothing but clay."

Silent Crow was dead. He was sprawled like a scarecrow dropped from its bracket and seemed no more capable of life than that. The tomahawk of Five Wolves was still lodged in his skull, the crown of which was cleft clean open, an inky fluid like blood and clots of gray matter having dribbled down his hideous, ridged face. There was a great hole in his brow, the back of his head blown apart. More of that dark fluid had oozed from the stump of his wrist. And a great quantity by the looks of it…it had pooled and clotted in a great, sour-smelling puddle.

"We should burn him," McComb said.

But there was really nothing to burn him with. Five Wolves, however, had lost interest in Silent Crow. He was intrigued by something just ahead. McComb followed him further over that tongue of rock, and what he had first taken to be a solid wall of rock was no wall at all. It was a huge, threadbare tapestry of tanned human skins that had been meticulously stitched together. There had to have been dozens of bodies used, and each pelt removed in one piece, like the others on the walls. Even the hands and feet were evident, as were the stretched faces with their gaping, empty eye sockets and distorted mouths that looked to be howling like those of ghosts.

Every time that McComb thought he could witness nothing more devastating than that which he had already seen, this catacomb brought him a fresh slate of horrors.

"We've done what had to be done," he finally said. "Let's make ourselves scarce."

"No," Five Wolves told him, motioning at the tapestry with his tomahawk. "The wife of Silent Crow lives."

McComb looked at it, noticed that it was moving subtly, as if some subterranean breeze were pushing against it. But there was no breeze that he could feel. Right then, his insides squeezing together with fright, he knew that there was someone on the other side of that tapestry, and there had been since they arrived. He caught a high, sweet odor like rotting hay. It was not the stink of death exactly, but more the smell of life so profuse and juicy it was decaying from the inside out.

That's the smell of what waits behind those skins, he thought then.

But he had no more time to think as he heard a sweet and eerie singing that was female in tone. It was lilting and shrill, melodious to hear, but underneath blank and profane, and it made something run cold in both men. As they stood there, unsure, shivering, muscles pulled taut, the voice grew louder and louder, weaving a cocoon of webby dream around them.

"It is she," Five Wolves said, breaking the spell. "The wife of Silent Crow."

22

McComb shook off the paralysis of fear that had gripped him, felt horror replaced by rage: "Show yerself, ye foul, witching cunt," he called out. "We've come to do ye a godawful hurt...."

The singing stopped in mid-note.

The tapestry fluttered like a wind had glanced off it.

Then, as they stood there helplessly, a single thorny claw punctured it from the other side and slit it right open. Then something misshapen and grotesque leaped out with a shrieking cry of hatred. It was wearing ragged hides that were blackened with age and stiff with dried blood and clotted fat. One angular, black-veined breast poked out, but it was

219

wreathed in a creeping gray moss that grew out of the numerous rents in the hides and grew up over her throat in a moist, crepuscular webbing.

Tongue-of-Serpents, Silent Crow's wife and the source of his power.

Both men were momentarily shocked. McComb saw something like a woman with a yellow, blurred face that was seamed and corded and punched with holes. It was a stitched together mask, seemingly composed of many faces, animal skins, and greasy scraps of fur. Neither human nor animal, but something composed of both. Her hair was long and black and braided with rodent's bones, her hands the gnarled, black talons of a beast.

But that was all he had time to see.

For as he raised his hatchet and knife to do some killing, Five Wolves knocked him aside and let out the whooping, wild war cry of the Crow Nation: *"Hooo-kiii-hiiii!"*

He dove at the woman, and she hopped at him like an insect, ready to disembowel him. Again, battle was joined. Five Wolves slashed and hacked at her with his tomahawk, and she tore at him with her claws, her huge distorted mouth filled with gnashing fangs. Her discordant cry was inhuman and hissing, and the reason for that was immediately apparent: she was alive with snakes. They came out of her flesh like worms from pork, coiling and striking, some green-bodied and slick, others black and shining, still others reticulated and yellow-eyed. They even emerged from her whipping, black hair in a living garland of serpents like Medusa of old.

They hit Five Wolves again and again.

This all happened in a matter of seconds as McComb pulled himself off the rocky floor and found his feet. And by the time he had, Five Wolves was down. Tongue-of-Serpents had gored him viciously, and his blood still dripped from her claws. The venomous snakes that corkscrewed from her oily skin had struck him countless times. Bleeding and envenomated, he had no more fight left in him.

He wailed out his death song as she lunged in, burying her face in his throat and tearing out his jugular in a hot spray of blood that steamed in the air.

He died fast, but not without inflicting injury: for the bitch was gashed open in a dozen places, pissing the same black blood as her husband. Many of the snakes had been beheaded, but still twisted and bled. And Five Wolves' tomahawk had succeeded in opening up her belly, her entrails hanging out in cold loops.

But she was far from beaten.

McComb's turn.

She looked up at him, her mouth bursting with knifeblade teeth painted red, her nose flattened and upturned like that of a boar, her eyes those of a stuffed python: glassy and black. The snakes which nested in her coiled and struck out at him again and again. McComb spun and ducked, darted and slashed with knife and tomahawk. His blades cleaved through the bodies of striking serpents, took the bitch's left arm off at the elbow, and opened her throat up in a wash of fetid blood.

Her claws laid open his cheek, his chest. The snakes hit him again and again. But he would not go down, not until it was finished. His saving grace was his heavy beaver coat and the buckskins beneath. The fangs of the serpents could not penetrate his garments, though they managed to bite him in the hands and the face. He could feel the cool sludge of their poison in his veins.

And then she staggered and went to one knee, horribly gashed and bleeding freely. She looked up at him with her corded, yellow face and those glistening, black eyes, vomiting out ribbons of her own blood. She snarled at him, gnashed her teeth, slashed out at him with her claws. Many of her snakes were dead and hung limp, and those that still lived moved sluggishly.

McComb let out a last resounding cry, and, gripping his tomahawk with both hands, jumped in and swung it with everything he had. The blade cut right through her neck with a wet, meaty sound, tearing through tendons and ligaments and muscle, and her head toppled to the ground, still alive, still hissing and biting and glaring at him with an insane hatred. Her body tumbled at his feet, shook a few times and went still.

The evil witch was dead.

McComb fell down on his ass, gasping for breath. He was hurting bad, his blood coming out through too many openings. Had it not been for the venom that filled him, he might have been able to stitch himself up and live to tell the tale. But then again, he was not a young man.

"Not by a long chalk," he said.

He clutched the corpse of Five Wolves to him, rocking the dead Indian lovingly. He was not ashamed of the hot tears that washed down his cheeks or the girlish whimpering that scratched in his throat. Five Wolves had died for him. He had lunged out at Tongue-of-Serpents, offering his own life in one last fury of death-battle so that McComb might be spared.

"Not to be so, m' fine old friend," McComb whispered to him. "Let us make fer the Crow graveyard where I will lay ye down so ye may commune with yer ancestors and be praised for the warrior and friend ye have always been."

It took some time and some doing, but McComb dragged the corpse of his brother from the catacombs and out of the caves themselves. Amazingly, his own horse was still there. Still waiting. The others had been slaughtered... but not his.

Not part of the plan, not part of the Great Mystery.

And as he loaded Five Wolves over his saddle, he could hear the thundering hooves of the ghost buffalo getting nearer. Filled with pain that was both physical and spiritual, Crazy Snake Boone McComb rode off into the chill, blowing night.

23

When Major Lyons woke up, he was in the tunnel with Corporal Coyles.

They sat with their backs to the walls, mummies to either side descending the passage and rising above in carefully articulated rows. There were five or six arrows still protruding from the corporal's chest and belly.

"Thought you died back there, son. Thought those Skull-Eaters got you."

"I crawled off to die while they busied themselves with Pearson and Standard," he said, breathing heavily with a whistling sound. "Kept crawling, I guess. Ended up here."

Lyons nodded, touched the shattered bones of his face. "We made it, though," he said. "By God, we did."

"Yes...sir." Coyles breathed again, as if he only needed to now and then. "We sure did."

He pulled a hand-rolled cigarette out from a tin box inside his tunic. An

222

arrow had dented it, but other than that it was undamaged. He scratched a match and took a drag. In the cigarette's light, Lyons saw plumes of smoke rising from the arrow holes in his chest. Coyles didn't seem to notice or care.

"What now, Major?" he asked. "What now?"

Lyons turned to look at him, the crown of his skull bashed in, a trail of dried gray matter at his forehead. "We'll rest a bit. Just close our eyes and wait a spell…then, then we'll know."

"Sure, then we'll know," Coyles said, smoke rising from him.

Understanding, but too tired now to weep, Lyons closed his eyes, going to sleep with the rest of them in that darkening tunnel.

24

There was little life left in Boone McComb after he stitched up Five Wolves in his own buffalo robe and placed him at the foot of a burial scaffold in the Crow cemetery. It was dark and windy, flakes of snow blowing in the air. He said what words he could over his old friend and left him there, in the bosom of his people, his ancestors, leaving him alone so that his spirit guide would appear to lead him away.

He was far too weak to do anymore.

Delirious and wrenched with stabbing pains, his lungs filled with needles, he staggered through the cemetery mindlessly. In the glow of the moon, he saw families interred in their shrouds, warriors and chiefs laid out on leaning scaffolds, all gone to skeletons now.

He knew he would not see another sunrise.

His blood running hot and cold in him, he finally collapsed at the foot of a spreading and gnarled dead oak whose branches were phosphorescent with the eye of the moon upon them. It seemed a fitting place. He loved these mountains. He loved the earth and the sky, the animals and peoples. Here was where the blood of the world ran hottest and the wind blew mightiest, and here was where he would surrender to the cold and the might of death itself.

To the wounds slashed into him.

The poison in his blood.

No more rendezvous. No more hunting and trapping and scraping hides. No more venison and elk roasted over fires. No more stalking and scouting and feeling the warm, copper flesh of a young squaw writhing beneath him. No more—

Listen.

Listen, ye old, deluded fool.

Fer it comes.

He could hear the distant thundering of hooves as the ghost buffalo finally came to claim him, to gore him with its horns, and carry his soul off into the next world. McComb was shaking as the ground shook, terrified but fascinated. This was what it all led up to, this was the crowning moment of any man's life. Do not shrink from it. Do not cower and languish with superstitious fear. Embrace it. Know it. Feel it. Make it one with yourself.

Glory to that, glory to that.

The ghost buffalo had arrived. It stood not twenty feet away, a supernal luminosity coming from it that filled the graveyard with ethereal light that shifted and danced. The ghost buff was huge, its great, shaggy head raised much higher than a man stood. Its white hide bristled with muscle and sinew. Steam blew from its snorting nostrils in great misting plumes. Its great humps of meat and fat trembled. Moonlight winked off its gleaming, yellow-white horns.

What say ye, White Spike? What say ye of m' time here on this plane?

McComb asked this with his rapidly fading mind that was becoming crowded with half-remembered boyhood memories, recollections of hunts and drunks and women he had loved and friends he had honored. His brain, at this last and final moment of spiritual purity, was more crammed with useless bits of ephemera than an old maiden woman's attic. And like her, he dared not throw any of those precious things away.

"Come on, then, White Spike," he grumbled under his breath, snowflakes melting on his worn, grizzled face. "I tire of the pain and the hurt of this world."

The ground rumbled with the hammering of the beast's split-hooves as it zeroed in on him, its huge, bony skull lowered, horns ready and unleashed for the taking of lives. With one last earthly scream of bestial terror, the ghost buffalo was upon him, and its massive spikes speared him straight through the chest, piercing out of his back, scarlet and dripping. He was raised up, shaken like prey, shown the fury and rage of killing for all the killing he had done. Shown the agony of flesh in its death-throes, his entire being a strident melody of electrified nerve endings. And lastly, speared like an olive, he was drowned in his own blood and made pure again.

Then that ghostly light faded, and there was only the wind moaning through the Crow cemetery and the corpse of a man named Boone McComb leaning against a dead oak as the cold leeched the pink from his cheeks and the snow enshrouded him and made him memory. In time, only the silence of the dead.

THE PLAGUE MAIDEN

1

It was an afternoon's entertainment.

The raiders gathered in a ragged, wolf-eyed, howling pack—Tartars, Mongols, and Turkomen—as the Uriankhai elder writhed on the ground like a headless snake, a foaming slime of blood and bile hanging from his mouth in gurgling loops. Punctuated by the cries of the villagers, his own moist screams were short and guttural. A half-dozen mongrel dogs were on him, vicious, slavering, and emaciated.

Yemura laughed.

The sound of infidels dying was sweet music to his jaded ears. As a true son of the Mongol Nation, he lived for battle, for the smell of blood and the death rattle of his enemies. There was no finer music on Earth than the hammer of hundreds of hooves and the manic war cries of his soldiers, volleys of arrows whistling through the air and the clash of swords, the shrieking and pitiful, mindless pleading of the vanquished.

That was, save for the game of death before him.

As the dogs ravaged the elder, Yemura's warriors wagered on the longevity of his death. Driven to new heights of bloodlust and depravity, they bet *bashliks* of silver, enough to buy dozens of fine horses.

The Uriankhai elder died slowly in agony. It was yet another game Yemura dreamed up with his dark, sadistic creativity. The dogs had not been

227

fed in over ten days. They were starving for meat, slat-thin and desperate. It was given to them—the elder's belly was slit open, his entrails washed down with a sweet seasoning of milk and honey. Then the dogs were given their feast. All four of them had hold of his intestines now, pulling them in four different directions, snapping and tearing with white foaming mouths.

Ah, it was but simple, mindless entertainment, but the men enjoyed it. And Yemura, as their leader, their *jagutu-lin-darga,* considered it his responsibility to keep them amused when possible. And today had been a day of great amusement for one and all.

There had been some 300 inhabitants in Khorta before Yemura's warriors arrived, now there were half that number. The Mongols roared in like demons on horseback, slicing and hacking those who dared stand against them, firing arrows into the unwary and innocent, and beating down any that begged for mercy.

All in all, a successful raid.

Yemura turned his back on the elder's last moments and the shouts of his men, touring the village, making his rounds. He was a fearsome character in black, plated lamellar armor and conical iron helmet, scimitar in hand. His very image struck horror across Asia, the very apotheosis of the Mongol war machine of the 13th century. Dismembered corpses were spread in every direction like scythed wheat, the heads of women and men speared on sharpened spikes. No less than thirty Uriankhai peasants were impaled on sharpened stakes, dangling six feet off the ground, the blood still dripping from them. Dogs licked at pools of it, flies lighting off red-spattered faces.

Amidst the carnage and death, warriors in goatskin jackets with blood-smeared swords in their filthy hands gathered around fires of sheep and goat dung, roasting mutton in boiling pots. They drank steel vessels of *kumass,* an acrid brew of fermented mares' milk, and scratched at the lice which infested them. The stewed meat was a welcome change from their usual diet of sour milk, hares and rodents, half-raw partridges eaten on horseback.

The village of Khorta would no longer exist after today and Yemura found pleasure in that, in the defilement and destruction of more enemies of the Great Khan.

It was little loss.

Khorta was a sprawling collection of clustered mud huts and primitive stone structures, all of which had been crawling with packs of human dogs, Uriankhai infidels, stinking hordes of them, fly-specked things living in the collected filth of their animals. The village was hemmed in to all sides by a forest of towering reeds, cut by trails and set with curious pagan altars of piled stones.

No, it was a blight on the land and would not be missed. Yemura stood before a heaped pile of corpses, watching several of his men drag a lone woman from a hut. They raped her one after the other. Her squealing child was seized by the ankles, its head smashed against a stone wall.

"A day of plenty for all," said a wizened voice.

Yemura turned and saw the Scarred One standing there, a powerful, bow-legged bull of a man in scaled leather armor, a bloody mace in one hand. He kicked the head of a child from his path with grim amusement, fixing his leader with his one remaining eye. The other had been pierced by the lance of a Cracovian knight on the Czarna Hańcza and was little more than a closed weal of scar tissue now.

"So it has been," said Yemura.

"We have taken oxen and goats, made a cruel sport of the peasants, but the treasure is but a fable."

Yemura bristled. The only reason he had diverted his men from more lucrative pursuits and come to this godforsaken wasteland was the promise of a cache of treasure hidden away in Khorta. It had supposedly been taken from the Holy Land by Christian crusaders. Gold or silver, no one knew.

"We will continue the search," he said, growing angry. "We will encamp here for two days."

"As you wish," said the Scarred One.

The sarcasm in his voice was evident. The only reason Yemura put up with him was because he was a great warrior, a veteran of countless campaigns. For this, he allowed the man's poison tongue. At least for the time being. But if it continued, he would cut it out.

2

The silence of the village elders angered the Mongol king to no end. He was not a man to be trifled with. Had he not vanquished armies of half-human, slobbering infidels from the Byzantine Empire to the Song dynasty in his meteoric climb to great heights of barbarity? Was he not known as the Black Blade of Baya'ud for the hundreds of men he had killed, the villages he had razed, the mongrel women he had ravaged and slaughtered like livestock, and the hordes of infidel children he had put to the blade?

It was so and as such, disobedience of any sort was not in his lexicon.

So when he demanded that the village elders of this dung heap known as Khorta provide him with their hidden riches and they denied knowledge of the same, it incurred his mighty wrath. It summoned the demon of vengeance from the dark, pathless wastes of his soul. Their very existence was a parasitic worm tunneling into his heart.

It took only a single wave of his hand to set things right.

A dozen of his Mongols—walking monstrosities in mail shirts and patched animal skins, reapers and death-mongers with lifeless eyes, cruel faces, and sabers in their fists—beat the elders to the ground. And not just beat, but battered and kicked, pommeling and goring them into subservience.

Still, they would not speak.

Examples they wished to be and examples they would become.

They were forced to their knees, hands tied behind their backs with ropes of catgut, heads forced down upon blocks of ancient stone.

While the villagers were held at bay by his troops, Yemura, Black Blade and corpse-maker, studied the dour faces of their loved ones, amused by their screaming voices and pleas for mercy. Grinning, he snapped his fingers.

His Mongol executioners raised bloodstained battle axes high into the air and shouted, "For the blood of the Great Khan!" and brought them down with brute animal strength. The blades, keen as razors, chopped through offered throats, severing muscle, tendon, artery, and vertebrae. Gouts of blood erupted high into the air, heads spinning to the dusty ground.

As shrieking, mindless screams ripped through the afternoon heat, Yermura laughed with deranged glee, seizing two heads by the hair. He held them aloft for all to see. Blood still spurted from their throats. Grimaces of horror twisted their lips like sun struck earthworms. And their eyes, only just touched by the glaze of oncoming death, rolled madly in their bloodless faces.

For a moment.

Then two.

As life ceased, he tossed the heads to the starving wild dog packs for sport.

3

Yemura moved towards the outskirts of the village where the hide tents of his soldiers had been pitched. Here he found his own tent, a black felt yurt of finely-woven yak hair. He urinated on the body of an infidel and stepped inside, sealing the skin doorway. Sighing, he removed his armor and weapons, collapsing on a cushion stuffed with horsehair.

His concubine, Khulgana, sat across from him, greasing her braid with rancid fat dipped from a pot. She came to him immediately, removing the half-*niqab* veil that covered her nose and mouth. Only in his presence would she reveal the lower half of her face. She offered him a plate of cold mutton and horseflesh which he did not want and a cup of black *airag* which he drained immediately.

"Many are my woes, my little mouse," he said, sipping from a second cup of the sour alcoholic beverage. "A man only has so many years to weave his destiny and the failures are abundant."

"The treasure?"

"Yes."

"But it was only a story."

Yes, a twice-told tale that he, Yemura, believed because he needed to believe it. In her dark eyes, he saw that she did not approve of the destruction of the village. She would never say so for he would have beaten her, laid her back raw with a horsehair whip, but she was thinking it, of course. He saw that much. Her morals and ethics, thinly concealed, were a never-ending source of irritation to him. He had bought her from a Turkic Kipchak slaver because she pleased his eye and satisfied his body, but slowly, quite unintentionally, he had grown to depend on her and, perhaps, even love her as a man like him *could* love.

"There will be other conquests, other days of glory," she said.

He did not reply to this. It was what she told him everyday, conditioned

231

by his brutality to tell him that which he wished to hear even though her eyes betrayed her.

He stroked his mustache, the tips of which extended beyond his jawline. "You do not approve of what has happened, do you, mouse?"

"The business of war is not my business," she said, very diplomatically, flashing her seductive eyes at him. "I am but a woman."

He laughed. *Ah, if that's all you were, my mouse.* "You are a woman who is being ordered to speak your mind."

"At what consequence?"

He swallowed the rest of the airag, wincing. "Speak, mouse."

The flickering light of the firepot played over her olive skin. "What would I tell you, the master soldier? The conqueror and vanquisher of many peoples?" That darkness in her eyes seemed to fill her now, describing her. "I can only say that in the village where I was born, there was one belief that no one ignored or dared make light of: that the harm you do in this life will be visited tenfold upon you in your last hours."

Yemura ground his teeth together. Heathen wench, what could she know of his destiny? The bones had long been cast. He had been trained for one thing his entire life: to conquer. There was nothing else. He was not a farmer, not an artisan, not a peasant, but a *warrior.* Before he even took his first steps, he had become one with his horse. As a boy, he was taught herding, hunting, and the warrior's creed that might always made right. He was a blooded member of the Mongol Nation. He feared no man, no god, but the Great Khan himself. His was but one voice of many tribes and clans that had risen from lowly beginnings to rule the Earth. From the windblown high steppes to the arid deserts of Mongolia to the fertile lands of the Rus, the confederation of Uyghar, Tartars, Huns, Hsien Pei, Turkomen, and Hsuing Nu had defeated every army thrown against them. Their way of life was the horse, archery, and the sword. There was no other.

He swallowed another cup of *airag.* She could never understand his ambitions. He commanded a force of 100 men, but he saw the day when it would be a *minqan* of a 1,000 and then a *tumen* of 10,000. And even that was the only the beginning. In the depths of his black, beating heart, he dreamed of becoming another Attila, of uniting all the tribes of the East into a single cohesive, deadly force that would sweep across not just the Great Wall, but into the very heart of Europe itself.

"Ah, mouse, you would have me die of old age like a pig in the straw and deny me my rightful place within the ranks of the imperial elite of the Khanate," he told her, practicing a tolerance that he was not known for. "You worry over the death of these simple animals like an old woman prophesying doom…but am I not a son of the great Khan and is it not my destiny to kill?"

Khulgana did not argue the point. If he said it was so, then it must be so. Yet, he could see that she did not believe this. In fact, she gave him a look of pity that incensed him.

He finished his *airag* and donned his armor. Sheathing his sword, he stepped from the yurt. Khulgana watched him leave, the pity in her eyes replaced by something closer to revulsion.

4

The Mongols were the greatest horsemen, the deadliest mounted warriors ever to thunder across the Asiatic steppe. Something the sniveling peasants of Khorta learned when Yemura's force charged into the village.

Now, they would learn that lesson yet again.

A group of some fifty women and children were herded into the village square like cattle paraded for auction. Mongol archers circled around them at a distance, hooting and shrilling and swearing their blood oaths to the Great Khan. Man and horse alike were armored in black leather scales. Though the innocents, of course, were of no threat, the archers practiced their craft as if they were enemy troops—circling them, pressing in on them, swarming them.

Like the Mongols themselves, their horses were small yet powerful, rampaging, highly-disciplined beasts bred for warfare.

The archers rode at top speed, standing on stirrups while guiding their animals with their knees. Each man had a quiver of sixty arrows and as the villagers cried out for mercy, they brought up their compound bows and fired shaft after shaft in a withering, deadly arrow storm.

Arrows punched through skulls in explosions of pink and gray mucilage. They punctured chests and riddled bellies and penetrated eye sockets.

Horrors of War

In less than a minute, the innocents were on the ground, wriggling in a communal pool of blood and anatomy. Very few arrows did not find their mark. And once in, their barbed heads were nearly impossible to remove without tearing free huge chunks of meat and gristle.

The archers immediately dismounted, jumping on their prey with horn-handled knives and slitting throat after throat. They accomplished this without hesitation, seeing no difference between a maid of fifty and a child of five years.

5

With two of his guards at his side, Yemura sought the yurt of the seer, the *qam*, the shaman who might divine the true nature of things. Her name was Fatima and she was a *udagan*, a female soothsayer, well adept at shamanistic ritual and practice. She routinely conversed with the spirits of the dead, held congress with frightening Earth and Sky elementals. She was one of Yemura's most trusted advisors and he counted on her for not only prophecy, but to heal the sick and counsel him in all matters.

Her tent was dim, lit only by flickering candles, the air smoky with incense and smelling of exotic spices. There were chests of dried herbs and vessels of curious liquids, boxes of dried insects and the ashes of crematoriums in stoppered bottles. Petrified birds, monkeys, and rodents dangled about her on strings of gut. Several cages held poisonous reptiles that hissed and slithered. She used them for divination and made the dreaded arrow poison, *mogain khoran* from their venom, particularly the steppe viper and adder.

"You have come seeking my insight, oh Lord Yemura?" she asked in her silken voice. "Then sit by me and we shall begin."

He stripped off his armor, helmet, and weapons, sitting across from her clad in his silks and woolens. She produced a fatty balm from a tin and daubed his forehead with it. It burned instantly. He did not like this place because he feared her power. He had known many shamans and most of them only told their masters what they wished to hear, but it was not so with Fatima. She spoke the truth, regardless how disagreeable it was, and was invariably correct.

As she stared into the fire, sweat ran down his face. It was stuffy and close in the tent, nearly claustrophobic, yet the heat did not bother her even though she wore a traditional heavy black *abaya*, a flowing cloak that covered her from head to toe. Only her eyes were visible and they were black as midnight, piercing as the fangs of a cobra.

He knew little of her other than the fact that she came from a long line of *qams* and had been taken during the Mongol campaign against the Khwārazmian Empire many years before. Although her wisdom was unimpeachable, she was no soft aesthete, but a wolf that regularly ate the meat of horses and dogs and had no scruples about eating human flesh when none other was available. She considered the afterbirth of a mare a delicacy.

"Throw the bones, old one," Yemura said. "My heart is uneasy. Dispel my fears or justify them as you would."

She nodded her head, muttering prayers, or perhaps curses, in ancient forgotten tongues under her breath. She reached into a hide bag and removed the ankle bones of sheep and the skeletal digits of monkeys. They were painted with ritual signs. She shook them in her hands, then cast them over a red felt rug.

"Ah," she said, touching them, running her long fingers over each, reading portent and omen. "Ah...*ah, such a gathering of darkness.*" She described symbolic patterns in the air with her hands. "It is not good, my Lord."

"Tell me."

She gripped his arm with ice-cold fingers. "What is cast is cast, what is thrown cannot be undone. There is great sorrow in this place and a dark evil witchery that gathers around us as death gathers around an old man in his final moments. I see terror and pestilence and a vile hunger that cannot be quenched, not in this world and perhaps, not in the next."

Yemura forced himself not to shiver with the fear she had seeded in his soul. "You speak in riddles, old one. Tell me what I need to know."

"Your way is dark and your path is the curse of the grave. You must put aside your greed and ride from this place before the circle closes. Once closed, there shall be no way out."

"No way out?" He laughed at the very idea. "And who is it that would stop me, old one? Who would dare stand in my way?"

She shook her head. "I have read the stars for you, my Lord, and consulted the entrails on many occasions. Why do you doubt me now?"

"Because you speak of enigmas. I cannot understand your words. Speak plainly."

She threw a sprinkle of powder into the fire that caused the flames to blaze high like licking green tongues. "My words have been spoken. The truth is in them."

He tried to get more out of her, but the more questions he asked, the darker her predictions became until she quivered with them.

But as he left her yurt, her predictions were obvious: the treasure he sought would be his undoing.

Outside the tent, he spat at the earth. "I will not be denied that which is mine."

6

There were tortures and then there were tortures.

Amongst the clan of Khorta, there was a woman of some repute named Gorhag, a healer, midwife, and, it was learned, a powerful voice within the village. It was she who goaded the lowly sheep to resist the relentless force of Yemura's tribe. And when she was caught attempting to incite a riot of sorts, she did not back down or recant her words that the Mongols were inbred dogs who worshipped a fecal swine god.

Not even when she was stripped and beaten.

Or branded with hot irons.

Horse-whipped or slit with blades.

When she was brought before Yemura to answer for her crimes, she spit in his face. Every man present grew uneasy because his malevolent temper was legendary. They had once seen him dismember a Uyghur with nothing but a hunting knife after suffering an insult.

But this day, he was calm.

He secretly wished this Uriankhai hag would submit to his will, because he had use of a hissing reptile like her. He admired her strength, her audacity, her verve. But since there was no breaking her by conventional means, a special sport needed to be made of her.

Upon his orders, an ox was brought forth and killed with a blow from a mace to the head. Under the Scarred One's tutelage, the beast was hollowed—organs, entrails, and bones cleaned out, the carcass scraped clean as possible inside.

Gorhag, still screaming obscenities at the invaders, was bound hand and ankle and shoved inside the carcass. All orifices of the beast were sewn shut, save for a four-inch incision in its belly and the hole which Gorhag's head poked from. The ox was hoisted up by the neck where it swung back and forth two feet off the ground.

Then Fatima was called for. She brought two cages of squeaking, squealing rats that had been starved into madness for several weeks. The crazed, voracious rodents were pushed into the carcass through the incision, all thirty of them. Then the incision was stitched shut. It was an ancient torture and an effective one. In their hunger, the rats would eat anything. In their fear, they would chew through whatever stopped their escape.

It began immediately.

The rats bit and clawed her from within, gorging themselves on her flesh. Her head thrashed from side to side as she screamed in agony. It took her nearly two hours to die.

7

"I have brought you yet another amusement," said the Scarred One, indicating an old woman in the dirt. "She was found in a chamber beneath a hut, hiding from us." He turned away from the other men, speaking quietly. "We believe her to be a witch of sorts."

Yemura swallowed. Like all Mongols, he was immured in ancient tribal superstitions, fearing witches and their spells, the terrible powers they could cast at will. And particularly today in the light of Fatima's prophecy.

"And why do you think that?"

"The chamber she resided in. There were symbols of a devilish nature scratched into the walls." The Scarred One studied her with his single narrowed eye. "She was drinking blood from a vessel fashioned from the skull of an infant."

A blood-drinking, child-murdering witch? Yemura did not like it. He sensed the despair and grim prophecy Fatima had forecast becoming a reality. He could not allow it. He would have this witch decapitated, her remains put to the flame.

"She claims information."

"Of what nature?"

"The nature of treasure."

Yemura felt his spirits lift. His heart began to beat again and the blood ran hot in his veins. His mouth watered. If he could find it, the tribute he would pay his superiors would grant him the first of many steps in his ascendency. This witch might live another day.

He stared down at her. She was a withered thing wearing rags of kidskin that crawled with beetles. Her face was sallow and sagging, pocked with open sores. One eye was milky white with a cataract, the other amazingly bright and cognizant. A smell of urine and feces wafted from her, but was certainly no more unpleasant than the stench of the village itself, the unburied human remains, and the Mongols themselves, none of which had seen soap and water in many months.

"This is Lord Yemura," the Scarred One said. "He is your benefactor if you tell him of what he seeks and your executioner, if you do not."

"Speak," Yemura said.

The old woman studied him with much trepidation. It was obvious that she knew she was a vole in a snake pit. The Mongols struck fear into all peoples of those ancient lands and Lord Yemura's love of torture and human sport was well-known.

She licked her yellowed teeth, smiling with lips split open by the dryness. "I can only tell you that which I know, my Lord," she said. "That which I know to be true."

"So, speak, you old whore," the Scarred One ordered her.

Groups of soldiers were massing now, intrigued by the idea of treasure *and* at what her punishment might be if she did not tell their master what he wished to know. They were a disparate, unsavory lot in fur breeches and Mongol boots. Some wore cuirasses of leather armor or shirts of mail, still others dressed in long woolen *deels* or dirty gowns of dog skin. They sported fur caps and Tartar helmets, sabers and spears, many with compound bows and bark quivers of arrows. They were men used to death and they admired morbid creativity of the sort that their commander routinely offered them.

Like starving livestock anticipating their daily feed, they grew excited, murmuring.

"I thirst," she said. "Water would lubricate my throat and loosen my tongue which is as dry as dung."

Yemura was amazed at her boldness. Here she was, scant seconds away from the blades that would chop her into dog meal, yet she had the audacity to ask favors.

Sighing, he motioned to the Scarred One who uncorked a leather water bottle and offered it to the old sow. She sipped slowly, perhaps expecting poison. Then licking her lips and realizing its purity, she emptied the bottle, water trickling down her pitted chin.

"Your kindness is appreciated," she said, settling back on her haunches. "So…you have heard of a treasure, have you? Spoils and riches? Oh, *ha, ha, ha,* so it is true. The treasure is here. It is worth the riches of all men. A treasure like no other…if you can find it."

Yemura gripped the pommel of his scimitar. "Old whore, I will have your head! I will peel your skin! I will sew rats up in your belly! You do not dare play games with me!"

"No, no, my Lord! Not games! Not games!" She shook her head vehemently. "What you seek is underground! As you found me in a chamber so shall you find it! It waits for you! It awaits the hand of the righteous! It awaits *your* hand, oh master." She held a single finger to her withered lips. "But it is a secret. One that even I cannot tell you for the location of the treasure is a mystery even to me. But it is here. You must find it."

Yemura did not care for the unknown and enigmatic. Such things enraged him. In this place, this festering asshole of the world, he was Khan. He considered his options. He could have the old witch tortured until she spoke the truth. Her skin could be peeled slowly. Her fingers could be chopped off. He could have her burned, roasted slowly over a pit of coals, or given to the dogs.

Pulling him aside, the Scarred One said, "Now that we know there are chambers beneath, perhaps we can search them out and if we find nothing, we can make a terrible sport of her."

Yes, that was reasonable. There was always time to kill the witch. He must proceed slowly. The treasure must be found.

"Very well. Set the men to searching. Those who find what I seek will be well rewarded." Yemura approached the old woman. "If the treasure is not found, I will have your life."

She smiled, cackling in a low voice. "Have no fear, my Lord, it shall be yours. What you seek awaits you and no other."

"You had best hope so."

He had already decided to flay her alive. To surgically strip the flesh from her body, then rub the raw meat beneath with rock salt. Her screams of agony would be sweet music.

8

Ten village men that had defied Yemura's orders that all weapons be turned over to his men were brought before him. He liked to believe that he was not a barbarian, not a man without a conscience or scruples. He was no animal, he told the guilty men. He offered them their only means of staying alive: they must swear allegiance to him and join the Mongol nation.

"You are fighters, yes? It is in your blood to raise steel against your enemies? Then join us now."

Several seemed to be considering it, even though it was obvious they held the Mongols in the lowest of esteem (perhaps ranking them somewhat above poisonous spiders but certainly beneath rutting hogs). That was, until Yemura told them that to belong there must be a blood allegiance to him and the Great Khan. It would be quite simple: each man would have to kill a villager, preferably a woman or child.

"You see, I am not the beast you believe me to be. Now choose your victims."

None would, of course, so Yemura's offer was rescinded. The ten, guilty of crimes against the omnipotent Khanate, were stripped and hung by the feet from a high rack used in the drying of hides. So that their screams would not offend Yemura's delicate constitution, their tongues were yanked from their mouths with tongs and cut free at the roots. One of the soldiers

240

gathered them, threading them onto a cord of sinew which he wore proudly as a necklace.

Bets were placed with shekels of Persian silver.

Which man would bleed out first? Silver changed hands. It was collected in a pot. Then without further ado, all ten throats were cut simultaneously. Afterwards, there was much drinking and celebrating. The winner, a lowly Yugur dressed in the lice-infested skins of wild dogs, was able to buy himself a fine shirt of mail.

It was a good day.

9

So, it began. Yemura's men made a highly intensive, careful search of the village of Khorta. None were excepted. They thundered amongst the many mud huts and crumbling stone edifices of the village, climbing over rooftops and exploring barrows and holes, peering down the mouths of wells and sliding into cramped crawl spaces. They had been promised great rewards if they found what their master sought. It was incentive and inducement. They knew that Yemura could be incredibly cold and calculating, brutal and violent, but they also knew he could be generous when pleased.

As they mounted their search, he lay in his yurt, drinking, eating, dreaming of great conquests and riches that would soon be his. Khulgana watched him as she always watched him.

"What is on your mind, mouse?" he asked her after a time.

She did not speak immediately. He did not believe it was because she had no words, but, probably, because she had too many. She chose them carefully, rolling them about in her mind and over her tongue. She was lovely with her shining black braids, high cheekbones, thrusting breasts, and her smooth olive skin. Again, he was struck by the improbable notion that he might love her.

"Well?"

She licked her lips slowly, not out of rising passion but as if to wet them so her words would flow more easily. "I wonder what Fatima told you," she said. "You are troubled and I sense it."

He sipped more *airag*. "She speaks in riddles and couches her meaning in

241

paradox. There is great woe unto me if I seek the treasure." He waved that away. "If it is so, then the bones of my fate have already been cast."

"You do not fear her portent?"

"I fear nothing, my mouse. I inspire fear; I do not shrink from it."

He knew she didn't believe that anymore than he believed it himself, but it was important that he conduct himself like a khan. He was the wind that shakes the bush, not the bush that trembles in its blow. One sign of weakness from him and his men would become unmanageable. They respected cunning and strength, but despised soft hearts and flaccid leadership.

"Fatima is often right."

He laughed dryly. "Yes, but she has been wrong on occasion. Let this be such an occasion."

10

Despite the scale of carnage to his people, the last of the village elders still would not submit. Yemura's demands were quite simple: he wanted the treasure. If it existed—and it certainly must exist, in his thinking—then it was owed him by birthright. As a Mongol warlord, that which he saw was his for the taking. All peoples must bow down before him. They were animals that existed to be exploited and enslaved. And the surviving elder was proving to be a difficult animal, one that needed breaking like a horse.

"You have but minutes to live, old one," Yemura told him. "I have come for the treasure hidden in this shit pile and I shall have it. I have no patience with dogs who stand in my way. Now, will you give me what is mine?"

The elder refused to reply.

"Very well, then. Let me convince you of my sincerity, my determination."

The elder's wife was named Chimeg and she was brought forth. He began to ask forgiveness immediately, but it did him no good. Only the treasure would sate Yemura. Nothing else existed for him. Fatima was called for again. From her collection of venomous reptiles, an Egyptian asp was brought forth. She handled it carefully as its hood spread in threat. She placed it in a burlap bag which was then pulled over Chimeg's head and knotted around her throat.

The snake, irritable and predacious by nature to begin with, was frightened

242

by the proximity of her face and began to strike at her without hesitation. It sank its fangs into her lips, eyes, cheeks, and tongue.

But even as she lay dying on the ground, the elder refused to submit. He seemed, in fact, more intractable than ever. Yemura was at the end of his patience. He screamed. He raged. One did not defy his iron will, particularly not a dirt-grubbing infidel like the elder.

If he wished to be peeled like an apple, then so be it.

In the skilled hands of an artisan, a knife can do many things. It can carve, it can render. It can even heal and lance. But in the hands of a sadist, it can only create screams. And so it was for the last of the Uriankhai elders. Yemura, surrounded by his eager savants of torture, used his bone-handled dagger with gruesome enthusiasm. While his bound victim screamed his mind away, the Black Blade of Baya'ud practiced his well-honed art of butchery, exacting agony for the disobedience shown him.

He cut.

He sliced.

He slit.

He punctured and perforated.

Carefully, with great exacting diligence, he peeled wafer-thin sections of skin from the elder's chest, throat, and thighs. He gouged free yellow globs of fat from his midsection and speared a single eyeball after slitting the lid free. With a violent corkscrewing of his wrist, he plucked the eye from its socket and displayed it to the other dogs of war by the bloody tissue of the optic nerve. Then with another twisting motion, he cut the elder's nose off in a single bloody flap of cartilage, tossing it and the eyeball and stem to the snarling wild dog pack that was ever-present. The dogs trailed the Mongols from siege to siege and massacred village to village like sharks following a ship, always certain to get their fill of human meat.

By that point, the elder lost consciousness, hanging limply by the ropes that bound his wrists. His face and torso were a grisly display. Ice-cold well water brought him around again for a fresh slate of horrors.

Yemura, following a brief swallow of wine to refresh himself, wasted no time.

Horrors of War

Sharpening his blade against a stone and wiping droplets of blood from his fists and cheeks, he flensed the elder's face, immune to the man's mounting hysterical screams. He peeled him from forehead to chin, taking his flesh down layer by layer, epidermis to dermis to deeper subcutaneous tissue, until his knife scraped against the skull beneath with a terrible grinding sound that made even his soldiers queasy.

By then, the elder had passed out again.

He came around when Yemura took his tongue. His mind was mostly gone by then, so the Mongol chieftain took his other eye as tribute.

The Mongol tribe pushed in closer now because they did not want to miss the penultimate act—the emasculation of the elder.

With Yemura's unflinching eye for detail, it took some time.

11

"Excuse my interruption, oh Khan, but something has been found and it defies description."

"Tell me," said Yemura, feeling revelation in his bones.

The Scarred One was disturbed. There could be no doubt of it. He was a seasoned warrior, a war horse of countless campaigns from Yunnan to Thrace. Yemura had never seen him alarmed and certainly not frightened. He charged into battle with steel in his fist and blood in his mouth against the most overwhelming odds…but here, in this dried-up, desolate scab of a village, he was scared.

Yemura was certain of it.

And regardless of how he plied him with questions, he would only shake his head at something far beyond his experience.

Together, they moved through the village to the far outskirts where soldiers were gathered outside a strange hut with a triangular roof. They were a restless lot, studying the ground, whispering to one another.

"What sort of foolishness is this?" Yemura demanded to know.

The Scarred One led him inside, pointing to a hidden passage that led below. It was discovered beneath a makeshift goat's hair bed.

"The men," he said. "I cannot compel them to go back down there. They are frightened."

244

Yemura had had enough. First, the Scarred One acting like a superstitious old woman and now his warriors had become scared little boys.

"There will be a retribution for this," he said. "I will go down first, but you will order the men to follow…if they do not, I'll have their heads."

The Scarred One bowed and nodded.

Exasperated and irate, Yemura took the steps down, grumbling. Halfway there, he paused.

There was a sound.

The weeping of a woman.

What? Another old hag-witch? He had had his fill. Any that stood in his way now would die. The passage was dark, suffocating. Something winged brushed against his face and he slashed at it with his sword.

"Bring a torch down here, you idiot!" he shouted, his voice echoing into subterranean depths.

He took another step down followed by yet another. Something crawled up his leg, tiny claws scraping against armor. He reached down to slap it away and cried out with disgust—it was plump and hairless, throbbing hotly against his hand.

"The torch!"

Now there was a smell he knew quite well, that of death. But not of a single lich, but mass death, of hundreds of rotting, maggoty bodies. It blew into his face like a breath from a tomb. Two soldiers came down bearing flaming torches. The firelight illuminated the passage, shadows crawling over the walls. Their faces were constricted with terror. Whatever was down here terrified them, but he knew that he terrified them just a little bit more.

Now Yemura heard—breathing.

It could be nothing else. A dry, terrible rattling of tubercular lungs. He heard squeaking, mewling sounds that set his flesh crawling. He would not show fear before his men. He would lead them as he had always led them… yet, he could not deny the mounting fear inside him that made him shiver, made his hand shake on his scimitar.

Now the passage ended, opening up into a large chamber hewn from solid rock. He saw something like a crude altar and…and, *dear God, what sort of madness was this?* A girl of maybe twelve or thirteen was chained to it, a cadaverous thing white as a slug, bones thrusting beneath a veneer of skin like the rungs of a ladder. Blowflies crawled over her. They nested in her hair and gusted from the black hole of her mouth in dark, buzzing clouds. Her corpse-white flesh was set with bulbous sores and festering ulcers. It looked soft as the skin of a brown apple. Though she should have been dead, she lived, staring out at him with shining white eyes like slimy frog spawn.

All of which was bad enough—but at her feet were dozens of twisted black forms: the corpses of infants rotting into mulch, some little more than collections of fine, pathetic bones, and others swollen and green.

"What you seek, I contain the secret of," the girl said. Yemura was impervious to suffering, immune to death. But what he saw before him filled him with crawling horror. The children…why were there dead children at her feet?

Yet, if this persecuted, victimized wench knew of the treasure, then surely it was worthwhile to release her from her bondage. Perhaps the elders kept her trapped in this sewer of human filth so she would not tell what she knew.

"Cut her free," he ordered.

The men looked at him. Why, they were terrified. Both of them were trembling.

"If I have to repeat myself, you forfeit your lives."

They handed him their torches. They stepped forward, the brittle bones of children breaking beneath their boots. Both of them made sobbing sounds. They could not cut the chains, but they did the next best thing, yanking them from the walls.

She was free.

"Now I give to you all that I have," she said.

What happened then was a reeling nightmare, a hallucinogenic madness that taxed Yemura's brain. The flyblown girl stepped forward and the dead infants at her feet *lived*—they moved, slithered, crawled, opening bleary yellow eyes and mewling from cracked gray mouths. From them were born dozens and dozens of pink crawling things, hairless fetal rats that crept over her, covering her in a busy feeding swarm.

Now the two soldiers began to shake and writhe, crying out in gurgling voices as black-red freshets of blood poured from their mouths. Their faces went blue, lips splitting open, eyes going pink as raw mince. Huge gangrenous sores erupted on their faces.

Yemura screamed and threw the torches. He scrambled up the passage, stumbling out of the hut where the Scarred One and the other soldiers waited.

"Plague," he said. "Dear God, the plague!"

But it was already spreading: men dropping, squirming on the ground as their faces went blue-black with spreading lesions and rising blood-filled abscesses which burst one after the other with coiling white worms. Black vomit spewed from their mouths. Dozens went down in a macabre, grisly chain-reaction. And those that didn't, lost their minds. Swords in hand, they chopped down the afflicted, slashing and cutting, turning on one another and hacking mindlessly until the village became a sea of blood and dismembered limbs, rolling heads and gutted torsos. Its waters washed up against the abundant corpses of the villagers.

It was going on across the village.

Even the Scarred One went down, infested and gagging out a stew of wriggling worms that slopped from his mouth in a noodly mass. Yemura raced away until he found the old woman. She had not moved. She waited there, a shriveled crone, grinning with delight. Her one good eye blazed with triumph.

"You have found her, you great fool! Or perhaps, she has found *you!*" She cackled, drool hanging from her mouth. She pointed at him with one skeletal, sallow digit. "Now you have found our treasure! Now you have released the Plague Maiden! The demon of pestilence! *Idiot conqueror!* Blind, stupid little man! Did you not know that every village for miles around has been wiped out by the plague? Only here, only in Khorta, did we thrive for we had the Maiden! She drew the plague off as a sponge absorbs water! As metal filings are drawn to a magnet, so was the plague drawn to her and away from us!"

Yemura was shocked by what she said and what he had seen. "Shut your mouth, hag! I'll have your hide for this, I'll—"

Her laughter boomed. "Oh, great conqueror! Master and commander! Subjugator! Lord of the running dogs! King of a horde of criminals, deviants, murderers, skulking sewer rats! Now you are beaten, bested, stripped of your manhood and made impotent before she who walks in the night! The hot breath of contagion! The cold chill of the grave! The foul stench of the crematory pit! Our lady of pestilence! Squirm before her, my Lord! Crawl in a lake of your own shit!" She shook with dry, derisive laughter, watching him cringe with unearthly contempt. *"She is the treasure brought to us from the dungeons of the holy land! We offered our firstborn to her as in the old days! We gave unto her, laid our bawling offerings at her feet, so that the curse would never touch us! And you have undone it, mongrel! Now reap what you have sown!"*

The hag was insane. She was a witch. A dark conjuror. Was he expected to believe that the Maiden drew the sickness from them so that they might live uncontaminated? That she was the treasure? A living, flesh and blood divinity that they sacrificed infants to? Feeding the malignant horror so that she would draw the plague from them as suction draws out the venom of a snake?

Men were screaming and shouting. Swords bisected flesh. Bloodstained axes splintered bone. Skulls were smashed by maces. Yemura was powerless to stop the destruction of his own army.

But he was not powerless against the witch.

As she cackled nonstop, he seized a battleaxe and split her in two. She died writhing in a pool of her own blood like a severed viper. And yet, her single eye never stopped glaring at him, piercing him with a hatred beyond anything he had ever known.

12

What possessed the men was an irresistible influence to destroy not just themselves but their comrades in arms. Its source, its epicenter, was something that moved amongst them—unknown, unspeakable, and as yet, unseen. It sent hot, flyblown currents of death and pestilence in every direction, enveloping the dying village of Khorta in a searing dust storm. And when it passed after a few moments, the green stench of carrion was so thick in the air that men dropped to their knees and vomited out tarry pools of black bile. Those of stronger constitutions stayed on their feet, answering the primal call of bloodlust. Without conscious thought, they found swords and battle-axes in their hands.

The rage spread man to man to man.

There was a clashing of steel. The sound of maces crashing into helmets and crushing skulls. Battle-axes glanced off leather armor and crunched through limbs. Spears punched through throats and impaled bellies. Horrendous, merciless battles went on across the village. Heads were cleaved free. Kneecaps shattered. Throats slit and bellies opened. Blood spilled and men went down, tangled in their own viscera. Severed hands still clutching sabers trembled on the ground. Men dragging greasy ropes of entrails skated through ponds of blood and human refuse.

The wild dogs, their innate viciousness accelerated by the slaughter, attacked the dead and dying with slavering jaws, biting and tearing.

The air was filled with screams of pure terror, shrieks of bloodlust and victory. Dogs howled and snarled. Men begged for death. Butchers in blood-glistening black armor shouted war cries and lifted speared heads high on javelins.

Khorta became a graveyard haunted by the dying, the deranged, and the disembodied.

And it was far from over.

13

What remained of his army rode from the village and Yemura went after them, screaming at them to stop, shaping their names with his mouth which was white with fear. But they were dogs running mad with simple terror, curs chasing their own tails. Once they had been the fearsome, blood-hungry warriors of the steppe and now they were mindless toys pulled along by strings.

They disappeared into the reed forest, shadows melting into shadows.

The reeds pushed in from all sides, rows upon rows of them, rustling and scraping together, whispering with a dozen sibilant voices. Even on horseback, they nodded above Yemura's head. Paths had been beaten through them that seemed to run in circles, turning back upon themselves, intersecting and forking in a claustrophobic maze.

He could hear men crying out, battle-hardened soldiers screaming like children. Their cries echoed in his skull continuously. They were nails

249

pounded into his temples. He would not submit. He would not fall down before the nightmare of the Plague Maiden, he would not be a candle snuffed out by the hot breath of disease.

There was motion in the reeds—the stealthy, furtive motion of crawling things and creeping things reaching out skeletal arms and grasping, black-rotted tiny fingers. It was the old woman, he told himself as he rode and circled and rode again. The witch had cast a terrible ravening spell upon him that was eating his insides out and devouring his mind, stripping it to bare bone. Even as small, swollen faces peered from the reeds, squealing with yawning black mouths, he told himself it was not real, that it could not be real.

He thought he saw the old woman waiting for him on the meandering path, withered arms reaching out like the spreading limbs of a dead apple tree.

But then she was gone.

A fly-specked shape took her place, its white flesh hanging from the bones beneath like a loose winding sheet. He saw a pallid face framed by greasy dark corkscrews of hair, holes eaten into it. Gnarled hands offered him twisting white worms.

He cut into another path away from the apparition and her offerings. A voice in his head—one that sounded decidedly weak and bloodless—told him that he was Yemura, he was strong, he was mighty, he was the demon wind that swept over the plains and he did not fear hallucinations from a witch's cauldron. And he realized at that moment that he had never been beyond terror, simply reckless in its face and now, oh yes, now it had him. It was a moon-flecked devil dancing in his head, a tumescent mass coming to term in his belly.

Shivering in his armor beneath the cold sweat of abject fright, he steered his horse to the left, to the right, this way and that, following one serpentine path after the other through the swaying, bobbing, crisping yellow reeds, avoiding the corpse-image of the Plague Maiden that revealed herself to him again and again like windblown cerements.

And then…and then—

He rode free of them and his lips pressed together, stemming the cry of victory he needed to set free because he was in Khorta again. The air was foul with the smell of decomposition as the bodies of villagers and soldiers alike bloated in the hot sun, popping with flies. He let out a cry of repulsion and fear, waving away black buzzing clouds of them that seemed to drone inside his skull.

Sliding from the saddle, his limbs gone to jelly, he dropped to his knees amongst the multitude of corpses. They were blackened from plague, faces ulcerated, gaping sores blown open like craters, all of them rotting and spawning maggots. But that was only part of it, for each and every one of them was knitted with the spiraling forms of long, slime-slicked white worms. They stitched numerous wounds and gashes shut like the laces of corsets.

The ragtag remains of his soldiers rode in, half as many as had ridden out. They dismounted, swords and axes in their hands. They were fighters, but what was there here to fight?

Yemura blinked his eyes, shaking his head from side to side because he could not be seeing this—the dead were beginning to move, slithering about with vermiform gyrations. One of them, a woman, sat up and began feeding on one of his dead soldiers. She ripped out loops of meat from his belly with her mouth, pecking away like a vulture.

It seemed to be happening everywhere now.

The dead were feeding on the dead.

Yemura knew death. He courted death. He worshipped and exploited death—but this was not the death he knew. It lacked its permanence. Death was the ultimate and what it left behind did not move. It did not contort and writhe in a bloody sea of remains. It did not nurture itself on the blood of soldiers and peasants and infidels. He was sick to his core, delirious. Perhaps he had been bitten by a snake or a poisonous spider, stung by a scorpion. Whatever had happened to him, the dead still moved and his bulging eyes were testament to that particularly ugly fact.

He saw the Scarred One moving in his direction. He was hacked and gutted. Half of his head was missing, yet he came on with sunken eyes, face blackened with plague, lips withered to wicker. Maggots swam in the corruption of his eye sockets.

It was happening everywhere.

Corpses walked. Limbs crawled. Fingers scuttled. Torsos inched forward and heads screamed. In whole and in part, death lived. Dead children with arrows still jutting from them like quills stuffed themselves with organs and guts, sucking gray matter from ruptured skulls.

His last remaining soldiers, all of whom were struck mad by that point, were screaming and hacking at the dead, doing everything to make them stop moving.

And Yemura screamed as the elder had screamed—the demented sound of a mind completely emptying itself, voiding reason and sanity.

14

The village was a black, seething womb of plague. It traveled on the hot breeze and contaminated the wells. It seeped from the blood-saturated earth and dripped from slit throats. It lived on the mites and ticks which infested the ragged pelts of wild dogs and teemed in the roundworms that twisted in their intestines. It crawled on the blood-sucking lice that clung to the filthy hides of the graveyard rats that fed on the multitudes of unburied corpses.

The plague was more than an infestation of disease, it was a single noxious entity that had invaded the corpse-fields of Khorta, spread by the Plague Maiden herself. She was no longer the pestilence that walketh in darkness, but an animate spawn of evil that had been set loose by the greed of the would-be Mongol king to walk the byways of man, generating death and blight.

For uncounted years, she had been a prisoner, a wraith called from the slime-dripping cellars of hell, an apotropaic against malignance, a living cauldron of disease that drew plague from the village as colloidal silver was used to draw out infection. She had been held in stasis by dark witchery and cabalistic conjuration. Now she released what she had absorbed in a charnel tempest.

Those Mongols that had not died in the reeds or hacked each other to death upon their return to the village, stumbled about mindlessly, eyes glazed, gripping bloody weapons and peppered by flies, some of which seemed as large and juicy as blackberries. Mad dogs snapped at them. Bodies swarming with corpse-fattened maggots were sprawled about them. Some of which moved and gnawed on others. Buzzards and vultures hissed.

Yemura watched it all with blank, unblinking eyes, a crooked lunatic grin on his face. He sobbed deep in his throat. He began to giggle, then cackle madly as he saw the head of Fatima speared on a spike. She stared at him with watery gray eyes like raw oysters. Then she opened her mouth and began to laugh.

The Plague Maiden had come.

A grotesque corpse bride in a moldering shift that blew around her like a cerecloth, rent and filthy with grave dirt. Her face was that of a cadaver three weeks in the ground—puffy, pulpous, squirming like a fat white grub. Framed by oily, dirt-clotted strands of hair, it was riven with wormholes and swollen with pockets of larva.

As Yemura cried out, she grinned with the shapeless chasm of her mouth, exhaling a buzzing cloud of coffin flies.

Men screamed.

They fell over each other trying to escape...but it did them little good. There was a terrible magnetism to her. She was the vortex of death, the eye of the storm which had turned the village first to a madhouse and then to a mortuary.

One after the other, the men—crying, whimpering, screaming out prayers—stumbled in her direction. They were drawn to her, pulled into her sinister orbit like rogue moons. She watched them with white, glossy eyes like glistening spider eggs. Pink fetal rats climbed her, crawling on her and nesting beneath her shroud. A multitude of sacrificed infants crowded around her, putrefied things with gas-blown bodies and gray skin.

As the men approached her, terrible things happened. They shook and shuddered violently with muscular spasms. Blood black as ink poured from their mouths, branching black veins spreading out under their skin like rootlets. Nodes and huge sores distorted their faces, each one erupting with puss, long sinuous worms sliding forth. They came out of their eyes and mouths and nostrils. By the time each man hit the ground, he was infested by them; a writhing, convulsive stew of plague worms.

Horrors of War

Yemura could feel her summoning him. The influence was practically electrical in the air. The need to go to her was irresistible.

Yet, he crawled away, sliding on his belly like a snake, dragging himself over heaped corpses gone prematurely soft with rot.

15

His yurt.

Yes, that was where he had to go. That was where safety lie and sanity would be restored. His thoughts whirling around in his head like stars, Yemura forced himself forward inch by inch. Perhaps he could have stood and ran, leap-frogging the dead, but he was afraid to stand up. Something told him to stay low, to scuttle away like a rodent. He tried desperately not to make a sound, but his armor creaked and a low, pitiful moaning came from his throat. Sweat that was both cool and hot ran down his face. It tasted sickeningly sweet on his lips.

He knew the Maiden was somewhere behind him. He could hear the squeaking and squealing of her attendant rats, the eerie wailing of the infants, and the perpetual buzzing of the blowflies that enveloped her. Worse, he could smell her—the fetid, noisome stench of plague pits and bloated bodies exploding with the gases of putrefaction.

No, he refused to look, to acknowledge the horror which had destroyed his mind.

The corpses he crawled over were in a much more advanced state of decay than they had any right to be. They were rapidly dissolving into a congealed pudding of carrion that was hot, flabby, and bubbling with ooze.

The constant squalling of dead infants was like a blade drawn up his spine. His heart pounded at his temples and in his sinuses.

Yemura no longer felt like a warrior, a Mongol or the feared Black Blade of Baya'ud. As his mind collapsed, who and what he was faded into some gray, haunted netherworld where he dreamed of days he would never see again. The tribes gathering. Herds of sheep and goats. The evenings spent listening to the old ones telling stories and singing songs of the mighty Mongol Nation. The fletching of arrows. Braiding horsetails into twine. And conquest. Oh, the hot-blooded feel of conquest, of swarming your enemies,

254

jaws locked and sharp steel in your fist. Horses thundering across the steppe in black, gleaming armor—

Around him, those things which would not lie still continued to feed upon human remains. The wild dogs glutted themselves. Armies of rats feasted and scavenging birds pecked away at dead faces and circled high overhead.

Yemura heard a terrible flapping noise and cringed. There was a dry, croaking cry and a buzzard landed on his back, picking at his neck and tearing a rut in his scalp. Another landed directly in front of him, cawing in his face. Its scaly claws tore at the abundant decay, huge wings spreading, its scabrous head darting in, nipping at his nose and lips.

"No, no, no!" he screeched. *"Not me, you damn bird! Can't you see that I'm not dead?"*

But the buzzards didn't seem to understand that at all. Several more landed on him, pecking and picking, making blood run. A beak tore a long string of flesh from his forehead. He jumped up, slashing at them with his dagger. They were everywhere. He ran until he reached his yurt and fell through the flap.

Khulgana was there as she was always there. She had made herself ready for travel, donning a heavy black *abaya* cloak that shrouded her and a *niqab* head veil so that only her eyes were visible. They were black and smoldering.

"You left me here to die, my Lord," she said in a tone of resentment he had never heard before. "Why would you do something like that? Have I displeased you in some way?"

Shaking, he peeled himself from his filthy armor, grabbing his saddlebag. It was made from a cow's stomach and could be inflated when crossing rivers. With madly shaking hands, he threw anything into it he could find—awls, a cooking pot, needle and thread, a file for sharpening arrows, a spare dagger, a short-handled axe, an extra pair of horse-leather boots.

"No, mouse. You do not understand. I cannot make you understand," he said, shaking his head from side to side. "I don't know why this has happened...this madness. I rode out after my men—"

"You were a coward. You ran like a child."

A distant memory passed through his mind of how he would have once beaten her for such talk, but now he only trembled on his knees before her. "No…I…I do not know who I am now…I cannot…*God, help me, but I am cold and barren inside…my flesh crawls…the itching…the terrible, terrible itching…*"

Khulgana was unmoved. "You are a coward and you will die a dog's death. May your bowels rot inside your body and the conqueror worm feed sweetly on your brain."

Terrified of her, of an insane world he no longer recognized, he crawled over to the horsehair cushions where he whimpered like a child. There was nothing left inside him but a raw seam of terror.

Khulgana stood before him. He watched her with heavy-lidded eyes and her image seemed to blur, to melt, to distort completely out of shape. She was like some animal bladder that had been blown up with air and was now deflating, becoming a limp doll-like form that drifted closer and closer. The *abaya* rustled around her. It seemed to be as empty as a desquamated snakeskin.

Her eyes were no longer black. They were filled with blood. Then, almost casually, like a dancing girl pulling away her veils, she revealed herself.

Yemura watched with fear-blanked eyes, a mind gone to warm suet. Fevers boiled in his brain and his mouth formed silent words.

Khulgana's *niqab* was stripped away and he saw her black, greased braid and her beautiful face that was beautiful no more. It was seamed and split, swollen and bulging with pestiferous boils and bone-deep ulcers, eaten away by the pox. Worms slid from them, gray-white, oily things that spiraled and looped in the air. A huge wriggling mass of them hung from her mouth like wet noodles.

He screamed, stumbling away. Crashing into things, tripping over his saddlebag, slashing dead air with his dagger.

In his head, her voice whispered, *"You will die in the dirt like a dog…foaming at the mouth while your insides become jelly and vermin infests you…"*

She moved towards him, seeming to be carried aloft by a wind of blood, disease, and decay. Deep inside her, there were terrible cracking, popping, and ripping sounds. The horrific contagion that had invaded her was destroying her now from the inside out. Her *abaya* seemed to flutter as her flesh became a curdled, bubbling pulp, a liquefied and steaming mass of putrescence that spilled to the ground in a convulsive pool of blood, bones, and *worms*…oh yes, because the worms owned her. They were not the little things he had seen crawling from the soupy ruin of her face, but gigantic monstrosities longer than a man's arm and bigger around than the shaft of a spear: coiling, squirming, literally boiling from the loathsome anatomical mess she now was. Dozens and dozens of them were tangled up in her remains like tree roots, reaching out towards Yemura with puckering mouths…

He stabbed his dagger into the wall of the yurt, slitting it open and forcing himself through, running, stumbling, seeking sanctuary in the madhouse of Khorta.

16

Alone.

The great Mongol conqueror had been alone for days. He was certain it was days because at each sunrise he had tried to escape the village only to get lost in the reed forest and be directed back into Khorta. He had done that at least four or five times now.

My God, he was in hell.

He was in purgatory.

He was trapped in the cage of the village which had become a great suppurating wound that was decomposing around him. Rats. Buzzards. Maggots. Flies. All feeding on the sea of corpses out there.

He was hiding in a mud hut with his dagger, his mind a slurry of psychosis. He itched. Every inch of his skin itched terribly. He had scratched himself raw with his fingers until he bled and even that wasn't enough, so he used the dagger—cutting, peeling, getting at the infested meat below, pulling out tunneling white worms with his fingertips. They infested him, but he would not give in. He kept cutting them free, digging rents in his torso and arms and legs. He had even tugged one from the head of his penis.

But he was Yemura.

And Yemura did not give in.

He would fight until there was nothing left to fight *with*. Let the infidels see how a man dies. Oh, yes.

He clawed at the soft, larval mass of his face, tearing out abundant maggots and countless flies that hatched beneath what remained of his skin.

The itching, the terrible incessant itching.

He was hungry.

God, he was so hungry.

When he peeled a section of worm-riddled skin free, it smelled like roast mutton, like boiled fowl, like juicy cutlets of horse flesh. And it tasted delicious—salty, sweet, succulent. His stomach growled. Drool overflowed his mouth. He couldn't make any of it stop until he licked the fine, offered meat, chewing it, biting into it with great, near orgasmic relish. He had taken most of his belly and all the flesh from his left leg by that point. He could no longer stand, just recline there up against the flaking wall of the hut, scratching, cutting, smashing worms and swatting flies and filling his belly—

But he would not surrender.

He was a soldier.

Oh God, oh God. That voice.

The Plague Maiden was outside, calling to him, inviting him to the final act. Already the hut was filling with the pink, pulsing bodies of her fetal rats. Yemura seized one after the other, crushing them in his hands until warm black juice squirted from his fingers.

The infants were coming in now; boneless, creeping things with reaching stick fingers and eyes like yellow seeds. Their suckering mouths squealed and bawled as they flooded the room.

The Maiden was in the doorway, infants surging over her, enveloping her, climbing her. She held one of them in her arms, a vermid thing, putrid and soft.

Yemura would not look at her. He would not give her power over him even as her vermin crawled over him, biting and suckling his wounds. She wanted him to scream, but he would not. He stuffed a bloated white mushroom in his mouth to keep quiet. He began to chew it. It was tender, spongy, and delicious.

By the time he realized it was his own hand, he was too far gone to even care.

PUBLICATION HISTORY

"The Rat King" is original to this book.

"Der Wulf" appeared originally in *Dark Animus #10/11, 2007.*

"The Chattering of Tiny Teeth" originally appeared in *Warfear,* 2002, Marietta Publishing.

"Hell Flies" is original to this book.

"The Procyon Project" originally appeared in *World War Cthulhu,* 2014, Dark Regions Press.

"Maggots" originally appeared in *Vile Things,* 2009, Comet Press.

"1867: The Skull-Eater Campaign" originally appeared in *Four Rode Out,* 2010, Cemetery Dance Publications.

"The Plague Maiden" is original to this book.

ABOUT THE AUTHOR

TIM CURRAN is the author of *Skin Medicine, Hive, Dead Sea, Resurrection, The Devil Next Door, Dead Sea Chronicles, Clownflesh,* and *Bad Girl in the Box.* His short stories have been collected in *Bone Marrow Stew* and *Zombie Pulp.* His novellas include "The Underdwelling," "The Corpse King," "Puppet Graveyard," and "Worm, and Blackout." His fiction has been translated into German, Japanese, Spanish, and Italian.

ABOUT THE ARTIST

BRAD MOORE'S artwork has been described as capable of leaving a lasting impression of graphic damage. His paintings and drawings are most often found on the album covers of death and doom metal recordings, and in the pages of outlaw, underground comix. The legendary "Alien" designer H. R. Giger invited Brad to exhibit at his castle, in Switzerland, and Brad's album cover for WORM, "Foreverglade," has been voted the number 11 best album cover of 2021. His famous quotes are: "The media is the gallery of the present," and "There are two kinds of people in this world, and they're both Bill Bixby."

www.ingramcontent.com/pod-product-compliance
Lightning Source LLC
Chambersburg PA
CBHW030359020726
47493CB00003B/888